The Tattered Web

by
Roger Thomas

To my blood brother in so many senses,
David Andrew Thomas
Fellow teacher and storyteller

Books in the *Watchful Sky* series:

Under the Watchful Sky
Rising Darkness
The Wounded Land
The Tattered Web

Published by JCK
Fort Gratiot MI

ISBN 978-1-7330809-2-7

Michigan's Thumb Region

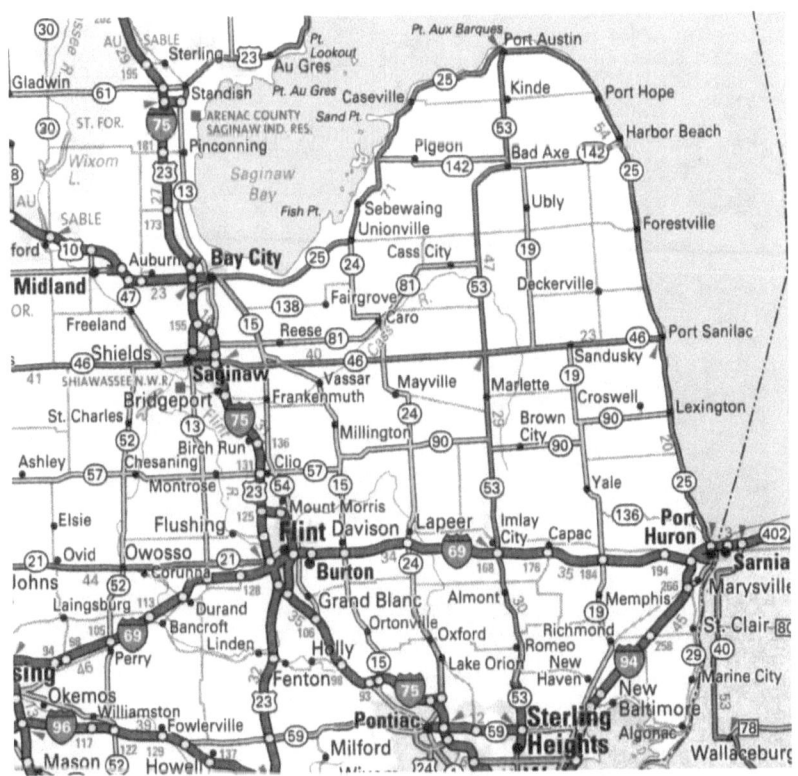

Northeastern Michigan

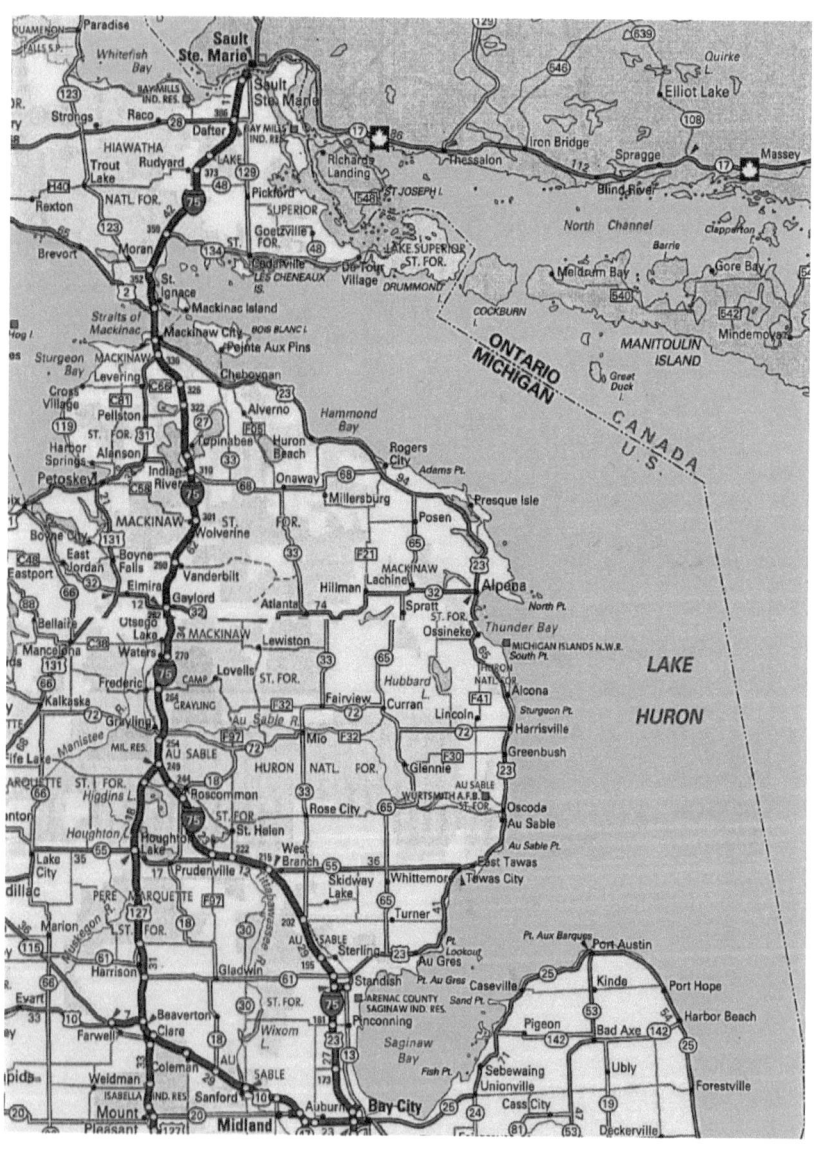

Amnesia

The atmosphere in the conference room was brisk but genial, which was what Cynthia had been hoping for. Too many issues were still unsettled, and all it would take would be for some overblown ego to start blustering or pounding the table to unleash a torrent of acrimony. But though there were plenty of overblown egos in the room, restraint seemed to be winning at this meeting.

"Thank you for your report, Director Buchanan," Cynthia said. "It seems like we're finally getting our feet under us in the Special Protectionary District, thanks to your able leadership."

"Thank you, Cynthia," Buchanan replied with just the right tone of modesty. "Your support, and that of Director Miller, has made all the difference. However, while getting our feet under us may be a good start, it is still short of walking, much less running – and running was what we'd hoped to be doing when we set up the SPD."

"Please, Director," Cynthia offered. "The SPD has only been in existence for four months. Give yourself some credit."

"Yes, yes," Buchanan acknowledged with a deprecating wave. "But the SPD initiative is supposed to be an exercise in nimbleness and responsiveness. With all the concept projects that DHS and HHS are hoping to roll out, we can't risk getting complacent. But one thing is clear to me, based on our experience in the District as well as the plans we've discussed today."

"What is that?"

"We need more robust compliance enforcement. Our completion percentages started strong but have begun slipping. We're going to need better policies and the staffing to enforce them, especially in light of the new initiatives being considered."

"We'll certainly take that into consideration," Cynthia replied, jotting on her tablet. "Do you have anything else for us, Director?"

"No, I've monopolized your time long enough," Buchanan said, rising to leave. Behind him, his aide Lieutenant Bonnie Hammond tucked away her tablet and headed for the door. With a few nods and handshakes, Buchanan followed. Some of the restraint in the atmosphere seemed to depart with him. The D.C. insiders glanced around with smirks and rolled eyes.

"Honestly," asked Roy Nicholson of DHS in a slightly exasperated tone. "How much do we need this Special Protectionary District with its pompous bureaucrats? How much protection does a rural corner of a minor Midwestern state require?"

"I grant your point, Roy," Cynthia replied. "The immediate answer is, not much. But protecting the region isn't the primary goal of this pilot SPD."

"Oh? What's it for, then?"

"It's a test bed, a proving ground for us to try out new policies and protocols. Some of the projects we'll be attempting will be bold, even risky, and we want to test them to iron out the kinks. But there's another reason."

"What's that?"

"We want to push some of these initiatives a bit aggressively in hopes of getting push-back."

"Really?" Roy asked. "You want to provoke response?"

"Sure," Cynthia explained. "HHS has been more in on this, since they've got more going on in the District, but the idea is to provoke challenges so we can get them in front of judges and obtain favorable rulings. Once a precedent is on the books, it's much easier to implement elsewhere. Same with policy rulings – with a few incidents resolved, the policies are that much stronger."

"So, who's going to be pushing back?"

"Doesn't matter," Cynthia shrugged. "Local officials, patient advocacy groups, the recipients themselves – it's immaterial. We've got the preliminaries all set up in anticipation of the challenges.

"You're right about the region. It's a sparsely populated, insignificant corner of Michigan, a complete backwater. Just look at their voting patterns over the past several election cycles! Nobody cares what happens there, and if anyone complains, nobody will listen. The vital thing is that it will afford the opportunity to get the rulings and precedents we need to strengthen our hand for when we have to roll out the SPDs where they really matter."

"I see, though I hope nobody tells Director Napoleon there," Roy replied, gesturing toward the door through which Buchanan had just exited. "From how he talks, you'd think he was running half the planet."

"Director Buchanan is useful for this stage of things, and his task is well suited to his talents," Cynthia said. "I'm certain that the day will come when the importance of his role becomes clear to him." Turning to the brown-haired woman sitting quietly near the end of the table, she asked, "Now, Carly, do you have any questions about the HHS side of all this?"

"Not right now," the woman answered. "We have an implementation plan mapped out. Natalie here has been appointed clinical compliance director, and we are confident that she'll be able to address the issues we've been encountering."

"Very good," Cynthia said, scanning her tablet. "Natalie…Griggs, is it?"

"Yes, ma'am," Natalie responded, then gestured to the blonde woman sitting beside her. "This is my assistant, Stacey Lang, who'll be accompanying me." Stacey smiled nervously and nodded, but said nothing.

"Excellent." Cynthia gave Stacey an encouraging smile. "We have every confidence in both of you. And you, Roy, are going to draw up a more comprehensive enforcement plan, as well as appoint an executive?"

"I'll have it to you by the end of next week," Roy promised.

"Superb," Cynthia tapped her tablet screen with finality and snapped the case shut. "That looks like everything for today. Thank you for your time."

The HHS representatives rose and bustled from the room, chatting among themselves. Roy hung back, organizing and tucking away papers until the room was clear of all but himself and Cynthia.

"I did have one more question," he said hesitantly.

"Yes?"

"About the first director of the SPD, the one who didn't last long," Roy continued hesitantly, as if broaching a difficult or embarrassing topic. "I...I heard he'd resigned."

Cynthia stiffened slightly, and her smile seemed to freeze. "Why do you ask?"

"Well, given how ambitious the SPD initiative is, and how far the implications reach, it might be...delicate...to have someone out there who was privy to so many sensitive secrets."

Cynthia was still for a minute, as if thinking, before she replied. "It's against policy for me to discuss personnel issues with uninvolved parties, but since he was technically DHS, and to set your mind at ease, yes, Mr. Pelletier did resign, but only after suffering a breakdown."

"A breakdown?"

"Yes. The clinicians on his case refer to it as a 'soft breakdown' – not total incapacitation, but severe damage to perception and judgment. It was quite sudden, and they think it can be traced to the stress he incurred while conceiving and implementing the elements of what eventually became the Eastern Michigan SPD."

"'The clinicians on his case'? So, he is receiving care?"

"Yes," Cynthia assured him. "He was taken into clinical custody to ensure he received proper attention. I don't know many details of his regimen, but my contacts in HHS who are familiar with his case assure me that he is in the best of hands. In fact, I understand that he is receiving treatment under a new protocol."

"New protocol?" Roy asked.

"Yes – an experimental technique that was developed to deal with advanced cases of PTSD. I understand it's a two-phase program, with the first phase designed to disengage the patient's personality from the negative memories, and the second phase reconstructing the personality without the detrimental components."

"Sounds sophisticated," Roy said. "I'm glad to hear he's receiving suitable care."

"Oh, certainly," Cynthia replied with a smile. "After all Mr. Pelletier did for us, he deserves the best we can provide."

*   *   *

He felt, rather than heard, the low hum of the door opening. He didn't know how that was possible, given the thick padding on his couch-chair and the thick sleeves covering his arms and hands. He certainly couldn't see anything through the thickly frosted visor or hear anything above the white noise flooding his ears. But even through all that, somehow he'd learned to detect the vibration of the chamber doors sliding open. Perhaps it was because an opening door was the only advance warning he got when it was time for a session. He preferred to know when those were coming.

It wasn't that he minded sessions. They were at least a break from the timeless, asensory hours he spent here in the darkened chamber. The sessions were always in the white room, and he was taken there by nameless attendants who never spoke. Usually there was an aide waiting in the white room, who'd give him an injection or some pills to swallow, after which things would get very vague and confusing. What came next varied. Sometimes the aide would ask him random, senseless questions, or a series of images would be projected on the walls, sometimes in rapid sequence and sometimes more slowly. There didn't seem to be any rationale behind the sequence or the images: some images were senseless, some were horrible, some were hauntingly beautiful. Sometimes random shapes were projected, all sizes and colors, some appearing abruptly and then vanishing, others appearing as dim outlines then brightening to almost unbearable intensity before fading away. Sometimes the images would appear in dead silence, sometimes they were accompanied by types of music, and sometimes they would appear against a background of raucous and random noise. Sometimes while all this was going on various odors would fill the room; some pleasant, some unremarkable, and some disgusting.

He had no idea what the sessions were supposed to accomplish, but they always ended the same way: all the lights would go out and he'd be left in silent darkness until they came for him. They'd put the heavy sleeves and frosted visor back on and lead him through darkened hallways back to the chamber. Usually he'd sleep following a session, but whether he did or not, eventually his brain would be filled with the images, and the noise or music would resonate in his mind. The most annoying thing was that everything seemed to dance right on the edge of familiarity. The images of city streets or landscapes would be almost, but not quite, familiar. He would nearly recognize a tune, but no, it wouldn't be exactly what he remembered. An aroma would nearly bring back something familiar, but exactly what remained elusive.

As a result, his existence was one of constant confusion. He didn't know who he was, where he was, how he had gotten here, or what was expected of him. The measureless hours he spent in the dark chamber were broken only by the meaningless sessions. In the chamber his visor prevented him from seeing anything, the sleeves kept him from feeling or manipulating anything, and the white noise filled his ears constantly. He was fed through a tube, the flow of which was controlled by the thumb of the large mittens at the end of his sleeve. The thick paste that came through the tube was tepid and tasteless, serving only to fill his stomach when he could bear the ache no longer. Washing, drinking, and other bodily functions were done in a corner of the chamber where there was a stool over a hole in the floor, and a hose with a spray head which dispensed water that was neither hot nor cold. It was clumsy working the hose with the mittens, and he often got wet, but he managed.

Most of his hours were spent lying on the couch-chair with images and melodies (or noises) whirling in his head and sometimes seeming to come to life before his eyes. Sometimes he'd recognize the images or sounds from a recent session, but sometimes not. It all merged into a giant, random, boundless ball of sensations that had no coherence or pattern or purpose. Everything was just images and sounds flowing around and through and over one another in a cataract that swept him along to wherever it was headed.

Except – there were some images that persisted, showing up at unpredictable intervals and passing swiftly. There were only four of these, with some appearing more than others. They never lasted long, but they were always accompanied by strong emotions. One image was of an older man with white hair and a moustache smiling and chatting genially while rocking in a rocking chair. For some reason this image was always accompanied by a sense of ominous foreboding, as if something dire was about to happen. Another image was simply of a well-trimmed yard containing a pond with trees set about it, and a gazebo not far away. This image was accompanied by yearning, almost an ache, as if he was desperately searching for something he could not find. Yet another image was of a woman in white, seen only from behind, walking through a gate or doorway into ominous blackness. This image came with a sharp sense of imminent peril overshadowed by a profound sadness that was so intense that he'd find himself weeping. The final image, which occurred less often than the others, was of a mysterious round golden thing that looked like a many-bladed fan, except that it had a small glass window in the center, though which could be seen a white disc of some nature. He had no idea what this thing was, but it seemed to hang before him, suspended in space and illuminated by brilliant light which either shone upon or emanated from it. This image was always the briefest, coming unexpectedly and lasting but a few seconds, but it always left him feeling naked and exposed and very small, like he was being scrutinized by a great, all-seeing eye. It was acutely uncomfortable, but for some reason, he longed for that image more than the others.

There was something different about these recurring images and the emotions that accompanied them. All the other images seemed nothing more than a random, jumbled stream roiling aimlessly and carrying him along with them. But those images – just those four – seemed anchored and purposeful. They meant something. He had no idea what it was, but he knew beyond question that they were of people and places and events that had some significance. He only hoped that he could discover their meaning before they were swept away by the torrent of meaningless images.

Other than those fixed points, his existence seemed to be merely a deluge of disconnected sensations. At first, he wondered if things would become more clear with time, and the reason for his being here and subjected to all this would come to light. Instead, the opposite seemed to be happening. Each session left him more confused and disoriented, until at last he gave up trying to figure it out, or hoping for clarity to emerge. Maybe this was just what his life was and would always be: lying here in the darkness with random images tumbling through his mind until they came to take him to another session.

Which was what seemed to be happening now, if his muffled senses weren't deceived. He sat up a little and cocked his head. Sure enough, firm hands grabbed his arms and pulled him to his feet. He prepared himself to be walked out of the chamber, but to his surprise, that wasn't what happened. Instead the hands undid the buckles that held the visor helmet on his head and the straps that held the sleeves in place, then both were removed, which never happened outside the session room. Startled and a little frightened, he looked around the dim interior of the chamber that he'd lived in but had never seen, and at the two men who had come for him. One was a black man and the other was white with brown hair. Both were dressed in nondescript blue scrubs and neither was looking at him, instead focusing on removing various items and pitching them on the couch.

"C'mon," the black man finally mumbled, taking his arm and leading him toward the door, which stood open, letting harsh white light stream into the chamber. He winced as they walked out into the hallway, not just from the brightness of the light but from the clean-edged objects he caught sight of as they passed down the hall: doorways and windows and signs and lighting fixtures that seemed so sharp they could cut you. He gazed about in wonder as his escorts walked him silently through the bright, empty halls.

Finally they turned a corner and he saw at the end of a hallway a dark gray door with a red exit sign above it. The men walked him down the hall but near the end stopped by a door that opened off to the right. The brown-haired man opened it.

"There," the black man pointed through the doorway. "Get in and change."

He stepped through the door and found himself in what appeared to be a small changing room. The walls were lined with lockers and a bench ran down the center of the floor. On the bench was a pile of clothing which turned out to be a pair of sweat pants, a hooded sweatshirt, a t-shirt, some socks, and some running shoes. He removed the hospital gown he was wearing and slipped on the t-shirt and pants. They were a bit loose on him, as were the shoes, but they would serve. Shortly he was back out in the hallway.

The two men said nothing, but took him by the arms and walked him the rest of the length of the hall to the gray exit door. One man opened the door and the other pushed him out into the cool evening air. The door was quickly shut, slamming behind him with harsh finality.

Inside the door, the brown-haired aide turned to the black man. "Well, I guess there was no funding for the second phase of the program," he said. The black man gave a grim chuckle as they turned their backs on the gray door and returned to their work.

Outside, he was lost and bewildered. He seemed to be in some kind of alcove between two buildings, with brick walls rising on both sides and a loading dock with large metal box next to him. He seemed to know that the metal box was for holding garbage, but he didn't know how he knew that. There were no other people in sight, though he could hear noises. Hesitantly he walked along one brick wall until he came to a corner, around which he cautiously peered.

His senses were overwhelmed with an onslaught of color, motion, and sound. He was looking across a street at some storefronts, but the people walking and the cars moving and the lights flashing and the breeze blowing were too much for him, so he quickly pulled back. Retreating down the length of the wall, he crouched in a corner behind the big metal box, which certainly smelled like it had something to do with garbage. Questions whirled in his mind: where was he? Why had he been taken out of the chamber and thrust out here? What was he expected to do? Would somebody come for him? He tried to focus on these questions, but they kept eluding him like a tomato seed slipping from beneath his thumb (where had that image come from?) His brain didn't seem to be working, and he didn't know what to do about it. He supposed he should do something, but it was all too much.

A wave of exhaustion swept over him. Too much, that's what it was. Too much for him. He'd figure it out, but not yet. Not just yet. His head slumped back into corner formed by the brick walls, and he dozed.

"Hey!" A harsh voice awakened him as something nudged his legs. "Hey!" The voice continued, and he stretched his cramped neck to look up and see a swarthy man with black hair and a moustache standing over him. The man wore an apron, and behind him a supply truck was backed up to the loading dock. It was dark and he was stiff – he imagined he'd slept the night through.

"Hey!" The aproned man continued in a harsh voice, nudging his legs again. "Get outta here. You can't sleep here. Go on."

He scrambled to his feet awkwardly beneath the scowl of the aproned man, who was acting like this wasn't the first time he'd done this. Walking along the brick wall, he turned the corner with some trepidation, remembering how overwhelmed he'd been. To his surprise, he had no such reaction this time. It was the same street, the same storefronts, the same wind-rustled trees, but now it didn't seem so intimidating. Granted, there was less traffic and fewer pedestrians, but the signs were still illuminated, making a bright visual impact. But for some reason it didn't bowl him over like it had before. His mind also seemed clearer. It was early morning, the beginning of a day, which was why there wasn't so much traffic. How did he know that? He just did.

He was still stiff from sleeping on the pavement, his mouth was dry, and he was terribly thirsty. He was cold, too – the wind was less gusty than it had been, but a pre-dawn chill hung in the air. He noticed a bench along a sidewalk, and went over to it, hunching as he sat and pulling his sweatshirt more tightly around him. Questions swirled in his mind, clamoring for attention, but his physical discomfort was overriding them. He had never been so thirsty. Noticing that the rubberized metal grating of the bench was damp with dew, he swept his hand across it and then licked the moisture from his hand. The moisture was gritty and had an odd taste, but he barely noticed, so welcome was it on his tongue. He did this again and again until he'd collected all the dew on the bench, and still his thirst raged. Then he noticed a wastebasket at the end of the bench, and soon he was pawing through that in search of anything to drink. He found nothing but paper and plastic, but another bench with another wastebasket up the walkway proved fruitful. There he found a discarded bottle that still contained a couple inches of water which he guzzled eagerly. There was also a plastic cup with a lid that contained the watery remains of some coffee drink. Just beside that was a true treasure – a bag that someone had carefully closed before discarding that contained the end of a deli sandwich and half a bag of chips. He drained the coffee drink, finally feeling his thirst abating, and gobbled the sandwich and chips. Unfortunately, other bodily needs were now clamoring for his attention, so he stepped behind some bushes, glad that the walk was still mostly empty of traffic.

The sky was beginning to lighten as he walked along, hunched against the morning chill, still stiff from his irregular night's sleep. His mind did seem clearer now, but that only made the questions easier to sequence – there were no answers yet. Where was he? What was he doing here? Why had he been so abruptly ejected from the chamber? What had he been doing there in the first place? And who was he, anyway?

He sat on a bench and watched the morning traffic build in the streets and on the sidewalk. Going to work, that's what everyone was doing. It was the start of a workday. More people were bustling by on the sidewalk as the morning light grew, talking on phones or looking at tablet screens, focused on the day ahead. Nobody seemed to notice him. He sat and watched, trying to corral the questions and images rolling around in his mind.

"Hey, buddy," a voice came from behind him. He turned to see a man in some kind of uniform, with patches on the shoulders and a radio on his belt. "Hey, buddy, you're going to have to move."

"Move?"

"Yeah. This bench is on private property, put here for use by the tenants." The man gestured to the office building behind him, where people were already bustling through the glass lobby doors.

"Oh – okay," he said, getting to his feet.

"All these benches are along this stretch," the man pointed up and down the walkway, where benches stood at the edge of the neatly manicured lawn surrounding the office building. "So just keep going."

He walked off along the sidewalk, looking for somewhere to rest, and hopefully something else to eat and drink. He found a short concrete wall to lean against for a while, but when a security guard emerged from a nearby building and headed in his direction, he just moved on. He found a small park that (oh, bliss!) had a drinking fountain where he quenched his thirst, but when he sat on one of the benches to rest, the women who were supervising the children on the play structure began to cast suspicious glances in his direction. Within fifteen minutes a police car drove by the park, slowing down as it passed where he was sitting. When the cruiser came back around less than ten minutes later, he took the hint and departed.

So the day passed with him wandering the sidewalks, perching briefly here and there, watching people and cars bustle past. Nobody spoke to him, nobody noticed him; he might as well have been invisible, except to the hostile eyes of watchers determined to drive him off if he lingered too long. Periodically he'd get an image, something right on the edge of memory, of himself as one of the bustling pedestrians, walking past people sitting forlornly on park benches or by storefronts, glancing at them but not seeing, focusing on his phone so he didn't have to meet anyone's eye.

Where had that image come from?

As the day wore toward evening, the hollowness in his middle grew more acute. Thirst wasn't as much of an issue, and the restrooms at the park solved the other need, but he had no idea what he was going to do about food. He guessed that digging through garbage cans would attract unwelcome attention very quickly, but if something didn't happen soon, he might have to resort to that.

As the dusk deepened toward night, he found himself sitting at a table in a pedestrian mall, surrounded by restaurants and coffee houses. He kept glancing at the diners around him, wondering if one of them would leave an incomplete meal on a table or casually tossed into a wastebasket from which it could easily be retrieved. He was so distracted by looking around that he was startled when a man sat down across from him. The man was middle-aged, with gray streaking the blonde hair that stuck out beneath his dirty baseball cap. He was unshaven and an earthy odor clung to him, but his eyes were bright.

"Howdy," the man said. "You're new around here, right?"

"I…ah, yes, I am," he replied.

"Figured as much. Been watching you wander around all day. I know most everyone on these streets, and I never seen you before."

"You've been watching me?" he asked. "I haven't seen you at all."

"Well, that's the trick, ain't it? You got a name?"

His brow furrowed, and suddenly the persistent image of the white-haired man with the moustache flitted through his mind. "Mike," he blurted out. "You can call me Mike."

"Mike, eh?" the man replied with a grin, then held out his hand. "I'm Keith." Keith had a firm grip and looked him right in the eye as they shook hands, which made him feel good about Keith. "Look here," Keith continued, all business, "I don't know how you got here, but it's clear that not only do you not know the ropes, you aren't aware there are ropes to know. You won't last the night if you hang around."

"Police?" Mike asked.

"If you're lucky, and even they're none too gentle. But it's the jackals you have to really worry about."

"Jackals?" Mike asked. Keith nodded and said nothing, but pointed down the street to where a group of noisy young men were hanging around a parked car, bantering and smoking.

"I can't say for sure that's a pack of 'em," Mike explained. "But there are some around just like that. They roam the streets at night looking for any kind of trouble, and they love to find people like us. Just a couple of weeks ago a man was found dead behind a dumpster out Fairfax way, beaten and cut up. The cops made the expected statement about not tolerating the lawlessness, bringing the perps to justice, blah, blah, blah, but truth is nobody cares what happens to street people. The cops will talk about cleaning up the jackals, but they really don't mind 'em. Word gets out that jackals are prowling about an area and the street people stay away."

"Oh," Mike said with another glance at the group of young toughs. "Sounds dangerous."

"Yeah," Keith confirmed. "You don't have anywhere to go, do ya?"

"No, I don't. Truth be told, I don't even know how I got here."

Keith looked at him and shook his head. "You're in bad shape, ain't ya?" He sighed. "First thing we gotta do is get you away from here, far enough away to be clear of danger. Sure, there's danger everywhere, but we can at least get you out of this frying pan. Here." He fished in his shirt pocket and brought out a nondescript green card and held it up. "Know what this is?" Mike shook his head. "This is a Metro card, for riding the Metro, the subway. Used to see a lot more of these, but nowadays people mostly use passes on their phones. Someone gave this to me a few months ago, loaded with a hundred bucks, and I tell you, it's been one of the best things I ever got. I been using it to get all over, and put money back on it when I got a few bucks to spare." He handed the card to Mike.

"You're giving it to me?" Mike asked.

"Yeah. Not much left on it, but it should be enough to get you clear of the area. You should take a line that gets you well out of town, like the Silver or the Red. I think Red would be best for you – take it to the west end of the line at Shady Grove, near Rockville. I haven't heard of any jackals out that far. There's still the cops, but it'll be better than sticking around here."

Mike looked at the card and at Keith for a long while before responding. "I...thank you. But what will you do?"

Keith shrugged. "What I always do: survive. Try to stay a step ahead. I figure they'll catch up to me eventually, but I can give them a run. Which is what you better be doing. There's a Metro station just a couple blocks that way. Remember: the Red line out to Shady Grove. Get goin'."

They shook hands, then Keith slipped away, leaving Mike to find his way to the Metro station. His stomach was still aching but his mind was clear. He seemed to have completely shed the sense of vague disorientation that had plagued him when he'd awakened that morning. Though he couldn't remember ever having been in a Metro station, the environment didn't intimidate him. There were the terminals on the walls that allowed him to verify the card's balance, and the turnstiles that swept the card through, and the platform where he waited with other riders for the train that would take him to Maryland. He got onto the proper train without incident, though he seemed to be the only one in the half-full car not fixated on a phone or tablet screen. He stared out the windows, one part of his mind gnawing on all the unanswered questions while another part was just weary of it all: the questions, the unfamiliar conditions, the walking around all day, the hunger. He just wanted to find somewhere to rest.

When the train emerged from underground, he saw that the rain that had been threatening all day was finally coming down, driven by wind gusts that rattled the rail cars. The rain lashed and spattered against the windows, causing him to wonder what he was going to do when he had to get off.

Unfortunately, there wasn't much he could do. By the time the train arrived at the Shady Grove station, the rain and wind had intensified. He stepped out onto the platform, which was clearly designed to discourage lingering, and scanned the area around the station while his fellow riders dashed for the parking lot. Spotting a glow of lights that looked like storefronts, he put his head down and headed out through the rain, hoping to find some kind of shelter.

He did. One of the storefronts was a diner with a counter, so he sat on the stool closest to the door. A big black guy sat two stools over, working his way through a cheeseburger combo, and the waitress behind the counter came over, eying him suspiciously.

"What can I get ya?"

"Oh...ah, nothing just yet," Mike stammered in reply. She eyed him again then walked away. The smells in the diner were tantalizing, and he was weak with hunger. His eyes kept straying to the almost untouched plate of fries sitting beside the black guy's cheeseburger. He toyed with the idea of asking if the diner needed any odd jobs done, or if someone would be willing to exchange the Metro card for a couple of bucks, just so he could get the cheapest item on the menu – something like the plate of fries, which were looking like the best meal on the planet just now.

"Here," the black guy rumbled, shoving the plate toward him.

"Really?" Mike asked. "You're sure?"

"Yeah, take 'em. I really don't need 'em," said the man with a grin, patting his ample gut.

"Thank you. Thank you very much," Mike barely got out before he was wolfing down the fries, which indeed tasted like the best meal he'd ever had. "I really...thank you so much."

"Damn, man!" The black guy exclaimed as he watched Mike eat. "How long since you ate?"

"This morning – some scraps," Mike said through mouthfuls.

"Damn," the man said again, gesturing to the waitress, who snorted in disgust but turned to her terminal. "I'm James," he said, holding out his hand.

"Mike," he replied, wiping his hand so he could return the shake. "Thank you again."

"So, you from around here? You got anywhere to go?" James asked.

"Not really," Mike shook his head, looking forlornly at the now empty plate. "I just got here on the Metro. A friend gave me a card so I could get away from the city – he said it wasn't safe."

"He was right about that," said James, shaking his head. "Not that here is much safer. Where you coming from, Mike?"

"I honestly don't remember," Mike admitted. "I think...I think I was in some kind of program, but suddenly they just threw me out on the street."

"Your insurance probably ran out. Damn rehab programs. No friends or family in the area?"

"Not that I can remember," Mike admitted, spotting a few crumbs around the edge of his plate and picking them up carefully. Just then the waitress, without speaking to or looking at him, put a cheeseburger, another plate of fries, and a large glass of milk on the counter. With an exasperated look at James, she stalked away while Mike gaped at the meal in front of him.

"Is this mine?"

"Yeah," James admitted with a touch of embarrassment.

"James – thank you so much! I didn't..." Mike trailed off, not knowing how to express his gratitude.

"Hey, man, it's just a burger. I know what hunger feels like. Just do the same for the next guy when you get a chance."

They chatted about minor things while Mike gobbled his dinner. As he was finishing up, James excused himself to duck outside for a few minutes. The rain had not abated, and when he returned his windbreaker was soaked.

"C'mon, Mike," James said, throwing a couple of bills on the counter while giving the waitress a stony stare.

"Where are we going?"

"To my truck. We need to talk," James explained. They dashed through the rain to where a gleaming blue semi tractor was parked behind the diner. They clamored into the cab, which was cluttered but clean.

"Listen, Mike, what I'm gonna suggest is stretching some rules and could get me in trouble back at HQ, but sometimes you gotta go with your gut," James said. "You're in a fix, and it isn't safe for you to be anywhere around here. All these eastern cities are cracking down on street people big time, and the suburbs and towns around them are following suit. You gotta get away from here, far away.

"I just picked up a load to run to Chicago, which is where my home and HQ are. I'm all rested and was planning to drive through the night. If you want to come with me, you can use the sleeper while I drive. I know it's not much, but at least it'll get you somewhere safer."

Mike was dumbfounded. "That's...but you don't even know me."

"Well, you don't know me, either, so we're both taking a risk, ain't we?" James replied. "But like I said, sometimes you just gotta go with your gut. My gut tells me you're no danger to me, but that you're lost and alone and need help. I seen my share of the ugly underside of life, and seen men who only needed a little help to get back on their feet. You look like such a man, so I'm offering the little help. You don't have to take it, but there it is if you want it."

Mike rubbed his face and tried to collect himself. "I don't have much choice, honestly. Thank you very much."

"No problem. The sleeping space is back there. I tidied up the bunk and spread out my spare sleeping bag, so you don't have to worry about getting the mattress wet. I don't care if you want to strip out of those soggy sweats and lay them out to dry. I seen guys in boxers before. All I ask is that if we're stopped, or if I'm taking on the phone or radio, that you keep back there and keep quiet. By regs I'm not supposed to have anyone traveling with me unless I sent in a form, and HQ don't welcome such requests."

"Sure thing," Mike agreed. He scrambled back into the berthing area, which was snug but not cramped, while James pulled the truck out onto the road. It was a relief for Mike to shed his drenched clothing and lie down on the soft sleeping bag. His long, stressful day followed by a full meal had left him exhausted, and sleep took him quickly.

They rolled through the night and the predawn found them pulling into a large truck stop at what appeared to be the intersection of two expressways. James had to take some mandated rest time, so they got breakfast, after which James picked up some basic toiletries for Mike, along with a couple more t-shirts and a cheap duffel to keep it all in. He also gave him a card for a shower, which Mike deeply appreciated.

"James, I don't know how to thank you for all this," Mike said.

"Aw, it's nothin' – whole mess didn't top forty bucks," James replied, slightly embarrassed.

"Still, I don't know how I'll ever repay you, for this and all your help."

"Forget it. Like I said, do the same for the next guy when you get a chance – I know you will."

After a shower for Mike and some rest for James, they were back on the road by later midmorning. "Now," James explained as they rumbled across northern Indiana. "We're gonna be meeting up with a friend of mine named Buck at a truck stop just east of Chicagoland. I been talking to him about your situation, and he's agreed to help. I can't take you all the way on this trip, 'cause I'm going to my HQ, and I sure can't take you home, 'cause of my wife. But if it's agreeable to you, Buck'll take you as far as he can. That should get you to a safer place, where maybe you can get some help, and get your feet back under you. It ain't what we'd like to be able to do for you, but it's what we can manage, given our situations."

"It's plenty, James," Mike replied. "I wish there was something I could do to express my gratitude."

"Well, just this: you've got a long road ahead of you, and when you're tempted to slip back, remember me and hold strong. If you want to thank ol' James, hold strong when you're tempted to cave in. Remember: you can't do it."

"I can't?" Mike asked, a bit mystified by all this.

"No, you can't – only your Higher Power can. Remember that, and always turn to your Higher Power for help. Mine, His name is Jesus."

"Right," Mike replied, still puzzled but grateful for the good intentions. "I'll definitely keep that in mind."

They met up with Buck at a truck stop near Gary. Buck was a grizzled, unshaven guy in a battered Cabela's hat.

"Please t'meet ya, Mike," Buck said as he sat down at the table in the diner. "James explained a little of your situation, and I'll help as I can, which won't be much. Seeing as how big cities are getting dangerous for street people, it's best to get you somewhere out-of-the-way where you stand a chance to getting help. I got a run to Hamilton, Ontario, over near Toronto. I'll take you along, but I don't want to file for approval for a rider, because my company would ask a lot of questions, so please keep it quiet."

"Be sure of that," Mike assured him. "And I appreciate any help you can give."

"Well, I've been where you are, and I know how tough it is to climb back," Buck explained. "Thing is, without any papers, I won't be able to take you into Canada. I'll have to drop you off at the border. We'll be running up I-94 to I-69, then east to Port Huron – open road all the way, avoiding city traffic. If we leave soon, we should be at the border by dinner time. Fair enough?"

"Fair enough," Mike answered. The men all stood, and Mike turned to James. "I can't thank you enough for all you've done for me."

"Pay it forward, man, pay it forward," James said with a grin, clapping Mike's shoulder. "You got difficult times ahead, but you'll pull through. Just keep looking to your Higher Power, take it one day at a time, and don't let setbacks keep you down. Just pick yourself up and start over."

With rough hugs all around, the men went their separate ways. Buck headed east out of Gary, and soon they were part of the heavy flow of trucks that ran between Chicago and Detroit. Traffic lightened up a little when they turned north at I-69, but there were still plenty of semis, particularly as they curved around Lansing and headed east. The scenery was nondescript, typical Midwestern farmland punctuated by stands of trees. Buck was genial enough, and would converse if prompted, but mostly kept to himself, leaving Mike to ponder where he was going, and what he'd do when he got there.

It wasn't until they'd passed through Flint that the surroundings began to catch Mike's attention. As they passed the exit for Lapeer, Mike nodded in recognition, then caught himself. Why would he recognize somewhere named Lapeer? To his memory, he'd never heard of the place. He pondered this for some miles until they came over a rise and saw another exit, this one for Imlay City.

Imlay City.

Abruptly, Mike was struck by an unexpected barrage of emotions. Tension and satisfaction and comfortable familiarity and distress all roiled within him, unmistakably associated with the town just north of the approaching overpass. What on earth? What about a small city in rural Michigan could possibly trigger such reactions? He couldn't remember even hearing of this place, much less ever being there.

But then, he couldn't remember much of anything, could he?

Part of him was tempted to ask Buck to pull off just to take a look at Imlay City, but he rejected that idea – Buck had a schedule to keep. But he strained his neck to see what he could as they passed, which wasn't much. He settled back in his seat, thinking hard about this, one more confusing and mysterious component in a confusing and mysterious situation.

Half an hour later they were approaching the end of the expressway. Buck avoided the lanes that would have taken him directly onto the bridge to Canada, instead taking an exit that put him on a city street. "I wanted to pull through the Duty Free anyway," Buck explained as they turned left into a fenced parking lot. They got out of the truck and Buck shook Mike's hand.

"Best o' luck to you, Mike. I don't know what's next for you, but I hope it all turns out for the best," Buck said, then pressed a couple of twenty dollar bills into Mike's hand. "It's all I can spare, but it should get you supper and breakfast. There are a couple of fast food joints you can see from here, and a donut shop just over there."

"Thanks, Buck," Mike replied. "I hope you don't get in trouble for helping me."

"If you keep quiet, I won't," Buck replied with a wink. "Good luck!" With that he headed into the store while Mike made his way out of the parking lot and onto the sidewalk. He was on a busy city street that seemed to be running north-south. Just to the south of where he stood the street passed under the bridge plaza, which was so big that the street seemed to be running through a short tunnel. To the east, above the treetops, he could see the steel arcs of two bridge spans sweeping up to the sky. He supposed that must be the bridge to Canada he couldn't cross. Looking at the spans, he felt another stir of *déjà vu*, as if he'd seen this before.

Mike shook his head. He was exhausted from trying to figure out who he was or where he'd come from. Right now something to eat sounded good, but not another burger. Something light, like a croissant and some coffee. Yeah, that sounded good. He hoisted his little duffel and headed for the donut shop.

District Troubles

State Senator Shawn Ramirez didn't like the way this meeting was going, not in the least. The problem was, there seemed to be nothing he could do to change it.

From when the federal government had first announced the Eastern Michigan Special Protectionary District about four months earlier, Shawn had been plunged into a nightmare of bureaucratic doublespeak and deflection. Ever since that infamous day last May, when online sources and his office phones had lit up with alarming reports of homes being raided, black-clad troops, and missile strikes, Shawn had been pushing for answers. But he might as well have tried to push over the Blue Water Bridge. All he'd gotten for his pains was delay and promises to get him more information, promises that to this point had gone unfulfilled.

Shawn was immediately concerned about the federal bureaucratic monstrosity because of the five counties that made up the SPD, three lay completely within his district – St. Clair, Sanilac, Huron, and part of Tuscola. The other two – Lapeer and the rest of Tuscola – were in the neighboring 26th Senate District, which was represented by Connie Rigney. But he knew better than to expect much help from Connie, who was focused on her race for the congressional district seat that had just opened up. The House representatives whose districts lay within the boundaries of the enigmatic SPD also wanted answers, but none of them had as much real estate in the game as Shawn did, so he usually ended up as point man.

The first thing Shawn had sought was official, formal definition of the SPD: what authority it was claiming, how that authority meshed with other state and local entities in the region, and what the District's purpose was. This had proved as easy as tracking unicorns by moonlight. All he'd been able to get out of the ever-changing crowd of bureaucrats was messages filled with vague definitions, assurances that his concerns were being addressed, and promises to deliver answers as soon as they became available. It didn't help that the whole situation had broken open just before the summer, when the Legislature went on recess and almost everyone returned to their districts to plan and run their primary or general election campaigns.

Shawn wasn't up for election this year, but party protocols expected him to be supporting colleagues in competitive districts. That, plus the planning for his daughter Maria's wedding, had diffused his focus over the summer. He'd met with some people about the topic, including a couple of times with the unctuous director of the SPD, Pierce Buchanan, and several more with grandiosely-titled underlings. He knew that bureaucrats could and did say anything in private conversations, so he discounted the mealy-mouthed platitudes of Buchanan and his flunkies accordingly, but he never got anything more substantial. Adding to his frustration was the fact that there seemed to be no sense of urgency in any corners about this power grab. When the SPD was first announced there had been a surge of coverage and commentary, but concern had quickly died down. The predominant impression, reinforced by the sparse statements of the SPD bureaucracy, was that the District was no big deal, business as usual, nothing to see here, folks.

Shawn wasn't buying it, and neither was his district staff member David Brennan, who actually lived in the district (which was apparently unusual for a district staffer.) From his home in Marlette, David made a point of getting out to local restaurants, businesses, and community meetings, where he was hearing quietly expressed concern about incidents and activities within the SPD that weren't being reported on any news sites. Despite superficial appearances and bureaucratic reassurance, it was not business as usual in the 25th Senate District, and Shawn wanted answers.

So Shawn had pressed and pressed for this meeting, only to run into an extraordinary amount of passive resistance.

Though all parties had professed eagerness to "clear the air" and "lay all the cards on the table", when it came down to finding a time to meet, the available periods had always seemed to be when Shawn had other commitments like Senate session or committee meetings. After it had become clear that he was being stonewalled, Shawn had resorted to deception: he'd publicly scheduled a hearing for a committee of which he was the chair, but quietly spread the word to his fellow senators that the hearing wouldn't happen. When the federal bureaucrats had miraculously all been able to meet right during the time of the committee hearing, he'd had his staff agree to the meeting with the understanding that Senator Ramirez would be sending a staffer. At the last minute he'd "cancelled" the sham hearing and had the satisfaction of seeing the bureaucrats' faces when he walked into the meeting they'd been working so hard to avoid.

But now that he was here, Shawn was finding his hopes for clarification still frustrated. He'd assembled a group representing local interested parties, including his chief of staff Kelly Anderson, David Brennan, Representative Wayne Osterland who represented the House District in the northern Thumb, staffers from House Districts more in the middle of the Thumb, a staffer from the state Attorney General's office, the head of the state's Department of Community Health, and three sheriffs from counties within the SPD. The feds had brought the SPD Director Buchanan and his aide Lieutenant Hammond, an official from Health and Human Services and another from the Department of Homeland Security, both of them flown in from Washington, D.C., the in-district head of Clinical Services, and a couple other minor functionaries. The conversation had been monopolized by the HHS official, who was behaving like the SPD existed to provide medical care. When the head of the state DCH had pressed to discover who would be paying for this care, the HHS rep had assured him that the federal government was directly assuming all expenses relating to clinical care within the SPD without any reduction in reimbursements to the state. This had generated some excited muttering between the DCH head and his assistant, and Shawn could understand why. By assuming complete financial responsibility for medical costs in the Thumb, the feds had just freed up millions in the DCH's budget that could be used other places in the state. It was a bribe of staggering magnitude, and it ensured that Michigan DCH would be putting up no resistance to the SPD.

This was not the outcome that Shawn had been hoping for. The SPD was an ill-defined and unprecedented intrusion of federal power into the lives of his constituents that left far too many questions unanswered and, in Shawn's mind, opened the door to serious abuse. Since it was the federal government, it would take a united front of state and local authority to push back, so having a substantial component of the state voice silenced by a giant payoff did not help.

"Look here," Sheriff Corrigan of Sanilac County broke in gruffly. "The main issue is not who's paying for the aspirin. The main issue is the constitutional rights of the citizens we're sworn to protect. This hastily-created 'District' raises too many jurisdictional questions for my comfort, as was amply demonstrated last May. What assurances do we have that spheres of authority will be respected?"

"I'm glad you raise that point, Sheriff...ah...Corrigan," the representative from the Department of Homeland Security replied in a soothing voice. "I think you'll be reassured by the answer. There is no question that the District was, as you put it so succinctly, hastily created, and that some of the earlier operations were laid on quite quickly with some ... ah ... distressing results. However, we resolved to learn from our mistakes, and are in the final stages of clarifying our policies *vis á vis* this issue. Our guiding principle is simple: SPD staff will be responsible for enforcing federal laws and policies within the District, while state and local authorities will be responsible for enforcing state laws and local ordinances. Not very different from current arrangements, actually."

"The 'current arrangements' didn't do much good last spring, when DTD troops waved loaded rifles in our deputy's faces and wouldn't talk to them at all," Corrigan challenged.

"Yes, well," the DHS representative replied with a note of exasperation in his voice, "to once again go over ground that has been covered many times, the incidents in question are undeniably regrettable, but have been traced to confusion at the leadership level between different federal units. In fact, that was part of the reason the SPD was created in the first place: to put everything under the same tent. We have rectified that confusion by personnel and policy changes, and it is Director Buchanan's foremost responsibility that those disturbing events will not be repeated."

"How?" Sheriff Tim Neal of St. Clair County chimed in. "What steps are you taking to ensure that? What changes can we expect to see?"

"I assure you, Sheriff...ah...Neal, that we are at least as concerned as you are about not seeing more incidents like we saw last spring. Though it would be inappropriate for me to divulge all the security measures we are implementing, I can apprise you that a new head of District security has been selected, who will be assuming control shortly. Furthermore, we're finalizing protocols for notifying appropriate authorities of imminent enforcement activities, so that everyone will be on the same page in the event that we need to take action. These are only two examples of the many safeguards we're putting in place to ensure that all spheres of authority are respected within the District."

Sheriff Neal started to respond, but at this point Director Buchanan closed his tablet case with an air of finality and announced, "I'm afraid we're out of time for now. Our out-of-town guests have more stops to make during their brief visit to the area, and other duties call me. I want to thank Senator Ramirez for arranging this meeting, and all of you for taking time to attend. Of course, you all have my contact information, and I am at your disposal if you have any further questions."

Stunned, Shawn looked at Kelly and David, who appeared as surprised as he was. "I don't know if we've quite –" Shawn began, but by now all the federal bureaucrats had stood and were packing up their materials. The state DCH rep and his assistant were already bustling from the room, talking excitedly, clearly eager to get back to their offices to begin planning how to allocate the unexpected windfall. The DHS rep was talking to the staffer from the Attorney General's office, and Director Buchanan was leaning over the end of the table holding a side conversation with Sheriffs Neal and Corrigan. Though Shawn had convened the meeting, the bureaucrats had summarily adjourned it.

Shawn managed to get to his feet in time to get a brisk handshake from Director Buchanan before he breezed out the door, followed by Bonnie Hammond tapping on her tablet. Most of the sheriffs had remained seated, and were glowering at the doors through which the feds had departed.

"Well, ain't that a load of deodorized Beltway bullcrap?" growled Al Corrigan. "Lots of flowery phrasing but nothing concrete."

"What do you expect?" Chip Keller of Huron County replied. "Notice they're subtly pushing their story again – nothing overt, but hints and suggestions."

"Yeah," confirmed Sheriff Neal, as if continuing an earlier conversation. "I noticed that."

Shawn glanced at Kelly and David, who looked puzzled. "What story is this?" Shawn asked. Neal gestured to Chip Keller, who replied.

"We were noticing over the summer that the mouthpieces for this SPD were quietly creating the perception that that the calamity that unfolded last spring was the result of a rogue executive who got too high-handed, and that the situation was defused by removing that executive and replacing him with this Buchanan."

"Yeah, that's the impression I got," Shawn replied. The sheriffs cast dark glances at one another before Chip continued.

"The reality is almost the exact opposite. There was an executive of sorts, but the strikes were executed without his knowledge or authorization. He worked to get them under control. We suspect that may be why he abruptly vanished to be replaced by Buchanan."

"Really? Do you have proof of this?" Shawn asked.

"Does the name Jason Pelletier mean anything to you, Senator Ramirez?" Chip asked.

"Never heard it," Shawn replied, glancing at his staffers, who shook their heads.

"He was the executive in question. He was pursuing an investigation of supposed domestic terror activities, and claimed to have plenary authority over all Domestic Terror Division activity within the region. When the raids began coming down last May, I called him. At that point he said that he had no knowledge of the activities, and that things weren't completely under control."

"Sounds like buck-passing," Shawn suggested.

"I thought so at first, but he said he'd ordered the troops to stand down, and recorded a video to that effect for our deputies to play to the DTD troops, instructing them to cooperate with local officials. It wasn't long after that – a few hours, I think – that the troops packed up and returned to their staging areas."

"Do you have a copy of this video?" Shawn asked.

"Right here," Chip replied, flipping open his tablet. Soon they were watching a self-shot video of a man with brown hair and brown eyes who looked to be in his mid-30s. He identified himself as Jason Pelletier of the Department of Homeland Security and spoke as if addressing people under his command. He explained that there had been a breakdown in communication, but was firm in his authority, giving clear orders to stand down. He gave the impression of someone striving to reestablish control over a situation that had lost it.

"And this Jason voluntarily recorded this video for you to distribute?" Shawn asked.

"Yes – I've got the phone conversations recorded, if you'd like them," Chip affirmed. "He spoke repeatedly about matters being out of control and needing to be reined in."

"What then?" Shawn asked. "Did he just vanish, or did you have any further conversations?"

"Well," Chip hesitated briefly before continuing. "That was our last official interaction. The next notification I received was of the creation of the Special Protectionary District and the appointment of Buchanan as director."

Shawn wondered at this carefully worded response to his question, but decided not to press the matter. "Have you tried to call this Pelletier?"

"Just once, out of curiosity. The number he'd given me showed as not in use."

"Well, that's…unusual," Shawn said, repressing the urge to say 'ominous'. "That recorded message doesn't sound like something a typical bureaucrat would say. It seems more like a desperation move attempting to do just what he claimed – get an out-of-control situation back under control."

"Yeah," Al Corrigan added. "And keep in mind the timing. This video was made, and Pelletier disappeared, two days before the SPD was announced, and Buchanan didn't show up until the following week. Kind of torques the impression they're pushing that the excessive activity was the result of confusion surrounding creation of the SPD."

"Tell me about this activity," Shawn asked. "I've heard plenty of rumors, and seen the official federal reports, and gotten hearsay from constituents. You and your people were on the ground – what exactly happened?"

"It's hard to give specifics, because much of it we only found out after the fact," Corrigan said. "We knew that there was Domestic Terror Division investigation underway in the area because Mr. Pelletier had paid us all visits. What we didn't know about, and thus weren't prepared for, were the coordinated dawn strikes on the morning of May 7th. Mr. Pelletier claimed that they took him by surprise as well, for what that's worth. We don't know exactly how many strikes there were. We suspect somewhere between eight and fifteen."

"What – you didn't get people calling you when their homes were assaulted?" Shawn asked.

"That's exactly what we didn't get. What calls we got were from neighbors alarmed by the activity, or even asking if the vehicles were ours. Some of our deputies spotted the DTD units on the move, but none of us had many cruisers out on the road that early in the morning. None of us got calls from the targeted homes."

"So, how did you find out what was going on in your counties that morning?"

"With two notable exceptions, we mostly learned after the fact, by the presence of federal troops securing sites that had clearly been raided. Once we knew something was coming down, we started looking more aggressively, and even put up some drones. Between that and the online reports, we eventually pieced together a picture of at least some of the sites that had been hit. There were probably others that we never learned of," Corrigan explained.

"Two exceptions?"

"One was the much-debated missile strike which is still being disputed by DTD. Despite numerous reports of a smoke trail followed by a fireball, the feds are still saying the investigation results were inconclusive and are spinning a story about a propane tank accident. Of course, they made further forensic evaluation impossible by bulldozing the site and burying it under several truckloads of sand just a few days afterwards, but my first responders verify that six bodies were removed from the accident site."

"Six bodies?" Shawn was shocked – this was the first he'd heard of fatalities.

"Yes, and three of them were children," Corrigan went on. "Another thing my deputies reported was that Pelletier showed up at that site and seemed to have a run-in with the guards."

"A 'run-in'?" Shawn asked.

"Yes. They said he tried to enter the site, but was denied access by the guard with an exchange of sharp words and even a pointed weapon. He drove off after a while, having never gotten past the guard."

"This is just plain weird," Shawn observed. "This guy claimed to have authority over all DTD activity in the area, but got pushed around by his own troops. At least that gives credence to his later claim that things had gotten out of control. Who were the victims?"

"Victims?"

"Yes – the victims of the blast, the six people killed," Shawn pressed, a bit puzzled. "Surely there's been some complaint or follow-up from family members?"

The sheriffs glanced at one another before Corrigan responded. "That's one of the strangest things about that morning – we don't know. With one exception, the families at all the raided sites had been quite reclusive, barely known even to their neighbors. We've had no calls from relatives or acquaintances, not even for the parties that we know were killed."

"But…surely there's some record somewhere?" Shawn protested. "Tax records? Post office records?"

"According to the local post offices, no mail was delivered to any of the sites we know were raided. Many didn't even have mailboxes. The tax records all show deeds in the name of various trusts, not families or individuals," Corrigan explained.

Shawn leaned back in his chair and attempted to digest this peculiar situation. "So, we've got mystery families raided at dawn by out-of-control troops, with you all only finding out afterwards, if ever, by the presence of troops guarding an empty property? Were there no eyewitnesses to any of these raids while they were happening?"

Corrigan glanced at Chip Keller, who nodded and responded. "We do have eyewitnesses to one of the raids – sons of the family who were at the back of the property feeding goats when the raid occurred. They saw it all and managed to escape out the back of the property. From them we learned how that particular raid unfolded, which turned out to be consonant with what we found at other sites after the fact. These raiding teams were clearly all working out of the same playbook."

"Sons who escaped? Where are they now?" Shawn asked.

"Safely within my jurisdiction," Chip replied. At Shawn's expectant glance, he continued. "Do you really need to know more?"

"No, no, I guess I don't. I presume you're taking all precautions."

"Yes," Chip assured him. "It's worth noting that Pelletier suggested on his own initiative to hide the boys once he heard we had them. A small matter, but it indicates two critical things: that he didn't trust his own organization, and that he wasn't sure he'd be able to regain control."

"And then he vanished," Shawn mused. "By the way, what happened to the people taken in the raids?"

Again, the sheriffs cast ominous glances at one another. "That's the most disturbing thing of all: we don't know," Tim Neal replied. "Often federal detainees end up being lodged in our jails, but not this time. We've no idea where those people were taken."

"And nobody has come looking for them?"

"Not that we know of," Neal confirmed. "Again, that's part of the irregularity of this whole situation. It's like these people were isolated from usual social contact, with no connections to their communities or neighborhoods – yet it was these very people that the feds came hunting, sweeping them away to places unknown."

"Even if nothing else about this was out of order, that would be," Shawn declared. "It's a violation of our most basic laws to hold people without charging them. Do you have any hints as to what might have happened to them?"

"Only speculation," Corrigan replied. "We suspect they're being held locally, within the SPD. That would make jurisdiction simpler, and enable them to invoke any contrived policies they can come up with to justify breaking the law."

Shawn stared at the wall for a minute, his mind racing. Clearly, he'd been unplugged from what was going on across his district for far too long. He needed to get back and see some of this for himself, and probably get Connie into the loop as well, congressional campaign or not.

"Is there anything else going on in my district that I should be aware of? Or in the 31st?"

"Well, there are the unexpected deaths," Tim Neal offered.

"Unexpected deaths?"

"Supposedly. There's nothing official, it's all anecdotal and mostly online. You're aware of the Rapid Care Centers and this UPAIR initiative, aren't you?"

"I dimly remember hearing something," Shawn admitted.

"That all preceded the announcement of the SPD by several weeks, but shortly after the clinics came online, rumors began circulating about people who'd been to them slumping over at work, or being found dead in their homes, or otherwise turning up dead. All word of mouth and online postings, though, no formal acknowledgement. The only official word about the clinics have been accounts of those who'd been there talking about the wonderful service."

Shawn cocked his head. This did sound fishy, but he'd learned over the years to be skeptical of anecdotal data. His office was plagued by people calling to report or inquire about something they'd heard about online. His staff even knew some of them by name, such as Judith from Port Huron or Fred from St. Clair, who called at least twice a week to discuss the latest online rumor. "Has there been any indication of higher mortality within the district?" he asked.

"Not yet, but it would be too early for anything to show up in the statistics," Neal acknowledged.

"Any complaints from relatives, or calls about unusual or unexpected deaths?"

"Nothing. Just online chatter and bar talk. And, older people with health problems do sometimes just die. What we don't know is whether they're doing it more often over the past few months, and if so, if the new clinics have anything to do with it."

"I'll tell you one thing, though," Al Corrigan added. "People are getting spooked, especially about the new clinics. They don't like the idea of being told where they have to get their medical care, and these rumors about unexpected deaths aren't helping. My deputies are hearing people say they'll flat-out refuse to go to them."

Shawn knew his constituents, and the streak of rural stubbornness that was so strong in many of them. He wondered how well that tendency was sitting with the carefully planned policies that their bureaucratic masters were crafting.

"Well," Shawn said with finality. "I clearly have a lot of catching up to do, but I don't need to chew up your valuable time while I do it. Thank you all for making this meeting. I want your offices to be in close touch with mine as we delve into this. There are far too many unresolved issues and unanswered questions about this federal initiative; what I've learned today has only heightened my concern. I don't plan to let this sleep."

With handshakes all around, the sheriffs departed, leaving just Shawn, Kelly, and David in the conference room. Shawn wondered if his expression looked as concerned as theirs.

"Of all the districts in Michigan," David moaned. "Why did they have to choose ours?

"And Connie's," Shawn reminded him. "But I agree – I can think of a few of my esteemed colleagues more worthy of this hornet's nest than us." He rubbed his face and looked at his staffers. "Of all these issues, I think the biggest stick to start beating people with is illegal detention. If people were taken away last spring, and are being held without due process, that's big. It's more than just unjust, it's something we could take to court and get publicity on."

"There are the two witnesses that Sheriff Keller spoke of," David pointed out.

"Yes, but they're minors, and I think him prudent to keep them hidden away until he can be certain of keeping them safe," Shawn answered. "But other than that, all we have is circumstantial evidence – guards outside home, rumors of people taken. No relatives or other interested parties have come forth to report anyone missing. It's hard to search for detainees when you don't know who you're looking for."

"Federal charges filed," Kelly said, looking up from her tablet.

"Pardon?" Shawn asked.

"Federal charges. If these people were arrested by federal agents, there should have been charges filed against them in the District Court in Detroit," Kelly explained. "We could review the records to look for a surge in charges last May."

"Bay City, too," David advised, checking his tablet. "Huron and Tuscola fall into the Northern District, so any charges against citizens of those counties would be filed there."

"Good thinking, Kelly," Shawn said. "Get someone on investigating that, will you? You can get precise dates from any of the sheriffs. Also, please draw up a couple of documents for me: a memo for Connie and her staff, informing them of what we're doing and offering them a chance to get involved. Nothing formal, just an advisory document. The other is a letter to Ruth's office, which should be more formal, advising her of what we've learned, our concerns, and what avenues we'll be pursuing. I want to see drafts by tomorrow afternoon." Ruth Becker was the U.S. House representative for the 10th Congressional District, which covered most of the Thumb area.

"Got it," Kelly affirmed, jotting on her tablet.

"David, I want you back in the district. Keep your ear to the ground. Try to find addresses of all the sites that the DTD raided last spring. If that takes you into Tuscola or Lapeer, apprise Connie's office but go anyway. Get any specifics you can about any people that were taken. Also see what you can learn about recent unusual deaths, okay?"

"Sure thing, boss," David confirmed.

Shawn leaned back and steepled his fingers as his staffers departed on their assignments. Good thing this was an election season – next week should be their final week of session here in Lansing before the legislature recessed for the final frantic weeks before election day. Even better, Shawn didn't have a campaign to run, since he wasn't up for election this year. He and his staff would be expected to lend assistance to other races as well as attend party functions, but none of that should be so intense as to interfere with his investigating what was happening in his district. He started berating himself for not getting on this mess sooner, for letting legislative and political and family matters elbow aside what he should have been on top of since last May, but shook that off. What had happened, had happened, and it had taken everyone by surprise. From the sounds of it, there were so many irregular things happening that the usual alerts had gone untriggered, so everybody had just proceeded with business as usual. Well, that was stopping today. He sighed – it would be easier if he had any idea what to do, or had confidence about his chances facing down the federal government. But what troubled him most was the question lurking behind the whole situation:

What they knew about sounded ominous enough. What might be going on that they didn't know about?

*   *   *

Captain Katy Touma pulled into the parking lot of the small office complex just east of Marlette with a set jaw. She didn't know if the choice of meeting site was mere coincidence or a deliberate gesture calculated to rub her nose in her disgrace. It had been at this location that she'd been humiliated in front of her troops by that sentimental, treasonous bureaucrat. She'd been forced to abort the carefully planned evolution, turning a promising beginning into a near total failure. She'd been sent back to her command in disgrace, and even though the investigative hearing had cleared her of wrongdoing, the taint of the incident had clung to her ever since.

But now, four months later, Captain Touma had been sent back to eastern Michigan without explanation: report to this place at this time for purposes that will be detailed upon your arrival. The site had been one of the Tactical Command Centers for the evolution last May, and was where Jason Pelletier had finally caught up with her and given her in-person orders to halt operations and stand her troops down. Now Pelletier was gone, nobody knew where, and the government had set up this Special Protectionary District, whatever that was. The Marlette site was clearly still in use, though for what purpose she could not imagine. She didn't even know who would be waiting for her inside, or what they would want of her.

Well, she thought grimly as she got out of the car and donned her beret, only one way to find out. She walked through the door to find a sentry seated at a genuine desk instead of the folding table that had been set up last time she was here, and using a workstation instead of a tablet. The

40

sentry saluted as she presented her ID. "Captain Katy Touma reporting as ordered."

"Captain Touma, yes, welcome, ma'am," the sentry glanced at his workstation. "Conference room three, just through the doors, fourth door on the left."

Touma passed through the door to the sentry's right, not knowing what she'd find on the other side. When she'd last been here, everything beyond the vestibule had been one big space which had been configured into a makeshift situation room, with workstations, projectors, and communications equipment scattered randomly about. She imagined that the area had been partitioned up into offices and cubicles like a more typical workspace.

She was surprised to see that she was only partly right. The space had been cleaned up, and some offices set up along the north wall, but the central area remained open, with desks and chairs placed around the perimeter and big screens mounted permanently on the walls above. In fact, most of the wall all around the room from waist level to the ceiling was covered with active screens, upon which were displayed outlines of the Special Protectionary District, of Michigan, and of the nation, with lists and charts scattered about. The central area was bordered by a set of movable partitions, set away from the wall far enough to create a makeshift hallway down which she was walking toward conference room three. There were occasional gaps in the partitions, allowing passage to the center space. Through these gaps she could see people walking about, consulting tablets or noting things from the projections on the walls. She'd obviously been wrong when she'd guessed that the TacComm had been dismantled. If anything, it appeared to have been established as a permanent site and properly equipped. Touma wondered what all the people in the central area were doing. And if this was what had been done to a makeshift Tactical Command, what had been done to the Operational Command?

Captain Touma came to the door of conference room three, knocked lightly, and entered. Seated at a conference table was an olive-skinned man in the uniform of the Domestic Terror Division whose insignia gave his rank as major, a heavy-set woman with short black hair, and a slender woman with bobbed blonde hair. Touma saluted the major, who remained seated and gave a half-hearted wave.

"Captain Touma, what a pleasure to finally meet you. I'm Major Serrano, adjutant for the SPD. This is Natalie Griggs of Health and Human Services, with her aide Stacey Lang."

The women did not rise to offer their hands, instead nodding at her, so the captain returned the nod. HHS? What could they be doing here?

"Be seated, captain, and let us get you up to speed," Major Serrano gestured to the seat beside him. "You're probably unaware that the proto-effort which was the forerunner of the SPD actually had two facets. One was what you were actively engaged in: the identification and attempt to uproot the clandestine terror network. But the other facet pertained to a highly classified HHS pilot project in the area. Not many DHS staff knew of this pilot project, but it was ramping up initial operations even as we were planning our takedown of the terrorist network. The…ah…high-level staff who were spearheading the DHS effort were also involved with the HHS initiative."

"Is that why our teams were told to call in follow-up staff from HHS after they'd secured the sites?" Touma asked. She'd wondered about that at the time.

"Exactly. That was a point of entry into the HHS program for some of the detainees," Serrano explained. "So it's been a joint effort from the outset. I'd better let Ms. Griggs take it from here, since she's the resident expert."

"Well," started the black-haired woman, "though the DHS effort suffered a setback after the initial round of activity, the HHS program was unaffected, and has been proceeding ever since. You should be aware that the current initiative is actually the reviving of an earlier pilot program that HHS floated in the area a few years ago, one that was brought to an abrupt and violent halt by the Imlay City blast."

"Ah, so that was the point of contact," Touma observed.

"Indeed," Griggs affirmed. "Without going into detail, much of which is still classified, the original project got off to a promising start then encountered unexpected resistance, some of which was related to the parties responsible for the blast. When the executive whose efforts led to the creation of the SPD was assigned to this area, his primary mandate was to solve the mystery of the blast. However, he'd been briefed on the motives and goals of the initial pilot, and figured out a way to jumpstart the HHS initiative using different tactics. In this, he was surprisingly successful, and within a few weeks of his arrival we had a prototype of the system operating in the area."

Touma clenched her fists a bit at this oblique reminder of the man whom she considered responsible for the failure of her operations and her personal disgrace, but kept her expression impassive.

"That prototype has been in operation ever since, and has been sufficiently successful that we've drawn up plans to expand it, both geographically and operationally. However, we now find ourselves facing a problem similar to the one the original pilot encountered: noncompliance."

"Noncompliance?" Touma asked.

"Yes – the intended participants in the program do not comply with essential components of its operation. The original project, the one that that was derailed several years ago, had been restricted to acute care facilities, but within a few months of its launch we began to see a drop-off in suitable candidates being admitted to these facilities. We learned later that this was due in part to a focused, concerted effort by a network of subversives to frustrate the project's goals."

"But…if the project was so classified, how did this network know how to frustrate it?" Touma asked.

"We don't know how many of the project details they knew, but they probably spotted the effect of the project in their communities. We do know that somewhere along the line one of the network members managed to plant surveillance equipment at the Imlay City site, which was used by project personnel. We don't know how much was learned by eavesdropping on staff conversations, but it's a fair guess that the surveillance equipment helped them time the blast."

"So, this noncompliance took the form of refusing to cooperate with the first steps of the initial pilot, but you don't know whether that was due to a breach in security or simply observations of the pilot's effect?" Touma asked.

"Precisely. And now that the project has restarted, we're seeing another upsurge in noncompliance. We think we can rule out espionage this time, but we could again be dealing with clever observers out there in the communities," Griggs explained.

"I wouldn't be so quick to rule out sabotage by insiders," Touma advised, remember how Pelletier had been so sympathetic to the targets on the day of the raids, even going so far as to empower local authorities to frustrate her plans and undermine her authority. She wouldn't put it past him to have leaked classified material to the locals.

"We aren't, but it doesn't matter just now," Griggs replied. "Because the new iteration of the project operates differently than the original pilot, noncompliance takes a different form. Before, it meant simply not going to the hospital. Now it can be done several ways – missing appointments, refusing treatment, not adhering to regimens of care, that sort of thing. This is where we hope to bring you in."

"Me?" Touma asked.

"Well, DTD in general, but you've been recommended for the project command."

This came as a surprise to Captain Touma, who hadn't thought she'd be recommended for anything after the debacle last spring, but she just nodded. "Command of what project? What could DHS DTD do to assist with HHS noncompliance issues?"

"Assist us in a supportive capacity. We have resources to facilitate things like transportation, but if patients get recalcitrant, it would help to have a little muscle around to enforce compliance," Griggs explained.

"I can see that, but wouldn't that be stretching the utilization of DTD personnel?" Touma looked at Major Serrano. "Doesn't this open us up to jurisdictional complications?"

"Under ordinary circumstances, it would," Serrano affirmed. "But these aren't ordinary circumstances. One of the purposes of the SPD is to dynamically reimagine government responsiveness. If that means discarding outmoded lines of delineation to construct a more agile and responsive team, then that's what we do."

"Well, certainly," Touma affirmed. "But what would be the manner of this support? Would we be escorts? Guards? Investigators? How could my troops help with the goal of improving compliance?"

"Those details remain to be worked out, which I hope you will undertake with Ms. Griggs and her staff," Serrano replied. "If you're agreeable, I'd like to appoint you as Principal of Compliance Enforcement for the SPD, reporting to Ms. Griggs, who reports directly to Director Buchanan."

"Actually, you'd be working quite a bit with Stacey here, who'll be the chief compliance strategist," Griggs explained.

"I see. What kind of resources would be at my disposal, and what tactical doctrine would I be following? Or is that yet to be determined?" Touma asked.

"I was expecting to assign you troops on an as-needed basis, but I imagine it won't be long before you have a good number under your command," Serrano assured her. "Perhaps as many as two dozen, depending on the need. As far as tactical doctrine, that's something you'll have to work out with HHS. I anticipate your role will be more policing than field operations, but that may change. That's part of the flexibility of the SPDs! You can work out whatever you need without having to fret about bureaucratic encumbrances. And you can be sure that your work will set precedent for other SPDs, so you'll be blazing new trails in that regard."

Touma pasted on a smile and nodded. What choice did she have? It was this or head back to Fort Wayne to supervise training drills and file reports. "Sound great, sir. When do I begin?"

"Wonderful," Serrano beamed. "Let's consider you assigned as of now. I'll talk to the supply staff about getting you some working space, and find you some quarters. I presume you came packed to stay?"

"My gear is in my car, sir," Touma assured him.

"Superb. If you could fetch your computer, we'll get you set up with Ms. Griggs and Lang here so you can get up to speed on the details of the situation."

Touma rose and headed out to her car, trying to keep her face fixed so it didn't show her disappointment. Damn! Once she'd been in charge of all the troops in the region, but now she was reduced to planning mall-cop level duties at the behest of HHS clinicians. No, no, she admonished herself, that was the wrong attitude. No percentage in dwelling on the past. She'd suffered a setback, but she'd recover. She'd get her career back on track. Her enemies wouldn't have the last word, she'd see to that.

*　　　　*　　　　*

It was the end of the workday, and DHS agents Brian Sanderson and Stanley Harris were sharing their usual end-of-shift coffee at the Horton's on Pine Grove. Though they spent most of their workday together, they still enjoyed the chance to spend time as friends, talking about matters unrelated to work – though avoiding discussing work was getting increasingly difficult, considering how things were going.

Just today they'd learned that all DHS employees within the Special Protectionary District would be offered the opportunity to become part of the SPD or apply for reassignment to other DHS locations. In a way, this news was welcome, because it put an end to months of rumors and uncertainty regarding their status *vis à vis* the poorly defined bureaucratic monstrosity that was the SPD, but it was not the outcome for which they'd been hoping. Since the area contained several international border crossings, there were many Department of Homeland Security employees, mostly Border Patrol. When the SPD had been announced, those employees had hoped they'd be permitted to retain their positions and reporting hierarchy. But no, the little tin gods who ran the SPD couldn't bear the thought of not having everything under their control, so they'd finally pushed this change through, leaving many longtime DHS employees facing a difficult choice.

"So, whatcha think, Stan?" Sanderson asked over his cup of decaf. "Going to bite? Or cut and run?"

"Dunno right now," Harris muttered. "I need some time to think. I'll talk to the guys about it, see what they suggest."

Sanderson nodded approvingly. "The guys" were a group of fellow alcoholics whom Harris had first met at AA meetings who got together regularly to pray for and support one another. For that reason alone, Sanderson hoped that Harris would decide to stay in the area. With the help of his AA group, Harris was making significant progress against his alcoholism, progress that might come undone if he was ripped from his support network.

"What about you?" Harris asked, and Sanderson grimaced.

"I don't know right now, either," Sanderson admitted. "Things with Kayla are kind of fragile – looking hopeful, but still fragile. Moving out of the area would be hard. On the other hand, I really don't want to be working under the SPD and whatever jokers are running it. I think I'll…"

Sanderson trailed off because Harris was clearly not attending to a thing he was saying. Instead he was looking over Sanderson's shoulder with a dumbfounded expression, his eyes unblinking and his mouth slightly agape.

"Tell me," Harris finally whispered. "Tell me that isn't who I think it is."

Mystified, Sanderson turned to see what Harris was staring at. It was immediately clear what had provoked that reaction, and his eyes widened in turn. Standing in the short line waiting to be served at the counter stood a slender man of medium height with sandy brown hair and a scanty beard. He was dressed in plain gray sweats and held a small blue duffel in his hand.

"Tell me that isn't Jason Pelletier," Harris asked, but Sanderson shook his head.

"That's him, all right, no mistake," Sanderson replied, continuing to stare. "Right down to the posture. But what is he doing here?"

Both men were a little spooked. The abrupt disappearance of Jason Pelletier had been one of the most ominous mysteries of the past few months. The prior May, Sanderson had been the last person to speak with him, by phone, before he had boarded a private flight down to D.C. Sanderson had been under the impression that the flight would be a quick jaunt, after which Pelletier would return to the area to resume his work. Instead, he'd dropped off the face of the earth – no return, no calls, no messages, nothing.

A new administrator had been appointed to replace him, and there had been no official mention of Jason Pelletier since.

But there he stood, in line at an ordinary coffee shop, looking about him as if his surroundings were unfamiliar.

"Are we sure it's him?" Harris asked. "He looks kind of lost."

"Unmistakably," Sanderson affirmed. One of the skills required by their jobs was being able to recognize faces beneath all sorts of disguising attributes like facial hair, glasses, or changes to hair and skin. This case wasn't even difficult – Pelletier looked just as he had, though perhaps a little thinner, and in need of a shave and a trim. "That's either him or his identical twin brother."

"You think he'll recognize us?"

"He doesn't look like he's recognizing much of anything," Sanderson observed. The man was now placing his order, paying with a rumpled bill.

"Maybe we should leave," Harris suggested.

"You can," Sanderson replied. "I'm going to talk to him."

"Why?" Harris asked. It was a good question. Neither of them had particularly liked Pelletier while he'd been their quasi-supervisor during his brief stint in the area. He'd been pushy, aloof, and obnoxious. His disappearance had been ominous enough; this quiet reappearance suggested things were awry. Getting involved could complicate matters, perhaps dangerously so. Staying well clear seemed the prudent course.

"I dunno," Sanderson admitted. "He looks really confused." It was true. A bewildered, derelict air clung to the man, quite unlike the forceful and aggressive personality they'd known.

"Whatever," Harris shrugged. "You do what you like. I'm staying out of it."

"Feel free to shove off," Sanderson said, rising to head toward the man.

"I'll hang here, just in case you need backup," Harris replied.

Sanderson made his way to the table the man had taken. "Excuse me, sir," Sanderson said. "It's good to see you again. We were concerned when we didn't hear from you for so long."

To Sanderson's amazement, the man looked up at him with his light brown eyes and said, "I'm sorry – have we met before?"

"Why, yes," Sanderson replied, shocked and a little bit frightened. "We worked closely with you last spring right here in the Blue Water area. I'm DHS agent Brian Sanderson, and Stan Harris is right over there."

The man gave a little nod as he looked back at Sanderson. "Then perhaps you can tell me who I am."

Rattled, Sanderson glanced back to where Harris was watching carefully. "Mind if I sit down?" he asked.

"Not at all."

Sanderson sat down and stared at the man. Beyond question it was Jason Pelletier, but the vague look in his eyes was unnerving. "Don't you remember? You're Jason Pelletier, a high-level DHS executive. You came here last spring, and we worked together on a project until you were summoned back to Washington in mid-May."

"That would explain how I ended up in the D.C. area," Pelletier replied pensively. "I just left there a couple of days ago."

Sanderson was now close to alarm. What the hell had happened to the focused, hard-driving supervisor they'd known? "Listen, sir, this is all very confusing. Maybe you could tell me the whole story, but first let me get my partner over here." He waved Harris over, and he came, looking mutinous, bringing their coffees.

"I hope you don't mind if I record this," Sanderson said as he propped his tablet on the table.

"Not at all."

"You mentioned that you've just come from the D.C. area. Can you elaborate on that?"

Jason recounted the tale of his travels, carefully not naming the truckers who'd helped him. The two agents listened, only occasionally asking clarifying questions. The account was quickly over, and when Jason had finished, Sanderson and Harris looked at each other with astonishment.

"If you could give us a minute, sir," Sanderson asked, and took Harris to another table to consult.

"Jesus Christ, what did they do to him?" Harris asked, his voice laced with fear.

"I don't know. From his description, I suspect he was in some kind of program that he was just thrown out of."

"What kind of program would produce that kind of amnesia? It's like his brain has been scrubbed."

"No idea," Sanderson replied. "But notice that he's been lucid ever since he was thrown out onto the street, or since the morning after. Maybe he was being given some sort of drug that was messing with his head."

"In case you didn't notice, his head still seems pretty messed up," Harris pointed out. "But who, Brian? Who would do this to him, and then just throw him aside? It's spooky."

"It's damn spooky," Sanderson admitted. "I'm guessing that whoever had him pitched out on the street in this muddled condition was expecting him to be picked up by the cops, or worse – you've been hearing about some of the measures they've been taking in those big metro areas."

"Yeah, I've heard," Harris said. "But...what can we do?"

"Well," Sanderson answered, glancing over to where Jason was finishing his dinner. "One thing we can't do is just leave him. You heard – he's only got about thirty bucks, no papers, no phone, no home. He'd be a sitting duck out there."

"Brian," Harris pleaded. "Think carefully here. My guess would be that the people who put him in that brainwashing program are the same ones running this district. As you say, he probably wasn't supposed to survive being thrown out on the street, and certainly wasn't intended to end up back here. If he's caught, you can guess what'll happen – and that will probably extend to whoever's with him."

"I know the risks, Stan," Sanderson assured him. "But we can't just let him wander off."

"Maybe, but what can you do?"

"I don't know, but I've got to try. I promise I'll try to offload him as soon as I can, but I want to make sure it's into safe hands. Who knows? Maybe this amnesia will pass, and he'll come back to himself."

"As if that would make things easier," Harris grumbled. "You do what you think best. I gotta go."

"Sure, Stan. See you tomorrow," Sanderson said as Harris headed to his car and he went back to where Jason was sitting. "Look, sir…ah, Mr. Pelletier."

"Please, if Jason is my name, then call me Jason."

"All right, ah…Jason. You say you've got nowhere to sleep for the night?"

"No, I don't."

"Well, if you'd like, I could take you back to my apartment. It's kind of small, and none too tidy, but it's a place you could bunk until we get something figured out."

Jason blinked in surprise. "That's very generous of you, Mr. Sanderson."

"Just call me Brian."

"Very well, Brian. But wouldn't your hospitality inconvenience you?"

"Not so much. I have people I can call, other places I can stay," Sanderson assured him. "But let's get you out of here."

"All right," Jason replied, starting to clean up his tray. Sanderson's mind was racing. He could call Kayla. She certainly wouldn't mind having him stay in the guest room for a couple of nights while they got things figured out. Right now, they needed to get out of sight. This donut shop was frequented by DTD and Border Patrol agents, and it wouldn't do to have some walk in and spot him with Jason. The possibility that someone would recognize Jason was slim, but it was there, and if he was recognized it would really hit the fan. Sanderson hustled Jason to his car and headed for his apartment, a little shamed by how much tidying he'd have to do to make the place usable by a visitor. Hopefully this would be a very temporary arrangement, but Sanderson was at a loss as to what he could do with the damaged man who had so unexpectedly reentered his life.

Shadow of Threat

Shawn was tying his tie in preparation for some campaign-related function he had to attend this evening when his phone chirped with a message from David.

You catching presser on SPD? Running now.

No. Send link to tablet, Shawn messaged back, and propped his tablet where he could see it while he continued his effort to tame the necktie. Shortly a video opened, showing Director Buchanan standing behind a lectern in front of a blue background spangled with the logo of the SPD and the icon for the UPAIR initiative. The press conference had clearly been going on for a while and Buchanan was well into his speech. Shawn sighed. This was a standard bureaucratic trick – scheduling a press release or conference for late on a Friday, when all the legislators and most staffers and reporters had left their offices. He and the area representatives should have received advance notice of the press conference, but this was how the SPD was operating. At least David was on the ball.

Shawn tried to focus on what Buchanan was saying. Mostly it was the expectable bureaucratic fluff and hyperbole, expounding at length about the success of the UPAIR initiative, and how that enabled them to expand the scope of the initiative to include other underserved and at-risk populations. He spoke of implementing new protocols that would streamline treatment for the elderly, expecting mothers, and families with young children.

Shawn had heard such platitudes many times before, and knew that the devil would be in the details. Anything could be made to sound magical at a press conference. How it was actually implemented – and paid for – was where things could get gritty. But Buchanan was concluding his statement and yielding the stand to a black-haired woman whom Shawn recognized as having been at the meeting earlier that week. Grates? No, Griggs, that was it – somebody Griggs. She was reading a statement about how pleased she was with the initiative's progress and how happy she was to be appointed to head up such a bold initiative, et cetera, et cetera. Shawn recognized the woman who stood behind her, against the backdrop, as her blonde aide whose name he couldn't remember. On the other side of the lectern, standing next to Buchanan, was a brown-haired man in a suit whom Shawn recalled seeing with Buchanan at meetings and hearings and was probably some kind of aide. Beside him, almost out of the frame, stood a short, trim woman with shoulder-length black hair and a stern, no-nonsense expression. She was dressed in the black uniform of the Domestic Terror Division, and was scanning the room as if watching for threats. Shawn didn't know who the woman was, but from the looks of her, he didn't want to get on her bad side.

Ms. Griggs finished her prepared statement and was taking questions as the camera panned the nearly empty room. Shawn guessed there would be no questions, given that there were almost no reporters, but in this he was wrong. A man was sitting a few rows back, and when he stood to ask his question, Shawn recognized him as Jim Roberts, owner/editor/reporter for the ThumbWay News out of Harbor Beach. Jim was one of those old-school reporters who seemed to think he was failing at his job if he wasn't coming across as everyone's adversary, but he was a decent enough person when he didn't think it his responsibility to be grilling you, and he was passionately honest.

"Yes, Mr…" Griggs recognized him.

"Jim Roberts, ThumbWay News. Can you address the persistent reports of patients dropping dead shortly after visiting your Rapid Care Centers?"

Shawn couldn't help but grin at the stunned expression that Ms. Griggs let slip for a moment. Wherever she'd come from, she wasn't accustomed to that kind of bluntness from the media. "Well, ah, Mr…Roberts," she stumbled to recover, "in case you weren't paying attention, I've just presented statistics on the first quarter of the UPAIR Initiative, and they all show moderate to significant positive impact on the overall health of the district. Given the state of care in the region before the initiative, we would expect a certain amount of residual…"

Griggs continued to blather, but Shawn's attention was distracted Buchanan's aide, who was leaning over to whisper to the woman in uniform while occasionally glancing at Jim. The woman was listening with a fixed expression but nodding from time to time.

"But, of course," Griggs was concluding in a condescending tone, "you'll never lack for rumors and speculation online. I'm afraid that's all we have time for. Further details, links, and contact information are all in the briefing packets. Thank you." She left the lectern before anyone had the chance to pose more questions. Shawn noticed that as she walked from the room, she was joined by a high-level executive from the state Department of Community Health. He wondered how closely MDCH was working with HHS on these initiatives, and what impact it would have on his constituents.

*   *   *

"If I could see your right arm, please, Mrs. Hood," the aide asked, and Bethany held it out to be swabbed with alcohol and then sprayed with some kind of oily liquid.

"What's that?" Bethany asked.

"Anesthetic spray," the aide explained. "It numbs the skin. We have to give it a minute to take effect, but it makes this easier." She held up a small beige plastic box about the size of a spice canister.

"What does that do?"

"I'll show you," the aide said, tapping Bethany's arm. "Feel that?"

"No."

"Great," the aide entered a few things on her tablet then held the box next to it until the tablet beeped. Then she took

Bethany's arm and pressed the bottom of the box firmly against her skin. She pressed a button and Bethany felt a jolt of pressure as the box gave a muted click. The aide swiftly discarded the box and pressed a gauze pad against a small cut that was starting to ooze blood. "If you could just hold that firmly, it should seal right up. We'll bandage it before you go."

"What did you just do?" Bethany asked as she pressed the gauze down.

"It's a new innovation, and you're one of the first to benefit from it," the aide said with a cheery smile as she tapped away on her tablet. "It's a small chip that will hold all your medical records."

"But...I thought the medical records were in your computers," Bethany replied.

"Many are, but many aren't yet, especially in underserved areas such as this," the aide explained. "This chip uses nanotechnology to store all your records here in your arm, so wherever you go, you've always got your full medical history right with you." She held the tablet close to Bethany's arm and got a chirp, which made her smile. "It looks like you're coming online just fine!"

"That's great, but if all my records are right here, won't anyone be able to..." Bethany began, but the aid cut her off dismissively.

"You have to have an approved reader to scan the chip and make updates, and approved readers are only issued to approved providers. And...you're all set! The doctor will be in shortly." The aide finished a few final taps on the tablet screen and breezed out of the room, leaving Bethany pressing the gauze pad against her numbed arm.

Bethany and Patrick had been thrilled when the two telltale blue lines had shown up on the home test four weeks earlier. They'd been trying for a while, and were just starting to feel a bit concerned, when the test turned up positive. Bethany had promptly called her gynecologist to set up a schedule of visits, only to be told that due to a new set of protocols announced by the government, all expectant mothers had to receive care through the UPAIR program. So Bethany had driven to the Rapid Care Clinic near Fairgrove, which was the closest one to their home north of Sebewaing. She'd been greeted, questioned, and escorted to an exam room. Though small, the room seemed to have been set up to accommodate pregnant women, because there was an ultrasound machine right by the exam table. Eventually a tech had come in, taken a couple of blood samples, and had had Bethany lie back for the ultrasound. The ultrasound machine had been one of the newer models, so Bethany had gotten to see a real-time enhanced image of their baby flipping and wiggling in his little sac of fluid. Then the tech had done something Bethany hadn't expected – using a long, thin needle and guided by the ultrasound image, she'd gone right through the skin and uterine wall to take a sample of some sort. When Bethany had explained that she and Patrick hadn't intended to do tissue testing on the baby, the tech had assured her that this was all part of the new enhanced care and that it wouldn't cost them a thing. She'd handed Bethany a storage chip with a video of the ultrasound image to show to Patrick and had sent her on her way.

That had been two weeks ago, and now Bethany was back in response to a message from the RCC asking her to come in as soon as possible. Patrick had been hoping to come along for this visit, but the appointment time had conflicted with his work, so Bethany had come alone.

Bethany's fingers were starting to numb from the effort of squeezing the gauze pad against her arm when the exam room door opened and a red-haired woman in a lab coat came in. She was looking at a tablet screen and wearing a grave expression.

"Bethany Hood?" the woman looked up and asked.

"Yes," Bethany replied.

"Have you had – I see you have," the woman said, spotting the gauze on Bethany's arm. "Oh, she should have –

here, let me take care of that." With an air of exasperation, the woman took away the gauze and applied a bandage to the small slit in Bethany's arm. Then she held her tablet close to the spot and got a confirming chirp. Only then did she sit down on the stool and fix Bethany with a serious gaze. Bethany noticed that the tag on her lab coat simply said 'Dr. Jean' and had one of those bar codes that looked like a block of dots.

"Bethany, I'm afraid I have bad news for you," Dr. Jean said gravely. "The results of your tissue testing came back and the fetus tests positive for neurofibromatosis."

"For...for what?" Bethany asked.

"Neurofibromatosis, or NF for short. It's an extremely rare but incurable congenital condition. It causes tumors on nerves, and can cause blindness, neurological complications, cardiovascular complications, and other more serious conditions."

"Can...can anything be done?" Bethany asked, her head spinning. Dr. Jean shook her head.

"There is no cure, and what treatments there are only address symptoms. It's a complicated condition with a high potential for expensive, burdensome care that only gets worse as time goes by."

Tears were now seeping down Bethany's cheeks as she struggled to grasp the implications of this ominous development. She wanted Patrick. She wanted her mother. She wanted everything to feel like it had last night, when she and Patrick had had a boisterous time suggesting names for the baby.

"I'm sorry," Dr. Jean continued with just the right note of sympathy, then her tone brightened a bit. "The good news is that the modern testing we use detected this so early. That means we can schedule the procedure quickly, and you and your husband can try again."

"Wait," Bethany shook her head in confusion. "'Try again'?"

"Of course. This pregnancy is futile, but you're both young, and the odds of two NF pregnancies in a row are very low. The sooner you're able to try again, the sooner you'll have a clean, healthy baby," Dr. Jean assured her while looking at her tablet. "How about next Tuesday? We have an opening."

"Please, this is all happening too quickly," Bethany gasped. "What are you suggesting?"

"It's a simple D and C – I'm sure you've heard of them. Takes no more than fifteen minutes. We'll have you in and out within an hour. Now, how does Tuesday work? We also have openings on Thursday."

"Please, I want to talk to Patrick. I need to talk to Patrick." Bethany was feeling lightheaded.

"Of course, I understand," Dr. Jean assured her. "But there's no harm in scheduling an appointment –"

"No, no, I don't want to schedule anything until I talk to Patrick," Bethany replied, standing and reaching for her jacket. "I need to go home. I need to talk to Patrick."

"If you insist," Dr. Jean said. "The front desk will call you tomorrow to set up an appointment. I'll have them send you a list of open time slots so you can decide which one suits you best."

"All right," Bethany said, reaching for the door.

"Understand this, Bethany," Dr. Jean said in a cold voice. There was no trace of sympathy about her now, just a hard glare. "This is the only place you can receive care for this pregnancy, and this is the only procedure we will provide. NF is classified as an unsustainable condition. The sooner you reconcile yourself to that, the sooner you and your husband can put this behind you and get on with your lives."

Bethany bolted from the exam room, rushing down the narrow hallway and across the crowded waiting room, fumbling in her purse for her phone. She had to call Patrick. She had no idea what to do. Patrick would help.

Later that day, Patrick and Bethany sat mournfully at the dinner table. Patrick had left work as soon as Bethany had called him, and they'd spent the afternoon crying and talking and holding each other. Patrick had comforted Bethany as best he could, bringing her tea and holding her hand and making a delicious dinner for which neither of them had any appetite. Afterward they sat at the table wrestling with the terrible situation they were facing. Then Bethany's phone chimed, and Patrick glanced at the reminder that had popped up.

"Oh – it's lesson night. I presume you want to cancel?" Patrick asked.

"Lesson night? No, I'd like to go. Mrs. Kyle comes all the way up to Sandusky just for three of us. It would be rude of me to cancel. Besides, music is calming, and Mrs. Kyle is such a soothing person. I'm sure it will help to clear my mind."

"If you're certain, then. I'll drive you," Patrick offered.

"Oh, Patrick, you don't need to –" Bethany began, but Patrick interrupted her.

"Bethany, I'm not going to leave you alone, not in the middle of all this."

"Thanks, honey," Bethany smiled through her tears and went to fetch her violin.

*   *   *

Dorothy Oldham enjoyed reading, especially to such a willing audience. Tyrone could read, of course, but he still had a long way to go before he was competent to read the books he most enjoyed. The books at his reading level had simple, hokey plots that swiftly bored him. His eager mind and fertile imagination could drink in much more elaborate tales, and Dorothy was happy to oblige.

Tyrone had been a blessing to the Oldhams. They'd taken him in on that crazy summer night just over a year ago, when they'd thought it would just be for a brief time until more permanent housing could be found. But he'd been such an eager, delightful young man that they'd ended up arranging for him to stay with them. He loved his new home, awakening each morning full of excitement for what the day would bring. He helped Ralph with chores around the house, was keen to learn, and almost painfully eager to please. He was a quick study in the kitchen as well, and was competent at cleaning all over the house. Once Dorothy had explained to him how his room should be ordered when he wasn't using it, he kept it that way diligently.

Tyrone never spoke about where he'd come from, and the Oldhams had been cautioned not to ask. It was an arrangement that suited everyone, for Tyrone seemed as ready to leave that dark chapter behind as the Oldhams were ready to welcome the sunny new phase of their lives as Tyrone's foster parents.

One thing that was clear to retired teacher Dorothy was that wherever Tyrone had been, his education had been sorely neglected. When he'd arrived, he'd barely known his alphabet and had only the most rudimentary mathematics. He had no history or geography, and literature was out of the question. Dorothy had an almost empty slate to work with, and fortunately she knew just how to fill it. She knew what sites to go to and what resources to order to put Tyrone on an accelerated course of study that would challenge his ready mind and make up for what he'd lost.

Stories were a central component of Dorothy's regimen for Tyrone, for they not only gave him exposure to good literature, but served as an incentive. He would sweat out math problems or map labeling for the reward of hearing Mallory or Scott or Lewis. They'd gone through the Arthurian legends and *Tom Sawyer*, the Gospels and the *Arabian Nights*. Tyrone listened eagerly, then he'd go off and draw pictures of the images that had formed in his imagination. He was a surprisingly skilled artist, and had almost wept when the Oldhams had given him a full set of colored pencils and a real sketch pad. His bedroom walls were papered with drawings of knights in armor, boys on rafts, and giants. He'd often draw special pictures for Dorothy and Ralph, delicate flowers or trees against the sunset.

They were currently working through *The Odyssey*. Dorothy had read Tyrone a prose version of the Trojan War, since it would be years before he was ready for the actual *Iliad*. Tyrone had sat enraptured during the reading, then had scurried to his room to draw pictures of long ships on beaches, high-walled cities, and a towering wooden horse. Fortunately, there was a prose version of *The Odyssey* that followed, and Tyrone was soon drawing pictures of cyclops and ships at sea.

Tonight, the story came to the arrival at Circe's Island, with the men going ashore to find the surprisingly docile wild animals. Dorothy read of the men finding Circe's hall and being invited in to dinner only to be turned into pigs and driven to the pigsty. She looked to see Tyrone's reaction to this comical image, and was surprised to see that he wasn't laughing or even smiling. Instead his expression looked vacant, almost stunned.

"Well, Tyrone, what do you think of that?" Dorothy asked jovially, but the lad didn't reply, instead gazing straight ahead with an almost burning gaze, his lips moving slightly. "Tyrone?" Dorothy asked, now a little concerned – this detached intensity was very unlike the lighthearted lad they knew. She set the book aside. "Tyrone?"

Abruptly Tyrone jumped up from where he'd been seated on the floor and dashed out of the living room and up the stairs to his bedroom, where Dorothy heard his door slam. Ralph, who was seated at the dining room table, watched the boy's passage in amazement. "What's going on?" he asked Dorothy.

"I've no idea," Dorothy answered. "I've never seen him like this. Come on."

They went upstairs to find Tyrone standing in the corner of his room, facing the wall, muttering to himself. It was clear he was highly agitated, his arms and legs jittering where he stood, his fingers working and clenching.

"Tyrone?" Dorothy asked gently, approaching him slowly. "Tyrone? It's just us, Dorothy and Ralph. Are you all right?" He did not respond, so she stepped closer. "Tyrone?" He gave no indication that he'd even heard, which was beginning to worry Dorothy. She looked over her shoulder and nodded to Ralph.

"Tyrone lad, it's me, Mr. Ralph. How'd you like to join me for some milk and cookies?"

Still Tyrone did not respond, and his trembling was getting more violent, now shaking his whole body. Reaching out slowly, Dorothy continued talking in her low, soothing tones. "It's just us, Tyrone, we're right here with you. We're your family, remember? How about some milk and cookies? I'll just take you by the shoulder and we'll go down to the kitchen." With that she gently laid her hand on his shoulder. He gave a little start, but reached up to lay his hand on hers. She gripped more firmly, and he gripped in response.

"We're right here, Tyrone, me and Mr. Ralph, we're right with you," Dorothy murmured, stepping a little closer.

"Miz...Miz Dorothy?"

"Yes, Tyrone?"

"Miz Dorothy?"

"We're right here, Tyrone," she assured him.

He turned toward her. Tears were standing in his eyes and his lips were quivering. "Miz Dorothy, I need to talk to the safety lady."

Dorothy glanced at Ralph, who returned her puzzled look. "Sure, Tyrone. Who's the safety lady?" she asked.

"The safety lady. She was there, that...that night. She brought us out. She was really pretty and really nice and I really want to talk to her. Please?"

The plaintive tone of Tyrone's plea nearly broke Dorothy's heart. This clearly meant a lot to him, and was somehow connected to his abrupt and extraordinary reaction.

If only they knew who he was talking about.

"Sure, Tyrone, we'll do everything we can. Do you remember her name? Where she lived?"

"I think she told me, but I forget. She was just – the safety lady," Tyrone replied. "There were three of them, but she walked with me, and then she led us on the long dance. She said she'd be in touch, but I haven't seen her."

Dorothy looked at Ralph to see if he could make any sense of this, but he simply shrugged. Fortunately, Tyrone seemed to be calming down now that he'd expressed his wish, so Dorothy urged him over to sit on his bed. She sat beside him while Ralph stood by and put his hand on Tyrone's shoulder.

"I just want the safety lady. I need to talk to her," Tyrone was muttering, barely audible. "I need to see her. Please."

"I promise, we'll look for her," Dorothy assured him, but he seemed not to notice, constantly muttering while staring straight ahead.

"How 'bout some milk and cookies, then?" Ralph asked cheerily. That was an enticement that had never failed to elicit an enthusiastic response, but this time it had no effect. Tyrone sat still and stared, muttering to himself over and over.

Dorothy kept vigil with Tyrone, sitting beside him on his bed. He never ceased his quiet muttering, staring straight ahead and fidgeting slightly. Not even milk and cookies brought right into his bedroom – normally a forbidden venue for food – tempted him. Long after his usual bedtime he finally quieted and slumped over. Dorothy and Ralph laid him out gently, easing his shoes off but otherwise leaving him.

"Should one of us stay with him?" Ralph asked.

"I don't know where," Dorothy replied, looking about the small, sparsely furnished room. There was only Tyrone's desk and chair, dresser, and bedside table. There wasn't enough room on the floor to throw blankets down as a makeshift mattress.

"Let's leave the doors open, and try to sleep lightly," Ralph suggested. "Do you have any idea who this 'safety lady' is?"

"Not a clue. I'll have to make some calls tomorrow. Rosemary was the one who first contacted me about taking him, so she might know who to call," Dorothy answered.

"If they're still there," Ralph answered darkly. The Oldhams were on the periphery of the secret activity about the Thumb. They hadn't sheltered any endangered parties themselves, but knew those who had, and now and again had assisted with minor matters like supply runs and transporting people. Some of their acquaintances had been more engaged, like Rosemary, who had called that summer night asking if they could temporarily shelter a homeless youth with no questions asked. It hadn't taken much deduction to figure out that there was a connection between hastily sheltered youngsters and the corrupt foster care network that had been exposed just days later, but they'd never asked anyone, least of all Tyrone, for any details. The lad had seemed perfectly content in their home, neither speaking of where he had come from nor asking where he was going. Not even the rumored events of the prior spring had disturbed them, though Ralph and Dorothy had pieced together that the long-hidden network had been compromised and swiftly dismantled. This had not directly affected them at the time, but now it raised the question of whom to call, and what they'd do if nobody answered the phone.

"What on earth set him off like that?" Ralph asked in a whisper once they'd stepped out onto the landing.

"I've no idea. I was just reading him the story of the *Odyssey*, and we got to the part where they arrive at Circe's Island, and suddenly he got all distressed and fled the room," Dorothy explained.

"Circe's Island? Isn't that where most of the crew gets turned into pigs?"

"That's the one," Dorothy affirmed. "It was like a switch flipped inside him and his whole demeanor changed. He got agitated and jumpy, and started asking for this 'safety lady'."

"Any idea who she might be?" Ralph asked.

"None, and I don't think he does, either. It's possible that she was someone involved in whatever operation extracted him from his prior circumstances. It's equally possible that there is no such person, and she's simply a construct of his imagination arising out of his difficult past. You know how creative he is."

"He seemed pretty specific," Ralph observed. "Spoke of there being three of them, and what they all did."

"I know, but I've seen lots of traumatized children over the years. Their imaginations working with their subconscious coping mechanisms can do extraordinary things. I remember one poor girl who spoke glowingly of her mother, how beautiful and kind she was. Turns out her mother was a psychotic drug addict who completely neglected the girl. The pristine image the girl was maintaining was an amalgam of an aunt and a helpful neighbor."

"You think that might be happening here? That Tyrone created an imaginary person?"

"I think it's possible," Dorothy admitted. "It's equally possible that there was an actual person whom he simply knows as this 'safety lady'."

"And you have no idea why he suddenly wants to talk to her?" Ralph asked.

"No idea, but my gut tells me that the answer might be so terrible that we don't want to know. Why don't you get ready for bed? I'll call Rosemary in the morning."

The Warrior's Message

Gerald Solomon grimaced at the rattle coming from the old van's suspension. If this was how it responded to smooth expressway surface, how would it handle some of the back roads it was going to have to travel on the Isabella Reservation?

Gerald shouldn't have had to be driving this van. His much newer, much nicer sedan should have been ready before he had to leave. But Rick and Jerry hadn't yet received the required part, and Gerald's too-often postponed trip to visit his sister down in Mount Pleasant was at hand, so he'd had to borrow one of the tribe's vans to make the trip. He'd taken one of the older ones so as not to discommode the regular drivers, but now was wondering if he'd made a prudent choice.

Gerald sighed. Though nobody was keener than he was about keeping business within the tribe, he couldn't deny that operations like Rick and Jerry's made it difficult. They were the only auto repair operation on the Garden River Reserve, and proudly trumpeted their status as an all First Nation operation. But they were also laid-back and lackadaisical, opening whenever they happened to get to work and closing when they tired of working, with little regard for posted hours. They were equally casual about answering their phone, and Gerald was certain that when he'd been standing at their counter listening to Jerry's apologetic explanation for why his car wouldn't be ready for another week, Rick's frantic activity on the workstation in the background had been the ordering of the necessary part. Gerald had to admit that even though the dealerships in neighboring Sault Ste. Marie were run by Canadians with brisk European efficiency, they did have your car ready when they said they would. Taking his car to the dealership might have funneled funds outside the tribe, but at least he'd have been able to drive his own car to Mount Pleasant and not a rattly borrowed tribal van.

Gerald was coming up on the ramps, and had to remind himself to take the exit that would carry him south on US-127 rather than continuing along I-75. He'd taken the I-75 route so often in the past six months that it was instinctive for him to just follow the expressway down to I-69 in Flint, then turn east to Port Huron, cross the Blue Water bridge, and take Canada 402 over to the University of Western Ontario in London. The conferences and symposia about the missionary diary were winding down now, but it had been an exciting period of consulting with many scholars and First Nation officials. It wasn't often that a new original document was found, and one nearly four centuries old and from the period of first contact was even rarer. The professors and historians had made their presentations and expounded their theories about European influence on First Nation culture, and Gerald had listened without comment. As he'd expected, the analyses had focused on the recognizable and measurable: economic and social metrics, theories about the makeup of migrating peoples, and so forth. What Gerald considered the most important revelation of the diary, the spiritual and supernatural elements, had been ignored, simply because the scholars didn't have any convenient categories into which to slot them. Well, perhaps under 'lore and superstition', but that was as good as a dismissal.

Gerald could understand the scholars' reticence to address the more mystical elements of the diary's tale. It was easier to discuss familiar and recognizable things like tribal life and migration patterns. The account of the menacing shadowed woods, the bone-deep dread of the tribe, and the spiritual warfare waged by the diary's author, Fr. Thomas, seemed to belong more to the world of magic and voodoo than to anthropological and historical studies. For that matter, Gerald hadn't completely reconciled the account himself. He could appreciate the missionary's account of early contact with Gerald's Anishinaabek ancestors, and the shadowed woods with their damaging effects resonated with his own experiences. But he still didn't know what to make of the end of the journal, which recounted how new Christian Jean LaPenseé had participated in Mass on a remote beach and then entered the accursed wood, never to be heard from again. That had been the end of the shadow in the woods as well, but were the two events connected? Had the sacrifice of the Mass driven away the curse of the shadow? Fr. Thomas had certainly thought so, but what he'd described had been unlike any religious ritual Gerald had ever heard of. Was any of this more than mist and moonbeams? Had something dark and menacing been haunting the woods north of the Sault four hundred years earlier that had required supernatural eradication? Or could a more natural explanation be found? But then again, why reject Fr. Thomas's account just because it exceeded the bounds of rationalistic materialism? Why accept at face value his record of migrations and tribal practices, but reject his account of the maddened Cree, or the explanation of the Anishinaabek of the reason for their fear? How Gerald wished he could question the participants directly – Fr. Thomas, Jean, Jean's Ojibwa wife Nikikouet, or the tribal lore masters. There was so much he wanted to ask, to help separate observable phenomena from legend and lore.

As he drove south, Gerald ruminated that the whole episode with the missionary diary, from the initial excitement at its discovery to the seminars he'd attended, had served to accentuate the dichotomy of his own identity. He was proudly First Nation, nearly full-blooded Ojibwa Anishinaabe, glad of his heritage and happy to walk in it. But in many ways, he was also a modern Westerner, trained in their attitudes and versed in their ways. He had matriculated at McMaster and beneath the spires of Oxford, yet he had also portaged the Ottawa River from Montreal to Lake Nipissing. He was as familiar with the conference rooms and presentation halls of academia as he was with the sweat lodges and *wigwa*. He knew he could walk into any position he liked – in fact, he'd received many offers over the years – leaving behind the poverty and petty tribal politics that marked First Nations reserves. But he wanted to be with his people, to help them in a way that transcended superficial measures like learning the language or singing the tribal songs or camping in *wigwa*. He wanted to help them find their place in a world they did not control and an identity that didn't require them to revert to a Stone Age existence, yet still distinguished them from modern Western culture.

But to help his people do that, he'd first have to figure out how to do it himself.

Which was one reason he was taking this little vacation to visit his sister Kim. They had grown up very close, and had kept in touch after Gerald had embarked on his educational ventures and other journeys. She'd married Jeff Masters of the Saginaw Chippewa and moved down to the Isabella Reservation in central Michigan. Jeff and Kim lived a modest life with their three children, with Jeff employed by tribal security and Kim working as an accountant for the casino/resort complex which the tribe maintained near Mount Pleasant. Gerald always found visits to their home relaxing, and adored his niece and nephews, who loved to roughhouse with Uncle Gerald and to hear stories of his exploits or of the Ojibwa people. He'd been planning this trip for a while, and had already postponed it twice, so he was determined that this time he'd actually do it. The peace and grounding he found in his sister's simple family life gave him a taste of the heart of tribal identity, which wasn't found in externals like dress or lodging but in family unity and belonging. He hoped that a couple of weeks of that would clear out the mental clutter he'd accumulated in a year or so of busyness.

Gerald arrived just in time for dinner, and his niece and nephews came out to greet him and "help" with his luggage (though he noticed that his eldest nephew Anthony was getting big and strong enough to actually carry one of his bags – when had that happened?) It was a merry meal, with the kids deluging him with reports of their school and other activities, Jeff reporting how work was going (which, distressingly, involved dealing with an increasing number of drug-related incidents), and Kim explaining how the tribal authorities were worried about the slow but steady erosion of both visitors and profits from the casino complex. It was impossible to ignore: fewer people were visiting the complex, and those who came spent less. If the trend continued, it would start to affect a number of tribal projects.

After dinner, with the kids dismissed to their homework and to play with the presents Uncle Gerald had brought them, Gerald sat in the living room with Kim and Jeff and told them of his involvement with the missionary diary project – how the diary had been found, which scholarly parties had taken an interest, how he'd been drawn in, and the various commitments the project had entailed.

"A new original document!" Kim said enthusiastically. "How exciting! Were you involved in the translation effort?" Kim was attuned enough to Anishinaabek history to find such topics engaging.

"No, my French isn't good enough," Gerald explained. "That was Olivia Picotte and her crew over at UWO in London. I got first peek at the translation, though, even before the tribal elders, and was able to go over it with the journal's owner and the scholar to whom he first brought it."

"Did the journal contain anything new and exciting?" Kim asked.

Wrestling with the difficulty that question posed, Gerald chose to downplay the dramatic and mystical aspects of the diary, especially with the pragmatic Jeff listening. Instead, he spoke of what had been learned of migrations and missionary efforts and European influence spreading among the tribes.

Eventually Jeff excused himself to attend to his online night study course while Kim busied herself about the kitchen tidying and packing some containers in a towel-lined box.

"What's that for?" Gerald asked.

"Snacks for Esther Fox. I'm taking them over shortly," Kim explained. "She doesn't like the meals over at Andahwod, and enjoys my cooking." Andahwod was the senior care facility on the Isabella Reservation. Esther had no children and had lost her husband years before, so had somewhat adopted Kim as a *de facto* niece. A look of concern passed across Kim's face. "I didn't want to ask you tonight, because I'm sure you're tired from travel, but I was hoping that sometime during your visit you could come with me to help."

"Help? With what?"

"Esther's been...difficult for the past several months. She used to be enthusiastic and outgoing, but now she's withdrawn, and mutters to herself a lot. Most of her muttering is in Ojibwe, using terms I don't understand. Your Ojibwe is better than mine, so I was hoping you could decipher what she's saying."

"I'll come tonight – I'm not at all weary," Gerald replied. "Let's go."

The Andahwod facility wasn't far, just beside the Ziibiwing Center where Gerald had attended, and given, lectures and seminars. Along the way Kim briefed Gerald about Esther's status in the tribe, how she was universally respected as a lore mistress and wise woman. Esther treasured the Anishinaabek heritage and encouraged all, especially the young, to learn the history and language of their people. She stayed busy in tribal affairs, and was so insightful that she was considered by some to be a true seer, a tribal visionary.

They arrived at Andahwod and made their way to Esther's apartment, where Gerald was surprised to see a woman who looked like the opposite of the description Kim had provided. Rather than being erect and vigorous and engaged, Esther looked small and shrunken in her recliner, wrapped about with shawls that bore stains from food and drink. She looked up and smiled briefly when they entered, and gave Gerald a weak handshake when he was introduced, but quickly lapsed back into semi-silence, seeming to withdraw back into her wraps while gazing at the floor and muttering under her breath.

Gerald pulled up a chair beside Esther and settled in to listen. Kim had assured him that Esther wouldn't try to engage him in conversation – she barely attended to even familiar parties like Kim – and that he'd be most productive trying to catch snippets of her mutterings. But this proved nearly impossible, as Esther's murmuring was just at the threshold of hearing. She'd occasionally pause to answer some question that Kim asked, but then she'd resume the steady stream of gravelly muttering, seeming to ignore her visitors.

This was fine with Gerald, who would have been distracted by having to break his concentration to converse. Esther's Ojibwe was oddly accented, and the low volume was maddening, but after listening for a while he thought he was starting to pick up patterns in her speech. Fortunately, Esther was very repetitive, uttering the same words and phrases again and again. Finally, he caught one phrase clearly enough to understand it. He blinked, and a chill gripped his heart.

"What is it, Gerald?" Kim asked in a concerned whisper, but Gerald waved her to silence – he needed to concentrate, to see if he could catch the phrase again. The visitors sat quietly for a couple of minutes, attending to Esther's ramblings, until Gerald was sure he heard the phrase again.

Miigaadenim geteayii – old or ancient enemy.

The chill inside Gerald grew colder, but given that context, he listened to the other muttered phrases more attentively. After some repetitions he was increasingly certain about other phrases: *minkimii makadewah* – clinging blackness – and *awan bishagiishkan* – dark fog. His hands gripped the chair arms painfully as he deciphered yet another – *gichi nitaagwin* – big or great murder; massacre.

"It's been great, Esther," Gerald dimly heard Kim announce. "I'll be back tomorrow." She stood and grabbed Gerald's arm, nearly lifting him from the chair. A bit startled, Gerald nodded to Esther, who smiled weakly and waved to the suddenly departing visitors. Kim pulled Gerald out into the hallway, where she stopped and turned to him.

"That was an abrupt goodbye," Gerald said with surprise.

"Gerald, what was going on in there?" Kim asked fiercely. "You were turning white as a sheet and nearly panting with anxiety. What on earth were you hearing that was so distressing?"

"I…ah," Gerald stammered, flexing his stiff hands. "Let's go in there." He pointed to a lounge just up the hallway, which was fortunately almost empty. Sitting across from his now-alarmed sister, Gerald looked at her gravely. "Kim, you said that Esther changed dramatically several months ago. Can you tell me when that happened, and under what circumstances?"

"I can tell you both, because I was with her," Kim replied. "It was on *Minookamin* – the spring equinox. Esther wanted to pay special tribute to *Waabanong Manidoo*, the Spirit of the East."

"The Grandfather, yes," Gerald affirmed, remembering the customary spring rite.

"She had a particular ceremony she wanted to perform, so she got permission to go to the *ezhibiigaadek asin* in Sanilac County. Of course, she needed to be there at dawn, so she prevailed on me to pick her up about 4:30 a.m. We got to the site and had to slog back through the snow to the enclosure – you remember what last spring was like," Kim explained.

"I do," Gerald assured her as he did some rapid calculating. The spring equinox, the latter part of March – no, the translation effort was only beginning, and he was just starting to go over the results with Pete and Dr. Harris. Nothing had yet been made public, so there was no possible way Esther could have known of the diary's contents.

"So we got back to the enclosure, where we had to sweep the snow off the rock, then Esther set her herbs and shed her shoes and began her songs," Kim continued. Gerald shuddered, remembering that some spiritual ceremonies recommended direct contact between the skin and the ground, and wondering how that must have felt for Esther standing on the ice-cold stone.

"Did you participate?" Gerald asked.

"I beat the drum for her. I don't know the songs well enough. Anyway, she went through the songs and dances, and had just offered tobacco to the Warrior Glyph. She was kneeling on the ground facing toward the sunrise when she froze. She'd been kneeling up, then suddenly curled over into a crouch and stayed that way. At first, I thought this was part of the ritual, because I could hear her muttering, so I just kept beating. But when she didn't move for a long time, I began to wonder if she was all right, or if the cold had gotten to her. I stopped drumming and called to her, and then she gave this kind of strangled cry, toppled over, and started flailing."

"Flailing? Like convulsing?" Gerald asked.

"More like thrashing, but only with her arms. It was like she was trying to ward something off, or push it away. She had a vacant, faraway look in her eyes, and she was saying all kinds of Ojibwe words that I didn't understand. I only heard one that I knew."

"What was that?"

"*Giiwedin.*"

"Hmm. North, or north wind," Gerald mused. "Nothing else?"

"Like I said, she was muttering a lot, but nothing very coherently, and I had other things on my mind. I didn't know what kind of fit or seizure she was suffering, and I was worried that I might have to call for medical help."

"Did she injure herself?"

"Just a small scrape on her cheek from when she fell over. She's a tough old gal, and eventually she recovered, though we were both quite wet from being down there on the soggy ground. When she'd settled down and gotten her breath back, I got the impression that she'd had a vision or seeing of some sort."

"Could you tell what the vision was about?"

"She didn't want to talk about it. Whatever it was, it clearly distressed her. She wanted to cut the ceremony short and leave right then. I helped her to her feet and gathered up her things, then we locked up the enclosure and started trudging back through the snow to the car. She was leaning on my arm and muttering. I noticed that she stayed on the south side of me."

"South side?"

"Yes – it was like she was keeping me between her and the north. It couldn't have been because of the wind, which was from the southwest that day. She hobbled along, crouched over and muttering to herself, sometimes raising her hand as if to shield her face."

"Shield her face?" Gerald asked, puzzled.

"Yes – like you'd do if the low sun was in your eyes, except she was shielding her face from the north," Kim explained. "I kept asking her if she was all right, and what had happened, and if there was anything I could do. She didn't want to talk, she just wanted to get home. She didn't talk much on the drive back, which was unusual – normally she's rattling on about how important the ancient rites are and how much she got out of the ceremony. This time she just sat there, staring straight ahead as if stunned and muttering to herself."

"And she's been different ever since?"

"Yes. She used to be engaged in all sorts of activities, leading many of them. Weaving, singing, language studies, you name it. After that, she remained involved in many of them for a while, but her enthusiasm seemed gone. Increasingly she'd cancel classes or make excuses not to attend, and by midsummer she'd bowed out of nearly all of them. Now she just stays in her room and mutters. I think that's part of the reason she wants me to bring her food. It's not so much that she objects to the meals here as that she doesn't want to socialize – it takes too much out of her."

"And in Ojibwe," Gerald said pensively. "She always talks in Ojibwe."

"Yes, which is why I thought of you. What did you hear in there? You seemed startled, even alarmed."

"I heard some things that alarmed me, yes, but I don't want to jump to conclusions," Gerald replied. "You indicate she doesn't converse much now – do you think she'd willing to talk to me, if we could speak Ojibwe?"

"Perhaps. English certainly isn't holding her attention," Kim said.

"My conversational Ojibwe may not do it, either – I'm pretty rusty," Gerald admitted. "Should we go back in?"

"Not tonight, I'm thinking," Kim suggested. "It's getting late, and she looks worn. She's always perkier in the morning. Let's try tomorrow."

So it was that the next morning Kim and Gerald came knocking just after breakfast. Esther was still sitting in her chair, wrapped in her shawls, but did look a bit more alert than she had the prior evening. They knew she'd moved at least a little because one of the food containers Kim had brought stood empty on the table beside her, and there were a few crumbs scattered about. Kim had picked up a plate of biscuits and fruit in the cafeteria, and set them next to Esther then went to make tea while Gerald sat down by the old woman.

"Good morning, honored grandmother," Gerald said in clumsy Ojibwe. *"I hope you had a restful night, and welcome the new day with vigor."*

"*Thank you, honorable warrior,*" Esther responded in the same tongue. Her voice was still soft, but was more audible than it had been the night before. "*I did sleep well, and am as vigorous as these old bones can expect.*"

Gerald smiled. "*Perhaps those bones are not as old as you may think. My name is Gerald, brother to your friend Kim. I was here last night, though you were too weary to speak much.*"

"*I remember you, yes,*" Esther assured him. Just then Kim set down cups of tea for them both, so they paused for a sip.

"*I am of your brethren who live up by the Rapids,*" Gerald continued, hoping to set her at ease. "*I am something of a scholar, though I can only hope to aspire to the mastery of lore found in a wise woman like yourself.*"

"*Yes, the Rapids, I have visited a few times,*" Esther replied. "*One of the stopping points of the Great Migration. And the Greatest Lake! What a wonder!*"

Gerald continued the light conversation for a while, encouraged by how easily Esther was speaking. Kim sat on the other side of her, nodding and giving encouraging smiles. He got the impression that this was the most the old woman had spoken in a long time.

They had finished their cups of tea, and Kim was preparing refills, when Gerald felt confident enough to broach the topic of the incident at the Petroglyphs. "*My sister tells me she took you to the Legend Stone last Equinox so you could observe the rites honoring the Grandfather,*" he mentioned casually.

"*Oh! Oh!*" Esther's response was swift and sharp. Grasping Gerald's forearm in a surprisingly strong grip, she fixed him with an intense stare. "*Oh, yes! What a dawn! What a day!*"

Gerald glanced at Kim. He'd been concerned that mentioning the events might cause Esther to withdraw again, she seemed eager to discuss them. Kim nodded encouragement, so Gerald continued cautiously.

"*Can you tell us about it?*"

"*Oh, yes! Oh, yes! What a morning that was! My bones are weak even remembering. What a day!*"

"*Did you see something?*"

"*Oh, yes! It was a miserable morning, very snowy and wet. But the equinox is ever so, and I sang the songs diligently, and made the offerings. I had just made the offering to the Warrior, and was singing the prayer, when my eyes were opened, and who should I see but the Warrior himself! He was striding through the woods toward me, the rising sun at his back, scanning the horizon as he came. He was dressed in fine deerskin intricately decorated, and held his bow and quiver in his hand. His face was painted for war and his eyes were like glowing coals. He towered so high in the morning sky that the tallest trees came only to the belt about his waist.*" Esther paused to rest – even the retelling seemed to tax her.

"*Did he look at you?*" Gerald asked after a minute.

"*Look at me? No, no, he did not, and it is a good thing, or I surely would have perished,*" Esther assured him. "*He looked over me, mostly to the north. So imposing was his stature that I would have turned my gaze aside from him, but I was frozen where I knelt, unable to turn or bend. I dreaded that he might look at me, but he never did. His word was hard enough to bear.*"

"*What did he say?*"

"*He warned me to beware, for the ancient enemy had been summoned by forbidden rites, and even now the clinging darkness dwelt among the woods to the north. He said there had been a great slaughter in the dark fog, and that the devouring hunger lurked among the tree trunks. It was contained for a time, but it was pushing against its bonds, seeking how it might escape. Beware, he warned me, beware, as he watched keenly to the north.*

"*As he spoke, I could feel from the north the waves of malice, and I knew the Warrior spoke the truth.*"

"*Waves of malice? What did that feel like?*" Gerald asked

"*It is hard to say,*" Esther replied. "*It was like...it was like...do you know how at sunrise on a warm spring morning, when the sun is well above the horizon, you can feel what direction it is just by the rays upon your skin?*"

"*Yes, I've felt that.*"

"*It was like that, except instead of a warm, lifegiving caress, it was red and harsh, full of hostility and hatred.*"

"*And you felt this harshness on your skin?*" Gerald asked.

"*Yes, and in my heart, I felt a shadow of dread.*"

"*Did The Warrior say anything else?*"

"*No. Having delivered his word, he stood silent, gazing. I was caught between heavy awe at the presence of The Warrior, and the evil radiance whose strength kept growing, and the deepening dread upon my heart, until I could bear it no more and darkness took me. I was wakened by Kim.*"

Gerald nodded – he knew what followed from Kim's account. "*Have you brought this vision to the tribal elders?*"

"*No,*" Esther shook her head. "*I did not know where to bring it, and it seemed too severe for casual talk. I have borne the weight of this word by myself ever since.*"

Gerald smiled wryly. He could appreciate Esther's dilemma. The tribal administration would have no mechanism for dealing with such a thing. He imagined trying to fit it onto a council agenda, perhaps between the budget considerations and the reports of the standing committees: "Message from Guardian Spiritual Entity." The elders of the Saginaw Chippewa were no doubt like the elders of the Garden River First Nation – pragmatic, businesslike, concerned with the mechanics of administering the tribe. Oh, they'd attend sweat lodges and acknowledge the importance of their spiritual and cultural heritage, but that lay in a partitioned area of their lives that did not touch their workaday concerns.

For that matter, it was like that for most First Nations, including Gerald. Even now he felt the tension as two separate, almost opposing, sets of perceptions warred within him. Was he hearing nothing more than the rambling imaginings of an old woman who was obsessed with tribal lore, and undoubtedly had been exhausted and perhaps dangerously chilled on that March morning? Was this nothing more than a hallucination? Or had she perceived something real, something that had no regard for the carefully bordered categories of modern thought? The "Oxford Gerald" struggled against the "Ojibwa Gerald", not wanting to be drawn in, not wanting to appear credulous, wanting to keep a safe distance.

But yet, Gerald was becoming aware of just how much his thinking had been affected by having read Fr. Thomas's diary. Fr. Thomas should have represented a force opposed to the Anishinaabek identity: European, Christian, and educated in Western thought. Yet Fr. Thomas had hailed from an era before Enlightenment materialism had tainted everything with rationalistic skepticism. According to the diary, when the Salteaux Ojibwa had learned of the dangerous shadow lurking in the woods to the north of them, Fr. Thomas had not dismissed the report as irrational legend or primitive superstition. He had instead evaluated the situation with all seriousness, considering both the seen and unseen realities, and had come up with a strategy to defeat the supposedly unbeatable foe. There had been no superiority or condescension in Fr. Thomas's dealings with either Gerald's ancestors or with the spiritual threat.

Having had this example, Gerald found himself considering Esther's account of her vision differently than he once might have. While there were some who might listen politely to the tale then dismiss it as the imaginings of a devoted woman who took her lore too seriously, there were others who would make much of the vision and the seer, hailing it as an expression of Anishinaabek spirituality. To Gerald, both these expressions seemed deficient, because they would be focusing on the phenomenon proper; Gerald wanted to consider the content of the vision.

The Warrior, or Hunter, held an important place in Ojibwa lore, and was considered by many to be a guardian spirit of the entire tribe. For him to appear in a vision during a *Midewiwin* ceremony would be remarkable enough; for him to appear unexpectedly to someone simply going through routine rituals was extraordinary. Esther had not been expecting such a visit, and seemed confused and distressed by the message. There was no question of her concocting this story to garner attention – she'd kept this to herself ever since. But if this was a legitimate message, what did it mean? Obviously, it was a warning, but it was couched in such vague and symbolic terms that it would need careful deciphering. He was glad he'd asked Kim to discreetly record the conversation on her phone – he'd want to review it more carefully, and he didn't want to stress Esther with many questions.

"Kim," Gerald whispered. "Could you fetch me a lightly dampened washcloth?" While Kim was attending to that errand, Gerald knelt on the floor before Esther and took a pinch of tobacco from his pocket. His internal disputes could wait; the Ojibwa Gerald would handle this.

Kim returned and slipped him a moistened cloth. Gerald looked solemnly at Esther then bowed as he sprinkled the tobacco on the floor at her feet. *"Esther Fox, I hail you as a true seer and a wise woman of the Original People."* He eased her slippers from her feet, and taking the washcloth, he continued. *"I wipe the sacred soil from your feet, and thereby take from you the burden of this vision."* He heard Kim give a quiet gasp as he bathed Esther's bare feet with the cloth.

"Are…are you sure?" Esther asked in English.

"Yes. You have borne it long enough, and have done so bravely and honorably," Gerald answered in Ojibwe.

Esther smiled and seemed to slump in her chair. Kim moved quickly to attend to her while Gerald folded the washcloth carefully. It had been an impulsive action, but his gut told him he'd done the right thing in taking the burden of the message from Esther.

Now if only he knew what he'd do with it.

Unexpected Meetings

Dear Rose,

First, my deepest apologies for taking so long to write to you, especially after you've been so gracious about keeping me updated with what's going on in your life. Things have been so busy here! But after your last letter, I decreed that I wouldn't let another day pass without at least starting a response.

So…it's done. I'm a married woman now, and have been for nearly a month. Nothing is quite as I'd imagined it would be: the wedding, married life, "wifehood" (if that's a word!) The wedding itself was rather anticlimactic, especially considering all the fantasies I'd had over the years. I suppose the tumult of the recent months buffered the impact, or I might have felt a bit cheated. No colorful array of bridesmaids (in which you would have had a place of honor!), no pageantry, none of the songs I'd dreamed of having, no giddy reception, no romantic honeymoon. It was a simple ceremony in the chapel at St. Jude's, with only my and Luke's families in attendance. Even with a Mass, it was over in forty-five minutes! The vows didn't add that much length to the ceremony.

And then, it was back to Luke's house – our house. I think he was embarrassed to bring me here, because it's so simple – an older cabin on forty partly wooded acres. He'd been living there since we came up here, and doing his best to fix it up, but he's not as handy as he wishes he were. I keep having to assure him that it's a fine house, and indeed it is, despite its simplicity. I've been trying to dress it up a little (Aunt Linda's right – not only do men have no eye for that sort of thing, they don't even know they have no eye!) I've also been trying to make decent meals in the less-

than-spectacular kitchen facilities. I think I'm improving.

Well, then – husbands. I begin to see why you were so circumspect in your descriptions of married life. There are some things that are hard for even the best of friends to share, especially when one is married and the other isn't, and both are trying to be discreet. Husbands have such unexpected needs, and I'm not talking about the expectable one. Luke (I keep thinking of him by his former name, but that has to vanish forever) is in some ways so competent but in others so needy, particularly emotionally, in ways he doesn't even see. Aunt Linda warned me, and I'm starting to agree, that there's a wound from his estrangement with his mother that he doesn't recognize. At our wedding it made me a little sad that she couldn't be there, but when I said that to him, he pragmatically pointed out that there was no way that could have happened, and left it at that. I don't think it's so easy to just dismiss a parent.

I don't want to sound like I'm complaining. Luke is diligent and responsible and eager to please. But he's also vulnerable and insecure, something that comes out particularly in times of deep intimacy. I think he's ashamed of it, though I keep trying to reassure him (in many ways) that I'm here for him even in his weakness. Sometimes he holds me so tight that I can almost feel the ache within him – then he usually rolls away, apologizing, which makes me sad for him. I suppose it's going to take a lot of patience.

Mom has been great, but Aunt Linda has been especially helpful and supportive. She's very wise (I think from years of experience), and warned me that marrying Luke would bring a special set of challenges. She also told me something I hadn't expected or considered: that wives can help heal their husbands' wounded hearts by means of their bodies. I think I'm starting to see what she meant, though it surprises me – but then, I don't know why it should! Thinking about it, I find that I unconsciously expected that healing a heart would be accomplished by conversation and counsel and prayer, while the bedroom would be for – simpler needs. I guess I'd let a little Manichean thought creep into my assumptions! Not that there isn't a place for conversation and prayer, but some things are easier to lure my husband into.

"My husband" – I'm still getting used to that phrase. But I'm starting to ramble, and the dough has now risen, so I must attend to my duties. Please don't stop writing, no matter how badly I lapse in my responding. I want all the details about your pregnancy, even the least pleasant ones. At the rate we're going, it may not be long before I'm in the same situation! God bless you, Rose!

Much love,
Catherine

Grace smiled as she folded the letter from Felicity. Communications with the "vanished" parties had to be handled very delicately, since all electronic communications were assumed to be actively monitored. Under these conditions, one recourse was old-fashioned paper letters, written (by hand, often as not) and stuck in an envelope with a stamp. They added another layer of security by using their confirmation names in their correspondence, and in Grace's case using Todd's father as a courier. He'd mail the letters from his office in north Metro Detroit and use that address for the responses. These roundabout measures meant that letters could sometimes take weeks to reach their destinations, but that only made them the more welcome when they arrived. Grace would use the time in Sandusky to begin her response, and might even finish it.

Felicity was right: communicating would come easier now that they were both married women. Grace and Todd had wed in late June in a ceremony that was almost as simple as Felicity and Luke's sounded. They'd moved into a cheap rental near Capac and Todd had let his employer know that he'd take as many hours as he could get. They'd obliged him with odd shifts and weekends, which was taxing on their schedule but helped pay the bills. It also meant getting creative with drop-offs, pickups, and ride sharing, since they only had one car.

In early August Grace had awakened feeling queasy enough to consider calling the doctor, but fortunately had called her mother first. Mom had suggested a pregnancy test, and sure enough, that was the source. Todd and Grace had to endure a few winks and teases about a honeymoon baby (not that they'd had a real honeymoon – a weekend at a chain hotel outside Port Huron had been all they'd been able to manage), but both sets of parents had been very supportive, and now they were looking forward to a date sometime in March to meet the new family member.

Grace's mornings were still rough (Mom had confided that her pregnancies had been similar), but usually she was on her feet and functional by eleven or so. Today she'd dropped off Todd at work, swung by his parents' house to pick up the mail, and then had come here to her parents' for dinner. The plan was that she'd run her mom up to Sandusky for her evening lessons, bring her back home afterwards, then swing over to pick up Todd after his shift. It was a long day for a pregnant lady, but she'd be able to sleep late tomorrow morning.

Mom had kept up her schedule of lessons even as her eyesight had deteriorated, though there were fewer students than there had been. Most of her students were school age, which meant that over time they grew up, graduated, and usually moved away. Of course, more students came along to replace them, but the demographics of the region meant that the pool of possible students was shrinking, and fewer of those wanted to learn violin, so the drop-off was steady. There had been a time that Mom could book three full afternoons in the Port Huron area and one full afternoon in the middle Thumb, near Marlette or Sandusky. Now she might get two sparse days in the south, and only had a couple students remaining in the mid-Thumb. But Mom persisted, partly out of dedication to her students and love of her art, but also (Grace suspected) from a determination not to let her failing vision define her life. She'd do what she could for as long as she could, and teaching music was something you could do with limited eyesight. Mom thought her sharpened hearing actually helped her as a teacher.

Grace tucked away Felicity's letter and gathered up her gear. It was almost time to head to Sandusky.

"No, no, that's not right," Bethany fumbled for the third time, halting her playing. "I'm sorry, I just messed up. Let me try again."

"It's all right, dear," Megan Kyle reassured her calmly, trying to mask her concern. Bethany was an experienced player, yet tonight she seemed unable to focus. It wasn't just a matter of fumbling the current lesson material, it was elementary things like posture and bow discipline, things that had been second nature to her for years. Megan wished she could read expressions as well as she'd been able to years before, because she guessed she'd be seeing distress in Bethany's face.

Again, Bethany's playing stumbled and faltered. "I'm sorry, Mrs. Kyle, I just don't seem to be on form tonight. I hate to waste your time, but…"

"Bethany, dear," Megan said gently. "Don't worry about me. Here, let's sit down. Something's obviously upsetting you. Is it anything you'd like to discuss?"

Bethany seemed to be trying to calm herself. Megan could hear her breathing coming in little gasps. She kept wiping her eyes, and she sounded stuffed up. "I...well...," she stammered, "You know that I'm pregnant, right?"

"Yes," Megan smiled. "You told me the happy news a few lessons ago."

"Well, today I went to the doctor," Bethany continued, "and they told me..."

Grace was sitting in the next room, rereading Felicity's letter and composing a response. Beside her sat Bethany's husband Patrick, whom Grace had just met that evening. For some reason he'd driven Bethany to lessons this evening, and though he was courteous, he was preoccupied with something that made him disinclined to converse. That was fine with Grace, who spent the time writing while Patrick worked away on his tablet. It was just occurring to Grace that it had been some time since she'd heard any violin music from the living room when Mom called to her.

"Grace?"

"Yes, Mom?"

"Could you come in here for a moment?"

Grace was puzzled. "You want me to come in there?"

"Yes. And bring Patrick."

Grace glanced at Patrick and shrugged, and they both went into the room where Mom and Bethany sat side by side. The violins were set aside, and Mom was holding one of Bethany's hands. Bethany's other hand held a tissue, her eyes were red, and she was clearly distraught. Patrick rushed over and knelt beside her.

"Bethany," Mom asked, "could you tell my daughter what you've just told me? Patrick, if you have anything to add, please do so."

*   *   *

"Todd, this is terrible! What if that were us? What if that was our baby?" Grace implored as they drove through the night toward home.

"Honey, I agree, it's terrible," Todd conceded. "I just don't see what we can do."

It had been several hours since Grace had heard Bethany's heartwrenching tale. She'd been shocked and distressed, but most of all frightened, and none of that had abated in the time it had taken to drive Mom home and pick up Todd at work. Such treatment of any family would rightfully alarm any decent person, but as an expecting mother herself, Grace was nearly panicking. They were going to need medical care through her pregnancy and afterward. What if they were required to go to those horrid government clinics? What if the clinic ran tests and decided that their baby was defective? Would they be pressured to choose the same terrible option?

"Todd, we've done this before," Grace persisted. "We snatched people right out of hospitals to save their lives. This is the same situation – in fact, it's worse. We can't just stand by. We have to do something."

"Sweetie, I one hundred percent agree, but I still don't see what we can do. The ranches were originally set up in secret, when nobody was watching for them. That's all changed now, which is why we had to shut them down and go into hiding. There's no network left to use, and nobody left to run it."

"That's not true, Todd," Grace replied. "Nobody's living in the network right now, but some of it's still being maintained. The communications system is still in place and functioning. Rivendell is still being kept up – in fact, I'm going there tomorrow to harvest some grapes. And yes, a lot of people fled, especially those close to Rivendell, but the Fangorn staff mostly stayed. Many people are still living around there."

"Yeah, but the circumstances have changed –" Todd began, but Grace cut him off.

"Todd, we have to at least try. We have to. There's nowhere else the Hoods can turn, and who knows how many other couples are being pressured like this? We have to try."

Todd sighed. He was still a rookie husband, but he recognized that tone in his wife's voice – she would not give this up. And he had to acknowledge that she was right. This was a life and death matter for the little baby Hood, every bit as much as it had been for the poor elderly whom they'd once rescued.

"All right," Todd conceded. "Let me make some calls."

*   *   *

Brian Sanderson knew that he had to do something about his unexpected house guest. He just had no idea what.

Four days had passed since that unexpected encounter at the donut shop, and Jason Pelletier had spent most of them holed up in Brian's small apartment while Brian camped out in the guest room at his old house. Brian had looked in on Jason before and after his shift, ensuring he was all right and stressing the need to lie low. Brian had provided a pair of sunglasses which, combined with a cap and an old jacket, had offered enough of a disguise to permit Jason to take walks around the neighborhood. Brian knew that the chances of Jason being recognized even without a disguise were slim, but he was taking no chances.

Jason had been a courteous and considerate guest, even cleaning up the unkempt apartment while he stayed there. He ate a lot and rested a lot, and was beginning to lose the scrawny appearance that had haunted him. Brian guessed that wherever Jason had been hadn't been feeding him adequately. Jason's alertness and mental ability had also seemed to sharpen, causing Brian to wonder if his system was still shedding some drugs that he'd certainly been given.

There were many questions about the situation that pointed in horrible directions, so Brian was disinclined to pursue them, but he was glad to see Jason improving.

But those very improvements intensified the question of what to do about Jason. Though Brian didn't mind camping at the house with Kayla and the kids, he couldn't do so indefinitely, but neither could he just fling Jason back onto the street. Ordinarily someone in such circumstances should be taken for medical examination and government assistance, but that was the last thing Brian was considering. Whatever had happened to Jason, putting him back into the medical system, particularly here in the SPD, was not the answer. But what was? Brian could hardly send him out to seek employment with no official paperwork, no skills, and no memory of his life.

Jason's memory – that was the critical issue. Though Jason's physical vigor and mental acuity had returned, his memory had not. He had accepted that his name was Jason Pelletier, but only because Brian had told him – he had no direct recollection of it. His memory extended no more than a week into the past. He had jumbled images of being in some kind of medical facility, then being given new clothes and being let out a door into an alley. The memories immediately following that incident were blurred and confused, though they became more distinct as time elapsed. He recalled the truck stops and conversations with the truckers who'd assisted him. Brian hoped this meant that Jason's capacity to remember hadn't been damaged, but it didn't help with the fact that all memory of his life before the mysterious medical facility had been erased. Jason recalled nothing of his time here in the Thumb just six months earlier, or of his career with DHS, or anything at all of his prior life. Brian's biggest question was whether this memory damage was permanent or whether time would slowly restore what had been lost.

Well, thought Brian as he parked outside his apartment, time to test out his idea. It was his day off, and though he regretted losing part of it to deal with this situation, there was something he wanted to try if Jason was agreeable. He let himself into the apartment to find Jason eating breakfast and watching a documentary.

"Good morning," Jason greeted him.

"'Morning," Brian replied, sitting down across from him. "How are you feeling?"

"Great, though a little confined," Jason admitted.

"Do you remember what you had for dinner two nights ago?"

"Two nights," Jason mused. "Wasn't that the night you brought pizza, pepperoni and mushroom, with a Greek salad?"

"Correct in every detail," Brian replied. "Listen, if you'd like, I'd like to take you for a drive this morning."

"I'll have to consult my busy social calendar, but I think I can manage it," Jason replied with a grin. "Drive where?"

"On a recollection drive, if you will. I'd like to visit some places you knew when you were last here, to see if anything jogs your memory."

"Sounds fine. Let me clean up and we can go. Where are we headed first?"

"A little town called Sandusky where you lived for a couple of months. It's about an hour's drive north. You chose it for an informal HQ because it was geographically central to the area."

Before heading north, Brian drove to a spot which provided a good view of the majestic spans of the Blue Water Bridge stretching across the St. Clair River to Canada, on the chance that it would spark a memory for Jason. It didn't, but Brian knew it was a long shot – he couldn't remember Jason having been that active in the Port Huron vicinity. Sandusky, however, was another matter. Jason had lived here and walked the streets, so Brian was hoping that something about the storefronts or sidewalks might trigger a memory. Unfortunately, nothing seemed to.

"Do you remember this house?" Brian asked as they parked in front of the bungalow where Jason had stayed, which was still empty and for sale. "This was your home base for most of your time. I attended several meetings here."

"I'm afraid not," Jason shook his head. "None of this seems familiar."

"Let's try driving around," Brian suggested. They cruised out west of town, past the fast food joints and dealerships, but nothing jogged Jason's memory. Turning eastward, they passed back through town along M-46, turning south to drive down M-19 until they came to open fields. Jason couldn't recall any of this, but Brian did notice that he had gazed long and intently at the courthouse in the center of Sandusky as they'd driven past, so he suggested they go back and walk around that for a while.

As they strolled the parklike lawn around the courthouse, Brian kept watching for Jason to exhibit some sign of recognition, particularly as they passed the courthouse itself. He wasn't aware of any business that Jason might have had with the Sanilac County courts, but he guessed that if there had been anything, it might serve as a trigger. But that hope proved futile, as Jason walked past the courthouse without giving it a glance. However, as they were passing along the southern edge of the grounds, approaching the gazebo that stood near the corner of the lawn, Jason abruptly stopped and stared at the bench along the gazebo's south side. He stood silent for so long that Brian finally spoke.

"Remembering something?"

"Not remembering, but...feeling?" Jason groped for words. "Something about this bench. Discouragement, and frustration. Feeling upset and exasperated, like something wasn't going right. Then – surprise?"

"Surprise? At what?"

Jason didn't answer at first, instead closing his eyes so he could focus. Images were flashing through his mind, images detached from any context yet for some reason familiar. A woman in white, with short red hair and a glowing smile. This bench, with trees standing all around, trees with no leaves. A whirl of emotions – surprise, mystification, then stunned disbelief. Another brief image, this time of the woman in white walking away in the sunlight, leaving him startled.

"I…I can't say for certain," Jason replied apologetically. "It's so frustrating. I just get flashes of images, or surges of emotion, but nothing that holds together as what you'd call a memory, like I remember the pizza for dinner the other night. There are images of a woman, though, a woman with red hair and a brilliant smile. It *may* have been here, but I can't say for certain."

"Well, I'd call that encouraging," Brian said. "I know you spent a good amount of time in Sandusky, so if something here is triggering recollection, that's a hopeful sign."

"The woman is important, I think," Jason added. "Possibly very important. I just wish I could remember more about her! It's so frustrating."

"Jason," Brian said, patting his arm. "Let it go. Don't get yourself worked up. It'll come back in time."

"Will it?" Jason challenged him.

"Why, sure it will," Brian replied with a confidence he did not feel. "Just give it time. For my part, I'm encouraged. It may be only bits and pieces, but it's a recollection of a place that you'd been before. You may not remember you'd been here, but I do, so every recovery is progress no matter how fragmented. Let's keep strolling to see if anything else shakes loose."

They walked for another half hour, all along the downtown streets, but they encountered nothing else that triggered any memories. Returning to the car, Brian pondered where else to take Jason. This strategy seemed to be bearing fruit, so he wanted to continue it.

The difficulty was that most of the other places Jason had been were government facilities like Selfridge Air National

Guard base, or DHS offices around Port Huron. Those were the last places Brian wanted to take the confused, amnesiac Jason. But where else might be helpful? Perhaps the motel where he'd stayed in Imlay City, or even the site of the blast itself? Visiting either would carry risks, though – the entire district was under constant aerial surveillance, and two people showing up at the blast site would probably trigger undesired scrutiny of the surveillance records.

There was one other site, though, an address that had repeatedly cropped up during the chain of incidents the prior spring. Brian had no idea if Jason had ever been there, but it wasn't far from where they were in Sandusky, and could be worth a stop. If nothing got triggered there, they could continue on to Imlay City. A slim chance, but Brian decided to give it a try.

As they pulled into the semicircular driveway in front of the brown farmhouse, it was clear to Brian that the property was vacant. There were no household items like hoses or garbage cans visible, and there certainly were no people. But he also noticed that the house didn't look abandoned. It was in good repair despite its age, the lawn was mowed, and the yard was free of broken branches and other detritus that would be expected with so many trees. It seemed someone was maintaining this property.

"Let's walk around," Brian suggested. "It looks like nobody's occupying this house, or the one next door."

As they strolled across the silent yard, Brian noticed that Jason was again looking around intently and seemed pensive. Going to the back of the house, they found themselves in front of a stable, beside which ran a single-story cinder block building that could have been anything from a garage to a workshop. There was still no sign of habitation, but everything looked trimmed and well-kept, as if the residents expected to return any day.

To the left of the stable and cinder block building stretched a yard that spread all the way behind the adjacent building. It was a broad space, easily four acres, with the smooth lawn giving way to a lightly wooded area wherein stood a pond and a gazebo. At the west end of the lawn a meadow stretched off into the distance, and along the south edge beyond the wooded area ran a bushy mass of some kind of clinging plant.

Jason's gaze was fixed on the wooded area, and he seemed to be muttering to himself as he began walking across the lawn toward the pond. Brian followed him, and was startled when he abruptly stopped and turned to look at a curious object that was standing in the lawn near the cinder block building. It was a white monument, about knee high, and surrounded by beds of flowers. It reminded Brian eerily of a tombstone, which made it seem even more strange standing in a back yard. Jason was staring at it with his head to one side, his expression focused.

"Remembering something?" Brian asked after a period of silence.

"Nothing so clear," Jason replied, shaking his head. "But definitely emotions, just like at that bench. Very confusing, even conflicting emotions: satisfaction, as if…as if excited about discovering something important after a long search. Amazement. Intense curiosity. Other feelings whirling about."

"But triggered by this stone, you think?"

"Perhaps," Jason replied.

"'Samson John Chapman. The Lord is my Strength.'" Brian read the inscription off the stone. "Does the name seem familiar?"

"No, but there's something about it that triggers that satisfied feeling. You know how you feel when you wrap up a big, intricate project? Like that. The name seems to be some kind of key to a lot more." Jason fell silent, again struggling with the incoherent whirl of emotions tumbling about inside him, emotions somehow associated with white stone, or what was carved on it. He was torn by an almost ludicrous conflict between feeling terribly unsettled, as if a great many things had been upset and thrown akimbo, and that surge of satisfied relief, as if some intractable problem had been suddenly and unexpectedly resolved. How these two emotional avalanches could not only coexist, but be associated with the same object, he had no idea.

Meanwhile, Brian was staring at the inscription and muttering to himself. "Samson John Chapman. Samson John Chapman. Wait a minute…" Something triggered in his mind and he hastily pulled out his phone and started searching. When he found what he was looking for, a thrill shot through him and his hands began shaking. It was gratifying to find another connection, but in a strange way frightening as well.

"That was the name," Brian announced, staring at his notes on the phone.

"Pardon me?" Jason replied.

"Samson John Chapman. That was the name you asked me to investigate on your second to last day here last spring." Brian pointed to his phone screen.

"I did? I wonder why I did that."

"You didn't tell me. I called you with my findings as you were driving to Selfridge to take the plane back to D.C. You thanked me for my research and hung up without explanation. It was the last time we spoke," Brian explained. "The only other time I've seen that name is right here, right now, on that stone."

"Well," Jason said after a moment's silence. "That's spooky. I'm glad to have more dots to connect, but it raises even more questions. Do you have any idea what this place is, that they'd have a stone like this in their backyard?"

"I thought of asking you the same things, but I knew it would be futile," Brian said. "The house where we pulled in was once occupied by a family we thought might be tangentially connected to the original blast investigation. In fact, we mentioned that address in a meeting once. Nothing ever came of it, but that's all I know about this property."

"There's more, I'm sure of it, but it's just out there beyond my mental reach. It's maddening."

"You were headed toward those trees," Brian pointed out. "Why don't we go over by that gazebo to see if it triggers anything. After all, we got lucky by one gazebo today!" So they went over among the trees, and around and into the gazebo, but no recollections of any kind came.

"Sorry, nothing here," Jason said.

"It is a beautiful and peaceful place, though," Brian said, breathing deeply. "Whoever lived here must have loved spending time in the back yard. Look at all those benches scattered about."

"Yes, look at them," Jason added, wondering what it was about the benches that seemed vaguely familiar. "Let's check out the house."

As they walked the gravel path toward the house, with its large deck and glass doors, Jason again felt beset by a storm of potent and seemingly contradictory emotions. Feelings of safety and security, even friendship and warmth, warred with feelings of outrage, terror, frustration, and…dread? But not quite – dread not for himself, but for someone else? What could that mean? They reached the deck and came to the back door, which was locked, but Jason tried it a few times anyway, running his hand across the glass as he tried to rein in the emotional tumult.

"Recalling anything?" Brian asked.

"No specifics, just the same flurry of emotions," Jason answered. "Something seems to have happened in or around this house, though I've no idea what."

"Let's try the front," Brian suggested, so they walked around the house. The door was locked, but there was a big picture window through which they could look into the house. It was clearly vacated, with empty bookshelves and only a few pieces of furniture in the room. One of the pieces was a large wooden rocker, the sight of which triggered another storm of emotions, only this time they were accompanied by an image – a familiar image, one of the persistent ones. It was the image of the white-haired man with the moustache, smiling and chatting genially while he rocked in a chair. Jason stared and stared through the window at the rocker, feeling like he was right at the edge of recollection.

Had it been *that* rocker? Who had the white-haired man been? And why had he been so important that his image endured through whatever Jason had been subjected to?

"Seem familiar?" Brian asked.

"Almost," Jason shook his head in frustration, "almost. I may have seen that rocker before, but if so, there was a man in it, a white-haired man."

"Wow – that's more detail than you've been getting," Brian said. "Anything more?"

"No, just a jumble of feelings. Whoever the man was, he was kind and reassuring, very much a gentleman. Yet it was all under a shadow of some threat, something looming over us. I admired him, but it ended tragically."

"Tragically?"

"Well, it feels that way. No details, just feelings of shock and outrage and terror and deep frustration. I've no idea what happened, but I think I was very upset."

"A white-haired man, eh?" Brian nodded. This was turning out much better than he'd expected. They'd come here on a hunch, and it was turning out to be a gold mine.

"Yes, with a moustache. Very friendly and easygoing."

"Too bad we can't get inside," Brian lamented, trying the door again. "Do you want to go to the next house?"

"No," Jason said after looking at the blue house. "No, I don't think there's anything there. Let's try out back again. There may still be something among those trees." So they made their way back around the house and along the gravel path to the rear of the property. As they passed the gazebo Jason began drifting toward the little pond, looking intently at the surface. He came to the pond and stood with furrowed brow, then started walking counterclockwise around the edge, muttering and scanning the far side. Brian followed, keeping quiet, until Jason suddenly stopped and pointed across the pond to the empty bank.

"Remembering something?" Brian asked.

"It's like at the bench in Sandusky," Jason said. "Flashes of an image, an image of the woman."

"'The' woman? The same woman, the woman in white?"

"Yes, but she was wearing black. It wasn't just her, but what she said."

"You remember her saying something? Can you recall what?" Brian asked. This was definitely progress, moving from emotions and brief images toward recollection of speech.

"No, but whatever it was surprised and distressed me. I wasn't expecting to see her, though I wanted to. I was pleased, but then regretful."

"Regretful?"

"That's what it feels like – sharp regret."

"Regret over what she said?"

"Perhaps," Jason said slowly. "It feels like – she said something that I ignored, and I regretted it badly later."

"This red-haired woman seems central," Brian began, but noticed that Jason wasn't listening. His eyes were closed, his fists were clenched, and his expression looked strained, as if he was concentrating deeply.

"You know," Jason said at last in a heavy voice without opening his eyes. "I wonder if it was the same woman."

"Same woman as who?"

"It just came back to me. There was another image. During the time…the time I've just been through. When everything else was confused and washed away, these images kept recurring, although they had no context and I didn't understand them. One was the image of the white-haired man in the rocker. The other was the back of a woman. She was dressed in white, and she had short, reddish hair, though it looked brown because the light was so dim. I think it was at night. She was walking through some kind of door or gate into deep blackness. That's all I remember. I never saw her face, only her back, all dressed in white walking into the black."

"Of course, no idea who or where or when," Brian added.

"Of course not, but –" Jason began, but cut himself short as he started staring pointedly at a spot over Brian's shoulder.

"What – are you seeing something that's reminding you of something?" Brian asked, turning to look.

"No. There's someone in those bushes over there. I thought I saw movement earlier, and I just saw it again." Jason pointed to the mass of leaves along the property line.

Brian looked where he was pointing but didn't see anything. "All right, let's check it out," he suggested, starting to walk toward the leaves. As they got closer he recognized them as vines clinging to thick wires strung along a series of strong posts. "I think these are grapes," he said, pointing at some heavy clusters hanging among the big leaves. There seemed to be three long rows of vines.

"A lot of grapes," Jason observed, but just then some of the leaves on the far side of the vines rustled a little. Brian's instincts kicked in, and he had to consciously restrain his hand from reaching for his sidearm beneath his jacket.

"Who's there?" he called gruffly. "Come out! Who are you, and what are you doing here?"

In response a woman's head popped up from behind the far vine. She had wavy brown hair, and was rather pretty, though she was scowling at them with fire in her bright blue eyes.

"I should rather ask," the woman said in a sharp voice as she stormed around the end of the row of vines, "who you are, and what are you doing here? I know the owners of this property, and am here by permission! You, whoever you are, seem to be trespassing!" The woman was petite, and carried a bucket mostly filled with grapes, but her expression and demeanor were so forceful that the men drew back a little.

"Oh, yeah?" Brian answered, not accustomed to retreating before challenges. "If you're so legitimate, why were you hiding back there?"

"These are dangerous times, and I'm here alone," the woman fired back. "What was I supposed to do when two strange men came strolling onto the property? I see now that I should have challenged you from the outset – you've been wandering around like you owned the place."

"Where's your car, then?" Brian asked, grasping for anything to knock the woman off balance.

"Parked where I could walk here under cover. Where's yours? Parked out front, in full view of every bird in the sky?"

"Look, we're sorry if we offended you," Jason interjected. "We mean no harm, and were just here for…for old time's sake."

"'Old time's sake'?" the woman asked incredulously. "What on earth –"

"Please, please," Brian said in an conciliatory tone. "I'm sorry I came on strong. It's a bad habit from work. Really, we meant no harm, and would have asked permission if we'd found anyone to ask. What my friend meant was that he thinks he's been here before. He's suffered a…situation, and we were coming back here in an attempt to get him to recollect his thoughts."

"You? You've been here before?" The woman asked. Peering at Jason, her expression softened a little. "Come to think of it, you look vaguely familiar. Have we met before?"

The men glanced at each other sharply. Jason didn't recall this woman, but that meant nothing under the circumstances. However, if she could recall something about him, that might be a major breakthrough.

"My name is Brian, and this is Jason. Would you mind if we asked you a few questions?"

"It depends on the questions," the woman answered. "I'm...I'm Marie."

"Here, Marie, let me help you with that bucket," Brian offered. "We could sit on that bench, if that's – wow, this thing is heavy!" He strained to lift the five gallon bucket.

"It's nearly full. I've another one back there. I was nearly done when you two showed up."

"How do you carry such heavy buckets to wherever you've got your car parked?" Brian asked.

"I have a yoke back there which makes it easier, but it's still a chore."

"This is a lot of grapes. What do you do with them? Make wine?"

"Some people do, but mostly we make jam. These are concords, which are sweeter. This much will make jam for several families, but it's not even a tenth of the number of grapes on these vines. Most of them will rot or be taken by the birds, with nobody to harvest them."

"That's a shame," Brian said as he sat down on the bench. "These houses look like they could hold a lot of people, yet they're empty. Where is everyone?"

The woman looked at them skeptically. "You said you were here looking for things that might jog his memory. What kind of things were you looking for?"

"Jason, it's your images and emotions we're working with," Brian said. "Tell the lady."

"It's difficult to know where to begin," Jason explained. "I guess...well, do you know an older man with white hair and moustache, who used to rock in the rocker in the living room of that house?"

The woman stared at Jason with widening eyes and a shocked look on her face. "Do I...a man about a head taller than me, late seventies, quiet but authoritative manner?"

"I...I think so," Jason stammered, but the woman had pulled a phone from her pocket and was manipulating the screen. Finally, she held it up to show Jason a picture of several people, including a white-haired man.

"Second from the left – is that the man?"

"Yes," Jason said with relief at finally getting something definitive. The face in the picture was clearly the same one that had kept showing up in his mind. "Yes, that's him. Do you know who he is, and where I might find him?"

Sorrow shadowed the woman's face. "His name was Mike, though most of us just knew him as Grandpa. He's…he's no longer with us. He was taken last spring, and we're pretty sure…we're pretty sure he's gone."

Fresh waves of sorrow washed over Jason, mingled with sharp, undirected outrage. It was wrong! They shouldn't have! "I'm sorry," he said.

"Yeah," the woman replied. "So were a lot of other people. He was a great man, and an inspiration to us all. But he did what he thought would help the most people, because that's the kind of man he was."

"Do you have any pictures of a woman with short reddish-brown hair, dressed in white or black?" Brian asked.

"With a brilliant smile," Jason added.

Now the woman looked genuinely alarmed, and looked back and forth between the two men quickly. "You mean Teresa?" she asked. "Are you talking about Teresa?"

"I don't know," Jason replied. "All I have is images flicking through my mind without any firm connections. There were two just today, one of her in white talking to me on a corner up in Sandusky, and the other of her in black walking by that pond over there. But the most persistent is one that's been with me…a long time. It's an image of her back – just her back – as she walked through some kind of doorway into darkness. She was dressed in white, and I couldn't see her face, but I'm sure it was her. I'm sorry I can't give you more details, but I've suffered some…memory damage, and I'm trying to piece things back together."

The woman was staring at Jason throughout all this, and continued to stare for a while after he trailed off. Then her expression cleared, and she looked at him with something like wonder.

"You were there. That's where I know you from! You were the guy who came late! She spoke to you just before she…went in. You were there, and you saw it all! In fact, you gave Luke a ride afterward. I never learned your name, but you were there!"

Brian and Jason looked at each other, and Brian gave a relieved chuckle. Now they seemed to be getting somewhere!

"Oh, my goodness – you don't remember that? What happened?" the woman continued.

"No, I'm afraid I don't remember anything but that image," Jason admitted. "I'm not exactly sure what happened. I certainly suffered some kind of trauma – what or why, I don't know."

"So, what are you doing here? What are you hoping to accomplish?"

"I guess to try to recover more of who I am and what I knew. As far as coming here, that was Brian's idea, but it turned out to be a good one, it seems."

The woman sat still for a long while, gazing at her hands. "Listen," she finally said, "my name isn't Marie – at least, that's my middle name, the one I give out when I need camouflage. My actual name is Grace, and I was there on that road last spring when Teresa went into the shadowed wood. I'm sorry it took me so long to recognize you, but you stayed on the periphery, and I had other things on my mind. You were one of only seven people who saw what happened that night."

"Really? What was that?" Jason asked.

"It's too long to go into here and now. But if visiting sites where important things happened is helping you recover your memory, I suggest we meet up again, and we can visit where it took place."

"Okay – when can we meet?"

"Let's see," Grace mused. "Not tomorrow, because Todd has to work. Would the evening two days from now work?"

"Don't see why not – I'll be on day shift," Brian said.

"Good. Give me your number, and I'll contact you with the exact time and place," Grace said.

Dark Secrets

Gerald leaned back in his chair and rubbed his eyes. The message that had just come in from his contact up at Garden River reported the same dismal results: nothing. This was getting tedious, and Gerald was beginning to wonder if the whole effort was nothing but a quixotic attempt to comfort an imaginative old woman.

Gerald had spent the last several days on the phone and exchanging messages with his contacts up near the Sault, as well as scouring sites and online reports. He was looking for any hint of a massacre, or even a series of unexpected deaths or disappearances. Of all the things in The Warrior's message that Esther had recounted, the massacre or bloodbath seemed the most likely thing to have been noticed and documented. Gerald's searching had turned up no such event in the past couple of years. There was the usual steady trickle of homicides, with most of the First Nation ones being sadly but predictably related to domestic violence or alcohol or both, but no sign of any mass murders. He'd contacted a friend who worked for the Garden River Security and had him check with the Ontario Provincial Police and even the Mounties, but that had returned nothing. He'd even searched as far west as Thunder Bay, since he didn't have a precise idea what The Warrior had meant by "north", but still found no results. Either this massacre had happened in secret or it hadn't happened at all.

As a last resort Gerald had imposed on a friend at Garden River to drive up Route 17 as far as the area of Michipicoten, most of which was now Lake Superior Provincial Park, and poke around for anomalies. He'd had a devil of a time describing to his friend what he should be looking for, but the friend had attended carefully and given it his best effort. His report, which was the message Gerald had just read, told how he'd driven up to and all around the coastal forests near Michipicoten, and had talked to hikers and park staff, but had heard nothing of mysterious fogs, or of people getting inexplicably lost or exhibiting aggressive behavior. Furthermore, all hikers, campers, and other visitors had been accounted for, and though there had been a couple of serious injuries, they were no more than would be typical for a summer season. Gerald was forced to conclude that the clinging darkness had not returned to the last place it was known to have been.

So, what to do? Unquestionably the words of The Warrior's message, which had stuck so firmly in Esther's mind that she'd been repeating them to herself for months, strongly resembled the terms used by the Ojibwa to describe the curse to Fr. Thomas. The fact that they'd matched so closely had been a clue to Gerald that Esther hadn't just been dreaming things up. But if there was no indication that the phenomenon had returned, what was he to do?

Gerald had accepted the burden of the message from Esther, which meant a lot to an Anishinaabe. He'd taken responsibility for understanding the message and taking whatever steps it necessitated. He couldn't just throw up his hands and walk away. He was honor-bound to give it his best effort. But how far did he have to take this? How far could he take it? Even if he drove back to the Garden River Reserve to make the calls and visits in person, that would produce the same results. If there was nothing there, verifying it personally wouldn't change that. He couldn't keep searching forever – but what could he do?

He grabbed his coffee mug and headed to the kitchen for a refill. Kim was there working at something on her tablet, and asked how things were going. He gave her the summary, and she patted his shoulder sympathetically.

"If it's any consolation, Esther is resting much better. She's not back up to her previous level of activity, but she's in good spirits."

"That is a consolation," Gerald assured her. "But it makes my work more imperative. If only I knew exactly what I was looking for."

"It's tough," Kim sympathized. "How literally was the message to be taken? Visions from the unseen side are often thick with symbol and metaphor."

"Yes, but this message wasn't symbol, it was words – quite familiar words, at least to me," Gerald reminded her. "Tell you what I'm thinking: that I need to visit the Memory Stone myself. It's not far, is it?"

"Driving? About two hours. Due east to Bay City, pick up M-25 on the far side, take that to Unionville, then turn east. It's about halfway across the Thumb and clearly marked. It's after Labor Day, though, so the pavilion will be locked up. If you need to get to the stone itself, we'll need to make some calls to the park service to arrange to get you in."

"No need, at least on this visit," Gerald assured her. "I think the fence will be close enough."

"There's one more issue to keep in mind," Kim cautioned. "The Petroglyphs lie within this new Special Protectionary District that the federal government has created. Our tribe has cautioned any of us going into that area to be sure to keep our papers with us."

"I always do on this side of the border, but I'll be certain," Gerald said. "What is it with that, anyway? Have you heard of any incidents in there?"

"I've heard of nothing, but mostly we just stay out. It's supposed to be all about suppressing domestic terror, and providing better government services to underserved populations. I've no idea exactly what that means, or how it's going."

"Well," Gerald said with a wry grin, "if our people's experience with government suppression and better government services is any indication, they're pretty much doomed."

Gerald stood outside the circular fence enclosing the sandstone rock on which were carved the ancient images. An open pavilion had been erected over the stone, with steel legs supporting a canopy-like metal roof, shielding it from the sun and direct precipitation. The tall fence protected the stone from vandals and careless visitors. The site was usually locked up, but during daytime hours in summer it was staffed by guides from the Michigan Park Service who would give tours and explain what was known about the glyphs, which wasn't much.

The Petroglyphs were one of those sites that Gerald had always intended to visit but had never gotten around to, and now he was locked out. As Kim had mentioned, he could have arranged to get to it if he'd wished. The stone was cared for by the State of Michigan, but since it was an Anishinaabek holy site, the Park Service worked with First Nations members to facilitate access, as they had for Kim and Esther. But Gerald hadn't thought he'd need access to the stone itself – just being at the site would probably suffice.

But what was he doing here? Did he expect to see a replay of Esther's vision? He looked through the fence at the shaded stone, then around the sun-dappled trees that surrounded the site. Everything looked so ordinary, a typical Michigan wood on a typical autumn afternoon. It was pleasant and peaceful, but not helpful for illuminating the issues Gerald was facing.

Gerald strolled around the fenced enclosure, and then on a whim went up the trail to a clearing about half a mile from the pavilion. Some of the guides told visitors that this clearing had been a ceremonial site, used by the tribes for pauwaus and trade gatherings. How anybody could know that was beyond Gerald, but it certainly could have been used that way. He poked around the clearing for a while then wandered down to the banks of the nearby Cass River. This, Gerald knew, would have been important, and was certainly why the Memory stone site lay where it did. He tried to imagine the days before the Europeans arrived, when the dense woods were passable only by hunting trails, and the waterways were the roads by which the Original People traveled. The Cass meandered across the Thumb until it joined with the Shiawassee and Tittabawassee to form the Saginaw River, which flowed out into broad Saginaw Bay, rich with fish and edged with marshland that housed great flocks of wildfowl. His people would have thrived in this land – when the Fox and the Sauk weren't attacking them. In fact, to this day the Saginaw Chippewa maintained a reserve on the west shore of Saginaw Bay and exercised their fishing rights. Gerald knew a man who kept a fishing boat there.

Having seen enough of the river, Gerald made his way back to the fenced enclosure. He'd come here on an urge – what had he expected to find? Pondering that question, he realized that the Oxford Gerald had been doing the looking, which meant he'd been expecting empirical evidence, things that could be analyzed and categorized. But if he'd been drawn here by intuition, he needed to be thinking and responding as Ojibwa Gerald.

He stood still and tried to quiet his mind. Whatever the real history of the Petroglyphs, there was no question that First Nations tribes had been here. He tried to reach out with his heart and imagination, asking those ancient visitors to help him. Six months ago, a significant spiritual event had happened at this site, and he wanted to attune his spirit to that. He closed his eyes and tried to imagine the scene at sunrise on the spring equinox – the snow and chill wind, the hypnotic beat of the drum, the wailing of the song in the cold pre-dawn.

Something wasn't right. Something seemed to be hindering his access to that rhythm. Gerald opened his eyes and looked around and down. Catching sight of his feet, he grinned – that was it. He bent over and removed his shoes. That was better. His shoe-coddled feet balked at the direct contact with the forest floor, but he was in touch with the earth. For good measure he took a pinch of tobacco from his pouch and, facing east, sprinkled it on the ground while singing an invocation to the Warrior for aid. He closed his eyes again and tried to let the Ojibwa Gerald take over. He was not expecting a vision – seeing was not his gift, and he had not prepared himself – but he was hoping to open his heart to whatever had happened here that spring morning.

"Show me the threat," Gerald muttered, his eyes still closed. "Make clear the enemy, O Warrior." He tried to envision what Esther had seen, the tall figure of the Warrior striding from the east, towering above the trees. Gerald realized that she must have been given a visionary's perspective for that, since actually standing here gave one a view of nothing but tree trunks in all directions, and the only sky visible was straight up. But in his imagination, he could envision a tall figure standing against the dawn, gazing steadily toward the north.

Then it struck him. He pulled his phone from his pocket and brought up the video of the interview with Esther. He cued it to the point where she was describing the vision of the Warrior, and there it was – she clearly said that the treetops reached about to his waist. Well, Gerald mused, the most mature trees in this area were thirty to forty meters tall. Thus, if the vision in any way reflected reality, that would make the figure of the Warrior sixty to eighty meters tall. And that meant, if a spiritual vision respected physical constraints – Gerald asked his phone a question and received a prompt reply – thirty kilometers. From a height of eighty meters someone would be able to see just over thirty kilometers into the distance.

He'd been searching too far north.

Gerald's heart sang. No trance, no vision, no ecstasy, but he knew this was what he had been drawn here to learn. Every detail of Esther's vision had meant something: not just the word spoken, but the fact that The Warrior was looking toward the north (which Gerald had picked up on) and the

Warrior's height (which he hadn't). Gerald realized that he'd just assumed the scourge would reappear in the vicinity of the Sault, because that had been the last place it had been heard of. But the Sault was much further than thirty kilometers away – in fact, thirty kilometers would barely bring the Huron coast into view.

What, then, did "north" mean?

Excited at the prospect of progress, Gerald started walking back, only to have the stone and stick-strewn path remind him that he was still barefoot. That remedied, he returned to his car and brought up a map on his tablet. The Petroglyphs were nearly at the northern border of Sanilac County, and north of that everything to the lake was – Huron County? Where the largest town and county seat was called Bad Axe, population 3,000? Gerald smiled – what a name for a town. There had to be a story behind that. The town had a library, and was less than half an hour away. Time to do some research.

A couple of hours later Gerald was almost ready to admit defeat. He'd pored over the news reports and checked out the court records and searched using every phrase and keyword he could think of, and had turned up nothing remotely resembling a massacre. The closest he'd found was a murder/suicide just over a year ago involving a family just a few miles northeast of here. But that had been in a house, not a wood, and tragic though it was, it didn't seem to Gerald to qualify as "great" bloodshed.

"Is there something else I can help you with?" the librarian asked as she walked past. She'd been most helpful to Gerald in setting him up at a workstation and getting his tablet connected to the library's network. She'd undoubtedly been watching his building frustration as his searches kept turning up empty. He was reluctant to discuss what he was searching for, but he was also running short on options.

"I'm not sure," Gerald admitted. "I'm looking for something that may not even exist."

"You'd be surprised how frequently people do that," the librarian said with a smile. "What kind of thing?"

"A possible incident or incidents involving numerous people being killed, or going missing," Gerald replied.

"Hmm, that is grim. In what time frame are we looking?"

"I'm not precisely sure about that, either, but I'm guessing within the past three years, possibly five."

"Well, there was the Jennette incident. That was sad – my daughter knew one of the girls who was killed."

"I spotted that," Gerald said. "I've reason to believe that it wasn't what I'm searching for."

"There was also the whole Wondercare exposé, though most of that played out in St. Clair and other counties," the librarian suggested, "but that was more about people being found than going missing."

"I caught that, too," Gerald replied.

"Well, I don't know what to tell you," the librarian said with a note of apology. "Things are kind of quiet up here in Huron County. It's not like Flint or Detroit." She fell silent for a minute, then looked at Gerald with a curious expression before speaking again. "You know, though, there have been some curious rumors floating around since the Wondercare matter broke just over a year ago."

"What kind of rumors?" Gerald asked.

Again the librarian gazed at him for a bit, as if evaluating him. She seemed to come to a decision, and sat down at the desk across from him. "Not everything that happens gets reported publicly, but you'll hear things if you know where to listen. Things like how there may have been a lot more to the Wondercare incident than made the news sites. Things about how a local family was deeply involved, and that that family may have had other bad things going on, even to the point of owning some of the county offices. Things hinted at in the ravings of a mad woman who was held in the county jail before being shipped off to the psychiatric prison south of Ann Arbor. Things like insane vagrants wandering into the county last autumn and spring, haunting the streets and towns until they just – vanished. Things like how drivers learned to avoid certain sections of the county for a time last year, because if they strayed into those sections, they'd get inexplicably lost, and spend hours trying to make their way clear."

"Sounds like Huron County might not have been so quiet after all," Gerald observed after the librarian had finished recounting this improbable litany. He guessed that the only reason she'd continued was because he had not yet dissolved into laughter or scornful smirking. In truth, the Oxford Gerald was tempted to do just that, but the Ojibwa Gerald was recalling that just hours earlier he'd been standing barefoot on the forest floor, offering tobacco and praying for wisdom to understand a mystic's ominous vision. The results of that had brought him here, where this librarian was risking her credibility to inform him that his search might not have been in vain. "I'd like to hear more about those things, if I could. They may help me with what I'm searching for."

The librarian nodded slowly. "Let me make a phone call," she said, getting up and walking away. She was back in a few minutes and handed Gerald a sticky note with a name on it. "My cousin Audra works over at the sheriff's office. They're only two blocks away, over on South and up Heistermann. She said he's got fifteen minutes he can spare you, if you're interested."

"I am. Thank you." Gerald took the slip and began gathering his gear.

"You must be the library guy," said a brown-haired man with a moustache and a brisk, friendly manner who was standing behind a chaotic desk.

"I am," Gerald replied, taking the offered hand in a firm grip. "You must be Sheriff Keller."

"Guilty as charged," the man replied. "Though I usually go by Chip, unless I'm slapping cuffs on you. Forgive the clutter – I'm catching a late lunch while trying to clear out this paperwork. The wife makes me salads, which aren't as good as a burger down at Pete's, but are easier on the budget and help with the perpetual battle." He slapped the waist of a slightly snug uniform shirt.

"Well, Chip, thank you for squeezing me into your day," Gerald grinned, handing Chip his passport and tribal ID. "My name is Gerald Solomon, and I'm a member of the Garden River Ojibwa up near the Sault. I'm down here visiting my sister, who lives over near Mount Pleasant on the Isabella Reserve."

"A pleasure and an honor, Mr. Solomon," Chip said, passing back the documents. "Home of the Soaring Eagle, eh? How's the casino doing?"

"My sister works there, and she says it's getting by. Not what the tribal leaders would like, but you know how that is."

"Dwindling pool of customers," Chip shook his head. "My wife's women's group used to go over every month, but as members have aged, they can't manage more than once a quarter, if that. But how may I assist an official of the Ojibwa?"

"Well, that's the question," Gerald admitted. "I've been thinking over how to explain the situation to you without having you think I was wasting your time with fairy tales."

"Fairy tales?" Chip asked, cocking his head slightly.

"I think it best if I just start at the beginning," Gerald replied, and launched into a condensed version of the events of the past several months: the finding of the missionary diary, the account of the shadowed wood and how Fr. Thomas had dealt with it, the vision that Esther had seen the prior equinox, and his journey to the Petroglyphs this morning. "And so," Gerald concluded, "I came here to Bad Axe to see if I could find any record of a bloodbath or mysterious murders around woods. I drew a blank at the library, but got talking to the librarian, who alluded to things that didn't make the news and sent me here to you. Now I can only hope you don't throw me out for burning up your time with ancient legends and dark Indian lore, though maybe you should."

Through the entire recounting Chip had looked at Gerald without any trace of emotion. Even after Gerald had finished, Chip continued to gaze silently, his eyes burning with a steady intensity that was difficult to read. Gerald hoped he hadn't offended the sheriff in some way.

"Mr. Solomon," Chip finally asked in a very different voice than the genial conversational tone he'd been using. "How much time to you have?"

"How much time do I have?" Gerald asked, mystified.

"Do you need to be back in Mount Pleasant or the Sault today? Can you linger in the area until evening?"

"My time is my own, and I have no commitments. I'm supposed to be on vacation," Gerald explained.

"There are things I'd like to tell you that I can't easily explain in this office or in this uniform," Chip said, plucking his sleeve. "But if you could meet me after hours, I'd feel freer to talk about things you might find…interesting."

A slight chill shot through Gerald's insides – this was not the response he'd expected. "I can stay as long as necessary."

"Good. I'll be tied up here with the county administrator until about six, and then I'll want to go home and change, but I should be free between seven and seven-thirty. Can you give me your number?"

"Sure," Gerald scribbled it on a piece of paper.

"I'll send you the location and the time to meet," Chip assured him. "When we do, I'll tell you some things that may answer some of your questions, but will surely raise many more. They certainly did for me."

"Thank you, Chip," Gerald said.

"Wait until after you hear it to thank me," Chip said ominously. "It's an incredible account with elements that I don't know what to make of even now. I'm still sorting some of the things out."

"Sounds intense."

"It's worse. But just now, I need to get back to work. If you can find something in or near Bad Axe to kill a few hours, I'll let you know when I'm free. The Sugar Bowl has decent dinners, but stay away from their corned beef."

*　　　　　*　　　　　*

Lawrence Stover sat at the desk in his office thinking sad thoughts and trying to pray instead of cry. He wasn't managing that very well, but he kept trying.

Annette's amyotrophic lateral sclerosis was proceeding more rapidly than the doctors had estimated. They were still trying various combinations of drugs to find the best mix, but in the meantime her condition was deteriorating rapidly. Things had seemed to level off in spring and early summer, but as autumn approached, the pace had picked up again, and milestones they'd been assured would take months to reach were taking weeks.　It wouldn't be too long now, and Lawrence needed to come to grips with that.

Lawrence didn't know if he was comforted or annoyed by Annette's seemingly unflagging patience and optimism. He hoped he'd be able to approach impending death with equal aplomb. But then, he didn't know how he was going to go on living without Annette at his side.

His musings were interrupted by a muffled noise coming from a drawer in the desk. It sounded like the chirp of a phone, but he knew his phone was in the next room. Bewildered, he fumbled through the drawers until he found the device, which only mystified him further. This was one of the phones that used the private communications network that had connected the ranches. The ranches had all been shut down last spring, and the communications network had lain dormant ever since. What signal could have awakened this old phone?

Only one way to find out. He answered with a tentative, "Hello?"

"Hello?" came a woman's voice that Lawrence didn't recognize. "Is this Lawrence Stover?"

"Yes. Who's this?"

"Oh, thank goodness. Rosemary gave me your number, but she wasn't sure the number would still work, because it's apparently some kind of special phone, and she was worried that the batteries might have died –"

"Well, they haven't," Lawrence interrupted, trying to be patient with this woman's chatter. "What I can I do for you? I presume you're not Rosemary."

"No, no, I'm Dorothy, Dorothy Oldham. I called Rosemary because she was the one who called me back then, to see if I could help. It was all so rushed, so I only talked to Rosemary, who really had her hands full..."

Lawrence sighed and prayed for patience as the garrulous woman rattled on. When he was finally able to get a word in edgewise, he asked, "What can I do for you, Dorothy?"

"Do for me? Oh. Well, it's about the boy."

The boy? Now Lawrence was really confused. "I...I'm sorry – what boy?"

"The boy we're fostering. Rosemary said it was you who called her that night, a year ago last summer, looking for housing for youngsters who'd been displaced somehow. We agreed to take Tyrone, and he's been with us ever since."

Ah, Lawrence nodded, context at last. One of the children rescued from slavery that summer night. "So, you were one of the families who took in one of the children. Thank you for your help."

"It's been our pleasure, and Tyrone's been a delight. So helpful and eager to learn!" Dorothy assured him. "Only, we seem to have run into a snag with him just recently, and we don't know what to do."

"Really? What kind of snag?" Lawrence asked instinctively, then instantly regretted it. He was hardly the person to be trying to help a foster family with whatever problem they might have run into with one of the kids. He should delegate this to someone.

"Well, I was reading to him the other evening, and he suddenly stood up and ran away to go hide in his bedroom. Since then he's been frightened and withdrawn, which isn't like him at all. He's sleeping very lightly, and is restless and unsettled during the day. That, plus he keeps asking for the safety lady."

"The safety lady?" Lawrence asked.

"Yes, and we haven't any idea what he means. He says there were three of them 'that night', and calls them the safety ladies. We guessed he was talking about the night he was found, or whatever happened – he's never discussed it – but we have no idea who this 'safety lady' is, or whether she's even a real person."

Lawrence closed his eyes and tried to recall that night. It seemed so long ago, and so much had happened since. There had been three women: Teresa, of course, and Mike's granddaughter – Felicity, he thought her name was. And there was one other young woman, too, though her name escaped him. They'd been the ones who had gone into the woods.

"…And he hasn't said what he wants with her, only that he wants her." Lawrence realized that Dorothy was still talking. "We figured that with this dramatic behavior change, we'd try to find her."

"Yes, yes," Lawrence assured her. "You're right about that – certainly worth a try. Listen, Dorothy, I wasn't deeply involved in the arrangements for the children that night, but I know some people who were. Why don't I make some phone calls and get back to you? Can I reach you at this number?"

"Yes, of course," Dorothy replied. "But…could you make it quick? He's quite distressed."

"I understand, and I will," Lawrence assured her in all honesty, knowing more about the tragic circumstances out of which the boy had been rescued. "It sounds like something might have triggered some traumatic memory. Any idea what it might have been?"

"None at all. Like I said, I was just reading him the *Odyssey*. He's never been like this before."

"If you don't mind my asking, what portion of the story were you reading him?"

"The part about Circe's Island, where she turns Odysseus's crew into pigs," Dorothy explained.

Lawrence sat up, fully attentive. "Yes. Yes, I can see how that…let me make some calls." Ringing off, he sat pondering for a minute. Circe's Island. That poor lad. He needed to call Steve.

*　　　　*　　　　*

"Dammit, I want some answers!" demanded Jim Nichol. "What am I doing here? Why can't I see Dr. Carey?"

"I promise you, sir, the clinician will be along shortly, and he'll be able to answer all your questions. Hold your arm still, please, this'll only take a minute." The medical tech had been swabbing his Jim's left forearm before spraying it with some solution, and now he was holding a small beige box, just a couple inches square, against the swabbed spot. He pressed a button on the box and Jim felt a bit of pressure and a brief sting.

"What was that?" Jim asked as the tech threw the box in the trash.

"Preparation, sir," the tech explained as he bandaged the spot. There was now a small slit in Jim's skin, just a few millimeters long. "This is the latest high-tech innovation in medical provision."

"Oh, yeah? What does it do?"

"It keeps your medical records with you at all times," the tech explained as he began packing up the little kit he'd brought. "The problem of consistent, accurate medical records has plagued the industry since the days of paper files. You might get treatment at three different providers, and each of their records might be accurate, but they don't synchronize with each other. Nobody knows what anyone else is doing. This chip," he gestured at Jim's forearm, "solves that problem."

"A chip? In my arm?" Jim touched the bandage.

"Don't worry, you'll never notice it," the tech assured him. "It's five millimeters square and wafer-thin. And the best part is that it never needs batteries." The tech was all packed up and heading out the door.

"But wait," Jim objected. "What if I don't want –"

"The clinician will be here soon, sir. He'll answer all your questions," the tech said over his shoulder as he departed, leaving Jim alone in the tiny exam room to think and fume.

Jim didn't know what was going on. He'd shown up at his endocrinologist for his appointment, only to be told they couldn't serve him. According to some new protocol, he had to go to some government-run clinic to get care. No, they couldn't make an exception. No, they couldn't refer him to another endocrinologist – he had to go to this clinic. So he'd gone, intending to give them a piece of his mind, but he'd been greeted as if they were expecting him and ushered into this exam room. One tech had shown up to draw some blood, then another had come in to do this thing with the medical records chip, but he was still waiting to see a doctor.

Jim waited so long that he was nearly ready to put his shirt back on and stalk out when a man in a lab coat came through the door. The man had a stethoscope around his neck and was staring at one of the ubiquitous tablets. He wore a name tag that said "Dr. Brad" beside one of those square bar codes.

"So, Mr. Nichol, about your thyroid condition," the man began, but Jim cut him off.

"Look here, doctor, I don't know what all this is about, but I'm not used to being told where I can and can't get medical care. I've been going –"

"Please, Mr. Nichol," the man interrupted in a bored tone. "I appreciate your frustration. Change requires adjustments, some of which can be stressful. With a little patience, I'm sure you'll manage just fine."

"But why should I have to?" Jim challenged him. "I didn't ask for a new doctor. I was happy with Dr. Carey."

"I understand, but sometimes we have to look at the big picture, and consider what's best for everyone," the man replied soothingly. "Haven't you been hearing about the UPAIR initiative?"

"I've heard of it – some kind of government program. I don't see what that has to do –"

"The UPAIR initiative," the man talked over him, "is intended to bring consistent, quality health care to populations and regions that have lacked them. To facilitate this, standardized protocols are being implemented to bring everyone under the same roof, so to speak. Furthermore, it will cost you nothing."

"I don't give a damn about your protocols," Jim snarled. "Dr. Carey was the best, my coverage let me go to him, and I was happy to pay the co-pays."

"Ah, but what of those whose coverage did not, or who had no coverage at all? You see, if we are to be equitable about care provision, we must level the playing field."

"Is that it, then?" Jim barked. "Because someone else can't see Dr. Carey, that means I can't, either?"

"Mr. Nichol, I admit I'm surprised to find you so indifferent to the plight of your neighbors," the man admonished. "I'd think you'd want everyone to enjoy the same quality of care that you do."

"I...I don't care if everyone goes to Dr. Carey," Jim replied, a little taken aback by the statement. "I just want to be able to keep going to him, and I don't see why I can't."

"Because you're within jurisdiction of the Special Protectionary District, which means you receive the benefit of the UPAIR initiative," the man said with a touch of exasperation. "I assure you our staff endocrinologist is more than qualified, and she'll –"

"I don't give a damn about your staff endocrinologist! I want to see Dr. Carey!"

"Mr. Nichol," the man said, looking up from his tablet with hard eyes. "You will not be able to see your old doctor. You will see our providers at our facilities. There is no other option for you, so you might as well get used to it."

"Are you saying –" Jim began, but the man cut him off.

"I'm setting up an appointment for you at this facility a week from Tuesday. You'll receive a notification on your phone. Do not be late – the doctor has more people to care for than just you." The man concluded with some taps on the tablet screen and walked out before Jim could respond.

Delores Nichol was surprised to find Jim home from his appointment when she returned from work. She was even more surprised to find him storming about the bedroom, pulling clothes from closets and drawers and stuffing them into suitcases that lay open on the bed. His face was set and he was muttering to himself, which was never a good sign.

"Jim, what on earth..." Delores began, but Jim cut her off sharply.

"Delores! Get packing. We're leaving now – today."

"Leaving? But...to go where?"

"Wayne's. I've already talked to him, and he's okay with us staying as long as we need." Wayne was Jim's brother who lived over by Grand Rapids.

"Why would we go stay at Wayne's?" Delores asked.

"In order to get proper medical care, that's why," Jim explained. "Didn't I warn you? Didn't I warn you when they came out with all this Special Protectionary District hogwash that this was just a veiled assault on our freedom?"

"Yes, Jim, you warned me," Delores assured him, accustomed to pacifying her husband's tirades. "But what does that have to do with medical care?"

Jim explained how he'd gone to his scheduled appointment only to be sent to the government clinic, and all that had happened there. By the time he was finished, even the normally calm Delores was a little alarmed.

"Maybe...maybe it was just a misunderstanding," she offered weakly. "Maybe if you called Dr. Carey's office –"

"I did. I spoke with Sandi, and she told me that I was one of their transferred patients, and they couldn't give me any more care. She even hinted that she could get in trouble just for talking to me, and asked me not to call back."

"That's...unsettling," Delores admitted.

"Damn right it's unsettling. That's why we're getting out of here today. Pack what you need for a couple of weeks. I've asked Danny to bring in the mail and watch the property. We'll worry about the rest of the stuff later."

The pickup carrying Jim and Delores Nichol and what goods they'd packed was making its way west on I-69 toward Lansing, where they'd pick up I-96 and head for Grand Rapids. They had just passed through Flint, and Jim allowed himself a quiet breath of relief. They were clear of the borders of the SPD, and only two hours from Wayne's, where they could get a good night's sleep then make some phone calls and try to get all this sorted out.

"Crimenently, now what?" Jim muttered as flashing blue lights filled his rearview mirror. He checked his speed, but it was pegged at the limit by speed control. Figuring the lights for an emergency vehicle that needed to get past, Jim edged over to clear the lane, but the lights stayed behind him, almost on his bumper, and were now flashing their headlights at him as well. Jim's heart began pounding, but he pulled to the shoulder, the vehicle with the blue flashing lights right behind him.

"Jim, what's going on?" Delores asked, her voice on edge.

"I don't know – I wasn't speeding," Jim assured her. "Probably a mistake." But even as he spoke, he realized that the vehicle which had pulled them over was a black SUV with no visible insignia, and the two men getting out of it were wearing what looked like combat fatigues, all black, with black ball caps and wraparound sunglasses even in the twilight. The one approaching Jim's window had a handgun prominently holstered on his hip, while the one coming up the other side of the car was holding something by his side that Jim didn't quite see. They were coming up both sides of the car with stern expressions. Jim cracked the window and asked with a dry mouth, "Is there a problem, officer?"

"James and Delores Nichol?" the man asked sternly, his hand resting on the butt of the pistol at his belt.

"Yes," Jim began, but was interrupted by a frightened cry from Delores. Glancing over, he saw the source of her alarm: the man at her window was holding, low against his leg where it couldn't be seen by passing traffic, what was unmistakably a submachine gun.

"Hey," Jim exclaimed, but the man on his side was opening his door.

"James and Delores Nichol," he said in a stern voice, "you're going to need to come with us."

*   *   *

Brian Sanderson's phone chimed with an incoming call from a number he didn't recognize. He was about to silence it, because answering unrecognized numbers usually meant having to listen to a recorded voice trying to sound human.

But then he remembered that he was expecting a call, so he picked up.

"Mr. Sanderson?" came a clearly human woman's voice.

"Yes?"

"Hi. This is Marie. We met the other day in the grape arbor. I wanted to see if you still wished to bring your guest to that site we discussed to see if it might help with his condition."

"Very much so," Brian answered.

"Good. I'm transmitting the address and coordinates. We can meet there at seven o'clock this evening."

"That sounds great."

"All right, then –" Grace began to ring off but Brian interrupted her.

"Before you go, there's something I need to bring up. I'm not sure how to broach the topic with you, but I'm in a fix and I don't know what else to do. My...guest, as you put it, really can't continue to stay at my place. Not only does it make my living situation very difficult, but it's not really safe for him."

"Not...safe?" Grace asked.

"I don't want to frighten you, but the situation is complicated and I need help," Brian explained. "You know the trauma that my guest spoke of? The condition that affected his memory?"

"Yes."

"I'm pretty sure it wasn't accidental. Something was done to him, I'm not sure what. I think those who did it didn't intend him to survive long on his own, and they certainly didn't intend him to end up back here."

"Who are these parties that 'did it' to him?" Grace asked.

Brian sighed. Telling her would almost certainly scare her off helping, but he couldn't blindside her. "When my guest left the area last time, which would have been shortly after you saw him, he went back to his headquarters. We thought it would be just for a couple of days, but instead he vanished without a trace, and a new guy was brought in to take his place. There was no word of where he was or what had happened to him, until the other day, when he showed up in borrowed clothes with no recollection of who he was, except for those disjointed fragments of memory he talked about the other day."

"That's spooky," Grace admitted. "So you think his employers had this done to him?"

"I don't know for sure, but it's a strong possibility. I'm very concerned that if they find him again, they'll engineer another disappearance, and this one won't be temporary. It would be safest for him if he were to get out of sight somehow, and my apartment is just too chancy."

"Hmm," Grace said. "Let me make some calls, and hopefully I'll have something for you when we meet. In the meantime, bring your guest to that address this evening and hopefully we can jog his memory a little."

"Oh…okay," Brian said, somewhat surprised at how casually she seemed to be taking such a potentially risky situation. Ending the call, he pulled up the geospatial information she'd transmitted to see where he was supposed to drive tonight. As he looked at the map and the address, a chill gripped his heart.

"Oh, my," he whispered.

*   *   *

Brady Shevnock was browsing the black sites. He did this from time to time just to keep his ear to the digital ground, to see if he could learn anything interesting or useful. He took all the precautions: running his network traffic through a utility that masked his device's address, tunneling through a router at a distant location, encrypting all his data, and otherwise making himself as invisible and untraceable as possible. His intent was to be a cyber-ghost, able to visit wherever he wished without leaving digital tracks.

The black sites were mostly online forums unknown to the name servers and search engines that managed most internet traffic. These sites could only be reached if you knew their device addresses, a series of numbers separated by colons that you had to key in. The sites were maintained by anonymous parties, and their purpose was anonymity. Visitors to the sites registered under pseudonyms and posted information that generated responses, leading to lengthy online conversations that made very interesting reading, if you were interested in the right things.

Many of the anonymous parties who frequented these black sites worked for big operations – software firms, telecommunications conglomerates, hardware manufacturers, and government agencies. In their employment environments they were usually bound by contract or employment agreement to keep their activities secret, so posting online under their real names would open them to disciplinary action or even prosecution. But on these secret sites, posting under assumed names, these tech wizards could safely spill some of the deepest secrets of their organizations.

And spill they did. For those who knew what to look for, the conversation threads on the forums were a gold mine of intelligence about the most leading edge technical innovations being worked on around the world. Forum members would candidly discuss details about their darkest projects for everyone to glean information from. They were driven by many motivations: some wanted to boast about the sophisticated work they were doing. Others felt maltreated by their organizations and posted insider information as a way of getting even. Still others had ethical qualms about what they were being asked to do and posted details to salve their consciences.

Motives didn't matter to Brady. He wanted to sift through the volumes of data for anything interesting or useful for his purposes. Since the black sites were, by definition, beyond the reach of commercial search engines that catalogued online content, Brady had written his own search engine to crawl through the articles and conversations and log them to a private database. It was this search engine he brought up, to see what the hot topics of discussion were since he'd last visited.

Brady skimmed a few summary paragraphs on topics he'd flagged in prior visits, then clicked over to examine the new topics. One discussion thread stood out as very active, so he brought up the initial post, which had been written by a programmer for one of the major phone manufacturers. It was a routine posting for the black site forums: a listing of features, fixes, and enhancements contained in the most recent update to the phone's operating system. Mostly this was deep tech stuff, interesting only to those immersed in the minutia of such things. However, there was one new feature on the bullet list that had sparked a firestorm of follow-up commentary. Brady read the initial post carefully, especially the provocative bullet point, to ensure he understood what was at issue.

Hmm. Brady leaned back in his chair and pondered, jotting a couple of notes to clarify his thinking. According to this post, one completely new feature added with the most recent software update for this company's phones was the requirement that the phone constantly "listen" for a particular digital pattern. If the phone detected this pattern, it was to encrypt and transmit it, along with the geolocation of the receiving phone and the time of detection, to a particular network address. That was it – technically, a very simple function.

The disturbing thing was that this functionality had been mandated by the federal government, who had also mandated that the feature be kept completely secret. With their FCC licensure at risk, the telephone manufacturer had swiftly complied.

Brady skimmed the comments that had been posted by other forum members. He spotted a couple of posts from techs who clearly worked for other telecommunications companies reporting that their firms had recently included the same functionality in their software updates, and for the same reason: federal government mandate. Another member posted an interesting tidbit: an analysis of the digital pattern which all domestic phones were now required to listen for and retransmit indicated that the pattern was nothing more than a hardware address of the type embedded in all network devices.

Brady considered this thread of information. On one level, this new functionality was minimal to the point of triviality. Simply listening for a signal then repackaging and retransmitting a few bytes would hardly tax the sophisticated pocket computers that phones had become. But the fact that this new capability had been mandated by the federal government was what most alarmed Brady. What was this device address that the feds were so interested in that they wanted phones listening for and retransmitting it? Where did that data come from, where was it being sent, and what was being done with it once it got there?

Brady took a minute to compose a set of criteria to submit to his search engine. His first few configurations turned up no results, but finally one got a hit. Sure enough, on another thread was a report from a hardware engineer who worked for a medical products firm, one that specialized in implantable electronics and control systems. He reported that his firm had perfected a new product, a miniature chip that ran off electricity generated by body heat. This device was wafer-thin, just five millimeters square, and was intended to be permanently implanted just beneath the surface of the skin. The chip's circuitry was primarily designed for simple storage and retrieval, with the intent of using it as a repository of patient information that would always be with the patient, eliminating the problems caused by missing or incomplete data. But one feature of this chip was monotonously mundane: it would regularly transmit its device address on a particular frequency. This was supposedly a safety feature. The rationale was that this broadcasting would enable manufacturers to build clinical devices and dispensing mechanisms with the capability to positively identify patients and avoid things like mistaken dosages. The comments on this post pointed out that with the amount of power generated by body heat, the transmission couldn't reach far – ten feet, perhaps. The hardware engineer from the medical firm confirmed that the specs stipulated a twelve foot transmission radius, though some of their tests had detected the signal as far away as twenty feet.

Reading through the posts, there were two things that stood out to Brady, and taken together they alarmed him. One was that the digital pattern which the implanted chip emitted matched precisely the digital pattern which every phone in the country was or would soon be listening for. The other was that the implantable chip had been developed under a classified contract with the federal government.

Brady sipped his coffee and tried to absorb what he was looking at. He could make no sense of it at all. These were two disconnected conversations taking place on completely different sites with nothing in common between them but the digital pattern, and the fact that the federal government was driving them both. They could be completely unrelated events. The feds had their hands in a lot of things.

But still.

Brady knew when he was stumped, at least for a time, and now was such a time. There were too many disconnected facts whirling around in his head. He needed a break. He saved the links to the two conversations, then posted links between them on both threads, so that readers of one could follow over to the other one. That kind of cross-pollination was one thing that made these online conversations so useful – other parties might know details, or make connections, that were escaping him right now. He shut down his connection and virtually erased any trace of his exploration of the sites.

He'd check back in a few days. Right now, it was time for a bath and bed.

*   *   *

Shawn, his chief of staff Kelly, and district rep David were sitting down for what Kelly called their "pre-week check". They all came into the office an hour early to go over what was on the schedule for the week, legislatively and otherwise. They used the time before the rest of the staff showed up to cover a lot of matters that were happening in the capital and in the district. Because this was the last week before session was supposed to recess for the campaign season and leadership had a number of bills they wanted passed first, legislative matters dominated the agenda. But toward the end of the time Shawn asked David for an update on how things were going back in the district.

"Well," David replied, bringing up his list, "the office has gotten a couple of calls from the Blue Water Physicians and Surgeons group. They're complaining about the increasing number of patients being denied care at their offices and being forced to go to the government clinics. They want to know when it's going to stop, because it's starting to cut into their patient load."

"I'm not sure I understand," Shawn said. "How are they being denied care?"

"Treatment protocols," David explained. "They're defined by the federal government. If the protocols say the provider can't treat the patient, then the provider can't treat the patient – or, at least, they won't get paid for any treatment they provide. The protocols are constantly being updated, and are pushed by Health and Human Services out onto the doctor's computer systems. Seems that an increasing number of patients are getting flagged by these protocols to be sent to government clinics."

"So, the computer systems are telling patients where they can and cannot go?" Shawn asked, incredulous.

"Apparently it's part of this new UPAIR initiative that the feds are trumpeting. The physician's group contends that it disrupts longstanding doctor-patient relationships, though it's clearly impacting their revenue stream as well," David explained.

"That's disturbing on several levels," Shawn said. "Kelly, can you contact somebody at HHS and find out what options exist with respect to these protocols? Is there any way of appealing them, or applying for exemptions, or whatever?"

"Sure, Shawn," Kelly replied, jotting something on her tablet while giving David her for-all-the-good-it-will-do glance.

"Another item," David continued. "Representatives from county-level realtor alliances want to meet with you back in the district at your earliest convenience."

"Realtors? Why would realtors want to talk to me?" Shawn asked in surprise.

"It seems that in the months since the feds announced this Special Protectionary District, real estate sales in the Thumb counties have dropped off a cliff. Granted, sales haven't been that strong for several years, but now they've effectively died. Nobody wants to move into the SPD until the implications are more clear, which means that people in the district can't sell their properties because there are no buyers. Even movement within the counties has slowed to a crawl, since anyone who might be able to sell their property is thinking twice about sinking the proceeds into another difficult-to-unload property elsewhere within the SPD."

Shawn and Kelly looked at each other. "Unintended consequences bite again," Shawn said.

"They're biting more than just the residential property market," David added. "Some business property deals have already been put on ice or flat-out cancelled, and there are rumors that landlords are having difficulty finding tenants for their spaces."

"What do they expect me to do about it?" Shawn asked.

"I'm not sure they know, and they understand that," David replied. "But they've talked themselves hoarse to the federal agencies, and in response they just get the press release line that the impact of the SPD on day-to-day life should be negligible."

"Yeah, tell that to the guy trying to sell his house," Shawn grumbled. "Get back to them and set something up in the next couple weeks. If all I can do is buy them coffee and commiserate, I'll do that. Anything else?"

"Well, Fred called again," David said with a grin as Kelly rolled her eyes. Fred was the district conspiracy theorist, always calling to notify the office of some hare-brained story he'd found on some fringe site, or ask them about some nonexistent bill or bureaucratic policy that was supposedly being stealthed through Lansing. Normally the staff buffered Shawn from having to deal with Fred directly, though he sometimes showed up at district events to buttonhole the senator and talk at length.

"What's his concern now?" Shawn asked with resignation.

"He's claiming that the feds are putting identifying chips in people's arms at these clinics, enabling them to track the patient's movements and maybe even their financial transactions."

"Chips, is it?" Shawn grinned. "Well, Kelly, can you add that to your list of things to ask the feds about? Then at least we can assure Fred that we've investigated his concerns."

"Sure thing," Kelly jotted another note on her tablet.

"All right, then, people, let's make this happen, shall we?" Shawn encouraged them, and the meeting broke up.

*　　　　　*　　　　　*

"I'm sorry, Mr. Stover, but there's nothing we can do," the receptionist said sympathetically.

"I understand," Lawrence Stover replied, which didn't make it any easier. Dr. Gupta had been their neurologist ever since Annette's ALS diagnosis. It had been worth the two hour drives down to his office in Troy to get the excellent care he'd provided. Lawrence had hoped that the fact that Dr. Gupta's office was so far away might mean they could escape the notice of the HHS protocols, but it had been a vain hope. When they'd arrived this morning and the receptionist had brought up Annette's records, they'd seen the ominous message warning that they couldn't provide care to this patient because she fell within the jurisdiction of the SPD.

"They've set up an appointment for Mrs. Stover at a clinic over by Saginaw," the receptionist continued as she handed Lawrence an appointment slip. "We'll forward all her medical records. At least it'll be a little closer."

"Closer, yes," Lawrence acknowledged. "But it won't be Dr. Gupta."

"I'm sure the doctor at the clinic will provide excellent care," the receptionist offered lamely, "but we will miss Mrs. Stover."

"We'll miss all of you as well," Lawrence replied. "Thank you for all your efforts on Annette's behalf."

"Our pleasure, sir."

Lawrence returned to where Annette was seated in the waiting room. "What's the matter?" she asked when she saw his downcast expression.

"Well, dear, the long arm of the UPAIR initiative has finally reached us," Lawrence replied in as lighthearted a manner as he could manage, though heaviness was settling over his heart. "Since we live within the SPD, we can only receive care at an approved medical provider, and Dr. Gupta isn't one of them."

"Oh," Annette said, then fell silent for a minute before speaking again. "Lawrence, what will we do?"

"We're being told what we can do," Lawrence replied, handing her the appointment card. "An appointment has been set up for you at a clinic near Saginaw next week."

Annette glanced at the card and then took Lawrence's hand. They sat silently for a minute, drawing comfort from each other. They understood the implications of this.

"Well," Annette ventured at last. "Another opportunity to trust, then?"

"Yes," Lawrence acknowledged. "Another opportunity to trust."

*   *   *

To Gerald's surprise, Chip asked him to meet at the far edge of the parking lot of one of the big-box stores north of Bad Axe. Gerald pulled up to find Chip out of uniform, standing by his pickup.

"I hope the location doesn't inconvenience you," Chip apologized. "Emma's or the Sugar Bowl are common meeting spots, but I wanted someplace we couldn't be overheard. We can sit in my truck if you'd rather not stand."

"No, I'm fine out here," Gerald replied. "At this point, I'd stand knee-deep in Lake Superior in April just to hear what all this is about. The dark hints and deferred explanations have certainly piqued my interest."

"Well, then, let's walk, and I'll tell you what's been happening in Huron County over the past couple of years. There's a lot I can't explain, and I won't even ask you to believe all of it, but I'll relate my experiences truthfully and let you sort things out."

"Fair enough," Gerald agreed.

"Let's start two and a half years ago, when I first spotted some unusual trucks on our county roads," Chip began.

"Trucks?" Gerald asked.

"Yes. I didn't know it at the time, but it was my first clue that something fishy was going on here in the county – as well as the thing that ended up getting me unseated as sheriff, at least for a while…" For the best part of an hour the men strolled along the edge of the parking lot while Chip related his incredible tale and Gerald's wonder and amazement grew.

"So, there was a massacre," Gerald nearly whispered when Chip told of the summer night just over a year earlier when the youngsters had been rescued from the factory, the night of the mysterious fog.

"Yes," Chip affirmed. "We don't know how many died in those woods. In fact, it was your relating how your wise woman saw that vision which convinced me that I had to tell you all this. When did her vision take place, by the way?"

"Esther's vision? Earlier this year, on the spring equinox."

"So that was late March," Chip mused. "Well, a lot has changed even since then, but I need to tell you about the aftermath of that night –"

Chip continued his account, telling of the lingering effects of the shadowed woods from the night when the fog appeared and the slaves were rescued. He told of the Zanies, the fence, the mysterious tendency of people to lose their way if they ventured too near the woods. As the story unfolded, Gerald increasingly felt like he'd stepped into the world of Fr. Thomas's diary, or of Esther's vision, where the distinction between natural and supernatural vanished, and the seen and unseen real intermingled freely.

"'The trails became confused'," Gerald muttered when Chip told of the frightening effect of the woods on the surrounding area and any drivers who happened into it.

"What's that?" Chip asked.

"Just…just something I was remembering from that diary," Gerald explained. "Something one of the lore masters told Fr. Thomas. It confirms to me that we're talking about similar, if not identical, phenomena."

"Yes – whatever we're talking about," Chip conceded. "But that was the situation until this past May."

"Oh? What happened last May?"

Chip told of the call he'd received from one of the men who'd gone into the woods, of his unusual request, and the midnight rendezvous on the dirt road. He explained how he had unlocked and cut open the gates to allow the white-clad woman through into the woods, and had locked the gates behind her.

"Wait –" Gerald interrupted fiercely, grabbing Chip's arm. "So this woman participated in a Catholic Mass, then walked into the woods?"

"I think it was a Catholic Mass – I've never been to one," Chip admitted. "I'm pretty sure it was Fr. Gabriel running things. I've seen him around."

"Did she eat something?"

"Did she what?"

"Eat something. As part of the ritual, did she at some point eat something?" Gerald asked.

"I...I think so," Chip replied. "There was one point where they were all kneeling, and Fr. Gabriel was putting something into their mouths. She certainly drank something, because he gave her a golden cup."

"And then she walked into the woods?" Gerald asked, pacing in agitation.

"Well, she took a minute to say some things to the others. It looked like most of them were friends, and she was saying goodbye. She also stopped to speak briefly to...another man who was there, but essentially, she took part in this ceremony then walked into the woods. She was holding some flowers."

"I've got to see. I've got to see," Gerald was muttering. "These woods – how far are they? Can we go there?"

"We could, but it'll be dark soon," Chip warned.

"We still have a good forty five minutes of daylight," Gerald said, scanning the sky. "How long would it take us to get there?"

"Inside ten minutes. It's only a few miles from right here."

"Let's get going, then," Gerald replied. "If you could drive, that would be faster."

Connections

"I haven't been back by here much since that night," Chip admitted as he parked across the road from the gate in the tall security fence. "Nathan Road isn't a main thoroughfare, and few people live in the area, so there isn't much call for sheriffs. For a while I tried to visit it regularly to inspect for…irregularities, but that hasn't been necessary since last spring."

"It looks very normal," Gerald said, walking to the gate.

"It is now," Chip assured him.

"Can we get through these locks?"

"I have the keys right here," Chip replied. "But I don't know if I'd advise going in so close to nightfall. It seems clean, but to my knowledge nobody's been in there since she went through that gate. I don't suspect anything's in there, but if I wanted to explore, I'd do it by daylight."

"I understand. I'd just like to stand in the gateway, maybe take a step or two inside," Gerald explained, so Chip unlocked the locks and swung open the inner gate, standing aside for Gerald to step through.

Gerald stood on the threshold of the woods. In front of him an overgrown two-track trail ran into the trees, curving away to the left to disappear into the greenery, which was growing wild enough to encroach upon the trail. The clear evening sun slanted through the foliage, bathing the woods in a golden glow. Birds fluttered among the branches, filling the woods with their calls. It was a scene of beauty and tranquility.

Gerald took a deep breath and tried to quiet his mind. Slowly he became aware that while he'd sensed nothing at the Petroglyphs, here he was feeling something in the atmosphere, an aura or aroma. It wasn't anything eerie or fantastic, though – it was instead a freshness, a clean wholesomeness that went deeper than unpolluted air and pristine woods. He bent to remove his shoes so he could stand barefoot on the soil to experience the purity more directly. Taking several more breaths, he surrendered to a sensation he'd only experienced twice before – once in a wood in the Laurentian highlands, and again on the shores of Lake Nipigon.

"This place is...clean," Gerald announced, searching for suitable terminology.

"Well, nobody's been here in over a year, except –" Chip began, but Gerald cut him off.

"No, no, you don't understand," he said excitedly, grasping Chip's arm. "This place is pristine, unsullied. It's as pure as the woods the Anishinaabe would have found when they first arrived in the region on the Great Migration, or like the Huron tribe would have found north of Georgian Bay. This land has been made clean again. Can't you smell it in the air? Can't you see the freedom with which the trees wave? I wish I had the time to walk the length and breadth, if only to have the experience of being the first to walk the original woods."

"Well, even if the hogs are gone, there'd still be the ruins of Ray Hubbart's operation –" Chip began.

"I bet there aren't," Gerald interrupted with finality. "Whatever happened here was so momentous that every taint, every trace was removed. Considering the magnitude of the spiritual foulness that was expunged from this place, the removal of some bricks and beams would be trivial. These woods have been restored to their original state, and I only wish I had the time, and the courage, to walk them. I'd feel like Nanabozho. Then again, perhaps it would be best left untouched, so all may come to it as a shrine. But I will ask one thing." With that he turned to a birch tree that stood to his right and, bowing and whispering a prayer of permission, broke off a thin branch. "This is not by way of desecration, but as a message."

"Okay," Chip replied, not understanding that last part. Just then a car pulled up outside the security fence and parked beside Chip's truck. Mystified, the two men watched as a young couple stepped out and stared at them.

"Todd?" Chip whispered.

"Todd? Who's Todd?" Gerald asked.

"He was one of the men who went into the woods that night. In fact, he was on the team that was supposed to rescue the slaves, only he was frustrated by the mysterious fog."

"Really?" Gerald asked eagerly. "Could I talk to him?"

"I'm sure he wouldn't mind if he has time. In fact, I think the woman who's with him was there that night as well, though I can't be sure – it was a hectic night. For that matter, I think both of them were here last May as well, taking part in that ritual."

"Last May? When the woman in white went into the woods?"

"Yes. I'm certain that Todd was here, because he was the one who called asking me to show up," Chip explained. "But I think I recognize her as well. I wonder what they're doing here?"

By this time the two parties, who had been walking toward each other, met at the gate in the security fence.

"Chip!" Todd gripped his hand firmly. "Great to see you! This is an unexpected surprise – we were sure that everything would be locked up. What brings you here?"

"I was about to ask you the same thing," Chip replied. "I was just showing the site to an interested friend, Mr. Gerald Solomon of the Garden River Ojibwa up by the Sault. Mr. Solomon, Todd Beck, friend and co-conspirator."

"An honor, Mr. Solomon. May I present my wife Grace?"

"Wife, eh?" Chip grinned as he shook Grace's hand. "Last time we met you weren't a married man. My congratulations to you both."

"Thank you," Todd said. "In answer to your question, we're supposed to be meeting some people here – in fact, that may be them now." He pointed up the road toward an approaching set of headlights.

"Meeting someone? Here?" Chip was mystified. "Why on earth would you do that?"

"It's a long story, and Grace is the best one to tell it," Todd replied.

"It's got to do with a man I met the other day," Grace explained. "He'd suffered some trauma that had damaged his memory, and was visiting places he'd been to before in hopes that familiar things would jog his memory. It had helped at the site where I met him, and I knew he'd been here, so I suggested we meet on the chance that it would help him some more."

"Here? He'd been here?" Chip asked in amazement. "When?"

"On that night – you know, the one last May, when Teresa went in," Grace replied. "You should remember, you were talking with him."

"Talking with him? I don't remember talking with anyone but Teresa and…oh, my God." The oncoming car had pulled over and stopped, and Chip watched two men getting out of it.

"You remember him, then?" Grace asked.

"Remember him? That's Jason Pelletier," Chip said sharply. "Why would you bring him here?"

"Like I said, he's suffered some trauma," Grace said. "He's forgotten a lot of things about himself, and visiting places he's been seems to help him remember."

"Trauma? What kind of trauma –" Chip began, but the men who'd stepped out of the car were now approaching. One was a tall, slightly heavy-set man with thinning brown hair. The other was unmistakably Jason Pelletier, but he gave no indication that he recognized Chip.

"So, Mr. Pelletier, I didn't expect to see you here," Chip grumbled.

"You remember me?" Jason asked. "That's good. Brian here tells me that my name is Jason, and I've had to take his word for it. It's good to get confirmation."

"You don't remember me?" Chip asked, a little alarmed. "Last time you were in the area, we had a few...discussions. The last one of them was right here on this road."

"So Grace tells me," Jason said, looking around. "Hopefully visiting here will help me recover a few more details."

"Sheriff Keller, this is Brian," Grace interjected. "He's been helping Jason out. Brian, this is Sheriff Keller of Huron County, and his friend Gerald."

Hands were shaken all around, then Jason turned to look at the inner gate that opened to the woods. The twilight was deepening and shadows were filling the space between the trees. Overhead, bats flitted against the indigo sky.

"This seems somewhat familiar," Jason mused. "Though it felt more...threatening."

"It was, until Teresa went in," Grace explained. "You were standing about over there, and Fr. Gabriel was saying Mass over here. Sheriff Keller was parked just here. You were the last person Teresa spoke to before she had him unlock the gates and went through them."

Jason turned toward the inner gate and began slowly walking toward it. Behind him Gerald leaned over to Chip to speak in a subdued voice.

"So, he was here that night as well? What was he doing?"

"I wondered the same thing at the time, and confronted him about it. He professed to only want to speak to the young woman – this Teresa – who went through the gate. He did, briefly."

"Confronted him? Why would you confront him?"

Chip sighed. "Jason Pelletier was the DHS official in charge of all activity in the area, and laid the groundwork for what became the Special Protectionary District. Earlier on the day that we met here on the road, DTD troops had raided about a dozen homes, capturing an unknown number of people and killing six civilians with a missile strike. Those troops were under his authority."

"Really? And he was in charge?"

"Officially, yes. In fairness, by the time I spoke to him, he pleaded ignorance of the operations and claimed they were happening without his authorization. He said he was working to get the units in the field to stand down, and even recorded a video for my men to distribute and show to the DTD troops, telling them they'd been ordered to cease and desist. Hmm…I wonder if that's what triggered them?"

"Triggered who?" Gerald asked.

"I'm just trying to connect a few dots here," Chip said slowly, stroking his moustache. "If Pelletier was right about the operation last spring being run outside his control, that implies serious confusion in his chain of command. Sometimes that's simple incompetence, but sometimes it's caused by too many chefs in the kitchen, so to speak, often with hidden or conflicting agendas. Given the full-on cluster the SPD has been since inception, with HHS and DHS and who knows who all tripping over each other here in the Thumb, I'm suspecting that it was too many chefs. That would imply that by recording that video, he executed a clever end run around his fouled command chain that may have earned him some powerful enemies. Maybe they exacted retribution on him by doing…that." He gestured toward Jason's back.

"What happened to him? Do you have any idea? That level of memory damage is frightening."

"Sure is," Chip confirmed. "Either Mr. Pelletier is the world's best actor, or something ugly has been done to him. I can only speculate as to who might be responsible. The last time I saw him was on this road that night. I didn't think anything of it when some other bureaucrat was announced as the head of the SPD – these appointments don't always make sense. I didn't hear from Pelletier, but then, I didn't expect to, and had no reason to try to contact him. I didn't know what happened to him and I didn't care – only I wouldn't wish this on anyone."

"He was definitely here that night? He was one of the witnesses?" Gerald asked.

"He was, and I suppose you could talk to him about it, but it doesn't look like it would do much good," Chip said grimly, looking at Jason. "Damn! What the hell did they do to him?"

Jason walked slowly toward the gate in the fence, looking at the trees waving above him. He couldn't remember details, but the outline of the treetops against the evening sky was triggering all manner of emotions – panic, dread, oppression, and desolation. One feeling kept surging within him that was kind of hard to identify. It felt like a mixture of sharp regret and deep sorrow and an almost desperate urge to connect. There was someone he had to find, something he had to explain, some calamity he had to head off. But he was too late, and all he could do was stand there and watch it happen, then try to cope with his grief and loss.

As this maelstrom of sensations whirled within him, Jason came to a halt just before the inner gate. Facing the deep dusk that lay beyond it, he closed his eyes and reached for the image of the woman in white, the image that had stayed stubbornly with him, the image that had kept returning.

And the image came, focusing the emotions he was experiencing in their rawness. He was seeing it again, feeling it again – the tumultuous mixture of hope and loss and regret that had overwhelmed him as he'd watched that figure walk through that iron gate, her head high, her carriage erect, her back to light and life and friendship, her face toward the accursed darkness, and her feet carrying her bravely forward to be swallowed up and lost.

Jason's eyes snapped open. The first thing he saw was the gate, looking just as it had after she'd walked through it. Something inside him clicked into place, and he knew. It wasn't just a whirl of undirected emotions, or a scattered montage of disconnected images. He *knew*, he remembered, it came back to him.

"I stood here." Jason murmured, then lifted his head and said more clearly. "I stood here. Right here – or, rather, somewhere over there." He waved at a spot just beyond where Chip and Gerald were standing. "I stood there, and she came over and spoke to me. She said...she said my path would be harder, then she walked through here and then there. You were standing right there." He now pointed to Chip then pointed to the right of the inner gate. "She...kissed me." He touched his cheek almost reverently as the memory returned.

"You're remembering!" Grace said, bouncing on her toes in excitement.

"Yes...yes, I'm remembering," Jason affirmed, looking about like he was just awakening. "It's not much, but it's certain. I stood here, and you all were here, and she went through there, into...into..." His voice trailed away. In one sense it was a small thing, just one memory, but in another sense it was momentous. He remembered. He'd moved from image and impression to recollection. Everything else he "knew" about himself and his present circumstances was because somebody had told him, even down to his name. But this event he remembered, and his relief was immense. He felt like a man in the grip of a rip tide would feel when his feet finally found solid ground beneath them. He remembered. *He* remembered. He could now hope that more recollection would follow, and that he might eventually regain himself.

"Well, this is promising," Brian said enthusiastically, rubbing his hands. Contact with these people was yielding more results than anything he'd tried. He turned to Grace and asked in a low voice, "Did you find out anything about...ah...accommodations?"

"Yes," Grace assured him. "We understand the delicacy of the situation, and have arranged somewhere for him. We came prepared to take him with us."

"Good, good," Brian said with relief. "Hopefully he'll continue making progress. I've got his duffel right here."

"Thank you," said Grace, taking the bag. "Will he have any need to stay in touch with you?"

"No, no, that shouldn't be necessary," Brian said.

"That actually makes things easier. Thank you for your care for him. We'll take it from here."

Meanwhile, Gerald was talking quietly to Chip. "Would it be possible for me to arrange to speak with those who were here that night – including you – to find out exactly what happened? I'd like to get as many perspectives as possible."

"It may be possible, but you might have to be patient," Chip replied. "You know how to get ahold of me, though I want to give you my personal number. I know how to get ahold of him," he pointed at Todd, "and from the looks of it, they'll know how to get ahold of Pelletier." Grace was tucking the duffel in the trunk of their car. "In the meantime, we don't want to linger here too long, lest we draw attention." He pointed to the sky, and at Gerald's puzzled look, continued, "These days, we presume 24/7 drone surveillance by the SPD authorities."

"Oh – yeah," Gerald said, shaken by this sharp reminder that he was not only in a foreign country, but in something like occupied territory. "Probably best to scatter for now. I need to get back to Mount Pleasant for the evening."

Jason was still standing inside the security fence, looking about in wonder. "Jason!" Grace called to him. "Is there anything else you'd like to examine?"

"No, no," Jason replied vaguely, still feeling a bit stunned. "It wasn't much, was it? I was standing there, and she spoke to me, then walked in. She kissed me."

"That was about it," Grace assured him. "I can tell you more from my perspective later. For now, you're going to be coming with us."

"With you?"

"Yes. We have a safe place for you to stay. Brian's been concerned for your safety."

"And I've imposed on him long enough," Jason continued.

"Oh, it's been no imposition," Brian replied semi-truthfully.

"Nonetheless, I thank you for your help," Jason replied, shaking his hand. "If I ever pull things back together, it'll be largely due to your help."

Brian muttered something inaudible in answer to this, nodded to everyone, and trudged off toward his car.

"I think we'd better head back," Chip announced. "You've still got my number, Todd?"

"Yes, and you've got mine, though let me give you an alternative," Todd said, handing Chip a slip of paper. "Keep that number quiet, would you? Jason's coming with us. He'll be in safe seclusion for a while. Mr. Solomon, a pleasure to meet you."

"Gerald, please. I'd like to speak with you and your wife, and hopefully Chip here, about what happened that night. It may prove surprisingly important."

"We'll try to be available, though it may be a while – we have other responsibilities." Todd nodded toward Jason.

While Todd and Gerald were talking, Chip walked over to Jason and offered his hand. "Mr. Pelletier, though I can't say I approve of what you got started here in the Thumb, I honestly believe that you never intended for it to get this far, and I thank you for the help you offered last spring to try to stop it. I'm sorry for your misfortunes, and hope you get back on your feet."

"Thanks, Sheriff,", Jason replied. "I'm sorry for any trouble I may have caused you, and if I ever get clear of this confusion, I hope to help set things right."

"Don't you worry about that," Chip assured him. "Just work on recovering as much of your memory as you can. Once you've done that, we can proceed from there."

As Todd was holding the car door for Grace, his phone rang. It was an unfamiliar number, but a local one, so he answered.

"Is this Todd Beck?" came a strange voice.

"Who's asking?"

"This is Steve McLean. I'm trying to reach Grace Beck about someone she may know."

"Ah." Todd knew of Steve, though they'd never met. "Just a moment, she's right here." He handed the phone to Grace, who took it with a puzzled expression.

"This is Grace."

"Hello, Grace, Steve McLean here. I'm trying to resolve a situation that I hope you can help with."

"What kind of situation?" Grace asked, thinking that the last thing she needed right now was another complication.

"Do you know someone named Tyrone?"

*   *   *

Chip dropped Gerald back at his van in Bad Axe, and soon Gerald was on his way back to Mount Pleasant. He pulled out his phone and called his sister.

"Kim, do you know if Esther will still be up in a couple of hours?"

"I'm not sure – she's been sleeping erratically," Kim replied. "Let me give her a call, and if she'll be up, I'll meet you there. I've been going over a few evenings a week to ensure she's doing all right."

Gerald was nearly to Unionville before Kim called back. "She's just up, though a bit sluggish. She'll be awake for you, and I'll be with her tidying up."

It was nearly 11:00 p.m. when Gerald pulled into Andahwod and made his way to Esther's apartment with his gift. Esther was sitting in her recliner while Kim bustled about the apartment's small kitchen. Gerald knelt before Esther and presented her with the birch branch.

"Seer of my people, I have been there. The Warrior's word was true in every respect. An ancient enemy returned, and there had been a massacre. But it has been cleansed by heroic effort and great sacrifice. I bring you a sprig of birch as witness to the purifying of the land."

With wide eyes Esther took the branch and held it to herself. She leaned back with eyes closed as a broad smile spread across her face. She appeared not just contented, but more relaxed than Gerald had yet seen her. After resting for a minute, she spoke in a quiet voice.

"Now I can sense it. There was turmoil and deep darkness, and great conflict in the distance, but it is now clear. There was something like a great flash of light, and the conflict was stilled."

"You should have been there, mother," Gerald replied. *"Even a dullard like myself could detect it. The woods were pristine, as fresh as if the Great Ice had just receded."*

"What happened?" Kim asked from behind him.

"A momentous event, not long after the Christian feast of Easter," Gerald replied with excitement. "I only learned a little about it tonight, but I hope to learn more. It could have amazing parallels to some of the things I learned during the diary research." He shook his head in amazement. "To think what might have happened in our very own back yard! Had I known, I would have given anything to be there."

"So…what happened took place after Esther had her vision?"

"Yes. Her vision was true and accurate at the time she received it. What I just learned tonight was that the resolution occurred only a few weeks later." Gerald stood and began pacing in his enthusiasm. "I must learn more of this. It is vital."

"Well, I hope this helps her rest easier," Kim said, gesturing to where Esther was now nodding in her chair, clutching the birch branch, a contented smile illuminating her face. "The whole affair has really unsettled her. She's let her living quarters slip, and that's never been like her. I'm going to be another hour cleaning and tidying."

"All right," Gerald replied. "I'll head back to your place, if you don't mind. It's been a long day, and I've a few things I want to jot down before I forget them."

Back at Kim's house, Gerald brewed some decaf while he scribbled notes about what he'd learned and thoughts about who he wanted to contact, and the questions he wished to ask them. This vacation was shaping up like a very busy one. He was just starting to think about heading for bed when his phone rang. He was a little surprised to see that it was Kim.

"Gerald, something's happened with Esther," she said in a worried voice.

"Oh? Do you want me to come back over?"

"No, I've got her settled now, but I thought you'd want to know. She was dozing in her chair like she was when you left, and I was just wondering if I should spread a blanket over her and leave her there when she jolted awake."

"Jolted?"

"Yes, it was the strangest thing. She came awake very suddenly, looked around, and started speaking in a very agitated manner. Half of it was in Ojibwe, so I didn't catch it, but she was very worked up."

"What was she saying that you could follow?"

"Many things, but it boiled down to, 'some escaped'."

"'Some escaped'?" Gerald asked.

"Essentially, yes. She was quite upset. She was clutching the birch branch and rattling on."

"But she's calm now, right?"

"Yes, she's calm now," Kim assured him. "I've put her to bed. I thought you'd want to know as soon as possible."

"Thanks. We can chat more in the morning – I'm about to drop here."

"I'll be a while yet, but the end is in sight," Kim said, and rang off, leaving Gerald staring at his phone and wondering.

Some escaped?

Maybe things weren't as settled as he'd hoped.

*   *   *

After a couple of days, Brady decided to revisit the dark sites to see if there had been any further postings on the conversations he'd flagged. Once he was connected, his notification log showed that the threads had sparked a firestorm of responses.

Brady checked the thread about the phone patches first. Most of the responses were of little value to him – highly technical discussions about this or that aspect of the fixes, or tirades about government interference in private corporations. But one thread of commentary caught his attention. It was posted by a user who hailed from the automotive world, and he claimed that a very similar mandate had been issued to manufacturers who sold cars in the United States.

Vehicles had effectively been rolling computers for several decades, especially so in the last twenty years, as manufacturers had added sophisticated interfaces and displays. And wherever innovation went, government regulation was sure to follow. Since all modern vehicles had to include geolocation capabilities, and also had to be connected to the standard communications network, it was a trivial matter to require that the vehicle transmit its location on demand – and usually it was the federal government that did the demanding, though state and local authorities could also make use of the capability. Most drivers didn't think about the fact that their location could be accessed at the touch of a button without their being aware of it. They considered even less, if they knew at all, that their cars could also transmit their speed, direction, and load weight to those who knew how to ask, or how remote signals could activate and monitor dash and backup cameras, potentially turning any car into a surveillance platform of its immediate vicinity – all without the driver's knowledge or consent.

The forum member who'd contributed to the discussion said that about a year earlier the federal government had published a requirement for capabilities in vehicles similar to those stipulated for phones: they were to listen for a particular signal on a particular frequency, and if they detected it, they were to repackage and retransmit the data along with the time and location. That was it.

As Brady pondered this, a sense of dread slowly crept over him. This revelation indicated two things, neither of them good. The first was that whatever was going on behind these government dictates was broader than just telecommunications devices. Cars and trucks were included as well, and Brady wondered what he might find if he investigated things like entertainment units or point of sale systems. The second thing was how far back this went. The posting said the mandate had been issued to the automotive industry a year ago. That meant that the roots of this project had begun years before that, and cut across a broad swath of government departments. The agencies that regulated the auto industry were different from those that monitored telecommunications, which were different again from those that oversaw health care – yet they were all displaying a disturbing pattern of seemingly coordinated behavior.

Whatever was going on here didn't look good.

Brady linked over to the discussion thread pertaining to the medical records chip and its mysterious capabilities. As expected, the posts had generated plenty of responses, some of them quite heated. Some members had followed Brady's link over to the discussion in the telecom forum, and had returned with a variety of comments that ranged from the thoughtful to the vapid. Brady skimmed over most of these, but one lengthy post caught his eye. It was written by a member who claimed to be a cybersecurity expert, with extensive experience dissecting multi-layered systems to find security holes. The post was thoughtful and incisive, clearly not something that had just been quickly tossed off.

'The capabilities of this compound system,' the member had written, 'cannot be underestimated. Those who follow the link to the other discussion and consider what they find there should clearly see the disturbing implications. Each element of this compound system performs a single function. The chip squawks its device address at regular intervals, nothing more. The receiving device listens for that squawk, and if it hears it, repackages the received address along with time and geospatial information and sends it along to the designated address. Considered independently, these functions seem innocuous. But considered together, it is clear that they are intended to be components of a powerful and ubiquitous location tracking system. Many commenters have dismissed the effectiveness of the chip because of its trivial transmission range. They're missing the point – the chip's transmission would only have to reach the nearest phone or computing device, which the person would probably be carrying. And it wouldn't matter if the person left their phone behind – if they came close enough to someone else's phone, in the aisle at the grocery store or in line at the coffee shop, that would suffice. This simple, elegant combination creates an almost inescapable tracking network that can pinpoint the location of anyone implanted with that chip so long as they're standing within range of a phone.'

Yeah, thought Brady – or driving in a car, or riding a bus, or even walking through a parking lot. But the post continued.

'Especially disturbing is that this capability is buried within a piece of medical data equipment. Over the past decades, federal government control of the medical industry has gone so deep that the industry has effectively become an arm of the government. Bureaucrats issue regulations which hardly get noticed, much less resisted. This chip, with its seemingly benign function of tracking medical data, is just the sort of thing that could soon become mandated. Once that happens, the government has a system that can track any person anywhere in the country using ordinary technical components that are already widespread. We could see this within two years – in fact, it may be being piloted already.'

Like right here in our back yard, Brady thought grimly. Since reading the first postings, he'd been attending more closely to the whispers and rumors that whirled around the medical offices he supported. There were questions about this mysterious chip that was being inserted into anyone who visited a UPAIR clinic, though none of them suspected its most ominous capability. He perused the rest of the conversation threads for anything that might be useful, finding only a few comments by what appeared to be testing engineers commenting on the chips, and how much more work was needed to make them sturdier and more stable before being used in the field.

Brady logged out of the forums and pondered. That had been a lot of things to learn. If that security specialist's hypothesis was correct – and it had certainly seemed both reasonable and plausible – this simple but effective tracking system had been in the works for some time. He supposed the Special Protectionary District offered an ideal environment for trial deployment. Brady wondered what other projects they might be testing on his fellow citizens.

Somebody needed to hear about this, and Steve McClean seemed the best choice. Brady reached for his phone, then stayed his hand. Wiser to keep discussion of this off the public network. He rummaged in his drawer for the other phone, the older phone, the one that utilized the faint but still operational private network set up to help manage the now-closed ranches. The phone needed charging, but Brady guessed it still had enough for one call.

*　　　*　　　*

The moderately busy legislative week was close to ending, with the critical bills passed and on their way to the governor and the less critical ones deferred to the post-election "lame duck" session. Shawn wasn't looking forward to that hectic period, but it was still weeks away, and at least he wasn't heading back to the mayhem of an election campaign in his district. He was conferring with Kelly and David to cover last-minute issues before shutting the office down to a skeleton staff until after the election.

"Your recess calendar has been loaded onto your tablet," Kelly explained. "It contains your in-district meetings, including those with the realtors and physician's groups."

"I don't know what I'll say to them, but I can promise to bring their concerns to Ruth's attention," Shawn said. "Any issues waiting to ambush me back in the district, David?"

"I can't promise that Fred won't hunt you down," David warned. "He's called twice more about these tracking implants, which he contends the clinics are putting into all their patients."

"Good ol' Fred," Shawn chuckled. "Kelly, in your talks with the feds, did that allegation ever crop up?"

"It did," Kelly said, glancing at her notes. "I spoke with an HHS rep, and got the usual blather about improving patient care through leading-edge technology, and obviating the need for obsolete and ineffective methods by leveraging innovation in recordkeeping. She assured me that the nanotechnology employed was safe and unobtrusive, and would increase safety and efficiency while lowering cost."

"Wait – what's unobtrusive?" Shawn asked, confused.

"The medical records circuitry they're deploying," Kelly explained. "Apparently it's new microcircuitry that holds the patient's entire medical history. It can be scanned by devices in use at the government clinics, though they have plans to release the scanning technology to all providers in the near future. Diagnoses and procedures are updated wirelessly with no significant radio frequency footprint," Kelly read from the notes on her tablet screen.

"So, medical records are being kept on circuity," Shawn affirmed. "Where is this circuitry? On a chip the patient carries around? In their phones?"

"No, apparently it's embedded subcutaneously in their left or right forearm. The HHS rep assured me that the procedure is painless and the circuit both inert and unobtrusive. Once in place, the patient typically forgets that it's there. They've tested this on infants without adverse effect."

"'Embedded subcutaneously'?" Shawn asked, slowly turning a sober gaze on David. "So, they are chipping them."

Newlyweds

Luke sat on a rusty porch chair outside his back door and surveyed his domain.

Such as it was.

The hasty evacuation from Eastfarthing the prior spring had necessitated many quick decisions and makeshift accommodations. Evacuees were placed where they'd fit and the summer had involved no small amount of reshuffling and relocating to get families into the best circumstances that could be arranged. The end result wasn't totally satisfactory for anyone, but people tried to be understanding and flexible. It may not have been much, but it was better than how things were back in Eastfarthing, if reports out of the Special Protectionary District were to be believed.

Luke couldn't escape the feeling that he'd posed an extra problem. As a single man, he should have been very easy to accommodate – a back room or small apartment over someone's garage would have sufficed. But after becoming engaged abruptly, he had posed more of a challenge. Luke was certain that his and Felicity's wish to marry as soon as possible had greatly complicated matters for Felicity's father Gil as well as for Jenny Yarborough, who lived in Mio and was the primary resource coordinator for operations up here in Northfarthing. Of course, Gil had put a game face on it all, assuring Luke and Felicity that everything would be arranged.

And arranged it had been. After some brief temporary accommodations, Luke had moved here, to an older cabin in a meadow on a largely wooded lot. The house had been standing vacant for some time, and needed a "new" pump for its well (which had actually been a less-used one salvaged from another site), the pipes flushed, and the septic tank pumped out. Luke wondered if the old propane furnace would even run, or if it would be safe if it did – it hadn't yet gotten chilly enough to need testing. The electricity was

165

serviceable but archaic, and Gil had muttered about rewiring when they'd done their first walk-through of the house, which had made Luke groan. Other household projects he could manage, but electrical wiring was beyond him.

Luke had taken possession of this house a few weeks after their flight to Northfarthing, on the understanding that this would be his and Felicity's home when they got married. He'd patched spotty plaster and repainted old window frames and aired out stuffy rooms. People had dropped by with used furniture and other household goods, and slowly the cabin had begun to resemble a real home.

Toward the back of the property stood an older pole barn, which was used to house ten horses and two beef cattle. They'd inherited custody of the livestock for the simple reason that the property had a fenced grazing area adjoining the pole barn. Though Luke chafed a bit at the mundane responsibilities that came with having large animals around, he realized how relatively easy he had it compared to what he'd have to contend with if Felicity got the wish she'd voiced casually from time to time, which was for a couple of head of dairy cattle.

Luke had swiftly come to realize the truth of what he'd been warned about: that while Eastfarthing, the Thumb region of Michigan, was rural, the northeastern corner of the state in which they now lived was almost empty. At least the Thumb, with its fields and patchy woods, had small towns and hamlets at regular intervals. Here in densely wooded Northfarthing you could go for miles without encountering any human settlements at all. In sparsely populated Alcona County, where Luke lived, he could count on two hands the number of named communities that appeared on the state map. There were many more rivers and lakes up here, and while the waterways tended to be lined by vacation and retirement homes, the woods filled entire sections with no more than one or two isolated homesteads per square mile.

Not that Luke minded the emptiness. He was naturally introverted, so solitude did not discomfit him. His was one of those isolated homesteads, and he enjoyed the quiet. The land itself was beautiful and peaceful, and so removed from human bustle that he was frequently visited by wildlife ambling through the meadow or drinking from the pond that lay beyond the barn. He'd seen herds of deer and flocks of turkeys make their way across the property, as well as less welcome visitors like pairs of coyotes and packs of feral hogs that troubled the area. He'd never thought he would live in a home that kept a shotgun in the stable! And besides, it wasn't like he was completely alone – in fact, he was less alone than he'd ever been in his life, thanks to one amazing person.

Felicity.

Sometimes, especially first thing in the morning, Luke found himself gazing at his beautiful wife with a sentiment approaching awe. He'd been smitten with her since their first meeting, and though in the years that had followed their life circumstances had worked against them spending much time together, Luke's fascination with Felicity had never faded. His breath would still catch when he first saw her, and he'd cherish every word of even the most passing conversations. Nobody had been more stunned than he on that fateful night when Teresa had placed Felicity's hand in his, and part of him had been braced for some event or decision that would nullify that decree, but none had ever come. Now he was married to the most beautiful, delightful, vivacious, caring, and wonderful woman he'd ever known.

Luke had been repeatedly warned that marriage would take some adjustment, and he supposed the day would come when adjusting proved difficult, but as of yet all the changes he'd had to adjust to had been positive. Of course, there were the "bedroom benefits" of marriage (to use Kent Schaeffer's discreet phrase), which were as wonderful as Luke had imagined, but there was also the blessing of regular companionship, the practical assistance (even with messy chores like mucking out the stable), and Felicity's cheerful and positive demeanor. When Luke had expressed his regret that he hadn't been able to provide her a better newlywed home, she'd dismissed his concerns, assuring him that someday they'd look back on these months as having been the best of their marriage. While Luke had trouble believing that, he certainly appreciated having a coworker to help run the house. It was still a delightful surprise to find his laundry clean and folded or his meals prepared. Felicity was a diligent worker, so much so that Luke at times felt like he wasn't quite contributing to the household as he should.

Luke's employment status was still being worked out. His function back in Eastfarthing had been ready-made for him as a roaming medical worker – all he'd had to do was step into it. But the situation up here in Northfarthing was different. Not only was everyone more spread out, but the families were poorer. The system of funding the ranches through creative pooling of trusts, retirement fund distributions, and proceeds from the sale of properties had come to a halt upon the abrupt flight from Eastfarthing. There were some residual funds, which were primarily dedicated to covering resettlement costs, but mostly the refugees who found their way to Northfarthing were cast upon their own scant resources and the generosity of the residents already there. Since this region of the state had always been economically slow, this meant that most of the families suffered a sharp drop in their standard of living. Hard cash was scarce, and desperately needed for those situations where it was absolutely necessary. Barter was increasingly used, which meant that when people showed up to receive medical services, payment might take the form of some dozens of eggs, or bushels of grain or vegetables. There was also the common, "I owe ya", which Luke was getting tired of hearing. But Felicity laughed and accepted the unusual payments gratefully, taking them as a challenge to her cooking skills.

Second to hard cash, the most welcome form of payment was fuel chits. In the scant living circumstances, fuel was everything. Fuel could heat homes, run electrical generators, warm water, and power transportation. One of the few industries that was active and reasonably steady in the region was logging, and small independent logging firms were always looking for good help. This was an avenue of employment for many of the men, but payment was a challenge since under-the-table cash payments could only get so large before drawing attention. But those firms all had to store and use all manner of fuels: gasoline, diesel, kerosene, propane, and others. When it became clear that the irregular employees would accept payment in the form of chits authorizing them to draw upon the firm's fuel stocks, an entire sub-economy based on fuel chits was born. When Phillip Schaeffer, who was one of the lumberjacks, came home on payday with a wad of chits good for gasoline or propane, the family could exchange these with other families or even businesses for other items of value. Luke always welcomed fuel chits as payment.

In fact, that was where Felicity was right now. Kent had turned in several chits to refill their pickup's transfer tank, and Felicity had strapped their empty gas cans onto their nearly-dry ATV to drive to the Schaeffers to get everything refilled. Luke would have accompanied her except that the Baxters were due to arrive, to see if Luke could do anything about little Robert's stubborn croup.

A big advantage to their living location was their proximity to the Schaeffers. Kent, Linda, and all of their children except Martha had been relocated to a house only about six miles away. The Schaeffers were Luke's *de facto* family, and they had undertaken the task of coaching him and Felicity through marriage preparation. During that period, Felicity had technically still lived with her family up by Fairview about thirty miles away, but since that was over an hour's ride by ATV and even longer on horseback, she had often come to stay with the Schaeffers during the months of their engagement. The Schaeffer home had recovered its joyful and loving atmosphere, after the dark and dismal time that had begun with their children being taken from them in the spring of the prior year. Getting clear of the oppressive and dangerous atmosphere that had been plaguing the Thumb region had seemed to have cleared everyone's head and emotions, and the family undertook to establish a much simpler lifestyle in their new environment. Kent was forced to get creative with earning a living, since as someone who had officially vanished, he could hardly open another insurance sales office. He did odd jobs here and there, but ended up finding an interesting niche as a reviewer of insurance policies for farmers and other small businesses. This involved examining their coverage to decipher the byzantine clauses and intricate regulations, and making recommendations for changes. This service wasn't highly lucrative, but it earned him occasional cash and other barter items such as fuel chits and food, as well as the good will of the local residents.

This pattern of adaptation was being repeated all across the scattered farms and homesteads in the region that stretched across about thirteen counties of northeastern Michigan. Roughly bounded by Saginaw Bay to the south, the Lake Huron coast on the east and north, and I-75/US-127 to the west, the area resembled the Upper Peninsula in that it had few permanent residents and little economic activity. To the tourists from the population centers in the southern part of the state, it was broadly described as "up north", though the eastern quarter lacked the pricey waterfront cachet of the communities further west along the Lake Michigan shore. The cottages, vacation homes, and hunting camps located here were more likely to have been owned by factory workers than executives, and most of them had been built toward the middle of the prior century. There was still some demand for property, but it had fallen off in the past couple of decades, to the point that even prime waterfront properties which recently would have been snapped up within a season now languished on the market for years. Though higher-value real estate and some economic activity could still be found along the thin strip of lakefront properties on the Huron coast, inland from that both population and economic activity dropped dramatically, to the point that many county administrators were facing the possibility of some of their communities becoming ghost towns.

In some measure this isolation suited the families taking refuge in the region, but it meant doing more with scantier resources, and learning to live more simply. Many old skills were being resurrected, including in the healing field, where Luke's access to modern medical equipment and pharmaceuticals was limited. Fortunately for the Petersons and the Schaeffers, they lived near a settlement of Amish, who were sympathetic to the plight of the displaced families and willingly taught them many skills necessary for simple living. Linda, Felicity, and the Schaeffer girls had visited Amish homes to learn skills like spinning, butter churning, and cheese making, while Kent and Phillip had been getting instruction in handworking wood and caring for livestock. Luke had been learning a few things himself, to the point that he was starting to wonder if branching out into veterinary medicine might be in his future.

But for now, the new Peterson family was content with a modest life lived at a sedate pace. They didn't have as many things as they'd once had, but in the glow of newlywed bliss, that seemed a minor matter. Luke glanced at his watch – Felicity should be heading home soon, then they'd have dinner, say prayers, and turn in for the night. That had become Luke's favorite time of day. Smiling, he got up from his chair and headed for the barn. It was time to give the livestock their dinner.

Over at the Schaeffer household, Felicity was indeed wrapping up her visit. The gas cans and the ATV had been refilled, a few staples added to the cargo crate, and a loaf of fresh bread carefully tucked away for a dinner table surprise. As much as Felicity loved the tranquility of her home and the attention of her husband, she relished these visits to the happy, hectic home of her extended family. The interaction with Linda and the children rejuvenated her in a way that even the most peaceful evenings at home did not, and she said as much while she was packing up to depart.

"Yes, that's a difference between you and Luke," Linda replied. "He's so introverted that he's almost a recluse, while you're outgoing and social."

"Luke? A recluse?" Felicity asked in surprise. "He never struck me like that. He's always active and engaged when we're over here."

"Ah, but we're like his family," Linda explained. "He's much more relaxed among us. But even here, he can only take so much people time. Periodically he has to retreat for some solitude to recharge. I've had to warn Tabitha and Matthew to leave him alone."

"I'd never noticed that," Felicity said, pondering this revelation about her husband.

"With just you two, the dynamic is less obvious. He sees time with you as intimate, private time. But even then, he's going to need occasional time by himself, especially as your relationship matures. Right now he probably gets by doing things like chores by himself, or by getting up early or staying up late."

"Sometimes he'll choose to do chores by himself, even if I offer to help. I can't understand that. I can't imagine that doing something alone would be preferable to having company."

"From his perspective, it could be preferable, particularly if he needs some alone time. Of course, he may not yet understand that about himself, and be confused by the tension created between his yearning to be with you and his need to have solitary time to recollect. It's a dynamic in your relationship that you need to be aware of, because it could cause tension over time," Linda explained.

"Oh, I don't see it as a problem, just a difference," Felicity said blithely.

"I didn't say problem, I said tension," Linda cautioned. "It's more than just a difference in how you do things, it's a difference in how you perceive and interpret life. Your temperaments and propensities will sometimes pull you in different directions. It'll only become a problem if you aren't willing to communicate with and change for each other."

"I guess," Felicity replied, wringing her hands as her façade of buoyant self-confidence slipped briefly and she continued in a distressed voice, "it's just that this marriage thing is turning out to be more difficult than I thought it would be. You're right – we do perceive life differently. Don't get me wrong. I love Luke and am committed to him for life. But there's no denying that if the choice had been completely mine, I would have chosen a different man – or, more precisely, a different kind of man, someone with a personality more like mine."

"Almost certainly," Linda assured her. "When we trust another's choosing, we end up with challenges and blessings we wouldn't have chosen for ourselves. That strains us in new and sometimes unpleasant ways, but it also offers more opportunities for the Lord to fill in what you're lacking."

"I'm sorry, I'm not sure I followed that," Felicity admitted.

"Our culture places much value on compatibility, that marriage partners should have similar tastes and inclinations. The motive behind this is to minimize stress in a relationship, since people with similar tastes and inclinations tend to agree on many things. But that perpetuates the illusion that we can make marriage work by our own efforts, so long as we can keep the underlying stress manageable. But we always need

God's grace to make up for our sinfulness and deficiencies, especially when our lives are so close up against someone else's. The sooner we realize that and learn to reach for that grace, the better off we are. If there's too much natural compatibility between partners, it can actually hinder the development of a good marriage, since the partners can live under the illusion that they can 'handle things' on their own."

"Wow," Felicity replied as she pondered this. "That's counterintuitive. But you and Uncle Kent seem to have such a harmonious marriage – you appear very compatible to me."

"You're seeing the results of decades of grace, guidance, and very good counsel," Linda said. "It wasn't always that way. When we were young, Kent knew of me but hadn't even considered dating me, much less marrying me. I didn't seem like 'his type', as he puts it. But after he had repeated failures in relationships, Mr. Holmes finally suggested that he ask me out. The first couple of dates were awkward, but we grew on each other. Apparently, it was Mr. Holmes who kept pointing out to Kent what a good wife I'd make until he finally popped the question."

"That's certainly not the typical pattern these days," Felicity grinned.

"No, it isn't," Linda admitted. "But it's worked out well. I had girlfriends whose courtships and weddings more closely fit the cultural stereotype, with the bells and flowers and flashy reception, but their marriages didn't last - most of them were divorced within five years. Admittedly, Kent can be high maintenance at times, but so can I. He's a good husband and wonderful father."

"Yes, I'm beginning to understand the meaning of high maintenance," Felicity admitted. "Luke can be very needy."

"Don't underestimate the burden of being raised without a father," Linda replied. "Thankfully it's outside your experience, but of all the difficulties Kent and I have faced in our relationship, the worst have arisen out of the void left in him by the absence of a father. Mr. Holmes did the best he could, God bless him, but there's no real substitute for a dad. Luke's in the same situation, and that will become more obvious over time. It's going to call for a lot of prayer and patience on your part."

"Just what I need," Felicity said wryly. "More patience opportunities. I'd better get going if I'm going to have dinner ready."

Arrangements

"So you see, Senator, there is no cause for concern. The implants are completely harmless and serve one purpose only," the HHS representative assured Shawn in a condescending tone.

Shawn glanced at Kelly, who kept her face impassive. They were on a three-way videoconference with David back in the district and this HHS rep, from whom they were trying to get answers about the chip implants as well as several other aspects of HHS activity within the SPD. As usual, all they were being given were platitudes and bureaucratic doublespeak.

"But you must admit," Shawn countered, "that not publicly explaining the purpose of these chips, as well as requiring everyone to get them before receiving service, is a violation of conditions of medical treatment. Everyone has a right to understand what's being done to them, as well as to refuse —"

"Senator," the rep interrupted, "I'm afraid the confluence of circumstances within the SPD leaves us few options. We're trying to accomplish many goals in a short amount of time, which sometimes means the formalities may have to be put on hold for a period. With implementation plans this aggressive, the policies and protocols are still being worked out. For my part, I'd think the prospect of having my medical records promptly and accurately tracked would be cause for gratitude, not paranoia."

"Dismissing my constituents' concerns as paranoia is not helping —" Shawn bristled, but again the representative interrupted in a slightly exasperated manner.

"I'm not sure where your constituents are getting their information, but I believe I've explained how the chips in question do not have the capacity to be used for the purpose they fear. The chips are powered by body heat, which gives them an effective broadcast range of about five feet. The devices reading them must not only be in immediate proximity, but must have the proper security and encryption circuitry to communicate with the chips. The data on the implants is extremely sensitive, and protected by several levels of safeguards. Fears about these chips being misused or improperly accessed are without rational basis."

Shawn bit back an even sharper response and sighed internally. It was clear they were getting the standard PR line on this matter, and would learn nothing new from this bureaucratic mouthpiece. Other issues were pressing, so he'd have to pursue alternatives to find out more. "Very well – thank you for your time," he said to the HHS rep.

"Always happy to help dispel misinformation, Senator. Contact me at any time if I can assist further," the rep replied, and rung off the conference call.

"The lady doth protest too much, methinks," David said, cocking an eyebrow at Shawn and Kelly.

"I agree," added Kelly, who had decades of experience dealing with bureaucratic evasion. "If I hadn't had any suspicions about those chips before, I would now."

"Right," Shawn said. "David, I'm giving you a tough assignment. Track down Frank and sit down with him for coffee. Listen to every rumor, speculation, and anecdote he knows about these chips, no matter how hare-brained. Try and learn where he heard them. I realize that's asking you to shovel a lot of mud, but there may be a few gold flakes buried there."

"A morning listening to Frank over coffee," David replied, rolling his eyes. "Thanks, boss."

"Write it off as a full day, and consider it a service to the district," Shawn grinned. "While you're at it, check out some other sources, especially ThumbWay News up in Harbor Beach. Jim Roberts hears some strange things. I'll be back in district tomorrow, but my dance card is filling up, and I've got family affairs that need attention. Let's stay in touch, and not let the election hype distract us from all this."

*   *   *

Grace pulled into the Oldham's driveway, not knowing what to expect, or how she'd deal with what she'd find here. She did remember Tyrone, and the brief conversation they'd had on that terrible, wonderful night as they'd walked through the cursed darkness to freedom. Her conscience smote her as she recalled the promise she'd made to him that they would stay in close touch and that she'd visit often – a promise that had not been kept, as she'd gone back to school in Canada just weeks later.

Still, Grace consoled herself as she walked up to the front door, Tyrone had been well cared for. A good home had been found for him, and he'd been happy and content with his foster family, at least until just recently. His foster mother, Dorothy, seemed like the chatty type, but perhaps that was just distress over Tyrone's situation. Well, maybe Grace could help with that. She knocked gently on the front door, and a white-haired man in wire-rimmed glasses answered.

"Hi, I'm Grace. I spoke to Dorothy about Tyrone."

"Ah, Grace," the man replied, opening the door for her to enter. "I'm Ralph Oldham. Dot is back here in the kitchen. Tyrone is asleep on the couch. He had another one of his fitful nights, but finally dozed off in the living room."

Ralph led Grace quietly past the sleeping Tyrone and through the dining room back to the kitchen where a plump woman with white hair wiped her hands on a towel and took Grace's hands. Dorothy's face was open and cheerful, but her eyes were haunted with concern. "Thank God you're here," she said, "Tyrone has been no end of distraught, and keeps going on about the safety lady. I'm hoping you're the one."

"I hope so, too," Grace replied. "I think I am, based on a brief conversation we had in the...that is, on the night we met. He was such a bright and friendly boy."

"And still is, and helpful, and gifted," Dorothy assured her. "You should see his drawings."

"I'd love to. Will he sleep for a while yet?"

"Hard to tell anymore. He used to sleep like a rock, but once this started – well, at times he'll sleep for hours, and other times he's awake within fifteen minutes," Ralph explained. "We've given up trying to enforce anything on him. When he's awake, he spends most of his time in his room sketching."

"It's his hobby, and he's very good at it," Dorothy added. "But his drawings have changed."

"Changed?" Grace asked.

"Yes. They had been beautiful works on natural themes, such as landscapes and still lifes. I've got a few here – they were so good that I framed them." Dorothy stood and took some pictures from the wall. Grace examined the sketches and nodded with approval. Though they were clearly the work of an untrained hand, they were balanced and detailed. There was one of a split rail fence along the edge of a wheat field, another of an old barn at sunset, and another of a sleeping cat.

"He's very good with perspective and lighting," Grace observed. "He gets all that detail with colored pencils?"

"He tried watercolors for a while, but couldn't get the control. These are typical of what he used to produce – bright, open, and delicate. Let me show you what he's been doing lately." They got up and passed quietly up the stairway, with Ralph taking a quick glance at where the still-slumbering Tyrone lay on the couch. They went into his room, which still had the blinds drawn. Papers were strewn across the desk, with a few scattered on the floor.

"Take a look at these," Ralph picked up some of the papers and handed them to Grace. One of the sketches was of a deep, brooding wood, thick with vines and shadows. Another was of an open space edged by what looked like a fence made of pipes, with a low, ominous-looking building standing along the far side and shadowy, ill-defined figures dotting the open space. The figures were all done in gray and charcoal, except for one sickly red blotch at one end of the space, near the fence, around which several of the shadowy figures were clustered. Grace recoiled – the garish blotch looked out of place in the monochromatic work, and had a shocking, almost obscene quality to it.

"Do you have any idea what this is?" Grace asked, showing Dorothy the picture.

"Not a clue. Disturbing, isn't it? So is this." Dorothy picked up a sketch of a grotesque looking animal that had the outlines of a pig, but its face seemed to morph into some feral beast with dripping fangs. Like the other, this image was mostly blacks and grays, except for scarlet highlights about the mouth and eyes.

"I agree, it's very disturbing," Grace admitted, her skin crawling a bit at the graphic realism. "What's that supposed to be? A wolf's head?"

"Looks a bit like a hyena," Dorothy replied. "Lately we've been covering Greek and Roman mythology, covering creatures like gryphons, chimerae, sphinxes, and the like. I was wondering if these sketches were his imagination working all of that out."

"Maybe," Grace mused, thinking that the image looked far too visceral to be an illustration from a story. She glanced through the other sketches on the desk, all of which reflected the same dark, ominous atmosphere. Trees with thick branches overhung shadowed trails that led away into murky thickets. Decaying buildings stood in desolate clearings, their dark windows looking like empty eye sockets. "He did all this in charcoal, didn't he?" she asked.

"Mostly. Some pencil," Ralph confirmed.

"Except for this one," Grace pointed out, noticing a flash of color amidst the scattered pages. She extracted an intricate and richly colored drawing of a young woman. The woman had olive skin and jet-black hair that was tied back at the nape of her neck, and was simply dressed in a black skirt, white blouse, and brown shawl that was so coarsely spun that it looked almost like the texture of burlap. Even drawn by an inexperienced hand, it was clear that the young woman was extremely beautiful, and she was looking out of the page with a gentle, pleading expression.

"Oh, my, I hadn't seen that," Ralph said admiringly. "That's the first person I've seen him draw. Not bad for a first attempt."

"No, it's not," Dorothy affirmed. "He's got some work to do on the facial proportions and body perspective, but it's very good for his level. I wonder who it's supposed to represent?"

"I think I know," Grace said, wonder touched with a little fear rising within her. "That looks like St. Rose of Lima. I have a prayer card with an image that looks almost identical to this drawing. Do you have any such cards around, or books of saints, that might contain a picture like that?"

"I don't think so..." Dorothy began, but she was interrupted by cries and calls coming from downstairs. They all bustled down to find a distressed Tyrone sitting up on the couch, clutching the blanket he'd been covered with and looking anxiously around the living room. Ralph and Dorothy hastened to his side but Grace hung back, uncertain of how to proceed, or of how the tormented young man would receive her.

"We were just upstairs, Tyrone," Dorothy was reassuring him. "Look, a friend has come to visit, a friend you haven't seen in a while." She pointed at Grace, who smiled but stayed where she was. Tyrone looked at her blankly, not comprehending at first. A confused expression crossed his face, as if he was trying to make some connections. Then his countenance lit up as recognition dawned, and he gave a cry of joy.

"The safety lady! You came! Oh, my goodness!"

"Yes, I'm here," Grace said, walking to him with a warm smile. "It took them a while to find me, but I came as soon as I knew."

"Oh, my goodness! Oh, my goodness!" Tyrone gushed, almost bouncing in his excitement. "I forgot how pretty you are! Are you really here?"

"Yes, I'm really here, Tyrone," Grace replied through tears, reaching out for his hands. He took hers gingerly, as if afraid he was doing something forbidden, but when she gripped his tightly, he shuddered with the intensity of the conflict within him. "It's all right, Tyrone, I'm here," Grace continued, and enfolded him in her arms.

Tyrone almost collapsed as a torrent of grief and tension was released. He clutched Grace close and burst into sobs that wracked his frame. She held him firmly, a little off balance from his height and weight but determined not to budge as long as he needed her. She was aware of Ralph and Dorothy fluttering about the periphery of her vision, fetching towels and chairs, but she kept her focus completely on Tyrone. Grace could tell he was working to regain his composure, but kept failing time and again. His sobbing and howling felt bottomless as all the grief and trauma he had endured seemed to come pouring out of him at once. At times his gasping would start to abate and he'd begin to relax, then a fresh flood of heartache would strike, and he'd dissolve into more weeping. Grace simply held him through all these bouts, rocking gently as tears of sympathy poured down her cheeks. Her arms were sore and her back ached, but she was determined to support him as long as he needed her.

Finally Tyrone slumped exhausted in her arms, and Ralph was swiftly behind him with a chair. Dorothy had one ready for Grace, who eased Tyrone down without letting go of his hands. He sat gazing at her in amazement through reddened eyes, as if still unable to believe she was present.

"I'm so glad you're here," Tyrone said. "It's been so scary, and I remembered that you weren't afraid at all, and I knew you'd be able to help. I can come with you, can't I? I can stay with you now, right?"

"Ah…" Grace stammered, glancing at Ralph and Dorothy. They hadn't had time to discuss just how she'd be able to help, and the prospect of Tyrone leaving the Oldham's care to come with her hadn't occurred to any of them.

"Nothing against Mister or Miz Oldham," Tyrone said hastily, noticing Grace's quick look. "It's just…I was hoping…"

"It's all right, Tyrone," Grace reassured him. "You'll certainly be able to come with me for at least a visit, and we'll see what we can work out." Internally Grace cringed at the thought of trying to explain this to Todd. They were already housing the mysterious amnesiac Jason in the room that was intended to be the nursery. Where they'd fit another unexpected tenant in their already snug bungalow was beyond her. But the fear and hope in Tyrone's expression was more than her heart could bear.

"I'll pack a few things in a duffel," Dorothy said as she bustled up the stairs while Ralph hovered nearby. Grace got Tyrone talking about his life with the Oldhams, his studies, and his art. She was intrigued that his reports were unhesitatingly positive – there wasn't a hint of any shadow or threat that might have triggered this uncharacteristic episode. Grace hardly wanted to start probing the matter now, and wondered if she ever would. But it was certain that something had changed, for the lad who had been so happy and contented was now dissatisfied if she was not around. Why did he need her, and for how long?

"Tyrone!" Dorothy called down the stairs. "Could you come help me choose some clothes?"

Tyrone looked at Grace with trepidation, so she patted his arm reassuringly. "You go ahead – I'll still be around. I've got to step outside to make a phone call, but I won't be far and I won't leave without you." Tyrone nodded and went upstairs while Grace headed for the door. The private network phone for this call, no question, but that raised the issue of signal strength. The phone indicated that she was right at the edge of reception, but there was enough signal for her to try the number. It rang, and her husband answered.

"Hello, Todd? I've got a situation here that's going to require us to flex a little. Yes, more flexing..."

Later that evening, while all the men in the house slept, Grace was still awake, caught in the pregnant woman's perennial battle between fatigue and hunger. Though Todd had been initially stressed by yet another demand on their little household, he had adapted quickly, seeing the need to accommodate Tyrone as a spur to seek swift resolution of Jason's situation. Grace had brought Tyrone home with her, where to her surprise and delight he and Jason had hit it off immediately. Even with his vague and uncertain personal circumstances, Jason had quickly established a rapport with Tyrone, reassuring and calming him. Grace had been so secure about this new friendship that she'd felt comfortable leaving Tyrone with Jason while she picked Todd up from work. They got home to find the two busy in the kitchen preparing a late supper. After enjoying that they'd all turned in, with Jason in the guest room and Tyrone sprawled on the couch.

Now Grace sat at the dining room table by the light of a flashlight, eating cheese and crackers quietly and trying not to fret about all the complications that had entered their life recently. To distract herself she opened the folder of Tyrone's sketches which Dorothy had sent along. She leafed quickly through the dark and depressing pages, hoping to find the drawing of St. Rose. Her eye caught a flash of color, and she extracted the drawing, but it wasn't the portrait she'd been seeking. It was a landscape of the type Tyrone excelled at – a richly colored sun setting behind a rise in a meadow, with a finely detailed little shed on the near side of the rise and a two-track trail meandering across the foreground. The colors of the sunset were masterfully done, starting with the rich gold on the horizon and fading through a tawny red to the faintest yellow blending into the indigo sky. It would have been just another well-drawn landscape but for an element that was so alien that it changed the pastoral picture into something resembling an image from science fiction. The sky above the placid meadow was latticed with a network of straight red lines crisscrossing each other. The lines were regular, extending from the horizon toward the viewer, and crossed by other lines stretching across the picture from edge to edge. The spaces between the lines were large, but the effect made it look like the sky was covered by an eerie red net.

A sense of unease grew within Grace as she examined this mysterious drawing with its jarring admixture of the peaceful and the threatening. This wasn't like the dark and frightening sketches that had risen out of Tyrone's distress, but neither was it like his earlier landscapes and still lifes. When had Tyrone drawn this, and what had he been envisioning when he did?

And why did the image disturb her so profoundly?

*   *   *

A quiet knock came at the door, and Steve McLean opened it to find on his doorstep a stocky man wearing a broad-brimmed hat and heavy-framed glasses. The man was clutching a tablet and a black leather folio.

"Brady?" Steve asked.

"Yes," the man answered. "You must be Steve."

"I am – please come in," Steve opened the door wider and the man entered, removing his hat to reveal thinning black hair. Steve had heard much about Brady but had never met him in person, so when he'd called on one of the private network phones asking to meet with Steve and Lawrence,

Steve had taken the request seriously. Brady had agreed to come after dark to Lawrence and Annette's home, and now they waited upstairs to hear what had him so concerned.

"Thank you for meeting with me," Brady said as he took a seat in the living room. "I wish it had been something I could have explained over the phone, but I don't trust even private encrypted circuits with this."

Steve, Lawrence, and Annette looked at each other with raised eyebrows. "That sounds ominous," Steve said.

"It is – and potentially dangerous," Brady replied, then launched into an explanation of what he'd found on the dark sites about the chip implants, and the mandated software patches for various networked devices, and the potential capabilities of these two elements working together.

"And when you combine all that with what I've been hearing about new treatment protocols in the region mandating that patients receive treatment only at UPAIR clinics, and those patients also getting implanted with chips ostensibly to store their medical records, it starts to look ugly," Brady concluded.

"Yes, we've already had a brush with that," Lawrence said, glancing at Annette. "When we went for our most recent neurologist appointment, we were told we couldn't receive treatment there, and had to go to a government clinic."

"Have you gone?" Brady asked.

"Not yet, but it's getting more difficult to put off," Annette admitted. "My condition isn't getting any better."

"I...I hesitate to propose this," Brady offered cautiously, "but this may offer an opportunity. We don't *know* anything for certain. All we have is a suspicious alignment of circumstances, what with these chips, and these mandated software patches. It may have nothing to do with our situation."

"Or it might," Steve replied. "What would you need to be certain?"

"I'd need one of those chips. Based on what I've seen on the dark sites, I can write up some diagnostics to test their capabilities to see if they match the online descriptions. I might not be able to crack the encryption on the medical records, but that wouldn't matter – the only thing I'd be interested in is whether these chips transmit their device identity in a way that could be picked up by other devices."

"Well," Annette said slowly, "maybe we ought to make that appointment."

"Honey!" Lawrence said sharply as Steve gave a similar cry of alarm.

"What?" Annette continued with an innocent expression. "I'm in need of medical care, and they're expecting me to make an appointment. If they really are implanting these chips in everyone who comes in, this seems a golden opportunity for us to get our hands on one for Brady to analyze."

"But...weren't you listening to what Brady was saying?" Steve pleaded. "If you get one of these, they might be able to track you wherever you are!"

"As if they can't do that already," Annette scoffed, gesturing toward the sky. "Think realistically – we all know that I have less than a year to live, possibly much less if things keep progressing as they have. What could they do to me? And if it gives us a chance to obtain a test sample of what they think is secret equipment, wouldn't that be worth some small risk?"

Lawrence looked at his wife, then at the other men with a desperate expression. Years of instinctive secrecy warred with the plain sense of what she had said. "I...but...maybe we could..." he stammered until Annette patted his hand.

"Come on, dear, you know I'm right," she cajoled. "Brady, we'll make that appointment first thing tomorrow, and let you know when it is. You can get all your gadgets ready to come test it."

"If you're certain," Brady cautioned.

"We're certain," Annette assured him.

*   *   *

Bethany's phone rang, and though she didn't recognize the number, she answered anyway.

"Bethany Hood?" came a clipped and official-sounding voice.

"This is Bethany. Who is this?"

"We see you missed your appointment yesterday afternoon. We have rescheduled you for next Thursday at 3:00 p.m.," the voice continued.

"No – my husband and I have been talking this over, and we –"

"Ms. Hood, it has been explained to you that this treatment is your only option," the voice interrupted sharply. "Delays only make the treatment more complex and difficult for you. You must keep this next appointment."

"But...but we haven't decided –"

"If transportation is problematic, we can make arrangements," the voice continued, "but we can have no further delays. Next Thursday at 3:00 p.m. at the Fairgrove Clinic. I will send a confirmation to your calendar." The call cut off, leaving Bethany staring at the wall in shock.

She and Patrick had expected some kind of response when they'd chosen not to keep the appointment. Patrick had suggested that they play along for a while, proposing various appointment times that wouldn't work, rescheduling and delaying until the pregnancy was too far along for an abortion. Bethany had doubted that such a strategy would work, but hadn't expected this blunt, unyielding reaction. There had been no dialog, only being dictated to.

What could they do now?

Then Bethany remembered what had been given her the night of her last violin lesson. After she'd poured out her distress to Mrs. Kyle and then to her daughter – Grace, yes, that was her name – Mrs. Kyle had slipped into another room and returned with an old-style phone and charger. She'd given Bethany specific instructions on what to do with it before sending her home. Bethany remembered the simple instructions clearly, though they seemed futile in the face of the threat they faced. But having no other recourse, she decided to try. Fetching the old phone, she set it on the table and dialed Mrs. Kyle with her own phone.

"Yes?" Mrs. Kyle answered.

"Mrs. Kyle, I'm afraid I'm going to have to cancel our lesson for next Thursday at three. A conflict has come up."

"I quite understand, Bethany. Call me when you'd like to reschedule."

Bethany rang off and sat staring at the old phone for a minute before shaking herself for being silly. Whatever was going to happen wouldn't happen instantaneously. She called Patrick and filled him in on the developments, sounding suitably distressed (which wasn't difficult) but not mentioning anything about her contact with Mrs. Kyle. Patrick was sympathetic and promised to get home as soon as he could.

Shortly after that conversation finished, the older phone rang. "Hello?" Bethany answered, uncertain who she'd be talking to.

"Hi, Bethany, this is Grace Beck. Mom said I should give you a call. What's up?"

"Well, I didn't keep the appointment at the clinic yesterday, the appointment to…well, you know," Bethany explained. "So they just called–" Bethany poured out the whole tale to the sympathetic Grace, who listened without interrupting.

"So, you've got a firm appointment set up for next Thursday at three?" Grace confirmed when Bethany had finished. "What do you plan to do?"

"I don't know, I don't know," Bethany fretted. "Patrick doesn't know, either. I suppose we could just run away, but I don't know where we'd go. Our jobs are here, what family we have is here. I've got some friends down near Indianapolis, but it's too much to ask them –"

"Bethany, Bethany," Grace said soothingly, sensing that Bethany was working herself into a panic attack. "Let me make some calls and see what I can find out."

"But...but Grace, what can you *do*?" Bethany cried. "They were so insistent, and so...*mean*."

"I don't know yet, but whatever I can arrange, it's going to be before next Thursday," Grace assured her. "Just hang in there, and don't do anything rash until I get back to you, all right?"

"Okay," Bethany replied quietly.

"Keep this phone nearby, and don't discuss anything sensitive over your regular phone."

"I won't."

Back at her house, Grace took a minute to compose her thoughts before calling Todd. They'd both been distracted from Patrick and Bethany's situation by the other complexities that had abruptly entered their lives, but the deadline the Hoods had been given wasn't that far away and the consequences dire. Something decisive had to be done quickly. She keyed the number of Todd's private network phone and hoped he kept it nearby.

"Grace?" came the swift response.

"Hi, Todd. Listen, the situation with the Hoods just got a lot hotter, and we need to do something," Grace began, and relayed what Bethany had just told her.

"Yeah," Todd admitted when she'd finished. "That sounds pretty serious."

"Pretty serious?" Grace asked, incredulous. "Todd, it's life and death! Not to mention the implications for us – I'm due for my next prenatal appointment in two weeks, and they're sure to send us to one of those UPAIR clinics. What if they find something 'wrong' with our baby and make one of those appointments for me?"

"Babe, I understand the severity," Todd assured her. "Let me make some calls and see what I can find out."

"You said that before," Grace chided him.

"Come on, Grace," the aggrieved Todd replied. "You know what our life has been like! We've had other demanding issues in our faces!"

"Yeah, yeah," Grace admitted, "but this one has become a lot more urgent."

"I know, and I promise I'll get right on it," Todd assured her.

"Thanks. And I'm sorry for snapping at you."

"Accepted. And I really will get right on those calls."

Todd rang off and pulled a notepad closer. He wanted to compose his thoughts before calling Steve McLean, of whom he knew but with whom he'd only spoken once or twice. This was a lot to dump on a stranger, and Todd felt apprehensive, but he gathered his courage and keyed the number in his private network phone simply labeled 'Fangorn'.

"Hello?" answered a man's voice.

"Hi, this is Todd Beck. Is Steve McLean available?"

"This is Steve," the voice replied, "and this phone has been ringing a lot more than I'd expected it to."

"Well, it may do more ringing in the near future," Todd replied. "I've got a situation to discuss – in fact, several situations."

"Great," Steve groaned. "As if we need more situations. Wait...what did you say your name was?"

"Todd Beck."

"Were you one of the guys who..."

"Yeah, I was on a team that night, for all the good it did."

"Well, that makes you a minor legend in certain circles," Steve said. "What can I do for you?"

Todd was surprised and a little gratified that his reputation had in a small way preceded him. "The first situation involves an unexpected guest who got landed in our laps."

"Unexpected guest?"

"Yes – one with amnesia, and apparently a rather complex and delicate past."

"Really?" Steve asked in amazement. "This sounds intriguing, at least. Tell me more."

Todd proceeded to explain about Jason Pelletier, and update Steve on the developments with Tyrone, and lastly to brief him on the situation with Bethany and Patrick Hood. Steve just listened, asking a few questions here and there.

"The circumstances the Hoods find themselves in sound distressingly familiar," Steve said when Todd had concluded. "Though, in its way, this Jason's condition is more alarming."

"I know it's a lot to dump on you, but we're at our wit's end," Todd pleaded. "We can only keep so many guests in our small home, but it looks like we're stuck with Tyrone, because he seems to need Grace's presence."

"We appreciate your help with that, and please keep us updated on developments," Steve replied. "As far as those other situations, let me see what we can do. Our resources aren't what they were, but we still have some, and not all of our experienced volunteers scattered to other Farthings. I'll make some calls and get back to you."

"Thanks," Todd replied. "I'll try to keep this phone with me."

*   *   *

"So," Shawn asked after they'd placed their breakfast order, "whatcha got?"

Shawn and David were meeting in Shawn's 'district office', which was a diner just north of Port Huron. Actually, Shawn had several similar sites across the district, coffee houses and donut shops and even a bar or two, places where his constituents felt comfortable talking about what concerned them. Of course, frequenting such places ran the risk of meeting those constituents inadvertently and getting his ear talked off, which was why this time he'd chosen a corner booth and sat with his back to the door while David opened his tablet to consult his notes.

"District hours went unremarkably, except for a couple of odd incidents, both at Sandusky. One was a couple of irate parents complaining that their child had been vaccinated at school without their knowledge or consent."

"Vaccinated? By whom? The feds?"

"You guessed it – another aspect of the UPAIR initiative. The parents complained to the school administration and school board, but were told the matter was out of their hands. When they contacted the SPD office – which wasn't easy – they were sent to a site where they could register a complaint. That yielded nothing, so in desperation they showed up at district hours."

"And I imagine the kid wasn't just vaccinated, he was chipped," Shawn said, his blood pressure rising.

"My guess would be yes, though neither the kid nor the parents were told of it. I asked some discreet questions, and the kid indeed had a small slit on his left forearm, well bandaged. The parents had just assumed that it had to do with the vaccinations, so I didn't tell them otherwise."

"So, we've got a federal operation performing overt and covert medical operations on minors without the parents' knowledge, much less consent, and no effective avenue for appeal or redress," Shawn growled. "David, this isn't how America is supposed to work." Shawn's mind was already starting to toy with legislation he could introduce to counter this trend. He also wondered if it was worth talking to the state attorney general about this. "Could you have Kelly – no, no, I'll take that up with her later. Keep going. You mentioned a couple of odd incidents – what was the other one?"

"A man named Danny Hines came in to talk to me, because he didn't know where else to turn. Seems his neighbor asked him to look after the neighbor's property during what looked to be a lengthy absence. Just the usual stuff – take in the mail, forward what seemed to be important, watch the house, and so on.

"So, this Hines guy is watching his neighbor's property. I presume if he was forwarding mail, he knew where his neighbor was?" Shawn asked.

"Yes. The neighbor is named Jim Nichol, and he and his wife Delores were going to visit Jim's brother over near Grand Rapids for an indefinite period," David explained.

"What's the problem?" Shawn asked.

"After forwarding the first batch of mail to the brother's house, the brother contacted Danny to say that Jim and Delores had never arrived. He'd been expecting them, but they never showed up, so the brother figured they'd changed their minds. The brother called Jim's phone but got only voice mail, so he left a message and thought no more of it until he got the batch of forwarded mail. That got them both alarmed, so Danny went and checked out the Nichols' house. No sign of them and no answer on either of their phones."

"I presume Danny and the brother have been in touch with police?" Shawn asked.

"Both of them have. The state police verified that there have been no accidents involving their vehicle, or crimes or mishaps involving either person."

"So, somewhere between their home and Grand Rapid, they vanished without a trace?"

"That's right. Danny wasn't expecting us to do anything, just wanted to know if we had access to more resources than the state police. He did mention one thing that the brother had told him, though: what sparked the sudden trip to Grand Rapids was Jim's dissatisfaction with how he'd been treated when he'd visited one of these Rapid Care Centers."

"That may have nothing to do with anything," Shawn mused, then grinned at David. "On a lighter note, how was your coffee with Frank?"

"Not too bad, actually," David admitted. "He didn't ramble all over the map like he usually does. The specter of the SPD gives him more than enough fodder. This time he was going on about the old Caro site being used as a secret prison for detainees taken by the feds within the SPD."

"What, the old mental health facilities over there? They've been mothballed for years, haven't they?" Shawn asked.

"They have, but Frank contends that they're in use again, and that vehicles with darkened windows are pulling in during the small hours to unload prisoners. He claims the locals know about it but are afraid to talk, lest they end up in there as well."

"Does he have any proof of this?"

"Just rumors – as he puts it, he keeps his ear to the ground. But I did some checking on my own and verified that something is going on at that site."

"Checking?" Shawn asked. "What kind of checking?"

"I drove over to eyeball the site. The old buildings look pretty much like they have since everything moved to the new facility – dark and empty, though I noticed the lawns are trimmed. There is a new construct on the back of the building, right up against what seem to have been loading docks. I got a shot with my tablet, though it isn't very good." David showed Shawn a distance shot of the back of a building across a vacant parking lot. Sticking out from the back of the building was what looked like a giant car port, except with black sides and what looked like a large black curtain draped across the back. The entire structure looked large enough to hold a commercial bus, maybe even a full-sized semi.

"Could you get a closer shot of this?" Shawn asked.

"I tried, and that's when I ran into the other oddity," David replied. "I fired up my recon drone and sent it over the fence to get a close-up, but when it got within fifty yards of the building it ran into a no-go zone and grounded."

"A 'no-go zone'?" Shawn asked.

"An area wherein somebody doesn't want drones flying. You create one by setting up transmitters that broadcast on the frequencies that are used for drone control signals. When the drone gets far enough into the zone that all control signals are blocked, it resorts to the default behavior for signal loss, which usually is landing gently."

"Are such zones legal?"

"Oh, sure, with limits on broadcast strength and range. Sporting events, concerts, even law enforcement sites will set them up, though usually they'll broadcast warnings that it's a no-go zone. Operators learn to detect when they're on the fringe of one and pull back. I wasn't expecting this one, so I plowed right into it."

"Did you lose your drone?"

"Yeah," David said ruefully. "Newer drones have better signal protection, and settings where you can have the drone fly back to the launch point in case of signal loss, but mine was older and cheaper. I never got my close-up."

"Who would be setting up drone protection around a bunch of abandoned buildings in Tuscola County?" Shawn wondered.

"My very question. I checked with Patti Rucker, the utility lobbyist, and she did some digging for me. Turns out the electric bill notification is being sent to some generic e-mail address, and the mailing address of record is some post office box in Sterling Heights. That's all she could tell me."

"That could be anybody, including a federal agency," Shawn observed. "Something's going on. I want you to replace your drone with one of the newer models. Bill it to the office, I'll notify Kelly. Get one of the better ones –

within reason – but ensure it has features that will protect it from this no-go interference."

"Ah…sure, boss," David replied in a surprised but excited tone.

"Anything else?"

"No, that's all I had," David said, snapping shut his tablet, then checked himself. "Oh, one more thing: you asked me to check out local news sites to see if they'd heard of any oddities. I tried to get in touch with Jim Roberts up at ThumbWay, but didn't get an answer. Left a couple of messages, sent some e-mails, even dropped by his office. Nobody's seen him, and his site hasn't been updated in about ten days."

"Really?" Shawn paused. "That's kind of unusual, isn't it?"

"The duration is," David replied. "Jim's an impulsive guy, and according to his landlord will at times just take off with his lady of the moment to Vegas, or go on fishing trips. But he's usually back within a few days, a week at the outside. He takes his journalistic responsibilities seriously."

"Hmm," Shawn mused, a chill settling in his middle. "Keep trying on that, would you?"

"Sure thing," David said, packing up and heading off, leaving Shawn to finish his breakfast and ponder the fact that he might have just heard about two mysterious disappearances in his district.

Forebodings

Steve McLean shook his head, rubbed his face, and sipped his coffee. He needed to focus on the issues at hand, no matter how much his imagination wanted to kite off chasing unknowns. Yes, there were mysteries and worrisome indicators, but he had concrete problems to address – which was, in its way, a relief. He scanned the list on the legal pad before him and tried to prioritize matters.

Steve had to find housing for the mysterious man named Jason. All manner of questions swirled around him, but the immediate focus was getting him out of the Beck household, preferably to somewhere very secluded. Eventually that should be one of the other Farthings, but since those households were still trying to digest the abrupt influx of refugees from the prior spring, that might take a while to arrange. For now, they'd just have to settle for a place to hide him.

Equally important, and even more urgent, was getting the Hood family to safety. That was going to require activating some parties that hadn't been called in some while, but Steve hoped they wouldn't mind – they might even find it exciting.

Then there were the implications of what Brady had learned. Mom and Dad had already made the appointment at the clinic, and though they were treating it like nothing more than a chance to get an experimental object for Brady, Steve was nervous. He'd have been nervous about having them go near a government clinic even before this SPD. There were also the ominous undertones of what might have been done to this Jason...

No, no, Steve shook his head again. Dispatch the problems he could address, don't waste time cogitating about those he couldn't. He had some calls to make, and wanted to talk to his wife about an idea he had regarding where to stash Jason.

*   *   *

Todd's private network phone rang, and he stepped outside to answer. Grace was sitting at the kitchen table with Tyrone, looking over some new drawings, and the incoming call might touch on matters best discussed out of earshot. It was still warm outside, with only a hint of the oncoming autumn chill. Jason was mowing their small lawn, so Todd wandered around front to escape the noise.

"Hey, Steve," Todd said.

"Hey, Todd. How are things going?"

"A little cramped, but we're getting by."

"Well, I think we can help with that. Do you think Jason would mind another move?"

"He's adapted well enough to this one. What do you have in mind?" Todd asked.

"Do you know Martha and Evan Stover? He's my nephew – lives by his folks over near Harbor Beach."

"I think I've heard the name, but that's all."

"They've got a little house they're about to vacate. They're moving up to Northfarthing for a while to escape the...ah...climate around here. They were thinking of just shuttering the house, but are open to the idea of having Jason stay there as a caretaker. Think he'd agree to that?"

"I think it would be great," Todd affirmed. "Despite his unusual condition, Jason is a very helpful and considerate guest. He'd be responsible and eager to help."

"And you don't think his living there alone would be any danger? To himself, I mean?"

"I don't think so. He seems competent with life skills and has plenty of common sense. He just lacks a bit in the memory department."

"It's not like he'd be completely alone," Steve explained. "Evan's parents live right up the road. They'd be available in case of problems. I'll have Evan come pick Jason up and take him over to meet everyone. Now, about the Hoods: can you

200

find out a little more for me about Patrick's routine? Where he works, what schedule and routes he follows, car model and license, the usual stuff."

"Sure," Todd replied. "I'll have Grace give Bethany a call."

"How's your youngest guest doing?"

"Very well so far. He hasn't exhibited any of the distress that so alarmed his foster family, and is cheerful and helpful. Of course, he's only been here a couple of days, but it's been smooth sailing so far."

"Great. We'll get back to you shortly about the other arrangements."

Inside the house, Grace was paging through the drawings Tyrone had done since his arrival. She was astonished at both his speed and skill. He'd done a beautiful line sketch of the stand of birches out back, and a very authentic color drawing of a bird feeder, complete with birds.

"I don't understand it, Tyrone," Grace said. "I know artists who struggle for years to master perspective, to draw things so they look on paper just like they do to the naked eye. Yet you seem to do it almost effortlessly, with no training. What's your secret?"

"I dunno, Miz Grace," Tyrone shrugged. "I just draw, and if it don't look right, I fix it until it does."

"That's a gift, Tyrone," Grace assured him, picking up the next drawing, which was his most intricate. It was a color-tinged sketch of the back yard of their house, from the perspective of the front yard. The left side of the drawing was the side of the house, but mostly it showed the wooden fence along the right border of the property, the small utility shed in the back, and the plants and pots scattered about the edge of the yard. There was a man standing along the fence toward the back, who Grace took to be Jason, since Todd wouldn't have been around when Tyrone drew this.

As intricate and realistic as the details of the sketch were, they weren't what captured Grace's attention. Drawn across the sky above the warm and natural scene stretched the harsh red lattice, dividing the sky into elongated rectangles. Against this lattice, in the distance near the horizon, was a lumpy figure that seemed to be suspended in the air. Furthermore, surrounding the figure of the man was drawn a light red-orange haze or aura – not so distinct as to hinder the detail, but unmistakable.

"This drawing is interesting," Grace said as casually as possible, not wanting to trigger a dramatic reaction. "How long did it take you to draw it?"

"About an hour, I think," Tyrone replied. "I was on the rock out front with my clipboard, looking back the driveway, and I just drew it. Mr. Jason came out toward the end and leaned against the fence, so I drew him, too."

"And these red lines – did you see them, too?"

"Nah, that was later. I was inside, adding the tints, and I just saw them, so I added them. That's when I saw this, too, so I added that." He tapped the lumpy figure by the far horizon.

"Just what is that?"

"It's not very good, and it's kinda hard to see," Tyrone admitted, leaning over to squint at the drawing. "But it's us on the back of a flying bull. We're escaping."

"The back of a flying bull?" Grace asked, puzzled. There were no livestock around.

"Sure – like Zeus and Europa," Tyrone explained patiently.

"Ah, yes. What, exactly, we escaping?"

"We're getting out from under, flying away to freedom."

"'Out from under'? Under what? The red lattice?" Grace asked.

"Yeah, that's…that's bad," Tyrone looked a little agitated, as if she was getting near a topic he'd rather not discuss.

"I saw you had another drawing with those red lines," Grace ventured cautiously. "Is that what you see? Is it always there?"

"Yeah. That's bad. That's real bad." Tyrone was glancing around and starting to fidget, so Grace decided to back off the questions.

"But we're escaping, so that's good. Doesn't Mr. Jason escape too?" She pointed to the figure standing by the fence.

"Mr. Jason? No, he stays. He stays and...burns. Burns all up."

"Burns up?" Grace asked, alarmed. "Isn't...doesn't that hurt?"

"No, no," Tyrone replied pensively, gazing at the picture. "Not that kind of burning. It's a good burning. Mr. Jason wants it. But you and me, and Mr. Todd, and the baby, we all fly away to where it's safe."

Grace stared at Tyrone in amazement tinged with fear.

She couldn't remember having mentioned to him that she was pregnant.

The following evening a pleasant young man showed up to take Jason to another house. Grace and Todd had explained to him that they didn't have the room to house him long-term (which had been obvious), and had asked if he minded staying at a place about an hour and a half away. They explained how the couple who owned the house was taking a long trip, and would appreciate a caretaker to live there in their absence. Jason had agreed to this, not having much choice, and when the man came, he said goodbye to the Becks and his new friend Tyrone.

The friendly young couple whose house he would be watching were named Evan and Martha, and they had a happy little baby named Leo. To Jason's eyes they seemed a little young to be married, but that wasn't his concern. They certainly seemed very mature and responsible, taking good care of the baby and working smoothly together. They were courteous and considerate toward him, but it was clear they were in the midst of major changes and didn't have many resources to spare, so he simply tried to stay out of their way.

From some comments and other indications, Jason got the idea that the couple's impending move was hasty, stressful, and forced by factors Jason didn't understand. Most of the sparse possessions in the house were packed away, either in suitcases or bins. Evan left Jason a few sets of work shirts and jeans as well as some cold weather gear. The nursery had been emptied out and a bed, desk, and dresser placed in it for Jason's use. Evan and Martha spent much of the time bustling about checking lists and hashing out details. It was clear that Jason would barely get to know them before they moved on.

The evening of Jason's second day in the new house, Evan's parents dropped in. Their names were Dominic and Julieann, and they lived about a mile up the road. Jason was told that if he had any problems or issues, he should get in touch with them. They'd also ensure that he was stocked with groceries and other necessities. Dominic and Julieann were friendly and gracious, but they'd clearly dropped by to see their children, so Jason stepped outside while tearful goodbyes were said. Jason continued to get the impression that this parting was unexpected but necessary, and that all hoped it would be short-lived. Jason didn't know what circumstances would have to change to end what seemed like a temporary exile, but he hoped they would change soon.

That night, well after dark, Evan and Martha and Leo departed, but in an unusual manner. As night fell, they all went into the house, said prayers, and extinguished all the lights just as they would if they were going to bed. But once everything was dark, they slipped out the side door, where under the car port canopy they got into their older minivan. Then, without starting the engine, Evan put the car into neutral, and he and Jason pushed it just enough to reach the top of the gentle incline of the driveway. Evan hopped in as the van rolled quietly down the driveway, gathering enough momentum to allow him to turn onto the road and roll for almost fifty yards. Only then did he start the engine, but he drove almost half a mile further along the dark road before turning on the headlights.

Jason stood in the driveway, watching the taillights recede. He couldn't remember much, but he knew enough to know that this was unusual behavior. Evan and Martha were acting like people secretly fleeing some abiding danger. Why were they leaving their home and family? Why the hurried, furtive nature of their arrangements? Even when they'd said farewell to Evan's parents, Jason couldn't help but notice that everyone was acting like the young couple was escaping some fear that cast its shadow over all their lives, while the parents remained behind.

Jason went back inside the empty house. He got undressed in the dark and went to bed, but sleep did not come easily. He tossed about, going over and over in his mind what he knew and what he was observing. He knew he'd been in this area before – that was confirmed by the clear memories of the gate into the woods, and the dirt road, and the people in the headlights. But other memories proved elusive, and he was left floundering amidst flashes of scenes that had no context and vague emotional flurries, like echoes of how he'd felt at earlier times. What had he done when he was here before? From hints and comments Brian had made, and how the sheriff had treated him, Jason had been in a position of authority, but something had gone wrong. Had he played a part in creating this atmosphere of menace that had young families fleeing in the dark of night? If so, what could he do about it?

*   *   *

The next morning Lawrence and Annette Stover entered a nondescript door in a strip mall outside Saginaw. There were no identifiers on the door, just an address, and inside there was a waiting room with stark white walls and bare plastic chairs. There was a reception window, but it was closed by a rolling metal shutter. An armed guard sat behind a desk to the right, but after giving them a quick glance he returned his attention to his phone. The only other party in the waiting room was a woman with a young boy, both of whom were also focused on their phones.

"Do we sign in, or register, or something?" Annette asked in a near-whisper.

"I don't know – let me look," Lawrence said. He parked her wheelchair and went up to the window. After looking in vain for a button or a phone, he knocked on the metal shutter.

"Hey!" came a voice from behind him, and Lawrence turned to see the guard scowling at him. "Hey, don't do that. No knocking."

"But I wanted to let them know –" Lawrence began, but the guard cut him off abruptly.

"They know you're here. They'll call you when they're ready. Just sit down and wait your turn."

Lawrence shrugged and went to sit by Annette and settled in to wait.

And wait they did. The time of their appointment came and went, but the metal shutter remained closed, and there was no activity or notification. After a while the shutter did roll up abruptly with a startling racket, and a dour-faced clinician barked out a name that turned out to be the woman with the boy. They went up to the window to hold a muffled conversation, after which they left and the metal shutter was noisily slammed shut again.

After an hour of waiting, Lawrence could tell that Annette needed to use the restroom, and again stepped up to the metal shutter.

"Hey –" began the guard, but this time Lawrence cut him off sharply.

"My sick wife has been waiting for over an hour, and needs to use the facilities. Since there are none in the waiting room, we either need to get behind that door or we're leaving."

"Siddown, siddown, your turn's coming," the guard growled, but seemed to be fiddling with his phone while Lawrence sat down to reassure Annette. Within a few minutes the shutter again rolled open and a different clinician called out, "Stover!"

"Right here," Lawrence answered.

"That door," the clinician pointed to a doorway on the far side of the waiting room, then slammed the shutter closed again. Lawrence maneuvered Annette's wheelchair over to the door, opened it with some difficulty, and struggled to turn the wheelchair in the narrow hallway. An aide stood by impatiently looking at a tablet while Lawrence managed this, then turned to lead them down the hall, announcing over her shoulder, "Exam room five, down the hall to the right."

Lawrence began to follow, but stopped when they passed a restroom door. Helping Annette out of the chair and into the restroom wasn't easy, but he managed it, and after taking care of her and himself, he helped her back out and into the wheelchair, all under the aide's impatient gaze.

"Are we ready?" the aide asked snidely.

"Now we are," Annette replied sweetly. Hiding a smile, Lawrence wheeled Annette down to exam room five, where the aide left them to what they imagined would be another lengthy wait.

The delay didn't prove as long as they'd feared, as within ten minutes a different aide came in with a tray holding some paraphernalia. From Brady's description, Lawrence guessed that the small beige boxes were the chip implanting mechanisms, though he was a little alarmed to see that there were two of them.

"This'll just take a minute," the aide said as she scrubbed then sprayed Annette's inner forearm.

"What are you doing?" Lawrence asked, wanting to hear the official explanation, and the aide happily provided it. They heard all about the convenience and security and safety of having the medical records kept in this simple, unobtrusive manner.

"In fact, sir, I could set you up with one as well, if you'd like. You'll be needing it eventually, and this way you'll be ahead of the game," the eager aide offered at the end of her spiel.

"No, thanks," Lawrence assured her. "I don't like to get poked until I have to."

"Suit yourself," the aide replied as she held one of the boxes against Annette's skin and pressed the button, producing what sounded like a little snap. "That didn't hurt, did it?" the aide asked when Annette gave a quiet cry. "The anesthetic should have taken effect by now."

"It didn't hurt, but it was a little startling," Annette replied as the aide taped some gauze over the site.

The aide picked up a tablet and held it near the implantation site, and after a few seconds it chirped. "That's good, it's responding already," the aide explained, then lay the tablet on the table beside Annette. "It'll be synchronizing for a while, so please don't leave the room. The practitioner will be in shortly." She departed, leaving Lawrence to examine Annette's arm.

"Did it hurt?" he asked.

"Not really – just pressure, like I said. It feels odd."

"You'll get used to it, I'm sure," Lawrence replied, then changed the subject. Years of discipline, as well as the certainty that the room was monitored, kept them from discussing their true intentions for the chip.

After a lengthy wait a woman breezed into the room. She didn't introduce herself, but her name tag said "Kimberly" just above the bar code. She had a stethoscope in her lab coat pocket and was staring at the screen of a tablet.

"So, Annette, I've been examining your records," the woman explained. "We don't have a neurologist currently under contract, but we anticipate that changing soon. How about we call you in a few days with an update, and if we can line up an appointment then, we'll do so? Your meds look good for now, so I'll just renew them," she tapped the tablet screen. "While we're lining up that neurologist, we can make an appointment with a life counselor to discuss all your options."

"Look here," Lawrence blustered, "we don't want to see any life counselors, we want to see a neurologist. We were told we couldn't go to our regular doctor because we had to come here. I don't want to hear that you don't have a doctor for Annette!"

"Well, I'm afraid we don't yet," Kimberly replied frostily. "Arranging care for such a diverse population takes time, and we're working as quickly as we can. In the meantime, I highly recommend setting up an appointment with a life counselor. As you both know, ALS is a complex, trying, and ultimately incurable condition. We need to examine all options."

Lawrence looked ready to launch into another tirade, but Annette patted his arm. "Thank you for your concern," she said to Kimberly. "Perhaps we'll consider that when we return to speak with an actual doctor. In the meantime, we'd best be on our way. Lawrence, if you will?" The courteous but firm authority in her statement silenced Kimberly, who had seemed to be gearing up to apply further pressure. She stammered a few things then stood aside as Lawrence pushed the wheelchair from the room and back down the hallway. They were in the car and headed home before they spoke again.

"That was a couple of hours wasted," Lawrence grumbled. "And I can guess what kind of 'options' their 'life counselor' would be pushing on you."

"Of course, dear," Annette assured him. "But we got the important thing, which was what we came for." She patted the bandage on her forearm.

"Sure, Brady will be excited," Lawrence admitted. "But I'm still concerned about *you*. If we can't go back to Dr. Gupta, but this new arrangement isn't going to provide you proper care, what are we going to do?"

Silence fell in the car for a moment before Annette spoke again, laying her hand gently on Lawrence's arm. "Sweetheart, we've known since we received this diagnosis that it was only a matter of time. It's all part of the cross we've been asked to bear – the deterioration, the inconvenience of the appointments, the bitter milestones. Whatever the circumstances, we can only bear them with patience and courage. The outcome is in Another's hands."

"I know, but I'm supposed to provide for and protect you," Lawrence replied. "I feel so helpless."

"That's part of the cross as well," Annette reminded him.

That evening Brady came up to the Stover's home in Ubly to test his theory. "Now, you were careful to bring only older phones to the appointment, correct?" he asked.

"Yes, Brady," Lawrence answered with some patience.

"Good. It's possible that after the initial implantation the device hasn't encountered any devices that would transmit its location, but that's what I'm here to test." He held up a phone. "This is an older model, too, so it hasn't gotten the official software patch. I did write a utility that will mimic the effect – it should detect the broadcast from the chip, but instead of transmitting the location, it'll display the data it would transmit here on the screen." Brady tapped at the phone screen to bring up the utility, watched for a few seconds, then smiled. "And there it is, plain as day." He turned the phone so that Annette and Lawrence could see the scramble of labels and numbers.

"Are we sure that's the chip in Annette's arm? Could it be something else?" Lawrence asked.

"I'm fairly sure," Brady assured him. "It's an uncommon protocol, which was probably quite deliberate on the government's part, and there's nobody else around with a chip, right? You didn't get chipped, did you?"

"No. They offered, but I declined," Lawrence assured him.

"Good. Of course, the best way to test is proximity. The chips can only transmit a short distance, so if I were to walk over here…" Brady strolled to the far side of the living room while watching the phone screen. "Well, look at that. There's signal loss, but I'm still picking up. How about over here?" He wandered into the dining room, stopping here and there to examine the phone. "Wow, that's impressive. The signal dies about here, which is a good fifteen, twenty feet from the chip. That gets out to twice the distance in the specification, and this is an older phone. A newer phone might get yet another five to seven feet."

"Is that good?" Lawrence asked.

"Well, it's impressive from a technical standpoint, but for our intents it isn't. It means the signals from these chip implants can be picked up at a greater distance than we thought. By spec, a phone in the pocket of the person standing in front of you in line at the grocery store could register this signal. These field tests indicate that a phone in the next aisle over could do it. It's possible that a phone in a passing car, or even the car itself, could detect it. I need to do a few more tests."

Lawrence and Annette sat patiently while Brady tried a variety of things – standing in different places, holding the phone at various angles, wrapping Annette's arm in several layers of cloth and then in foil, all the while recording a battery of readings. At last he ducked into the kitchen and returned with a damp cloth folded on a saucer. He knelt beside Annette wearing a hesitant expression.

"I've finished gathering the data I can, so we've come to the part that's going to hurt a little. I need to extract that chip from your arm. When it was implanted, your skin had been anesthetized and the operation was quick. I don't have any anesthetic, and I may have to fish around inside your arm to get a good enough grip." He held up a pair of tweezers. "Are you sure you want to go through with this?"

"Of course, I'm sure," Annette assured him. "That's the point of all this, isn't it? I don't want to walk around with this thing in my arm constantly transmitting my position."

"Sweetheart, it's going to be rather painful," Lawrence said in a concerned tone. "Are you sure you're up for it?"

Annette smiled at Lawrence and patted his arm. "You boys should try childbirth some time. Go ahead, Brady, I'm ready."

Brady tried to be as gentle as possible in extracting the small chip, but he still winced in sympathy when Annette's expression tightened as he reached into the fresh incision. She gave Lawrence's hand a squeeze and took some deep breaths as Brady felt about. Finally, he got a good grip on the chip and extracted it triumphantly, holding up the tiny square that looked like a flake of tinted glass.

"Here it is," he said, tucking it into the folds of the damp cloth and pressing a gauze patch against Annette's arm. "Now comes the real test: how well does it do outside of a human body, and for how long? This cloth is about at body temperature." He took the saucer over to the dining room table and took a reading with his phone. "If you still had any questions about this device being the source of the signal, consider them answered. However, signal strength is dropping off quickly." Brady watched his phone for a few more seconds, then extracted the chip from the cloth and held it between his fingers near the phone.

"Well," he finally admitted, laying the chip down. "I'm not sure if I damaged it on extraction, or whether it needs body fluids as well as temperature to work, but the chip stopped transmitting within a minute after being removed. These things appear to be very delicate."

"Will the fact that it's not transmitting any more cause a problem?" Lawrence asked. "Will someone come after Annette?"

"I'm not certain, but I doubt it," Brady replied. "If the online comments are any indication, these chips have a relatively high failure rate. When they stop receiving signals from this implant, they'll probably just chalk it up to a bad chip. Of course, if you go back, they'll notice that it's not transmitting and will implant another chip. You weren't planning on going back, were you?"

Annette glanced at Lawrence. "No, we weren't planning on going back."

*   *   *

The next morning Patrick Hood was standing in line at the gas station with his cup of coffee and muffin. The usual workday crowd was bustling about him, but he didn't even notice. His mind was dominated by a date on the calendar, the next Thursday, and what he could possibly do to protect his wife and baby. Bethany wasn't sleeping well, and was bursting into tears at unpredictable times. Patrick was feeling distraught himself, but tried to maintain his composure for Bethany's sake. He kept groping for things to say to encourage her, to suggest reasons for hope, but his imagination was failing him. He felt so helpless.

Having paid for his items, Patrick returned to his car for the drive to work. He was just buckling up when he heard a chime and felt a vibration somewhere by his waist. He instinctively reached for his phone, then stayed his hand – his phone was in his shirt pocket, and that wasn't his usual ring tone. The chime came again, clearly from his right side, so Patrick fished in his jacket pocket to find an unfamiliar phone. It was an older model, but in good condition and well charged. There was a message on the screen.

Patrick. Drive to the shopping center south of town, park in the lot, and wait for a call on this phone.

What the hell? How had this phone even gotten into his pocket? He looked at the stream of people passing in and out of the convenience store. It was just the usual crowd of off-to-work folk, nobody he recognized. Yet, he guessed, one of them had slipped this phone into his pocket.

Why? And what was this message about? Why should he drive to the south of town? It was the opposite direction from his route to work. And why should he need to? What was wrong with calling him right here? Then he glanced at the signal indicator, which showed barely 10% strength. Maybe that's why they wanted him to drive south, because there might be better coverage. But Patrick knew all the phone carriers had moderate to strong coverage all over the area. Why was the signal so weak?

In his frustration and short temper, Patrick was tempted to just pitch the strange phone out the window and drive to work – he had enough worries. But something was nagging him, and he was a little curious, so he drove south to the shopping center. He'd barely pulled into the parking lot when the phone rang.

"Patrick Hood?" came an unfamiliar voice.

"Who is this?" Patrick asked.

"My name is unimportant, but I'm a friend. Do you want to save your baby's life?"

"My baby?" Patrick was momentarily puzzled, then remembered. "Yes, yes we do. Can you help?"

"Perhaps," the voice replied. "Are you willing to make radical changes to your life, if that's what's required?"

"What kind of radical changes?"

"Fleeing with your family. Abandoning your home, your job, your neighbors, your relatives. Going into hiding, possibly for a long time."

"I...I," Patrick stammered, taken aback by this blunt summary. "Yes, I guess I am. I know Bethany would be."

"Good. We can't promise anything, but we'll do our best to try to arrange an extraction. Your wife's appointment is next Thursday, correct?"

"Yes."

"We're working to pull something together before then. Keep this phone near you and well charged, but keep it turned off. Turn it on at three hour intervals between 6:00 a.m. and 9:00 p.m. by this phone's clock. If anything develops, we'll send messages with further instructions."

"I...okay," Patrick was still uncertain.

"Good. Turn the phone off now, and check again at nine, noon, three, and so on. You might want to set an alarm. We're doing what we can, and will be in touch. Goodbye." The call ended, leaving a stunned Patrick to stare at the phone, a thousand questions swarming in his mind, the foremost being, who was "we"?

Danger Signs

"Good morning, Captain Touma, Lieutenant Fraser," Natalie Griggs hailed cheerily as Katy and her aide entered the conference room. Fraser, of course, gave an upbeat response, and started chatting up Natalie's assistant Stacey as they went to fix coffee. Touma simply nodded cordially and took her usual seat. She found these weekly status meeting tedious, but attended anyway, because the director wanted HHS and DHS to be working "hand in glove" here in the Special Protectionary District – though he left unclear which party was the hand and which was the glove. There was some consolation in the fact that the meetings were so small, since in Touma's experience more participants meant more extended chatter. By HHS protocol the meeting proceedings were Classified, and DHS considered them Secret, so it was simpler to keep the attendee list short – usually only Griggs and Lang from HHS, and Touma with possibly Dylan Fraser representing Domestic Terror. There were no aides to keep records or fetch coffee, though Captain Touma noticed that Lang always had a recorder going.

"Are we ready, then?" Griggs continued as Lang and Fraser found their places. "Shall we begin? How about we begin with you this week, Captain Touma? Anything new to report?"

"Not much," Touma shrugged. "Other than the handful of compliance detainments and disruption pickups you've called us in on, we've mostly been conducting training exercises and running day drills."

"Yes, and my people have greatly appreciated your assistance and professionalism," Griggs assured her. "But you've certainly been busier than that. What of your work at the detainment center?"

Touma smiled thinly, not wanting to let slip that her soldiers considered guarding a prison to be trash duty.

"That's under control. We recently had a minor security incident, but it turned out to be nothing."

"What kind of security incident?" Griggs asked with a touch of concern.

"A drone flyover. Small, cheap drone with very limited capabilities, the type you can buy online."

"Are you certain nothing was spotted?"

"Fairly certain. There was no activity on the site at the time, and the drone was grounded at our security perimeter. Probably just a local hobbyist canvassing the area. We're running a serial number check to be sure," Touma explained.

"Let us know if anything unusual turns up," Griggs said. "I can't tell you how much help it is to have DTD operate that center for us. I know it's makeshift, and strictly speaking outside your mandate, but my legal advisors assure me that keeping all detainment within the borders of the SPD immensely simplifies our mission. Without detainment facilities under the SPD umbrella, our efforts would be diffused by a battery of distractions. Thank you."

"Yeah, whatever," Touma dismissed this bone tossed her way. "We'd been planning to start regular patrols, but that's been delayed – again – by the director's office."

Griggs smiled sympathetically in acknowledgement of her colleague's frustration. "Well, I'm happy to report that our implementation plan is on schedule. We're seeing more patients, and are encountering no more than the usual hiccups with some patients and providers. We're mostly hitting our targets."

"That's great," Touma said flatly. It was hard to fail when you made yourself the only game in town.

"I've also heard from our legal staff that they expect some action on the judicial front soon – favorable rulings that should free up all of our hands."

"That would be welcome," Touma replied. "How are your facilities holding up under the influx of new patients?"

"There's no denying that facility capacity and provider availability is lagging a bit right now, though we're addressing that," Griggs admitted. "We're trying to alleviate that by carefully timed deployment of our new protocols so as to keep the number of new patients within our ability to manage. We do occasionally miscalculate, and end up with patients we don't have room or expertise to handle. But these kinds of wrinkles are to be expected in an implementation of this size and complexity. We're learning as we go, and the experience will be invaluable when it comes time to apply this concept to a bigger venue."

"I wish I could say the same," groused Touma.

"Well," Griggs replied slyly, pulling a paper from a folder with the air of someone producing a surprise gift. "Hopefully you'll soon be able to. I'm going to be proposing an initiative that I hope will offer you and your troops opportunities more in line with your abilities."

"That would be welcome," Touma said. "Which initiative is this?"

"As the scope of the UPAIR project expands, noncompliance becomes a bigger problem," Griggs admitted, slipping the paper across the table. It had a few paragraphs at the top and some tables and graphs scattered across the page. Touma gave it a glance then handed it off to Fraser. "The earlier UPAIR protocols targeted populations that were disposed to compliance, which kept our noncompliance rates low. But as we're rolling out the new protocols, the selection pool has expanded to include a broader swath of the population, which inevitably includes more elements prone to noncompliance.

"Since our compliance numbers are a critical metric for this pilot project, it's vital that we address noncompliance decisively. Up to this point our response has been strictly reactive – we have to wait for a noncompliance event before taking action. You know all about this, since your people have been helping us deal with some of those events."

"Of course," Touma said. "But what are you proposing?"

"I'd like us to get more proactive with our noncompliance posture, and am proposing a modification of response protocols."

"Proactive? How can you know that noncompliance is happening until it happens?"

"We can't *know*," Griggs responded. "But we can reasonably project. Based on a variety of clinical and demographic factors, as well as treatment history and interaction reports, we can use predictive algorithms to identify elements prone to noncompliance and give them special attention."

"That sounds great, but where do we come in?" Touma asked.

"Our tactics for proactively addressing probable noncompliance involve an element of disruption. We expect we'll have to establish protocols that anticipate the noncompliance and take steps to head it off."

"What we soldiers would call striking first," Touma interjected.

"That's one way of putting it," Griggs admitted. "We think of it more as keeping problematic elements off balance. But we have a concern for the safety of our staff. Such problematic elements are notoriously…unpredictable."

"So, you're looking for us to…" Touma prodded again.

"Act as safety escorts, basically. The primary purpose would be to ensure the safety of HHS personnel."

"But in case any of the problematic elements got feisty, we'd be right at hand for the takedown," Touma added.

"I might not describe it in those exact terms, but that captures the gist of it," Griggs said.

"I understand the concept, but unfortunately, I'm not sure you'd want us along," Touma advised.

"But, of course…why wouldn't we want you?" Griggs asked.

"Because of the latest operational directive from the SPD administration that just came out the day before yesterday. Going forward, any time we deploy for anything other than training, we have to issue a field activity alert bulletin at least two hours in advance, preferably four."

"A field activity alert bulletin?"

"Yes. Apparently one of the sore spots with the locals during our deployment last spring was that everyone was taken by surprise. Now, I'd have thought that was one of the points of the whole evolution, but a lot of local officials got all hot and bothered, and came whining to the director. To appease them, he's issued this directive that any time we're going to be operating in their back yards, we have to give them advance notice."

"What kind of advance notice? What do you have to tell them?" Griggs asked.

"That we'll be operating in their jurisdiction, and the operational time frame. We have to state the gist of our operations in general terms, but we don't have to give particulars."

"Who's 'they'? Who would receive these bulletins?"

"First responders – police, sheriffs, fire units, EMT operations. Those were the parties who cried the loudest last spring," Touma explained.

"So, no county agencies or departments other than first responders?" Griggs asked.

"Right, unless you consider a sheriff's department a county agency."

"So," Griggs mused. "If you notified the sheriffs and fire departments that you were planning act as safety escorts from, say, 4:00 p.m. to 10:00 p.m. on a given day, that would suffice?"

"Yes, I guess that would," Touma replied.

"And this directive only applies to DTD personnel, correct?"

"As far as I know – it was given to me at our last meeting."

"I think we can work with that," Griggs said. "You wouldn't have to publicize who you were escorting, or why. If the director pressures us, I think we can make the case that broadcasting our intentions would be fundamentally detrimental to our mission. Besides, I don't think there's much chance of the elements we'll be targeting learning of our movements from first responders, unless the responders publish these field alert bulletins."

"They shouldn't," Touma explained. "I asked the director about that, and he said that he'd gotten assurances that they'd keep the bulletins quiet. If they don't, I'm sure I'll be able to make a case to the director that we should stop them."

"Fair enough. I don't see this as a hindrance," Griggs concluded.

"So, when do you see these…ah…proactive noncompliance responses beginning? How should I prepare my people?"

"Our analysts have been evaluating our expected activity for the upcoming weeks, and are preparing a list of cases with a high potential for noncompliance. The team is working up a solution protocol to propose. Once that protocol is approved, we should be able to firm up a plan. As far as preparing your people, I don't think you'll need to do much – it really will be escort duty, standing by to handle any trouble we might encounter. Nothing that your people aren't already trained to do."

"Sounds like it," Touma said. "Keep us in the loop regarding the timetable. Remember, we have to publish those alert bulletins."

"Ah, yes," Griggs said. "We aren't yet certain, but my advisors have floated next Wednesday as a possibility for an initial foray."

"Next Wednesday? That soon?"

"Yes. I mentioned that the noncompliance incidents are slowly but steadily increasing. That's a trend we cannot allow to continue."

"Well, let us know as soon as you know for certain, so we can prepare the alert and get our teams assembled. Anything else?"

"Actually, there's one thing our analysts recommended I bring up with you," Griggs took out some papers and passed them across to Touma. "It's an ambitious idea, and they've written up the details for you, but they think the suggestion would be better received if it came from Domestic Terror rather than HHS."

"What are they suggesting?" Touma asked, glancing over the papers.

"Constant near-real-time monitoring of all network traffic into and out of the SPD, with interdiction capabilities."

"Near-real-time monitoring? What does that mean in this situation?"

"Our techs have been talking to the National Security Agency and...other agencies since the summer. These agencies see the SPD as an ideal venue for some ideas they've been considering for years. All information these days moves by computer network, even voice traffic such as phone calls. This network traffic ultimately gets passed along a few major data pipelines to routers and data centers before being moved along to its destination. These agencies propose intercepting that traffic to evaluate it for threat indicators."

"I'm not sure I understand," Touma admitted.

"The tech who gave us the briefing explained it like this," Griggs replied. "If the data passing into and out of the SPD can be thought of as water flowing through a pipe, they're proposing putting a digital 'shunt' on the pipe that would divert the 'water' through a 'filter' to be evaluated for contaminants. The 'filter' would be artificial intelligence programs evaluating the data stream for suspect content."

"Really? *All* of the data for the entire SPD? What about the fact that some of it is encrypted?"

"I asked the agency tech the same questions. Apparently, they have some quantum computing clusters ready to devote to the evaluation and decryption effort. The data volume doesn't daunt them – they see it as a proof of concept, a trial run to hone their tools and protocols in anticipation of larger rollouts in bigger venues. The SPD is a convenient test bed for them, and I got the impression they were itching to give their ideas a try."

"Diverting all data for evaluation?" Touma mused. "Won't that delay things? Won't people notice the interference?"

"They don't think it'll be very noticeable, though that's one of the things they'd like to test. People might see a slight lag on their online connections, or a bit of hesitance in phone conversations, but the agency techs don't think it'll affect response speed all that much."

"Wow – completely filtering all network traffic. What would it buy us? Would we get advance warnings? Recordings?"

"The deliverables would be something you'd have to discuss with them. I got the impression that, with all the region's data passing through their filters, the sky's the limit. Traffic patterns, threat analysis, network reconstruction, anything you could wish. One immediate advantage is that it would give you a kill switch over data traffic for any portion of the SPD at any time."

"A kill switch? As in cutting off traffic?" Touma asked.

"Apparently so. Complete data interdiction governed by arbitrarily complex criteria. The tech went on and on about it."

"The ability to throttle data traffic on a moment's notice," Touma said. "That might prove handy."

"I thought you might find the idea alluring," Griggs purred.

"Are they ready to go with this? What would I have to do to activate?"

"The contact information is on the technical summary I gave you," Griggs pointed to the sheaf of papers she'd handed the captain. "The agency techs said they've got everything ready to go when you give the word. I've discussed this with the director, and he's all for it. I'm guessing it would take the NSA techs a little while to bring your techs up to speed, but you could probably have that done before the weekend."

"Thanks," Captain Touma said, waving the papers and handing them off to Lieutenant Fraser. "We'll get right on this. If it works, it may have the potential to really simplify our lives."

"And our lives could all certainly use some simplification," smiled Griggs.

Back in her office later, Captain Touma stared at the papers she'd been handed in the meeting and the reports on her workstation, her jaw set and her mind smoldering with anger. Dammit, she hated taking orders from clinical administrators! She hated having to stand in line to wait for her assignments to be handed through that supercilious Natalie Griggs! *She'd* discussed this with the director, and he was all for it! Any matter of security, data or otherwise, should be primarily under Touma's domain, not that of an HHS bureaucrat!

But that was the way it was here in the SPD – not the way it should have been, but the way it was. The Domestic Terror Division should have had a place at the table – hell, should have been at the head of the table – when the decisions and policies were made to form the District. But because DTD had been missing at the crucial time, HHS had stepped in to fill the gap. As a result, what could have been a working model of efficiency in dealing with subversion and domestic terror had instead become a giant clinical lab, with trained domestic terror troops acting as traffic cops and prison guards! What an opportunity lost; what talent wasted!

Captain Touma's thoughts flicked back to the prior spring, when things had looked so promising for a few weeks, only to have everything collapse in the space of a few hours. It was all Pelletier's fault! It wasn't just the humiliation of being publicly castrated in front of her troops, or even being sent back to Fort Wayne in disgrace to face that inquest. It was the fact that he'd crippled the entire evolution right at the critical moment! Her troops had identified the hidden network of subversives, and they'd had the strikes all planned out. They could have eradicated the traitors in one day, rounded them up and put them away. But no, Pelletier had chosen just that moment, the critical hour, to go soft on the mission. He'd tied their hands and ordered a general stand-down. She'd done her best to deflect his interference, trying to at least get through the day in hopes that their success would convince the higher-ups to override him and allow them to continue, but he'd gone around her, using local officials to undermine her authority with her own troops. He'd even grounded the recon drones, blinding the operation for almost a week! That had given the subversives plenty of opportunity to go to ground, something they were very good at. Now she was left to deal with the messy aftermath.

Damn him! If Pelletier hadn't caved at the critical time, not only would the original evolution have been successfully completed in a matter of days, but DTD would have had more voice in the formation of the Special Protectionary District, and the configuration probably would have looked very different. Whatever had happened to Pelletier – and she'd heard some dark rumors – wasn't bad enough. To think of the trouble and cost and downright danger her people had been put through because of his vacillation, not to mention the shame of the inquest and the shadow over her career, just for the crime of being a diligent and efficient soldier.

It was a mess, and it wasn't her fault, but it fell to her to clean it up. Dutifully Captain Touma turned to the administrative work awaiting her, longing for the day she could get out and be a real soldier again.

*   *   *

Shawn was sitting at his kitchen table scanning the day's messages when his phone rang. It was a Lansing number, but an unfamiliar one. Probably some colleague's staffer fishing for more resources for campaigning.

"Senator Ramirez? This is Jordan with the state attorney general's office. I called Kelly with this, but she suggested I call you as well."

"Oh?" It was unusual for Kelly to have a party call him directly – usually she'd distill the report and give Shawn the summary. "What's the issue?"

"A couple of things, sir. First was regarding the suit we filed on behalf of the family whose child was vaccinated without their approval. Since the legal climate within the Special Protectionary District is kind of vague, we named HHS as the defendant. But when we filed the suit, there was no movement on their part to even discuss the case, much less negotiate."

"That's unusual?"

"For government agencies suing other government agencies, it is," Jordan explained. "Normally once there's notice of intent to file, somebody calls somebody to discuss the case, examine the issues, try to come to agreement, or whatever. In this case, though, there was stone silence. One of their lawyers was present at the filing, and he seemed almost satisfied. It's like they'd been waiting, even – no, I shouldn't say that."

"Say it anyway," Shawn encouraged him.

"Well…" Jordan hesitated, "it's like – this is just my subjective impression now – it was almost like they were hoping we'd file, and were satisfied when we did."

"Really? Can you articulate what it was that gave you that impression?"

"That's the hard part, sir, and why I was reluctant to speak. It wasn't any one thing. His demeanor, I guess, and what he didn't do. It's hard to explain."

"No, I understand perfectly," Shawn replied. He had too much political experience to discount the intuitive insights of seasoned people. "What was the other thing?"

"It's about that search warrant that you wanted us to look into, for that property over by Caro. I sent your request on to the Director of the State Police, who has more experience in such things. He explained that their usual protocol was to look into the paperwork filed on the site and send a letter requesting access for inspection. Depending on the response to that, they evaluate whether it's worth pursuing a warrant."

"All right, if that's the procedure," Shawn conceded. "We don't have any concrete evidence of anything illegal happening there, but we do know there's something going on."

"Right, sir, which brings me to the next point. It is legal under Michigan law for a party to maintain an electronically enforced no-fly zone over their property, so long as the enforcement field doesn't interfere with other electronics, or with emergency or law enforcement efforts."

"That's what David thought. Anything else?"

"That's all for now, sir. I'll get back to you as soon as I hear from the State Police," Jordan said, and rang off, leaving Shawn staring into space and doing a slow fume. Dammit, this stuff was happening in his district, to his constituents! Well, some of it was happening in Connie's district to her constituents, but he and Connie had always seen the Thumb area as something of a joint responsibility, and he knew she'd be just as infuriated as he was. He really should call her or write up a report or memo to keep her abreast of everything he'd learned. Kelly could handle that, but first he wanted to check in with David, so he keyed his field rep.

"Hi, Shawn," came David's prompt response.

"Hey, David. Have you got that new drone yet?"

"On order, and should be in soon. It's got the coolest capabilities, listen to this…"

"Later," Shawn interrupted. "Have you heard anything else from anyone, particularly Frank?"

"Well," David replied hesitantly. "Frank has gone missing. Nobody's heard from him, or knows where he is."

*   *   *

Strangely, Jason enjoyed living by himself in the little house. It was a simple abode and the rhythm of his life was simple. He cooked basic meals then cleaned up, and fed the little flock of chickens and ducks, and mowed the lawn. He read books from the shelves and took walks. Most days he could count on a short visit from Dominic or Julieann or both, stopping in to drop off some groceries or collect eggs or deliver something or other. One useful item they delivered was a bicycle.

For his part, Jason was content to take life slowly and try to remember. The firm certainty of remembrance that had come to him outside the woods had a clarifying effect that strengthened over time. It wasn't that he experienced more or clearer memories, but his personality felt anchored. Before, he'd felt like an escaped balloon being wafted around the park by the afternoon breeze; now he knew he was Jason, and that he'd been here before. He didn't know how much of his past he'd ever recall, but he knew himself for who he was.

As Jason's surety grew, so did his confidence. He took walks and, eventually, bike rides which reached further and further along the long, empty country roads. From the way his body responded to the increased activity, he suspected that whatever his life had been like before, he'd been more physically active, and that during the mysterious lapse not only his mind but his body had fallen out of shape. The sore muscles and shortness of breath were a price worth paying to feel the slow return of vitality and strength that he hadn't realized he'd lost.

The air was beginning to cool as the season made the final turn from summer to autumn, so Jason tried to maximize the time he spent on the bike before chill rains made it impossible. One mild evening he went for a long ride that took him well out among the ripening fields of corn beneath the glow of the long sunset. Even as the evening light faded, Jason pedaled along, confident in being able to find his way home in the bright dusk.

The road Jason was following ended in a three-way intersection, with the crossing road reaching away to his left and right. He could not go straight, since beyond the intersection the land dropped down sharply to the shore. The blue waters of Lake Huron were rippling under the light evening breeze, and above the eastern horizon a large, bright moon was rising. It didn't look quite full, but it was brilliant enough to almost hurt Jason's eyes and cast shadows on the ground behind him. The moon's light made a bright streak of white along the water's surface that seemed to be pointing straight at Jason.

As he beheld this majestic spectacle, Jason felt a surety that he had been here before. Maybe not at this exact spot, but he'd stood on this lake shore and seen such a moonrise at some point in his past. He could recall no specifics, but the emotional echoes he felt were thick with relief and joy and the sense of having escaped something dark and dangerous. Whatever had happened, the last time he had stood on this shore under such a moonrise, he'd just avoided some looming peril. The bright moon over the clear water was how he had known he was safe.

Then alongside, or within, the emotional impressions came a certainty that his escape had not been accidental, that he had been protected and guided out from under whatever that threat had been. And beyond that, he had been guided back here again, to this shore, under this moon. There was a sense of…not inevitability, but surety, that sometime in the past some will had brought him here once to testify to his rescue, and had brought him back again on this evening.

This realization sobered Jason even as it reassured him. It was disquieting to think that even while his reason had been muddled and his will shattered, some other reason and will had been guiding him. It did make him feel a little less like human debris, but it also raised some profound questions. If his steps had been guided here once, and then guided back here, where did his path lead going forward? And what choice did he have in the matter? He hadn't been thinking much about his future, having enough trouble with his past and present, and the days before him were as open and vacant as his memory.

What did lie before him? And what, if anything, should he be doing about it? He had no answers, but as he gazed upon the brilliant white moon floating over the dark waters, something in his memory triggered and he again saw the image of something white and round and – glowing? Illuminated? He couldn't tell, exactly, but the image was important for some reason. A round white thing, suspended or elevated so it was clearly visible. Was that the key? Was that how he knew who had been guiding him and watching his steps? What did it mean?

Jason shook his head. Clues and hints, that's all these were, but he could drive himself mad trying to assemble them into a coherent whole. All he was getting was fragments, and he had to be content with that for now. Maybe he'd get more, and maybe he wouldn't. If he'd been guided back to this shore to witness another moonrise over the lake, he trusted he'd be guided wherever he needed to go. For now, it was enough to have a few more clues to ponder. Perhaps with enough of them some pattern would start to emerge.

With the sun well down and the breeze starting to blow cool, Jason decided to return to his temporary abode. Zipping his jacket, he turned to follow the lake shore road south to find a westbound road that would take him straight back. The brilliant moon would light his way home.

*   *   *

"Are you certain she's ready for this?" Gerald asked Kim as they pulled up to Andahwod.

"As certain as I can be," Kim responded. "Since you last saw her, she's been sleeping a lot, more soundly than before, but still disturbed and uneven."

"Has she spoken much about what's distressing her?"

"Not to me. She'll sit in her chair and mutter to herself, or potter about the apartment murmuring under her breath, but she only talks to me if I ask her a direct question, and then only briefly."

"So, she's preoccupied?" Gerald asked.

"That's a good way of putting it," Kim confirmed. "She's not as distressed as she was before, but something is still on her mind. There's another odd thing she's doing."

"What's that?"

"Remember that *wiga* branch you gave her? She keeps it with her wherever she goes. By her bed when she sleeps, by her chair when she sits, in her hands when she's wandering about."

"Hmm," Gerald mused, unsure what to make of that. "Well, let's hope she'll talk to me." They got out of the car and, as they approached the facility, Gerald tried to adopt a different attitude. What was needed here wasn't Gerald, Kim's brother, or even Mr. Solomon, scholar and activist. What was needed was a tribal elder of the Ojibwa coming for an audience with a seer and wise woman who had received visions. He tried to picture himself approaching a *wigwa* on the edge of a settlement where resided the village *mindimooyenh*, honored and respected and a little feared. He didn't fear Esther, but as they approached the door of her apartment, it occurred to him.

Maybe he should.

They found Esther dozing in her recliner, holding the birch branch draped across her. To Gerald's surprise, it still retained most of its leaves, which moved gently with Esther's light breaths.

"It seems a shame to wake her," Gerald said.

"Yes, but she wanted to see you," Kim replied, tapping Esther's shoulder gently while calling "Esther! Esther! I've brought my brother to see you."

Esther came awake with a small jolt, and after looking around in confusion, settled down quickly when she saw that it was Kim. After some reassurance and explanation, she smiled and nodded to Gerald while Kim fetched her a cup of water.

Gerald stood by Esther, closed his eyes, and tried to ignore his immediate surroundings, to see beyond the apartment walls and furniture. He was on ancient ground, hunted by his ancestors centuries before any European landed on the Atlantic shore. He was of the tribe of the *miigis* shell, the people of the Great Migration. He belonged here, even as he belonged at *Baawitigong*, and this woman had received visions for his people. To accept them, he needed to prepare himself.

"Good afternoon, Mr. Solomon," Esther said after taking a sip of water. "Thank you for coming."

"Lady Esther, it is an honor," Gerald replied, then knelt in front of her and sprinkled tobacco at her feet. He switched to Ojibwe. *"I hail you as a wise woman and seer of the Original People, and have come to sit at your feet to receive what you have to impart."*

"*Thank you*," Esther replied, then continued in English as she patted the seat beside her. "But surely you can make yourself comfortable while you do so. Kim, you as well." The two sat while Esther gripped the birch branch and continued. "I have seen things since your last visit, Gerald, often between waking and sleeping. Nothing so powerful as the word from The Warrior, but swirling images."

"Like…dreams?" Kim asked.

"Similar," Esther replied with a smile. "We all know those crazy pictures that run around in our brains when we're just dozing off. But these images are more…insistent? It's like they keep elbowing their way in, insisting on being heard."

"What are the images saying?" Gerald asked.

"I can only tell you what I discern," Esther cautioned them. "Images can be very difficult to interpret. I see the wound that was in the land; red, raw, and throbbing. I can sense the wicked will that made it, the desire to dominate, to crush and enslave, to devour. Above I see what I thought at first were clouds – long, thin, gray clouds. They are very straight and regular, crisscrossing the sky. I came to see that these are not natural clouds, that would bless with rain or shade, but rather a net."

"A net?" Gerald asked.

"Yes, like a giant net cast over the land, a net of malice and disregard, a net to control with no regard for the people or the earth. A net that would scoop up people like minnows and cast them aside as casually."

"Something our people would be familiar with," Gerald added. "Do you know who is casting this net?"

"No," Esther admitted. "I do not know who made the wound, either. But the net was vast, stretching from horizon to horizon, with wide openings. It was a very large net. And between the net and the wound there was an…attraction? A similarity?" Esther seemed to be struggling for words.

"An affinity?" Gerald suggested.

"Yes, yes, that is a good word. The wound and the net were similar, like two drummers beating complementary rhythms. This...echo drew them together. I do not know if the net came down, or the wound rose up, or if any such thing was necessary, but the gray net became tainted with red, and the red slowly crept across the net. That was what I meant when I said so clumsily that some had escaped."

"I see," Gerald said, though he didn't exactly grasp what she meant. "Have any other images come to you at any time? The Warrior, or any *dodems*?"

"I cannot say that they have," Esther admitted. "Only the image of the polluted netting stretching across the sky, covering the land and entrapping the people."

"That is plenty enough," Gerald said, bowing again. "Esther, I thank you and salute you. You have passed along your burden."

"Thank you," Esther smiled. "I'd planned to do some weaving, but I think I'll sleep a bit."

"I'll fix you some tea shortly, Esther," Kim said as Gerald stood. She went out in the hallway with him, her face etched with concern.

"Could you make any sense of all that?" she asked Gerald. "All that talk of nets and wounds – it doesn't sound at all like her vision of the Warrior. Do you think she's starting to lose it? Is anything she says trustworthy?"

"Oh, I think it's trustworthy, it's just a matter of properly understanding the symbols and metaphors being used. Deciphering that is the key. From some things I've learned recently, I can see a tenuous connection between her vision of the Warrior and what she's being shown now."

"Really?" Kim asked. "I could make no sense of any of it."

"I'm not sure I can, either," Gerald assured her. "I may just be spinning fancies. I won't have a clearer idea until..." He trailed off, his mind racing.

"Until what?" Kim prompted after a few moments, accustomed to her brother's mannerisms.

"Until I talk to as many witnesses as possible," Gerald replied absently, his focus still elsewhere.

"Witnesses? To what?"

"Listen, Kim, you had a few things you wanted to do for Esther, didn't you?"

"Yes, but they shouldn't take me long."

"Fine. I've got some calls to make," Gerald said, reaching for his phone. "I'll be in the lounge when you're done."

Strange Visitor

Luke turned Kilroy onto their road and urged him to a canter. He'd been careful to preserve the horse's strength and stamina during his rounds today, but the animal needed some exercise – as did Luke, as demonstrated by his puffing at the effort to stay balanced in the saddle. He was getting home a little later than he'd expected, which he hoped would mean a hot dinner waiting for him rather than the other way around. Felicity would be excited to hear how he'd been paid at his last stop, which had been the Deming farm. Andy and Josh Deming worked part time for one of the local lumbering outfits, so they had plenty of fuel chits with which to pay him. He now had enough to get their propane tanks refilled, which should ease Felicity's mind. She was always concerned about using too much propane when cooking, which Luke was certain lay behind the recent spate of dinners cooked over the fire pit. Having more propane in the tanks should make her happier.

As much as Luke wanted to dash into the house to see his wife, he forced himself to ride to the stable, remove Kilroy's tack, give him a perfunctory rub-down, and ensure that his food and water were filled before heading in. From the couple of times he'd just tied his horse by the door, he'd learned that Felicity wouldn't be at ease until the beast was properly stabled, so he had resigned himself to taking care of the matter first thing whenever he returned.

Entering their little cottage, Luke saw that his desire to avoid distressing his bride had been in vain – she was distressed already. She was sitting at the unusually messy kitchen table, her hair in disarray and her apron stained, sobbing into her hands. Luke dropped his pack to run to her.

"Sweetheart, what's the matter?"

"Oh, Luke, this afternoon has gone all wrong! I wanted to make roast chicken with homemade bread, but the dough wouldn't rise, and I did such a terrible job of preparing the chicken that it's just a bloody mess that can't be cooked into anything!" She dissolved into sobs again while Luke tried to console her. "It...it was my first chicken, and I was so sure I could do it. Rebecca made it look so easy, and I watched carefully, but I made such a mess when I tried it myself!"

Rebecca was an Amish woman whom Linda had befriended, and Luke knew that Felicity had gone with Linda a few times to visit Rebecca for fellowship and lessons in living simply. One of those lessons must have been on how to turn live chickens into dinner, because live chickens were the only kind they had. Luke figured that somewhere along the sequence of catching, slaughtering, plucking, cleaning, and cooking, something had gone desperately wrong.

"And...and I so wanted to have a nice dinner ready for you when you got home, because you were sure to be hungry," Felicity was continuing.

"Sweetheart, it's all right, it's only a meal, it's not that big an issue," Luke murmured semi-truthfully, trying to set his hunger aside so he could attend to his wife. "I'm sure we can salvage something here – let me clean up a bit for you." He'd learned that clutter tended to dispirit Felicity, so he bustled about picking up bowls and wiping counters. There was indeed a chopped-up and bloody heap of meat and bones and a few feathers in the sink, and a bowl with a solid-looking lump of dough sitting in the bottom. Luke started rinsing and separating the chicken parts until Felicity came to take over while he tidied some more. When he took the garbage out to the fenced enclosure they had to use to keep the bears and raccoons off, he saw the place by the fire pit where Felicity had done the first part of her dinner preparations. There were bloodstains on a log and quite a few feathers scattered about.

"There, now," Luke commented when he got back inside and saw the bowl of chicken pieces that Felicity had extracted from the mangled mess in the sink. "That's plenty of meat to make a hearty chicken noodle soup, or creamed chicken to go over biscuits. And you can boil the bones for stock."

"You're right," Felicity said, leaning against him. "Or I could try chicken and dumplings. I just thought it would be nice to have a beautiful roast chicken on the table for you when you got home."

"I won't deny, it would have been nice," Luke admitted. "But we'll get there. In the meantime, those green beans look good, and you could slice up a tomato, and we've got crackers in the cupboard and cheeses aging in the barn. Let me bring one in – that'll make a fine dinner."

"It'll have to do under the circumstances," Felicity conceded, patting Luke's cheek. "Thanks for being flexible."

They made a decent dinner out of what they could scrape together. Luke told how his rounds had gone, and cheered Felicity with news of the fuel chits he'd earned. They decided that they'd tackle the next chicken-slaughtering jointly, perhaps at the house of someone who had more experience.

"And to think I had visions of having enough time to bake up some shortcake today," Felicity sighed. "I'm sorry there's no dessert for you tonight."

"Oh," Luke smiled as he reached across the table to caress his wife's cheek, "I don't know about that."

The next morning Luke was standing in the kitchen, sipping his coffee and waiting for Felicity to finish up in the shower, when he spotted something at the back of the property by the pond. The morning air was clear but there was a mist along the ground, so he couldn't see clearly, but it looked like somebody was prowling around back there.

Drat! Luke was angry but a little frightened as well. He knew what kind of rough-edged people could be found around here, and while he didn't relish facing down a trespasser, he couldn't have a person of unknown intent and abilities lurking about when Felicity was here alone so often.

On the other hand, maybe it was just some wandering fellow passing through – there were plenty of those as well. Glancing down at his bathrobe and pajamas, he decided that if the figure was still there when he'd finished his shower, he'd go confront whoever it was. Better not mention this to Felicity, though, lest she get nervous.

Luke hastened through his shower and dressed quickly while debating internally whether he should pick up the shotgun from the stable on the way back to the pond. He didn't want to provoke something by appearing too belligerent, but neither did he want to go unprepared. Was showing up armed considered a provocation in these parts, or was it just considered prudent? Not for the first time, he wished they lived closer to someone. He wanted to call Kent for advice, but was sure that would make the older man want to come over, and Luke didn't want to impose on him. Maybe the trespasser would have gone away by now. His insides churned at the prospect of marching out to confront a potentially hostile stranger, but he thought of Felicity's safety and steeled himself.

"Honey, I thought I'd go out to the stable and…Felicity?" Luke strode into the kitchen expecting to find his wife but saw that it was empty. Where was she? Oh, Luke realized, maybe she'd gone out to collect some eggs, and maybe that stranger had spotted her, and – oh, God! Luke rushed to the kitchen window and looked back toward the pond. It was still too misty to see clearly, but it seemed that there were now two figures back there.

Oh, no! Luke grabbed his jacket and rushed out, still torn between going straight to the pond and detouring to the stable for the shotgun. As he ran through the dew-drenched grass, he could see that the distant figures were standing close together, and he was certain that was Felicity's dress. What on earth?

They must have heard him thrashing across the meadow, because the figures turned to look at him. He was close enough now to see that one was indeed Felicity, who smiled and waved at him. The other was a strange man, dressed in worn and tattered clothes, with a short, scruffy beard and blond hair sticking out from beneath a knit cap. The man was standing beside a couple of white things that Luke now saw to be plastic five gallon buckets of the type that could contain anything from paint to spackling. Who was this guy, what was he doing by their pond at dawn with a couple of buckets, and why was Felicity talking to him?

Wary, but wanting to get within arm's reach of his wife, Luke came near to the edge of the pond. "Felicity," he gasped, his breath short from running, "what are you doing out here?"

"Hi, Luke!" Felicity smiled at him with her usual cheerfulness. "This is Bob. I saw him out here and came to say hi. Bob, this is my husband Luke."

"Howdy, Luke," Bob touched his dirty cap and nodded. "I'd offer to shake yer hand, but mine are a bit cold and slimy at the moment, so maybe I'd best not."

"Ah, I...what are..." Luke stammered, taken aback. "Hi, Bob. What...ah...brings you out so early in the morning?"

"I beg yer pardon," Bob nodded, seeming at least a little cognizant of proprieties, "but nobody's lived in th' house fer years. If I'd'a known, I'd'a come knockin' to ask permission."

"Permission?" Luke asked, still puzzled. "Permission to do what?"

"My harvestin'!" Bob explained, as if this was an obvious thing. "I been harvestin' this pond fer years. It's one o' the best on my circuit!"

"Harvesting? Harvesting what?" Luke was still confused, and a little irritated that Felicity was turning aside and seemed to be giggling into her hand.

"Why, leeches! This pond's perfect fer 'em, and I ain't been back here since last spring. Did right well this mornin'," Bob gestured to the two lidded buckets at his feet. Luke noticed a metal plate of some sort and some light chain lying in the grass by the side of the pond.

"Leeches? Are you serious?" Luke asked.

"O' course," Bob assured him with a sly grin. "Not somethin' most people think of but bait shops in these parts pay fifteen, twenty bucks a pound for nice, fat leeches. Terrific bait, just terrific. I can harvest fifty, sixty pound outta a pond like this before 9:00 a.m. Deliver 'em to the bait shops, get paid, go home and take a nap!" Bob lifted the lid from one of the buckets, giving Luke a glimpse of a mass of black sluglike things sitting in brownish water.

"Leeches? You're harvesting leeches from our pond?" Luke asked.

"Sure, he is!" Felicity broke in before Bob could respond. "Isn't it great, Luke? Here's this pond we aren't doing anything with, and Bob figures out how to support himself from it! I think it's wonderful, don't you?"

"I...ah...sure," Luke stammered. "I...uh...wouldn't even know how to harvest leeches."

"Aw, there's nothin' to it –" Bob began, but Felicity gently broke in.

"We'd love to hear the details, Bob – why don't you join us for breakfast? I was getting ready to cook up some pancakes and bacon, and we've got fresh coffee brewed."

"Breakfast sounds great," Bob lit up, but then glanced at his still-dripping hands, which had clearly been up to the elbows in the stagnant pond. "But I –"

"Oh, you can wash up by the stable there," Felicity assured him. "There's a spigot and soap – Luke can show you where."

Luke accompanied Bob to the wash station, where he had a good scrub. As the initial shock and surge of indignation wore off, Luke found Bob an interesting and almost likeable character. He seemed totally devoid of rancor and suspicion, accepting the presence of the young Peterson family without resentment and presuming they'd accept him with similar openness. He was intrigued by all the livestock in the stable, and from the way he spoke about them, was clearly familiar with the care and use of horses. From the eagerness with which he anticipated breakfast, Luke guessed that he didn't get many proper meals. From his general aroma, Luke guessed that he didn't get many proper baths, either, but he was courteous enough at the table, removing his cap and bowing his head for grace and not making a pig of himself despite his obvious enthusiasm for the meal. He downed three stacks of pancakes, several mugs of coffee, and as much bacon as he was given, all the while regaling them with tales of his life and exploits.

Bob had grown up in the area and lived here and there across the seven easternmost counties of the region. He'd traveled a bit, as far as Florida and Texas, but had never found a place he liked as much as his home turf, so he kept returning. He didn't like to be described as 'homeless', but rather as one who slept where he chose. In the summer that was often beneath a tent or a lean-to that he'd constructed beside a shed. He was a little vague about what he did during the cooler months, and Luke got the impression that he wasn't above squatting in empty houses and outbuildings, of which there were many scattered across the area. This somewhat refreshed Luke's uneasiness about Bob, but it was difficult to harbor suspicions about somebody so simple and free of guile.

Bob related how he'd been taught to harvest leeches by an older friend who'd done it for decades. Only certain ponds served, and they needed to be primed ("seeded") with raw liver, which also served as bait to lure the leeches onto the flat metal tray which he used when it was time to harvest them. He had a circuit of ponds which he worked, and Luke guessed that their locations were a closely guarded secret. Bob also had a keen sense of resource management – he'd harvest from a pond several times over a few weeks, then toss in a good amount of raw liver and depart for the season, giving the stock a chance to rebuild.

Luke listened with fascination and Felicity with delight to this plain-speaking, rough-cut man who defied categories. Sometimes he seemed simple enough that he needed someone to look out for him, while other times he displayed a sharp cunning that bespoke hard lessons learned in some of life's harsher classrooms. Luke was surprised to hear Bob lament that he'd never learned the skill of raising medical leeches, because those could be sold for five to seven times the price of bait leeches.

"I gotta say, Luke," Bob said when Felicity left the table to prepare another stack of pancakes, "you got yerself a beautiful wife there."

"Uh…yeah, sure," Luke stumbled, a flicker of suspicion rekindling inside him.

"No harm meant, no harm," Bob backed up, holding his hands open to attest to his pure intent. "Never touch another man's wife, no sir. It ain't done. But she's a pretty lady, and has a sweet heart."

"That she does," Luke confirmed.

After finishing off what Felicity later described as "three square meals" for breakfast, Bob finally sat back, replete, and protested that he really needed to get moving to his clients with the day's catch in order to fetch the best price. He thanked them fervently for their hospitality, and obtained permission to return for a couple more harvests from their pond. Felicity and Luke watched him walk away across their meadow to where his buckets of leeches awaited pickup.

"How does he get them to the bait shop?" Felicity asked as he picked up his gear and started walking off. "Does he carry them all the way?"

"He never said," Luke replied.

"Well," Felicity said with a chuckle, "my mother always said that this world is full of colorful characters. Bob the leech harvester certainly qualifies."

Several days later Luke was attending to morning chores in the stable while Felicity wandered along the far border of the meadow looking for apples. A couple of overgrown apple trees stood right on the edge of the woods. They'd undoubtedly been planted by earlier residents of the property, but had gone untended for so long that they were a riot of tangled, unkempt branches that bore fruit so small and scabbed that it was good for little more than deer feed. Luke made hopeful noises about someday pruning back the branches and trying for a proper crop, but with all the more urgent work the property needed, Felicity suspected it would be years before that happened, if it ever did. Still, she liked to comb through the branches in hopes of finding a few apples that were large and sound enough to enable her to make a pie for Luke.

Felicity had gathered about half a basket of reasonable apples when her attention was caught by a breathy, scratching sound coming from the underbrush to her right. She parted some bushes and was startled to see several piglets rooting about, undoubtedly searching for the same crop Felicity was. Recovering from her surprise, she watched them with interest – she'd been told there were wild hogs all over the area, but had never seen any this close. The piglets were barely taller than her ankle, covered in soft gray hair, and tumbling all over each other as they squealed and nosed about for dropped apples. Felicity smiled – they were cute little things, and clearly hadn't noticed her presence yet. She wondered if she could manage to back away quietly enough that she didn't disturb them.

Even as she began her slow retreat, Felicity heard a louder rustling and low huffing noise behind her. Turning, she saw a full-grown hog emerging from some bushes beside the trail. Her first response was excitement – she'd never been this close to a wild animal! Then a jolt of fear ran through her. The big hog wasn't as cute as the piglets; in fact, it looked menacing, staring at her with small black eyes and making strange movements with its hindquarters. It suddenly dawned on Felicity that this must be the sow that went with those piglets – and she was standing between them.

Felicity's vision narrowed as adrenaline surged through her system. Instinctively holding her basket between herself and the sow, she began stepping away slowly, not sure whether she should continue this steady pace or turn and bolt, whether she should stay quiet or call for help. The sow didn't seem to care – it was still focusing intently on her, even though she was no longer in the way of the piglets, and the twitching and jerking of the beast's hind legs seemed to be intensifying. She wondered whether that was what hogs did just before charging, and what she should do if this one did.

Just then Felicity heard great shouting and hollering toward her left. She looked to see a man running full-tilt toward her, bellowing and waving his arms. Luke? No, Luke was in the stable behind her. A detached part of her wondered if he was trying to warn her about the hog, and how silly that would be, because the hog was plainly visible right in front of her. The man continued sprinting directly toward her, howling and calling and waving his arms.

Then everything seemed to happen at once in a confusing, terrifying blur. She'd just turned from the distraction of the running man to see the hog start charging right for her. She shrieked and turned to flee, but stumbled and dropped her basket, which got tangled in her feet. Part of her brain wondered when the hog would hit her, and how badly it would hurt, when with a great shout and solid thud the running man cannoned into the side of the charging beast and everything dissolved into confusion. Felicity was scrabbling in the dirt, trying to get far from the shouting, squealing mass of man and hog. Her hand fell on a rotten branch lying among the weeds and, feeling like she should do something, she grabbed it and stood to face the melee. The man and the sow were struggling on the ground, looking like they were both trying to escape but were unable to. The hog was thrashing its head about, and at one point snapped at the man, who was pushing her head away. Felicity jabbed at the hog with her stick, then stepped back to try to get distance for a good swing, when the mass suddenly disentangled. The hog scrambled to its feet and ran off squealing into the underbrush. The man got onto all fours before toppling to a sitting position. He was covered with dirt and slime, was clearly favoring one leg, and was holding his left forearm, down which blood was dripping into the dirt.

It was Bob.

Luke was just finishing up a stall when he heard Felicity's shriek. He dashed for the doorway while shouts and what sounded like high-pitched screams came from the direction of the woods. He threw open the stable door, then checked himself long enough to grab the shotgun that stood beside it. Pelting out of the stable and up the small rise toward the meadow, he noticed that the noises had ceased.

"Felicity!" he called, his heart pounding as he looked around for her. He spotted two figures, one of whom was his wife, but the other seemed to be grabbing or groping her. It was a man, and he was clinging to her, while blood stained the front of her dress. Her face was contorted in what looked like a grimace. Looking more closely, Luke saw that the man was that Bob fellow they'd caught back by the pond the other day.

"Hey!" Luke called sharply. "Hey, you, what are you doing? You get away from her!" Instinctively he pointed the shotgun to signal his intent, then with chagrin realized that he wouldn't be hitting anything, because he'd left the shells back in the stable. But his indignation did not abate, and he started running toward the pair. Felicity had spotted him and was gesturing and shouting something he couldn't yet hear. The thought of anyone manhandling his wife filled him with rage, and he decided that if he couldn't shoot the scoundrel, he could club him with the barrel.

"...hurt! Help..." some of what Felicity was shouting was starting to get through. She was waving to Luke to hurry, then he saw the man stumble, nearly falling to the ground before Felicity caught him. Luke's mind whirled in disorientation as he realized that he'd totally misread what he was seeing. The man was hurt, and Felicity was trying to help him.

A different set of instincts kicked in, and Luke threw down the shotgun and ran as best he could through the tall grass to where Felicity was helping Bob to his feet.

"S'okay, s'okay," Bob was mumbling as he tried to wave away Felicity's ministrations. "Just a little sore, I'll walk it off."

"What on earth happened?" Luke asked as he came to Bob's side and got a hand under his arm.

"Bob charged a hog that was attacking me," Felicity explained breathlessly as she lifted Bob from the other side. "His arm is bleeding and something's wrong with his leg, and I don't know what else might be the matter."

"A hog?" Luke asked in amazement. "You're all right, aren't you?"

"I'm fine. I just got knocked down. It's Bob who needs the help."

"Let's get him to the stable and I'll give him a look-over," Luke suggested. "We can move him to the house once I've done some first aid."

"Aw, don' bother 'bout me," Bob muttered. "I'll walk it off."

Once they had Bob settled on some hay bales, Luke dashed to the house for his medical gear. Bob kept up the steady stream of assurances that he was fine, but Felicity noticed that he wasn't protesting too much, and was glad to relax against the hay while Luke looked him over.

"Well," Luke finally pronounced, "all things considered, you got off lightly. That gash on your arm looks nasty, but it doesn't go deep, and your leg joints don't seem to have been damaged. I hope that turns out to be nothing more than impact trauma."

"I think she sat on it when I was down on th' ground," Bob explained. "I tussled with a lot o' critters in my time, but this is my first match with a wild hog."

"We have to presume that arm gash was caused by her teeth, so after I clean and bandage it I'll want to give you a tetanus shot," Luke explained, hoping that tetanus was the only worry, because he didn't have any rabies serum.

"What, are you a doctor?" Bob asked.

"A physician's assistant, technically, but I'm as close to a doctor as some people get around here. I wish I had some topical anesthetic to give you while I clean this out, but I don't, so brace yourself."

"I taken worse in my time," Bob grimaced as Luke scrubbed the arm wound.

"All right, the worst is over," Luke said as he rinsed the spot clear. The wound was shallow, not even reaching muscle, and all the bleeding was capillary. "This part is going to sting, but it'll be over quickly."

"Wait – whatcha got there?" Bob asked, pointing at the bottle in Luke's hand.

"This? Cheap vodka," Luke explained. "Not as concentrated as medical grade alcohol, but strong enough to disinfect, and it's cheaper and easier to obtain. Don't worry, it's safe and effective – I use it all the time."

"Here," Bob reached for the bottle. He took two great swigs then gave it back. "Next time, gimme that in the first place."

"Okay," Luke grinned as he doused the wound and started bandaging. Over Bob's shoulder Felicity was laughing into her hand.

"Can't figger it out," Bob went on as Luke taped his arm. "I never seen a hog act like that. Usually yellin' and wavin' drives 'em right off."

"I was between her and her piglets," Felicity explained.

"Piglets, that make sense," Bob nodded, then added with a hint of a wink. "Y'know, if y'can ever catch a piglet without mom around, they roast up nice. Wonder what they were doin' there?"

"Looking for the same thing I was – apples. I was hoping to gather enough to make a pie, and they were rooting about at my feet. I didn't even notice them until mom spotted me."

"Mmm, love me some apple pie," Bob reminisced with a broad grin.

"I've got you patched up as best I can for now," Luke said. "Why don't we get you into the house where you can rest, and…"

"Aww, now, no need for that, no need," Bob assured him. "I'm real comfy out here. Not th' first time I slept in a haymow, and this is a real nice 'un."

"Oh, Bob, you can't sleep out here," Felicity objected. "Besides, I was hoping to wash and mend your clothes after they were so badly treated by that sow."

"Oh," Bob said, glancing down at his smeared and torn garb. "Well, that's a point. I would appreciate that, truth be told – but you could just bring some blankets t' wrap in, an' I'll be snug as a bug."

When it became clear that despite Luke and Felicity's protestations, Bob was intent on staying in the stable, they conceded the matter and went inside for blankets. When Luke took the blankets back out to the stable, he watched covertly as Bob stripped off his battered clothing, looking for any further signs of injury. Bob's wiry frame had some bruises and scrapes from the run-in with the hog, but from the scars Luke could see, they were hardly the first he'd received.

"Felicity's preparing lunch, which I'll bring out," Luke said as Bob handed over the grubby pile of clothes.

"Ah, lunch'll be welcome."

"Are you sure you'll be warm enough out here?" Luke pressed.

"I'll be fine," Bob assured him. "Comfiest bed I had in a while, an' with a nice lunch made up by yer pretty wife, I'll be right set."

"Well, she'll have that ready soon," Luke said, then extended a hand to Bob. "Thank you for coming to her aid. I shudder to think what damage that animal might have done to her if you hadn't been around."

"Ah, nothin' you wouldn't've done," Bob replied.

"Thank you nonetheless," Luke said, then headed into the house to drop off the clothes and bring out lunch, wondering as he went whether Bob's statement was accurate. Would he have found the courage to charge a wild beast, even if Felicity was threatened? He hoped he would, but honestly wasn't sure.

"Here," Luke said to Felicity as he dropped Bob's clothes into a basket when he got inside. "Take your time with those – I want to pin him here overnight so I can keep an eye on him. He may have a concussion, or some internal injuries, which haven't manifested yet."

"Trust me, cleaning and fixing those is going to take a while," Felicity said, then leaned against him and let him wrap his arms around her. "Oh, Luke, that was terrifying. What a providence that Bob was there." Her frame was trembling as she buried her face in his shoulder.

"Indeed," Luke murmured, his mind still gnawing on the question of what he might have done had it been him.

Bob devoured the ample lunch which Felicity prepared, then wrapped himself in his blankets and dozed off, waking just in time for a large supper. Luke was glad to see that he showed no signs of bleeding or internal pains, though after dinner he suggested that his arm was feeling a bit sore, and another application of antiseptic might be in order. This remedy Luke provided with a grin, seizing the opportunity to administer the tetanus shot. Then Bob begged for his clothing back, not only for warmth but in order that he might move about more freely. Luke agreed to this, and fetched the clothing that Felicity had spent the morning washing and the afternoon mending. He made Bob promise that he'd spend at least the night in case of hidden complications. After helping a little with evening chores, Bob again wrapped himself in his blankets and nestled into the hay, answering Luke's protests with assurances that he was "snug as a bug."

Luke spent a restless night as his imagination ran and re-ran variations on the near-tragedy that had taken place. He finally dropped off to sleep in the small hours, with the effect that he slept later than he'd intended. He awoke when sunlight was filling the room and Felicity had already risen. He was just coming out of the bathroom when she came seeking him, her face etched with concern.

"Luke, Bob's not in the stable."

"What, he left?"

"Looks like it. I went to take him breakfast and found the blankets rolled up in the hay and him gone. I looked all about the meadow and the pond, but found no sign of him."

"I wouldn't have thought he could walk far with that leg," Luke admitted. "Well, he's a big boy, and if he wanted to go, we could hardly keep him. We can only hope that there aren't any hidden complications lurking that might clobber him, and that he checks in before long."

Bob indeed checked in before long, pulling into their driveway in the early afternoon pedaling a battered old bicycle that was pulling a rickety, makeshift trailer loaded with what looked like grocery bags.

"Sorry I didn't leave a note when I left this mornin'," he said apologetically when Luke and Felicity came out to greet him. "But I didn't have nothin' to write on, or with, an' I didn't wanna wake you."

"It's all right," Luke replied. "It was you we were worried about. How are you feeling? Any dizziness or body pains?"

"Naw, I'm fine," Bob dismissed Luke's concerns by handing him a couple of bags and taking some himself. "I'm a tough old bird. My leg's a mite sore, an' I think you'll wanna look at that bandage after supper, but I been hurt worse than that. Besides, those leeches wanted harvestin' an' my customers were waitin'. The Good Lord sure smiled on me today, 'cause I gathered over seventy pounds, an' the shops were so desperate they paid top dollar. An' so," he pulled a thick wad of bills from his pocket and lay it on the table, "that's in payment fer th' medical care you gave me yesterday."

Felicity and Luke both erupted in protest that they couldn't accept payment for treatment of injuries received while protecting Felicity, but Bob remained adamant. "Look here," he said at last, "I been poor, and I seen poor, and ya can't deny ya need it. I'm bettin' that you give plenty o' medical care to people who can only pay ya in eggs or lumber. I been there, and I know. Take it like it was from them."

"Well, then, all right," Felicity allowed. "But what's all this for?" She waved at the bags covering the kitchen table.

"Well," Bob said a little sheepishly. "I may've gone a mite overboard, but it's been years since I had some, an' I used t'love it when my mom made it, so I was wonderin' if I could prevail on you t'make me a meatloaf."

"A meatloaf? That's all?" Felicity asked.

"An' an apple pie, if it ain't too much trouble," Bob pulled out a large bag of apples that had been hidden in the grocery bags.

"Oh, Bob, of course I'll make you a meatloaf!" Felicity grinned. "And I'll make you an apple pie all your own! And, of course, a pie for you as well," she teased her husband when she saw his crestfallen expression.

"Oh, boy!" grinned Bob.

So it was that Bob became a semi-regular visitor to the little homestead, dropping in from time to time for a home-cooked meal or to bunk down in the stable. He was rough-cut and plain spoken, but worked hard and had a firm, if quirky, sense of honesty. He knew a lot of unusual people, and was familiar with many activities in the area that seemed to escape official notice. He was also very good with livestock, particularly horses, and was skilled with saddles and tack. Occasionally he'd help Luke and Felicity take the horses out for rides to ensure they all got enough exercise. He was always welcome and, as Felicity pointed out, proved the truth of her mother's adage that the world was full of colorful people.

Warnings

Patrick Hood had been diligent about turning on the old phone according to the stipulated schedule, but as of yet no messages had come in. This silence was starting to make him nervous, since the scheduled day for the procedure was inexorably approaching and he and Bethany had no alternative but to trust the nameless and mysterious parties who were giving him instructions over the phone that had been had slipped into his pocket. At times his anxious imagination toyed with the idea of just packing a couple of bags and jumping in the car with Bethany to drive as far away as they could get. Sure, he'd leave behind his job and some property, but what was that against his child's life? People had started over before; they could, too.

This morning, though, the phone gave a telltale chime when he turned it on at six. It was a simple message giving him a number and time to call. He decided to go to the parking lot at the shopping center south of town to make the call. An unfamiliar male voice answered.

"Patrick?"

"Yes," Patrick replied. "Who's this?"

"Call me Pippin if you must. We're sorry we haven't been in touch sooner, but arrangements are taking longer than expected. Still, we anticipate everything will be ready on time."

"Is there anything I should be doing?" Patrick asked.

"No. It's important that you and Bethany maintain your usual schedules and activities as long as possible. Don't do anything out of the ordinary, and be sure you don't mention any possible changes to anyone, even close friends and family. It should appear like you've accepted the inevitable, and intend go to the appointment next Thursday without dispute."

"All right, but...what do you mean, appear? Is someone watching who might notice anything different?"

"Patrick, assume that all your movements are being constantly monitored," the voice replied. "You're being watched even now, and all your communications are subject to inspection. That's why we're using this phone. From now on, you should keep it on all the time, and don't let the charge drop below seventy percent. We hope to be back in touch with you soon with a timetable and information about your evacuation contacts."

"Okay, but..." Patrick began, then fell silent.

"But what?" Pippin finally prompted.

"It's just...listen, I don't want to sound ungrateful, or suspicious, because I appreciate what you're doing, but try to see things from my point of view."

"All right, I'll try," Pippin said patiently. "What's your concern?"

"No offense, I hope, but it's almost as scary entrusting ourselves to an unknown voice on a strange phone as it is going to that clinic. We don't know you at all, and this is a big step."

"I understand your concern. I hope it reassures you that we hope to have at least one of your contacts be a familiar face. Maybe not a close friend, but known to you."

"Really?" Patrick asked. "Who?"

"I can't tell you, in case plans have to be changed at the last minute," Pippin explained. "But we've done things like this a few times, and appreciate how hard it is for you. We'll try to keep the trauma to a minimum."

"Thanks," Patrick said.

"That's all for now. Keep the phone on and nearby, even when you're sleeping. Keep some light bags packed. The call may come at any time."

"All right," Patrick replied, and the line went dead.

*   *   *

Todd Beck was driving home from work by a very circuitous route. He didn't like leaving Grace without a car, especially with Tyrone in the house, which was why he usually had her drop him off and pick him up. But today he had to meet someone, so he'd warned Grace that he'd be home late and not to wait up.

Turning onto Nathan Road still made him a bit jittery. With all that had happened there, his emotional response to the familiar fields was a mixture of tension, dread, joy, and amazement. He wouldn't have arranged to meet here but for the fact that it was a place that both parties knew, and one where his companion wouldn't be spotted by anyone else, for the simple reason that nobody came this way.

Todd reflexively doused his car lights for the final two miles, out of both cautious instinct and the desire to see better. There was little danger of other cars along this stretch, and as his eyes adapted, he could discern the patch of wood ahead, dark against the gray of the low cloud cover. By the side of the road beneath the trees was parked a familiar pickup. Todd pulled up behind it, and a man got out to greet him.

"Chip," Todd grinned as he gripped the man's hand firmly. "Thank you for agreeing to meet me so late."

"No trouble on my part – I'm accustomed to odd hours," Chip Keller replied, "though I was a little surprised at your choice of rendezvous spots."

"I know," Todd admitted. "We avoid this place for nearly a year, and suddenly it seems we're back here every other week. But I wanted somewhere we both knew that was also secluded."

"This is about as secluded as it gets. What can I do for you, Todd?"

"I wanted to give you something," Todd replied, taking a device out of his pocket and handing it to Chip. "It's a phone, but not one like your personal or official phones. As you can see, it's an older model, and it's tuned to use a private network that's active in the Thumb region. The private network is gated to the broader telecommunications network, so you can make calls in and out, but for security reasons we suggest you don't unless you must."

"Okay," Chip said warily, turning the phone over in his hands. "What advantage does this give me?"

"The communications that remain internal to the private network don't pass through the circuits maintained by the major providers, which are all monitored by the federal government," Todd explained. "If I were to call that phone using my private network phone, the signals would all go through private routers and switches."

"Am I officially hearing about things I've only unofficially heard about to this point?" Chip asked wryly.

"Well...semi-officially," Todd admitted. "It's not illegal to set up private networks, but it is suspect, since it's the sort of thing bad actors can do. But private networks can also be used for innocuous or even beneficial purposes."

"I'm presuming this network was set up for beneficial purposes by parties who...weren't bad actors?"

"A safe presumption," Todd replied. "I can provide a few more details if you really want them, but..."

"No, no," Chip waved his hands, "if I really need to know more, I'll ask. What am I supposed to do with this private network phone?"

"Keep it nearby, but keep it off most of the time. Turn it on at three hour intervals to check for messages, starting at 6:00 a.m. There are two numbers in the contact list – myself, under the name of Bree, and another named Pippin. If you need to contact me, or if I need to contact you, it's best to use that phone."

"I see," Chip mused, still examining the phone like it was a sleeping rattlesnake. Then he looked at Todd with a burning gaze. "Why are you giving me this, Todd, and why now? Even if it's legal, it's still risky, especially for you. As a sworn public official, I may be required to tell others about this, which could expose your operation, or whatever it is."

"I know, Sheriff. If you think possessing it might compromise you professionally or personally, I'll take it back. But you've proven yourself trustworthy. We don't have anything to fear from you. As far as why *now* – let's just call it a hunch, or an urging. Without going into detail, this communications network was brought up to support a network of covert operations that was abruptly shut down last spring when the feds put the heat on it. Most of the network elements either fled the area then or have lain dormant since, but some of them are having to reactivate to help parties who are being...oppressed by elements of the regime in power over the region."

"I certainly sympathize, but where do I come in? You can't expect me to participate in a clandestine operation."

"No, but you may want an untraceable way to communicate with us. We suspect that federal surveillance within the SPD is getting tighter, and that's based on what we're aware of. We can only guess at what's going on behind the scenes. The ability to communicate without being monitored is becoming a rare and precious thing."

"You got that right," Chip affirmed.

"You don't have to take it, Chip," Todd repeated. "If you have qualms or reservations, just hand it back, we walk away, and this meeting never happened. But if you think it might prove useful, particularly since the need for clandestine communications might be reasserting itself, then keep it."

"I won't deny that I've heard rumors over the years," Chip admitted. "Do you think it's coming to that, though? Needing to get people away to safety? Or are you just preparing for the possibility?"

"It's upon us. There's a situation I know of that will require action within days to save a life. The problem is that we're flying blind. We have no idea what kind of resources the feds can bring to bear, or how they might deploy them. You saw last spring just how ugly that can get. We'll have to make some of it up as we go along, and with lives at stake it helps to have as many resources as possible."

"I can't promise I'll be much good as a resource, but I will hold onto this," Chip held up the phone. "Having a secure channel for reaching you will be worth the risk."

"I hope you never have to use it," Todd replied. "Any standard charger will serve. Needless to say, don't leave it lying around."

"Needless to say," Chip echoed. "Thanks."

"Thank you. Maybe we can get together for coffee sometime when things aren't so crazy – and hazardous."

"Hasten the day. That'd be great – you can fill me in on how married life is treating you."

"Well, it'll be treating me better if I get home soon, so I'd best be on my way," Todd replied.

The Beck household was quiet when Todd pulled in, but Grace was in the kitchen scooping peanut butter with celery sticks and swilling grapefruit juice.

"Hi, hon," Todd gave her a kiss. "I was hoping you'd be in bed."

"So was I," Grace assured him, "but Junior here decided that my dinner wasn't enough and wanted one of his own. You're home late."

"Yeah, I had an errand to run."

"Anything to do with the Hoods?"

"No, unfortunately. I haven't heard a word," Todd replied.

"I hope somebody's doing something," Grace said grimly. "Their appointment is this week, and I don't know how the clinic staff is going to respond if they miss another one."

"It's probably taking more time to spin things back up than they anticipated. Also, resources in Northfarthing take more time to line up. They're poorer and more spread out up there."

"Be that as it may, I hope somebody gets off the dime soon, because their baby's life is at stake."

*   *   *

Shawn was on his second cup of coffee and reviewing election prognostications when a call came in from Kelly at the office.

"What's up?"

"Just heard from the state police on the matter of that search warrant for the old mental health facility over by Caro," Kelly explained. "In response to their letter of inquiry, they received an official communique from the Legal Affairs Office of the Special Protectionary District. They advised the state police that the site is under the authority of the SPD and is outside state or local law enforcement jurisdiction. No requests for inspections or search warrants will be honored. Furthermore, the site has been declared a no-surveillance zone, and overflights by private or public equipment will be denied – as David discovered."

"Did they give any rationale for all this?" Shawn asked.

"Apparently not – just 'reasons of security', according to the state police. They forwarded me a copy of the communique, if you'd like to see it."

"No, but archive it," Shawn said. "This is pretty creepy."

"No kidding," Kelly agreed.

"Anything we can do about this? Contest it? Appeal it?"

"The state police were pessimistic. We'd need to file suit, and because it's the feds it would have to be in federal court, and we'd need both cause and standing, and at best we'd only obtain the right to obtain a warrant – then we'd have to go justify the warrant," Kelly explained.

"Uphill all the way," Shawn said. "Anything else?"

261

"Well, speaking of federal court, I had some research done about charges brought in federal courts last May."

Shawn probed his memory, trying to recall what that was about. Ah, yes. "Right, right, just after the alleged detainments. What did you find?"

"Nothing. There was no increase in filings in either the Detroit or the Bay City courts. If a lot of people were arrested, they weren't charged in federal court. Filing traffic was completely typical – if anything, a little slow, especially in Detroit."

"And we know there wasn't a rush of charges filed in circuit or district courts," Shawn added. "So, if people were arrested, what happened to them?"

"That's the question, isn't it? Oh, one other thing – David submitted an expense for the replacement drone. It's...quite a total."

"Pay it. Keep me posted on any developments, particularly from the attorney general's office."

"Sure thing."

Shawn returned to the political analyses, but couldn't concentrate on them – his thoughts kept returning to the getting-more-mysterious Caro facility, and what might be going on within them. It wasn't even in his district, but hell, this kind of stuff wasn't supposed to be happening in America! He was just pondering whether he should call Connie to try to enlist her help when his phone rang again. This time it was Chip Keller from up in Huron County.

"Sheriff Keller?"

"Hello, Senator. I hope I'm not disturbing you – your office told me to call you at home."

"No disturbance. What can I do for you?"

"I wanted to let you know that our office has received an advisory memo from the office of the Director of the SPD. It boils down to official notification that SPD personnel may, at their discretion, engage in 'compliance enforcement evolutions' within our jurisdictions. The nature of these evolutions, and what kind of compliance is being enforced, is not detailed," Chip explained.

"Is that unusual?" Shawn asked.

"For federal law enforcement, it is. Usually if they're operating in our back yards, they consult with us at least, if not actively cooperate, unless there's good reason not to."

"So, you're completely left out in the cold?"

"Not completely. They say they'll send out an 'imminent activity bulletin' when they're about to engage in one of these compliance enforcement evolutions, but they don't give any details on what the bulletins will contain. My guess is that we won't know where, or when, or what kind of force they'll be deploying – just that they'll be doing something."

"What good does that do?" Shawn asked.

"I don't think these bulletins are as much for our sake as for theirs," Chip explained. "The biggest backlash from that debacle last May arose from the fact that it was essentially a surprise attack. Everyone was caught flat-footed, including first responders. By issuing these bulletins, DTD can claim that they gave us advance notice, probably without telling us anything of substance. My guess is that it's just coverage for them."

"And the director of the SPD sent this out?"

"Well, it was under Buchanan's letterhead, but it was actually from a Captain Touma of the Domestic Terror Division. Apparently, she's the compliance enforcement supervisor, whatever that is."

"I think I've seen her," Shawn said. "Listen, I'm back in district now and will be until after the election. If you get one of these bulletins of imminent activity, could you notify me immediately? If possible, I want to see one of these compliance enforcement evolutions in progress."

"You sure, Senator?" Chip asked skeptically. "If last May is any indication, things might get a little rough."

"Yes, dammit, and it's my constituents they're being rough on!" Shawn nearly barked, then checked himself. "Sorry, Sheriff, I didn't mean to snap at you."

"No offense taken, Senator," Chip assured him. "I appreciate your concern, and just wanted to ensure you understood the potential risk. Also, if I or my men end up in a difficult situation with you present, they might feel obligated to protect you even if it means compromising their effectiveness."

"You can tell your men that if I'm along, they're to ignore me and protect my constituents. I wouldn't be along just for thrills, Sheriff. I want to witness, and possibly record, any actions taken by the feds within the SPD. There's been too much happening in shadow within this arbitrary district the feds created. I intend to start turning on some lights."

"I'm with you there, Senator. I'll keep you updated," Chip assured him, and rang off. Shawn tried to return to the articles he'd been browsing, but soon gave up and snapped his tablet shut. He was too distracted mulling over possibilities and considering options. Every nerve in his being cried out to do something, but he couldn't figure out what. After all, this was the federal government, and ultimately, they held all the trump cards. What could he do to protect the people of his district?

He'd never felt so impotent.

Back in his office, Chip rocked in his chair, gnawing on the problems that had landed on his desk. The memo from the SPD made him nervous – the memory of last May was still fresh in everybody's mind – and now a well-intentioned but over-eager state senator wanted to be kept in the loop, possibly so he could ride along. Despite Shawn's assurance that he wanted no special treatment, Chip knew that the instinct to safeguard dignitaries was too ingrained in his deputies to be set aside casually. Would the senator's presence prove a hindrance during a field operation? Still, the senator had a point about being a witness, and if anybody had a right to be present, it was an elected official. Besides, it would be hard for even the feds to silence a sitting state senator.

Which didn't mean they might not try.

Chip's eyes strayed to where his uniform jacket hung behind the door. Tucked securely away in a zippered inner pocket was the phone that Todd had given him, the untraceable device that used the private communications network. Chip knew that such a device wasn't illegal, but he couldn't shake the feeling that even possessing it put him on the border of a murky and ill-defined world – the kind of place he never liked being. Of course, he'd deliberately approached that world, back when he'd gone to Lawrence Stover with his suspicions about what was going on in northern Huron County, and then when he'd enlisted his aid to execute that operation against Raymond Hubbart's slave-staffed factory. *That* had been murky and ill-defined, far more than he'd anticipated.

But he hadn't been sheriff at that time, Chip reasoned, and now he was again. He'd always taken a dim view of elected officials who behaved as if the obligations of their oath of office ended with working hours. As far as Chip was concerned, being in elected office meant upholding every aspect of that office and setting an example, even on weekends or on vacation, which meant avoiding even a hint of suspicious or marginal activity.

But what to do when those around him ignored those principles? His office gave him power over his fellow citizens, but that power was bound by strict laws and protocols, and even stricter principles of courtesy and fairness. Yet others with even greater powers were operating all around him with no regard for any such restrictions. How was he supposed to respond when his hands were tied by constraints that other parties disregarded? What was he supposed to do when injustice was inflicted by those who were supposed to uphold justice? Did that justify turning to the murky, ill-defined world for help?

Even as he considered this, his phone rang. Picking it up, he saw that it was Gerald, the Ojibwa official from Canada.

"Good morning, Gerald."

"Good morning, Sheriff," came Gerald's voice. "I hope you slept well. I have a favor to ask, which I hope won't prove too onerous."

"What might that be?" Chip replied guardedly.

"If possible, I'd like to meet with the parties who were witnesses of the events at the woods last spring. There are some things that I've learned that might be further illuminated by the accounts of actual participants."

"Well, I was one of those witnesses, but I think I've already told you everything I can," Chip said.

"I agree, but by your own admission you were a peripheral player that night. I'd like to talk to some of the people who were more involved, especially those who knew the woman who entered the woods."

"Teresa? That'd be a pretty short list, but I'll see what I can do," Chip replied. "But it'll have to be later in the day, after I'm off work."

"That's fine. The sooner the better, though, if possible – my vacation is supposed to be ending soon. I'm not anticipating anything too taxing, maybe just meeting them by the woods for an hour or so."

"That doesn't sound like too much to ask, though I can't answer for scheduling complications. Let me contact them and get back to you."

"Thanks, Sheriff," Gerald said.

Chip rang off and looked at his jacket again. With everything else coming down, he now had this visiting scholar to try to accommodate. Well, it wasn't much of a request, and he'd just fob it off on Todd. It would give Chip an opportunity to test that private network phone, which was why he wanted to make the call after hours. He was willing to serve as a go-between to set up this appointment, then hopefully that would be the end of it.

*   *   *

"Hey, honey," Todd Beck gave his wife a kiss as he got into the car, then glanced in the back seat. "You didn't bring Tyrone?"

"No, he was in the middle of some drawing and was comfortable being left. He's been quite stable recently, and is familiar with my picking you up from work, so I figured it was worth the risk. He has my number if something comes up," Grace explained. "How was work?"

"The usual – tiring," Todd replied. "They want to start training me on a new press." He fell silent for a minute before speaking again. "Chip called me at break on the secure phone. Seems this Gerald wants to meet up with some of us sometime soon."

"What for?" Grace asked.

"Apparently he wants to talk to witnesses – people who were there last May. He wants to meet at the woods to interview us, as soon as he can. Chip says he hopes to keep it under an hour."

"Witnesses?" Grace asked. "There weren't many. Luke and Felicity are unavailable, and I doubt Fr. Gabriel could make it. That leaves you and me – and Jason, come to think of it. What did you say?"

"I said I needed to talk to you, but I presumed we could make it. Since time is an issue, I told Chip we could make it tomorrow after work, if Gerald didn't mind meeting in the evening. You could pick me up and we could go straight there," Todd said.

"If he's looking for witnesses, we should be able to provide plenty of background, since we were there not only last May, but the prior July, when the shadow – that is, when the slaves were freed," Grace pointed out, then added. "For that matter, we could bring Tyrone. He wasn't there in May, but he lived in the compound, and may be able to answer some questions we couldn't."

"A thought," Todd admitted, "as long as the questions don't get too stressful, or we keep him out too late. Any word from the Hoods?"

"Nothing – I was hoping you'd heard."

"Nope. I've been tempted to call Patrick, but I don't want to stress him."

"I hope something gets moving soon. The appointment is the day after tomorrow in the later morning. I know snatches are played close to the chest, and they like to time them tightly to preserve an appearance of normalcy as long as possible, but this is shaving it pretty close."

"They may not plan to involve us at all," Todd reasoned. "If all goes smoothly, the Hoods will simply vanish for the right reasons, with the help of the right parties."

*　　　　*　　　　*

The following night Gerald was waiting at the gate in the fence outside the woods when Todd, Grace, Jason, and Tyrone pulled up. The sun was well down, but the night was warm for early October and the few clouds that drifted across the clear sky were eerily illuminated by the nearly full moon that was rising in the east.

"Thank you for coming, especially at this late hour," Gerald greeted them.

"I'm sorry there couldn't be more of us, but Fr. Gabriel's schedule wouldn't allow it, and the other two witnesses are unavailable," Todd explained. "We'd like you to meet Tyrone, who is a witness of a different nature. He was one of the workers in the complex in the woods who was liberated the night that…well, the night the fog appeared. Tyrone, this is Mr. Solomon of the Garden River Ojibwe tribe."

"A pleasure, Tyrone," Gerald greeted him. "Whatever you can tell me may be especially helpful as I try to learn about what actually happened here in light of some other things I've learned."

"I'll help as I can, sir," Tyrone replied. "I just worked the line here until I was rescued, then I been living with Mister and Miz Oldham, until coming to live with Miz Grace."

"Why don't you begin by telling me what life was like inside the compound?" Gerald asked. "You don't have to tell me anything that stresses or upsets you, but anything you can remember would be good."

So, under the October sky, with wispy clouds scudding across the stars, Tyrone told in dispassionate detail what the brutal life at the factory had been like. Grace's heart ached, and an occasional tear seeped down her cheek, as the lad recounted the harsh work schedules, the beatings, and the rest of the cruelty. She stayed close beside him, occasionally holding his hand, ready to step in the moment the memories got too painful to relate, but that moment never came. To Grace and Todd's increasing amazement, Tyrone exhibited none of the skittishness or reluctance that they'd been worried his memories would trigger, nor did he shy away from telling of even the most traumatic incidents. Grace almost turned away, and even the stoned-faced Gerald winced, when Tyrone told of the trips to the bleachers and what they'd been forced to witness there, but the lad kept speaking.

When Tyrone concluded with the account of the night the slaves were freed and how he'd ended up being fostered to the Oldhams, Gerald clapped him on the shoulder. "You've been very brave to tell me all this, Tyrone. I know it must be hard to relive that terrible experience, but you've done very well. I have a couple more questions. One is, do you remember anyone around the complex who looked like me? Anyone with dark, straight hair, dark eyes, and brownish skin? Anyone who looked Native American?"

"Mostly it was people who looked white, like Mr. Nick and Mr. Nathan. Somebody told me they were mostly related," Tyrone said, thinking. "But…there was one day – it was the second time I went out to the bleachers. By the hog pen, on the other side, there was a short man who was watching. He was skinny, and looked kinda like you say – dark hair, dark skin. I couldn't see his eyes 'cause he was too far away."

"A short, skinny man," muttered Gerald as he looked into the distance. "Maybe. Maybe. Can you tell me more about the mysterious fog that filled the woods the night of your escape?"

"Nossir, not really," Tyrone admitted. "We were in the barracks when the yellow lights started flashing, and I was supposed to push the button, but the pretty lady didn't want me to, and she stood in the way. Then all the lights went out, and then the safety ladies came in and took us through the woods out to the road. I remember it was foggy, and Mr. Nathan found us and came out with us, but I don't know much about the fog."

"Todd would probably be the best person to ask about that," Grace explained. "He was in the woods when the fog started."

"All right. Thank you, Tyrone, for your courage and cooperation," Gerald said. "Hopefully your story will help someone in some way."

While Todd related how they'd learned about what was transpiring within the fenced woods, and had assembled an informal strike team to try to liberate the workers, Jason was wandering along the security fence. The detailed histories with names and places meant little to him, but for some reason the security fence caught his attention. The relatively new links glistened brightly in the clear moonlight, a silver web encompassing a patch of simple woods, woods that no longer held shadow or terror. Yet as the others spoke of the mysterious fog that had risen and thickened among the trees on that summer night, it seemed to Jason that the fog that had clouded his memory was thinning and lifting. Yes, he *had* been here before, he knew that for certain, but details were becoming clearer. He was getting past ungrounded flashes of emotion and tantalizingly brief scenes flicking through his mind. Entire memories, complete with details and antecedents and context, seemed to be emerging from the mental mist that had plagued him. He strained to hasten the thinning, to discern more clearly what these recollections were, but his straining was in vain. The unveiling was progressing at its own pace, and he had to wait for it.

One thing was becoming clear: these woods were pivotal. Though miles from anything, and reachable only by dirt roads, the intentions and efforts of so many parties had converged here. The half square mile enclosed by this fence had been the locus of great and terrible deeds, tremendous evil countered by great good, malice that had been unleashed but promptly contained, a sinister intelligence that had bided its time, testing its bonds, seeking channels of escape.

Jason was coming to realize that nothing had been as it had appeared. Even if he were to recover his memory completely, the details would still deceive, for he would not be recalling the true reality, the forces behind what could be seen and manipulated. He'd been to this place more than once, had driven right along this stretch of fence, all the while oblivious to what lay behind it, to the entities that had been summoning him, ensnaring him, manipulating him to their own ends. Nothing had been as it had appeared, and the hidden reality had been the greater. The true vision lay just beyond the reach of his recollection. It was slowly becoming clearer, but there was nothing he could do to hasten it. Faces were appearing in his mind, and names to go with them, along with emotions which were sometimes sharp. A black-haired man named Ethan, associated with feelings of anger and betrayal. A dark-haired man in uniform, oily and ambitious – Collins. A sharp, angry woman, also in uniform, apparently named Touma. He clutched the fence and closed his eyes, pressing his forehead against the cold links, trying to block out the talking behind him, surrendering his efforts to force things along, accepting the slow pace at which recollection was returning.

Meanwhile, Todd was concluding his tale of the night that the fog had risen to thwart their plan. Gerald nodded slowly, his face grim.

"Can you make any sense of that?" Todd asked. "I'd never seen anything like it."

"And you can pray to your god that you never will again," Gerald replied. "I can only speculate, based on some things I've learned, and what I've heard here tonight. What happened here may have been what some might call black magic, as black as it gets, possibly involving human sacrifice and cannibalism, and the calling of the darkest evils known to my people."

"Your people? But it was the Hubbart family..." Todd began, but Gerald interrupted him.

"Hubbart may have been the mastermind, but I suspect the execution was done by another. The comment Tyrone made about seeing a man that looked like he was First Nation – that, and other things, make me suspect a hidden actor, someone behind the scenes, working his evil in the shadows." Gerald sighed. "There are such people, there have always been such people, in every race and nation. Some in our tribes try to gloss over it, to dismiss the darker chapters of our history as European propaganda, to perpetuate the mythology that before European influence we were an innocent and benevolent people. Those few of us who have delved deeply into our lore know better. I'm sure there has been propaganda through the years, but there were also tribes known for their corruption and brutality long before the Europeans arrived. The Aztecs with their bloody rites would be a glaring example, but even in this area the Munsee had a reputation for dabbling in the dark arts. And though some would contest it, even the Anishinaabe have had members and families who sought the darkness. These factors, plus other…messages I have received, make me strongly suspect that a First Nations party was involved somewhere. Wait – Todd, did you say that all of your people were rescued that night?"

"Yes, though Dan committed suicide some months later," Todd replied. "And none of us were…unaffected."

"And all the workers were rescued," Gerald mused. "But then – wait, what about the staff at the factory? Chip said there were several."

"Yes, there were," Tyrone confirmed. "Line supervisors and guards and others."

"How many would you guess were on the site that night?"

"I dunno, honestly, sir. I think about two dozen regularly around the factory. Can't say about outside – we weren't allowed outside."

"I'd guess between two and three dozen to run a complex that size with that many workers," Gerald said. "Did any of them get out?"

"Just Mr. Nathan and that other man," Tyrone said.

"Joe. Joe somebody, I forget his name," Grace added. "There were two of them on the path. We met them on the way in and again on the way out. They were guarding the path, and were…blinded. Nathan knew them. We offered to bring them both with us, but only the Joe guy accepted."

"There were lots of sounds in the fog," Todd said. "Screams and crashes and gunshots. They were far away, but very scary as I sat there blind, waiting to be rescued. Eventually the sounds trailed off, but the silence that followed was even more ominous."

"And none of them came out, except two," Gerald muttered. "A massacre indeed." Then he seemed to shake himself and turned to Grace. "But you alluded to your experiences. Could you elucidate a bit more?"

"I suppose it all started with a strange and frightening incident that occurred when Felicity and I were coming home from school…" Grace began.

*   *   *

In a conference room at a DHS facility south of Marysville, Captain Katy Touma stood before a screen upon which was projected a map of the Special Protectionary District. A faint grid overlay the map, and little clusters of numbers showed up here and there. About a dozen bright red spots were scattered across the screen. Rows of chairs were set up facing the map, and in the chairs sat black-clad troops with sidearms, their attention focused on the captain.

"All right, people, we've just received word from the clinical side that all our targets are safely where they're supposed to be. Our objective is to bring them all in for the treatment they seem to have so much trouble showing up for. To reiterate, the objective tonight is detainment with as little disturbance as possible. We slip in, detain the targets, and slip away to deliver them to the clinical staff. Ideally you won't even wake the neighbors. Questions?"

One of the troops in the third row raised his hand. "What's our threat level for this evolution, ma'am?"

"Officially, the threat level is the same as the entire SPD, which currently stands at low. However, I'd like you all to comport yourselves as if the level was moderate. All the targets are known noncompliers, and though we can't know for certain how much overlap there is between them and the hiding terrorists, I'd prefer you to err on the side of caution. I'd rather explain to the director how a couple of noncompliers got handled a little roughly than explain how some of my troops got wounded or killed. Of course, if we all do our jobs smoothly and the targets come along quietly, no explanations will be required, will they?"

Another soldier toward the rear of the room raised his hand. "How much overhead cover will we have?"

"Every team will have eyes overhead watching the evolution. Unarmed, for obvious reasons," Touma said with a wry expression. "The birds are standing by at Selfridge, waiting for our go-ahead. Coordinating our movements with drone control is one of the touchier aspects of this exercise. As explained in your op orders, this is a timed action – we want to keep all the strikes within a five minute window. Each team has its target location and optimal route pre-loaded into its devices, and those teams with geographically closer targets will have to loiter until teams with more distant targets get into position. And when I say 'loiter', I mean do so inconspicuously, so no donut shops. Drone control has our schedule and will time their launches so that the birds arrive over the targets shortly before execution time. I'll be in Marlette with reserve forces, so if we hear either from you or through drone control that you need help, we can dispatch them. Any further questions?"

There was no response to this, so the captain stepped aside for Lieutenant Fraser to issue final orders. "Mission clock starts now. Get to your positions. When we see everyone's in place, and the birds are overhead, we'll green-light your move on target. Dismissed."

There was a general rustle as the troops rose and made for the exits. Captain Touma was speaking to a technician who sat before a workstation at a side table, an earpiece in her ear.

"Comms, I'm shifting to TacComm Marlette now, so keep me posted on any developments, particularly from the clinical side. Also, send that notification I had prepared."

"Yes, ma'am," the tech answered.

"And contact NSA to tell them to activate the data interdiction plan we'd worked out."

"Yes, ma'am."

"Very well. Come on, Sickles, let's get going," Touma said to her driver, who had been standing by.

*   *   *

Chip Keller was tidying up the kitchen and setting up his coffee maker for the morning when his phone rang. It was Angela over at the dispatch desk.

"Hey, Angela."

"Hey, chief. Sorry to disturb you so late, but you said to call you immediately if one of these ever came in, so I am."

"One of what?"

"A notice from the SPD that they're carrying out compliance enforcement evolutions."

"What, tomorrow? Does it give a time or location?" Chip asked.

"Nope. It just says 'commencing immediately'," Angela replied.

"At ten thirty at night?" Chip said incredulously. "Why would they send something like that out at a time like this? They have to mean first thing in the morning."

"I wouldn't bet on it, chief," Angela cautioned. "The message reads like boilerplate, and is flagged as routine, but if you read carefully the timetable says 'immediately'."

"In the middle of the night?" Chip was still astonished.

"My cynical instincts guess that you weren't meant to see this until you got in tomorrow morning," Angela explained. "I'll admit, if you hadn't left clear instructions, I would have just tucked it in your folder."

"Who else got this message?"

"All the sheriffs in the region – you, Corrigan, Morris, everyone. Port Huron and Lapeer police. A few others."

"So, it's a general bulletin."

"Looks like it."

Chip's internal alarms were going off. He remembered last May all too clearly. This whole thing smelled. "No geographic information? No addresses or specific locations?"

"Nope. Just 'within your jurisdiction'," Angela confirmed.

"Okay, Angela, I'm heading back out. Call the dispatch desk of every entity on that list, and if they haven't notified their principal, *strongly suggest* that they do so immediately. I'm certain Al and Amanda will want to know, and I'm pretty sure Tim will as well. Who's out behind the wheel tonight?"

"Tom just went on at 20:00, and Ron's on till midnight."

"Call Ron and tell him to be prepared to stay out longer. I want you out there, too, if you can – call Bea and ask if she'd like some overtime. If she does, get her in – if not, find somebody else. I want as many eyes on the road as possible."

"Okay," Angela replied. "What are we watching for?"

"I'm guessing they're not crazy enough to try a full-on assault like they did last spring, but watch for black vehicles traveling together, possibly in convoy. Everyone knows the look of those DTD vehicles."

"Oh, sure, chief. We can spot SPD goons a mile away."

"Well, here's your chance to spot them in the dark. All sightings to be broadcast and tracked. These jackasses are up to something that they don't want seen. We're going to do our best to find out what it is."

"Got it, boss."

Chip rang off, fuming. Late night notifications. What a slimy trick. Spotting his uniform jacket hanging by the door, he remembered something. Fetching the phone Todd had given him from the zippered pocket, he keyed the contact labeled "Bree". A familiar voice answered.

"Sheriff?"

"Listen, Todd – you told me unofficially that this network of yours was working on some imminent activity. You might want to hurry along whatever that is, because my office just received notification that the SPD is going to be performing some compliance enforcement evolutions tonight."

"Tonight, as in right now?" Todd asked.

"No times were given, but the wording of the notification indicates that they're currently in motion. Maybe they're hoping to get a jump on everyone; they certainly tried to slip the notification past my office. If you had something in the works, you might want to advance the timetable."

"Thanks, Chip. We'll take action on this," Todd assured him.

"I don't need details, but if you could tell me the approximate vicinity of the impacted parties, I could vector in some resources to at least keep watch for them. The feds know where they're targeting; we don't."

"These parties are located in the Sebewaing area. I'll be advising them to move quickly, probably toward the east."

"You might suggest they stay within Huron County, at least initially. I have some of my people out looking for the feds. Tell your parties that if they see a sheriff car, to flag it down and stay with it. I'm alerting the other counties, but I can't predict how those sheriffs will respond."

"Thanks, Chip. I'll call them."

Chip rang off and stood pondering. He was itching to get back into his uniform and get out on the road, but something was nagging him. Someone had wanted a call – Senator Ramirez, that was who! Chip wavered – he wasn't sure the senator would appreciate a call at this time of night. But then, he'd given Chip strict instructions to be notified; what he did with the notification was his business. The senator lived down in Port Huron, and Chip doubted he'd want to drive up here to the upper Thumb at this hour. He reached for his phone and was about to key the senator's number when he paused and looked at the private network phone. Todd had said that it was gated to the public phone system, but it wasn't monitored. Deciding that would be the better choice, Chip brought up the senator's number and keyed it into the private phone. It rang for a long time before a sleepy voice answered.

"Hello?"

"Senator Ramirez, this is Chip Keller up in Huron County."

"Sheriff Keller?" The voice came more awake. "This isn't your phone, is it? I almost didn't answer because I didn't recognize the number."

"I'm calling from a secure phone, sir. Sorry to be calling so late, but you asked to be notified when we received a notice that the SPD would be doing compliance enforcement activities, and we just did."

"What, they just notified you now?" Shawn asked.

"Our dispatch desk received the message about fifteen minutes ago," Chip explained.

"This is for tomorrow, right?"

"No times were given, so we're assuming that the message should be taken literally, and the activity is taking place right now."

"In the middle of the night? That's fishy." Shawn said.

"That's what we thought," Chip replied. "I've got a few deputies on the road, and hope to have more soon. I've told them to watch for federal forces moving in the area."

"Wait – you don't know where they're going?"

"We weren't told details regarding time and location, just that there would be activity within our jurisdictions," Chip explained.

"That's beyond fishy – that's ugly," Shawn growled.

"Agreed. Hopefully we'll have more information soon, and I'll keep you–" Chip began, but Shawn interrupted.

"Wait, Sheriff, I'm coming up there."

"Are you sure, sir? This late at night?"

"Yes, I'm sure. I understand that you may not even find any federal forces, but if you do, I don't want to be an hour and a half away."

"If you're certain," Chip cautioned.

"Very much so. Where should I come? Your offices in Bad Axe?"

Chip pondered for a moment. "Tell you what – take I-69 west to Imlay City, then go north on M-53. I'll contact the other sheriffs along your route so they can send escorts – that way you can drive as fast as you feel comfortable. I'll meet you at the county border."

"Sounds good."

Chip rang off and headed back down the hallway to where Erin was already in bed. He kissed her cheek and started pulling on a fresh uniform shirt. "I've got to head out again. Something's come up," he explained.

"Mmm. Any idea how long?" Twenty six years of marriage to a law enforcement officer had gotten Erin accustomed to the fact that 'something' always came up.

"No idea. I hope to be back by midnight, or shortly thereafter."

"Be safe," Erin murmured.

"I'll sure try."

*   *   *

Todd was listening to Grace recount her experiences that dark night when they were all interrupted by a clear, sharp cry. They looked over to see Jason, who'd been standing silently by the security fence, stepping back from it with his hands raised and a startled expression on his face. His eyes were open wide, and to Todd he looked more alert than he'd ever been. There was no hint of vagueness or confusion about him, and his voice was clear and firm.

"I did this," Jason announced to his startled companions. "All of this is my handiwork."

Grace and Todd looked at each other in bewilderment, but just then Todd's phone rang. Seeing that it was Chip, he stepped aside to take the call while Grace answered Jason's assertion.

"Jason, what do you mean? We've just heard how Ray Hubbart and his family had this going for years. The night when the slaves were freed, when the fog appeared, was long before you were in the area."

"No, no, I don't mean that," Jason gestured toward the wood. "I mean this – all this." He waved his arms toward the sky, further puzzling everyone. "I just saw it all, for the first time, I think. I didn't know I was doing it, but I was…"

Just then Todd stepped back to the group wearing a grave expression. "That was Chip. The SPD is moving – now – and he strongly suspects they're going to try to pick up Patrick and Bethany. I'm calling to warn them right now, and then calling Steve. We need to get moving." He keyed the number for the phone Patrick had been given.

"Hello?" Patrick swiftly answered. Todd suspected the Hood household wasn't getting much sleep that night.

"Patrick? This is…ah…Bree. You need to get out of your house immediately. We've gotten word that the feds are moving, and are probably heading for your address. You need to get out now."

"Are you sure they're coming for us? The appointment's tomorrow."

"We're not completely sure, but do you want to take a chance?"

"No. Where should we go?"

"Anywhere. Come east. Try to stay within Huron County for now, and if you see a sheriff car, flag it down and stay with it. Avoid other official-looking vehicles."

"That's all? Just get in the car and drive?"

"Yes!" Todd nearly barked with impatience. "We're working out details to get you safely out of the area, but right now, as you love your wife and child, get moving."

"All right," Patrick replied. "We have some bags packed, just in case."

"Fine, but no electronics, other than the phone you're holding. I'll be back in touch," Todd rang off and keyed Steve McLean.

"Bree?"

"Yeah," Todd replied. "We have a crisis. I just scrammed the current case. We got credible word that the feds are executing 'compliance enforcement' in the region, and though no specifics were provided, I figured it would be better to be safe."

"At this time of night?"

"Yup. My source speculated that they might be trying to catch everyone off guard, and I concur. Since our case has been non-compliant at least once, I figured they might be one of the targets if the feds are doing some kind of sweep."

"Oh, hell," Steve replied. "I've been on the phone with Northfarthing finalizing details. We were planning a staged stealth removal tomorrow morning about the time the husband would be heading to work. We wanted to be as unobtrusive as possible."

"That's probably been shredded, so find a Plan B. I've got them out of their house and on the move, but we need a safe destination and route to get there. County law enforcement has offered sanctuary if they're spotted, but even that's chancy, and is certainly temporary."

"Right," Steve affirmed. "For now, keep them moving while I try to work something out."

"Work quickly, okay?" Todd urged, then rang off and returned to the small group that was looking at him with anxious expressions.

"Crisis?" Grace asked.

"Pretty much," Todd replied, then gave them a briefing on the situation.

"Given my heritage, you have my sympathies," Gerald said. "Not to seem obtuse, since I'm sure there's good reason for this, but why don't they just drive away? Get in their car and head for Vegas or somewhere?"

"They could try, but we're almost certain that they'd get nabbed before they got too far," Todd explained. "You may not be aware, but every vehicle sold here in the States is required by regulation to respond with its geolocation if it receives a triggering signal, which the federal government can send. We know how to disable that ability, but we haven't done it with the Hood's car. But even if we had, or if they'd done something like switch cars, they'd probably be spotted. Especially since the SPD was created, we suspect that surveillance efforts have been stepped up significantly. The roads are being constantly monitored."

"*All* the roads?" Gerald asked skeptically. "The Thumb is a big area to watch, even for the feds."

"With vehicular traffic, you don't have to watch all of it," Todd replied. "The region is bounded by expressways and rivers. The expressways are under constant video surveillance, and we suspect they've added active-trigger monitoring as well."

"Active-trigger?" Gerald asked.

"They can set the monitoring stations to ping every passing vehicle, and sound an alert when a sought vehicle goes past. Whether they've activated that capability or not we don't know, but we do know that every overpass and underpass on every expressway bordering the SPD has been rigged with monitoring stations. The bridges over the Saginaw River have long been watched. You simply cannot drive out of the Thumb without passing under a government camera. We also presume constant high-level drone surveillance, so there's no place to hide, unless you get under some kind of cover – trees, parking structures, or the like."

"But couldn't you drive through an urban area like Flint or Bay City? Sneak out on surface streets?" Gerald suggested, but Todd shook his head.

"Urban areas are even worse. Cameras watching all the streets, traffic monitors recording every passing car – all sorts of things you want to avoid. Plus, it's the Thumb, so even in the city the harsh reality is that you will eventually have to cross an expressway or river to get out, and all those crossings are monitored."

"Damn," Gerald grinned. "For a moment I was entertaining dreams of them slipping across over at Bay City and running up the west Saginaw shore to the reservation north of Pinconning. It's small, but it's sovereign Ojibwa territory, and they could seek refuge there."

"Good thinking, but if we could get them that far, we could get them farther to our hideaways in northeast Michigan, the area we've dubbed Northfarthing," Todd explained. "The problem is getting them out of the Thumb without being tracked. Other parties are working on that, so our immediate tactic is evasion – keeping us and them out of hostile hands."

"But isn't that a futile effort so long as they're driving their car?" Grace asked. "That'll be known to the SPD authorities, and it can be geolocated at any time."

"Yes, which is why we have to arrange a car swap as soon as we can. Maybe Steve will come up with something quick, but for now we should try to meet up with them so they can ditch their car."

"How can we manage that? We barely have room for us," Grace asked, looking at their small car.

"I'll help. My van can hold a lot of people," Gerald offered.

"Gerald, we couldn't. This isn't your problem, and we don't want to get you in trouble," Todd said. "I was just about to suggest you get out of here as quickly as you can. This could get very ugly."

"I fully understand that," Gerald replied, "but as I said, I have great sympathy for anyone caught in the grip of government machinations. It gives me no joy to see that Europeans are as good at oppressing each other as they are at oppressing non-Europeans. Besides, it may help you to have an observer at hand who is neither American nor, strictly, Canadian. It may give them pause."

"Or they may just sweep you up with everyone else," Todd cautioned.

"I'll accept that risk. What's our next move?"

"I've been pondering that," Todd said, examining a map on his phone. "I'm trying to think of a good rendezvous point, given our guidelines."

"What are your guidelines?" asked the perpetually curious Gerald.

"Avoid urban areas and main roads, because both are more likely to be watched," Todd replied tersely as he scanned the map. "Get far away from areas where you're expected to be. Seek as much cover as possible. We hope we got them away from their home quickly enough to avoid hot pursuit, so now we want to put as many miles between them and their address as possible, trying to remain within Huron County for the time being."

"What good will that do if the authorities can remotely interrogate their car to discover their location?" Gerald persisted.

"Gerald, we realize the SPD is essentially a police state," Todd replied with strained patience. "There just aren't many good options. We have to seize opportunities when we can. If it takes DTD twenty minutes to discover that they've fled, that's twenty minutes during which we can work on alternatives. There – Ruth. Let's have them meet us in Ruth. We can shuffle about there. Hopefully Fangorn will have come up with an exit strategy by then."

"Why don't most of us travel in my van?" Gerald suggested. "Not only is it completely foreign to the area, it's Canadian, so the circuitry won't have the same triggers and responses as American cars. Plus, it's roomier."

"All right," Todd said. "I'll lead the way, but don't follow too closely. If I get stopped, turn aside and try to get away."

With that they piled into the two cars and headed for the little crossroads of Ruth, about half an hour to the south and east. Todd called the Hoods to inform them of their destination. Gerald drove in pensive silence, muttering to himself, but Grace's curiosity was burning.

"Jason, before we were interrupted by those phone calls, you had been saying something about this being your handiwork. I got the sense that you'd made some sort of breakthrough. What did you mean by that?"

"I did make a breakthrough, or was given one, I think," Jason replied. "Many of the details of my last time in the area came back to me, almost like snapping into focus. Not all of them – parts are still vague – but enough to tie some vital things together."

"Oh, how exciting for you!" Grace said. "Can you tell us some of these details?"

"I can relay what I understand, though I think my new perspective may not exactly match how I looked at things before. I was sent to the area to resolve an open issue of some type, a calamity about which there were unresolved questions. The details of that escape me, but I think that's because they're irrelevant now. I think it had something to do with the monument in the back yard by the pond."

"Sam's monument?" Grace asked.

"If that's the one, yes. I saw it on the day I met you. But the more important thing I came to accomplish was to get a stalled effort working again. This was the thing that mattered most. If I succeeded at getting this effort going, it would gain me great favor and advance my prospects substantially. That's what I put most of my effort into, and I was – tragically – very successful."

"Tragically?"

"Yes, because what I was setting up was a system for eliminating people – unwanted, unwelcome, expensive people. That's what the earlier system had been for, the system that had gotten stalled, except that it had been limited and inefficient."

"I think I know the system you're talking about," Grace said.

"Maybe. I put much effort into building a better system to replace it, streamlining and focusing the effort. When I was done, I'd created an optimized killing machine that reached every corner of the region.

"But I hadn't known about what had happened in the woods back there. I did come too near a couple of times, and was entrapped by the menace that lurked there, but I had no idea what it was or where it had come from until I heard Tyrone's account tonight. I did see the final night, when Teresa walked into the darkness, but even then, I didn't grasp the damage I'd done."

"I'm still not comprehending, Jason," Grace insisted. "I mean, I understand your role in setting up the clinical network, but I don't see the connection to the spiritual damage that took place in the woods."

"I didn't understand, either, until just now," Jason replied. "You have to look at it a certain way, but when you do it makes perfect sense. The two events had the same foundation – a very utilitarian outlook, a callous disregard for people. The spiritual damage, so to speak, had already happened when I began my work. The nature and intentions of the two were so similar that there was...I don't know how to describe it...an alignment? A synchronicity?"

"A harmonic resonance?" Grace offered.

"Yes, that would be a good term," Jason said. "A resonance between them, so even though the savagery in the woods had been contained, it could still exert influence over what I was building all around it. Yes, that is a way of putting it."

"That sounds like something one of our seers might say," Gerald said.

"Very clumsily put, but how can one describe such things?" Jason replied. "It helps explain why things got so brutal so quickly."

"What do you mean?" Grace asked.

"Even last May, when the forces were let loose to eradicate the domestic terror network I'd been told was here, I was shocked and dismayed at how brutal everyone was. Maybe I was just a fool. I knew there would be coordinated activities and field teams and arrests, but I was envisioning people knocking on doors and serving warrants. When it turned out they were kicking in doors and smashing windows and even firing missiles, I was aghast. But it makes more sense now. If what I'd built was getting tainted by whatever was contained within the woods, then one would expect inordinate savagery."

"So that's how some of it escaped," Gerald muttered.

"What was that, Gerald?" Grace asked.

"Nothing, just making another connection," Gerald said. "I'm hatching an idea here, though – how long to our destination?"

"From right here? Maybe another fifteen minutes," Grace said.

"And then maybe another fifteen, and then…" Gerald replied, then announced, "I'm going to pull over for a minute. I need to look up a number and make a call." He pulled onto the shoulder of the road and dug out his phone. It took some searching to find the contact he was looking for, but he finally found it.

"Hunh?" came the grunted response.

"*Lean Bear*," Gerald said in Ojibwe. "*This is Gerald Solomon of the Garden River Tribe. We have met. I am brother to Kim Masters of Mount Pleasant.*"

"*I think I remember you, cousin,*" the voice answered.

"*How has the fishing been?*" Gerald asked.

"*You call me this late to ask about the fish?*" the voice growled.

"*No, but to request your aid. I invoke tribal emergency. The murderous Europeans are at it again. How soon can you get to your boat, and how much fuel do you have?*"

"*Twenty minutes. I am half full, good for twelve to fifteen hours, depending on speed and conditions. Who is in danger? Our people?*"

"*No – some Europeans, and perhaps an African. Can you get to your boat and fill up? I will cover the fuel.*"

"*The Europeans are eating their own now?*"

"*When have they not? The plan is still being worked out, but if I need you it will be swiftly, and you will need to be close at hand. Please fill up and get underway. Make for the eastern shore of Saginaw Bay. I will contact you with more details.*"

"*You ask much, Gerald Solomon.*"

"*Lives are at stake, Lean Bear. We cannot look aside. I will make good all your expenses, and will commend your deeds to the elders.*"

"*Hunh,*" Lean Bear's grunt made clear his opinion of this last incentive. "*Could this expedition get me into trouble with that new government operation that they have set up over there?*"

"*Almost certainly,*" Gerald assured him.

"*Hunh. I'm on my way.*"

"*Thank you, Lean Bear,*" Gerald rang off and turned to the others. "Forgive the Ojibwe, but that was a man I've only met once, a fellow member of our tribe, who takes great pride in our heritage. I guessed he'd be more receptive to my request if I posed it in our own tongue. He has resources that may help, depending on how our plans develop. I wanted to mobilize him in case we can use him."

"But...we don't have any plans yet," Grace replied.

"Oh, I'm always planning," Gerald explained.

In the car ahead, Todd's private network phone rang. "Hello, Pippin?" he answered.

"Ah…Bree, have you met up with your subjects yet?"

"No, we expect to be at the rendezvous in fifteen or so. I expect them arrive ten to fifteen minutes after that."

"This is going to take some delicate handling, because I just realized something. The woman has been to a clinic recently, hasn't she?"

"Yes," Todd affirmed. "That's what precipitated the crisis."

"Then she's probably been implanted with a chip that allows them to track her. They say it's for caching medical records, but it also alerts nearby phones and other smart devices to its presence, and they transmit the location to the government."

"Just modern phones?"

"And cars, and probably other devices we don't yet know about. Our tech has been researching this – it's insidious," Steve explained.

"But we use older phones that have been patched, and older cars as well. If we keep them away from…" Todd began, but Steve interrupted him.

"No good. These things can be picked up by passing cars, phones in the pockets of people nearby, and probably lots of other things. Maybe if she stood in the middle of a forty acre field by herself, nothing would be picked up, but that doesn't help us. We need to get her out of the district, and that'll involve passing potential transmitters. The minute she does that, they'll squawk her position."

"Damn," Todd said. "Let me check with her once we meet up. Maybe she didn't get this thing. And speaking of getting her out of the district, how are those plans proceeding?"

"Haltingly. I'll keep you posted, and in the meantime, keep moving, through low-population areas as much as possible."

"We'll do our best," Todd replied, and rang off. He tried to pray, but found it hard to concentrate under the suffocating feeling that events were closing in on them far too quickly.

Pursuit

Captain Touma and her driver arrived at the Tactical Command center in Marlette to be greeted by a sergeant who provided a status report on the deployment. She nodded in satisfaction to hear that her teams were moving into place without complication.

"Oh, and we've received word from HHS that one of the targets is on the move," the sergeant added almost as an afterthought.

"What?" Touma snarled, wheeling on the man. "On the move? Why wasn't I notified immediately?"

"They...they just informed us shortly before you arrived, ma'am," the sergeant replied haltingly.

"When did the target start to move? Where did they start from, and in which direction did they go?" Touma demanded.

"Ah," the sergeant fumbled with his tablet, "they...they were Target Seven, near Sebewaing. They departed their address about forty minutes ago, apparently heading east."

"*Forty minutes?* And it took them this long to tell us? Damned incompetents," Touma growled. Stepping over to where a map of the SPD was projected on the wall, she located Target Seven. It was only thirty minutes east of Bay City. Toward Bay City would be the most direct route for someone seeking to escape the SPD, yet the target had driven in the opposite direction. It was almost as if they had known, or suspected, that there were troops stationed on the bridges and along I-75 poised to pounce on anyone foolish enough to try to bolt. But why east? West made sense, or even south – not that they didn't have that covered as well – but east? What could they be thinking?

Maybe they weren't thinking. Maybe they were just fleeing in panic. But if so, their timing was damn suspicious. What if they'd been alerted? What if they were being guided, aided by some parties who had a plan in mind? What if they were in touch with the domestic terror network that had been in hiding since last May? This might be her chance to get a lead on that elusive enemy.

"Where is the target now?" Touma demanded. "Why isn't its location being displayed on our tactical maps?"

"I...uh, just a second, ma'am," the sergeant fumbled, stepping over to talk to a technician wearing a headset. After some discussion, the sergeant took the headset to speak to someone on the other end. Eventually he returned to the increasingly impatient Touma. "The last position was just east of Ubly, ma'am, and still heading east. Apparently, the HHS system can't transmit live data directly to ours."

"Then have that tech get regular verbal reports and manually plot them on our maps," Touma growled. She examined the map and tried to mentally plot the target's trajectory. East of Ubly? There was nothing east of Ubly but farmland that ran to the lake. What were they intending? When they reached the shore, they'd have to turn north or south. North would get them nowhere but around the top of the Thumb and eventually back to their starting point. South would take them to Port Huron, which she had well covered. A desperate dash for the Canadian border, perhaps? Foolish and hopeless, but maybe they were trying it. But then, that was a long coastline, and this was a maritime area – perhaps they were thinking of a water escape? Could the terror network have resources for that?

"Sergeant!"

"Yes, ma'am?"

"Send that dispatch I'd prepared to Coast Guard Air Station Detroit. I want a chopper in the air in fifteen minutes. Meanwhile, divert some recon drones toward the eastern coast, and notify any nearby teams that I may need them as backup – but only after they've subdued their targets. How close are we to trigger time?"

"Most teams are in place; furthest units are ten minutes from their targets. Anticipate all teams in position and ready in fifteen," the sergeant replied.

Touma tapped her foot in agitation. She wanted to get out after the fleeing target, possibly to catch whoever was aiding them. But the entire evolution was poised to execute, and if she was on the road, it would be more difficult to deal with the inevitable screw-ups. Oh, Fraser could address them from secondary in Marysville, but she didn't trust him to straighten out a paper clip. No matter how strong her urge to head out in pursuit, prudence dictated she stay here until they'd bagged the targets they could.

"Very well," Touma said. "Let me know when all teams are in position and ready. Instruct the team that was assigned to Target Seven to head east and stand by as primary backup. That notice did get sent out to local law enforcement, didn't it?"

"Yes, ma'am," an aide replied.

"Any response?"

"No, ma'am."

"Very well." Touma tried to settle in and watch the amber dots on the map turn green as the teams reported in. One dot over by Sebewaing glowed bright red, and a blinking red dot now flashed slowly on the map just east of Ubly. Touma glared at this only anomaly in her well-planned evolution. Oh, you just wait.

*   *   *

Gerald followed Todd into Ruth, turning south along Ruth Road. Todd turned immediately into an elevator complex that stood there, parking between two giant silos.

"This is good for now," Todd said as he got out to greet the others. "A drone would have to be directly overhead to spot us, and even then it would have a hard time seeing past the conveyer pipes. Patrick and Bethany should be about ten minutes away, but we have a complication." He explained what he'd learned from Steve about the chip implanted in Bethany.

"So, this thing is always transmitting her position?" Grace asked.

"Apparently it works with phones and other smart devices," Todd said. "Steve didn't go into detail, except to say that if she was isolated from those types of things, this chip would be ineffective. But that's not realistic, since any path of escape is probably going to take us through relatively populated areas, which will have devices that can pick up this chip's signals."

"Do they have a path of escape in mind?" Grace asked.

"Steve says they're still working on it. They'd had something nearly planned out, but this nighttime sneak attack knocked it into a cocked hat. I'm not sure what they're considering now."

"Actually, I have an idea to offer," Gerald chipped in. "But this tracking chip may cause problems if we can't figure out what to do with it. Do we know she has one?"

"Not clear yet," Todd admitted. "We'll have to wait for them to show up, which should be any minute."

*   *   *

The U.S. Coast Guard was organizationally close to the Domestic Terror Division, a connection the Coast Guard was reluctant to admit in public. They were both divisions of the Department of Homeland Security, so it was easier for DTD officials to swing their weight around when it came to requisitioning Coast Guard assets – which didn't mean the Coast Guard had to like it. Air Station Detroit was located at Selfridge Air National Guard Base on the shore of Lake St. Clair, about twenty miles north of the city of Detroit. The Air Station always maintained a helicopter in ready state and a crew on standby in case of a search and rescue call. Tonight, the duty pilot was Lieutenant Commander Erick Dunne, with his copilot Lieutenant Shannon Lock and flight tech Petty Officer Robert Fleury. They were all in a briefing room talking with their commanding officer Commander Rhodes via videoconference about the DTD directive that had just come in. A simple search and rescue call would have had them in the air in ten minutes, but Lcdr. Dunne had (correctly) judged that the CO would want to be awakened to discuss this irregular mission.

"So they want you to fly the coast of the Thumb to look for 'suspicious vessel patterns'?" Cdr. Rhodes asked as he examined his copy of the directive. "What the hell is a 'suspicious vessel pattern'?"

"No idea, sir," Dunne answered. "Perhaps they'll provide clarification."

"And just along the coast? Not out over the water? No search patterns?"

"So it would appear, sir. Just up the Huron coast and down the perimeter of Saginaw Bay," Dunne affirmed.

"This would be simpler if they told us what the hell they were looking for," Rhodes grumbled. "What have we got ready?"

"One of the older Super Jays, sir," Lock said. "It's fueled and checked out."

"Fine, then, take it," Rhodes waved. "Nice clear night for flying."

"Very well, sir," Dunne replied, and they rose to make their way to the helicopter.

*　　　　*　　　　*

Todd called Patrick and Bethany to let them know where to find the little group. The Hoods pulled into the shadow of the silos and clamored out of their car, holding small duffels and looking panicked.

"Bethany, when you went to the clinic, did they implant a chip in you anywhere?" Todd asked first off. "Inject or insert anything?"

"Yes, in my arm," Bethany held out her forearm. "They said it was for tracking medical records."

"Yeah, but it's for more than that," Todd explained. "It also broadcasts your position using networked devices like phones and newer cars. We should be all right because we've got older cars and special phones, but if you even drive past a newer phone, it'll pick up the signal and transmit it."

"Is this phone new enough to worry about?" Patrick held up his recent model, and Todd looked at him, stunned.

"Patrick! I thought I told you to bring no electronics except the private phone!"

"You...I'm sorry, I thought you meant no electronics in the bag," Patrick held up the duffel he was holding while Bethany guiltily produced her phone.

"Oh, God," Todd groaned, nearly tearing his hair. "This probably means they tracked you all the way here! We have to get rid of those immediately, and then figure out what to do about that chip..."

"Wait!" cried Jason, who had been spending a lot of time since their arrival by himself, walking back and forth in the shadow of the silos. "There may be a better way. How much do we know about these chips? How are they powered? What is their range?"

"I don't know – I'd have to call Steve," Todd replied.

"Then call, and quickly."

"Ste–er, Pippin," Todd asked when Steve answered. "These chips – how are they powered?"

"Body heat. It creates a trickle of current, enough to transmit about a dozen feet, though they can reach as far as twenty."

"What happens if you remove it?"

"It dies pretty quickly. They seem to be quite fragile."

"What if they are quickly and carefully placed in another body?" Jason had Todd ask, evoking stares of astonishment.

"Not certain – that hasn't been tested," Steve replied. "What are you thinking of trying?"

Jason waved at Todd to wrap up. "No time, Steve. Do you have a plan yet?"

"We think so, but we're poking holes in it right now."

"Hurry up. If they've tracked us here, we have minutes," Todd said, then rang off and turned to Jason. "Okay, Jason, what were you thinking of trying?"

"I know these operations," Jason explained. "If you kill the signal abruptly, you'll telegraph that you're onto their secret. They'll fall back on other resources, and come after you much more aggressively. They'll send drones to monitor the last known position and vector in troops to entrap you."

"But we have to do something," Grace said. "We can't have them tracking us, either."

"We need to decoy them until it's too late for them to do anything about it. Yes, we need to get that chip out of Bethany's arm, but we need to put it in another arm, then send it off, *with* Patrick and Bethany's phones, while you all escape in a different direction."

"Send them on a wild goose chase!" Grace exclaimed. "Brilliant, Jason! Only – who do you figure would be the goose? Whose arm were you thinking of transferring the chip to?"

"I was thinking mine," Jason replied, evoking stunned looks from the others. Gerald was the first to respond, stepping up to Jason and bowing deeply.

"That is a noble act, worthy of an Anishinaabek warrior. I salute you, sir."

"But…Jason, we can't ask that of you," Bethany pleaded.

"You have no choice, if you want your child to live," Jason replied bluntly, rolling up his sleeve. "More importantly, you have no time. We must do this swiftly, or they will find us and it will all be moot. Does anyone have a knife or sharp edge?"

"I do," Gerald said, getting out his pocket knife. "The blade is sharp, but I can't guarantee surgically clean."

"Let me get my first aid kit," Grace said, dashing for her purse. As a medical technician, she kept an unusually complete kit at hand, which fortunately included several alcohol wipes.

"Here, let's get under the headlights," she encouraged them all. She wiped Gerald's blade and Bethany's arm then felt for the chip.

"It's right here," Bethany pointed to a small square spot on her skin. "The incision healed cleanly, but you can just see the scar."

"That probably means some tissue has grown around the chip, which I'll have to cut loose," Grace warned. "This'll hurt."

"Get on with it," Patrick said, and Bethany nodded. Grace sliced into the skin right at the edge of the square, then slipped the blade tip under the skin, mindful of the warning that the chips were fragile. She could see beads of sweat breaking out on Bethany's forehead while Patrick held her other hand.

"There," Grace handed the blade back to Gerald, "hopefully that got it. I'll try to work it free with my tweezers. I may have to separate more tissue, so brace yourself, Bethany."

"Meanwhile," Gerald said, turning to Jason, "we need to prepare your arm to receive the chip."

"A simple slit won't be enough," Jason advised. "You'll have to run the tip under the skin to make space in the subcutaneous tissue." Jason held out his arm, and Gerald swiftly cut a short gash, then pushed the blade under the slit. Jason only gasped lightly.

"There," Gerald said. "Maybe too much, but I figured swift was better."

"Thank you," Jason said in a thin voice.

"And here's the chip," Grace said, holding up a small, blood-traced item.

"Slip it in quickly," Jason urged, offering his arm. "We don't know how long it'll keep working outside a body." Grace tucked the chip into the gash then fumbled in her kit for some gauze and tape.

"What next?" Todd asked as he bandaged Bethany's arm.

"Now I show them what they expect to see," Jason replied. "I take Patrick and Bethany's phones and drive off in their car. Hopefully the SPD units will follow me, leaving you all to drive away safely."

"But...what will happen if they find you?" Bethany asked.

"*When* they find me," Jason corrected. "I'll have to deal with that as it happens. The important thing is that you all escape."

"For the time being," Todd added glumly. "It's very possible that it will be a very short time. Not to make light of your sacrifice, Jason, but the bad guys are still out in force, with assets on the ground and in the air. Even with you decoying them, there's a good chance they'll catch us anyway, especially without a good plan, and possibly even with one."

"I have a thought on that," Gerald offered. "The problem is that the land exits are all tightly monitored, true?"

"We presume so," Todd affirmed.

"How about a water exit?"

"We've done that kind of thing in the past, but we don't have any boats available right now. Besides, water lacks cover – boats are easy to monitor with overhead surveillance."

"I have access to a boat," Gerald said. "In fact, I've already requested the master to get underway. He's an acquaintance of mine, a Saginaw Chippewa who fishes in Saginaw Bay and Lake Huron. He's currently heading across from the Pinconning area, and should be able to pick you up somewhere on the eastern shore of the bay. It won't be something they'd be looking for, especially if they're being led off in the wrong direction by a decoy." He nodded to Jason.

"But...we couldn't do that!" Todd protested weakly.

"On the contrary, you can do nothing else, and you must be about it quickly," Gerald replied, and laid his tablet on the hood of the car. It was displaying a map of the upper Thumb, with their location in Ruth showing as a glowing dot. "We are here. I recommend you go south a few miles to Forester-Bay City Road, and turn west. Head for the northwest shore. There are many ports there. I will contact my friend to find out which is the best, and we can arrange for you to meet. He can then take you to wherever you wish. You should take my van – it will hold you all, and I can recover it later."

"I...but, aren't you coming with us? Todd asked, staring at the keys Gerald was holding out.

"Actually, I hope to accompany Jason, if he'll permit," Gerald replied. Now it was Jason's turn to look stunned.

"That could be hazardous, Gerald," he warned.

"I understand, but I think it would be more hazardous for you without a witness by your side. Of us all, I'm the best candidate. Besides, a First Nation helped create this problem. Even if he was a renegade, it is fitting that a First Nation should help repair it."

"But...there's no guarantee..." Todd began, but Gerald cut him off sharply.

"*Time*, Todd! We have none! Get moving! You talk to your people, I'll talk to my friend on the boat, we'll work something out. Right now, you need to go!"

"But they'll track the van!"

"No, they won't. It's Canadian, and doesn't have to conform to all those protocols your government requires," Gerald assured him, jingling the keys again. "Take them and go!"

Todd grabbed the keys and hustled the others toward the van.

"Leave your keys and phones!" Jason called to Patrick and Bethany.

"For that matter, Patrick, leave them the private phone you were given – you'll have mine," Todd said, and a bundle of items was handed to Jason.

"God bless you, and good bye!" Grace called as they clamored into the old van.

Gerald waved as they drove away, then pulled out his phone and keyed a number. Listening for a bit, he rang off and tucked the phone away. "That's good, I hope. No response from my friend, which should mean he's in the middle of the bay, out of signal range. Now," he turned to Jason, "what do you have in mind from here?"

"Thank you for accompanying me," Jason said. "I think it foolish and unnecessary, but I appreciate it. As far as our route – well, I once drove a road to freedom on a night much like this. I'd like to retrace it in the other direction, if I can, which will mean going east from here to the lake shore and then turning north. Somewhere along the way, the lake shore road is intersected by one that leads west back to the woods. I'd like to take that, if we're able to drive the entire distance without being intercepted."

"That is a circular symmetry which my Ojibwa soul appreciates," Gerald replied. "Let us be on our way."

*   *   *

"HHS reports the target is moving again," the technician reported, tapping his keyboard to update the location of the blinking red dot.

"Which direction?" Touma asked sharply.

"East, ma'am."

"Let me know what they do when they get to the coast," Touma ordered.

The strikes on the targets had gone well enough, with no more than the usual number of communications mix-ups and troubles with the detainees. Touma was glad she'd stayed at the TacComm to sort these out as they'd arisen. Fortunately for her, their one fleeing target had chosen about that time to take an extended break, halting at a crossroads about five miles from the shoreline. The target had remained stationary for about twenty minutes, but just when Touma was starting to wonder if they'd gone to ground, they'd started moving again. She'd reassigned two drones from completed strikes in the area to overfly the site where the target had lingered for so long, so now the birds could tail them visually. She felt vindicated – the target's movement surely signaled that they were seeking either a water escape or to run down to the border crossing at Port Huron. She had them either way, but with visual oversight she might be able to pick up any more contacts they made.

"HHS reports the target has reached the shoreline and has turned north," the tech reported.

"Understood," Touma responded, gazing at the map. North? She hadn't expected that. The best harbors along this coast were Port Sanilac and Lexington, which lay to the south. To the north lay Harbor Beach and Port Austin, both of which were less convenient for a run across to Canada. Unless they planned to try to make connection outside a harbor? Perhaps a beach pickup? But even that would make sense further south, where the lake was narrower. But they might be up against resource constraints...

There were too many unknowns to guess the target's intentions from their movements. Touma decided she needed to get out there herself, to be on site when these scofflaws were nailed. Things here were sufficiently under control – most of the targets had been turned over to HHS and were on the way to the detainment center. "Is that Coast Guard bird in the air?" she barked.

"Ah...yes, ma'am," the sergeant replied.

"Tell them to give extra attention to Harbor Beach when they get there, and Port Austin as well. Any suspicious vessel activity, I want to know about."

"Yes, ma'am."

"I'm heading out. Keep me regularly posted on the target's location and progress, understand?"

"Yes, ma'am," the tech replied.

"Come on, Sickles."

*   *   *

The Sanilac County sheriff cruiser pulled to the side of the road just across the county line and shut off its flashers. Shawn got out of his car, thanked the deputy who had escorted him, then walked over to greet Chip, who was waiting beside one of the Huron County cruisers.

"Thanks for arranging the escort, Sheriff," Shawn said. "I've always wanted to drive up M-53 at that speed."

"Happy to help a good cause," Chip replied. "You can take the front seat. I've moved as many electronics out of the way as I can, but there are some that can't be moved, so it'll be a bit cramped. Of course, you could always take the perp seat in the back, but I'd rather have you accessible.

"I'll deal with the close quarters," Shawn replied, getting into the passenger side of the cruiser. "Any word from any quarters regarding DTD activity?"

"Nothing yet," Chip admitted. "I've got three cars canvassing the county – well, four, including this one – and we haven't yet seen any DTD presence. Of course, we're a large, thinly populated county. Also, we don't know how many sites they're targeting. If we presume they're covering the entire Thumb, and that they are hitting about the same number of sites as they did last spring, that might be only one or two in all of Huron County, given our proportional population."

"Do you know if they're hitting any at all in Huron?" Shawn asked.

"I don't think we would have been included in the broadcast if they weren't planning to do something here," Chip explained. "And I have information from other sources indicating that at least one location may have been targeted."

"Do you know where?"

"Only generally, and I'm reluctant to ask for specifics. However, I may call the source in question to see if he's heard anything. Which reminds me," Chip reached into a jacket pocket and pulled out a phone which he handed to Shawn.

"What's this for?" Shawn asked, turning the phone over in his hands.

"It's a special phone that's harder to trace. It's what I called you on earlier this evening. It uses a private phone network. I didn't know it was even possible to have a private network, but apparently you can. My source gave it to me. Hold it for me in case he calls, would you? I suspect I'm going to have enough distractions without managing that as well."

"Sure. Where are we headed?"

"Lacking better information, I'm heading back to Bad Axe. It's central to the county, and we have communications resources there. If we don't hear something soon, though, I might chance contacting my source," Chip said.

"Okay. Let me call my aide David. I thought of him while passing through Marlette. I want to get him and his surveillance drone up near us in case it proves handy."

"He won't mind being called this late?" Chip asked.

"Not if it gives him a chance to play with his new toy," Shawn grinned as he keyed David's number.

*   *   *

Jason was driving the Hood's car north along the lakeshore under the clear moonlit sky. They'd decided to run the risk of having him stopped for driving without a license, especially since a sheriff's car was one of the things they most hoped to see at the moment. It also freed Gerald to make phone calls, the first of which was to Lean Bear.

"*By my radar I'm about twelve miles from Sand Point,*" Lean Bear reported on their weak connection.

"*What is the best port to get in and out of?*" Gerald asked.

"*Along the east shore? Caseville. Long jetty. Lots of big river entries.*"

"*How about for picking people up directly from shore?*"

"*Oh, is that what I'm doing? Caseville works. Can pluck them right off the jetty, if they don't mind getting a bit wet. Where would I be taking them?*"

"*We're not certain yet. How far away are you from Caseville?*"

"*Figure forty-five minutes.*"

"*Good. I'll call you back.*"

"*Hunh.*"

The next call was to Todd. "Gerald?" came the answer

"Yes. Where are you now?"

"Just passing into Tuscola County. Gagetown will be the next town."

"Good. Follow our plan. Past Gagetown, turn north toward Owendale and head for Caseville. I've confirmed my friend will pick you up on the jetty there."

"Wait – 'you'? I thought we were just sending Patrick and Bethany."

"I recommend you all go. Patrick and Bethany certainly, and Tyrone as well – can you imagine what would happen to him if they found him? And if he goes, you two should. If they catch either of you with the slightest clue that you helped them escape, it's over. Just get out."

"But...my job? Our house?" Todd asked.

"You can straighten that out later. Maybe you'll get lucky and be able to return in a week. But with troops on the ground and drones in the air, I strongly suggest you all just get clear until things settle down, at least," Gerald said.

"You're probably right," Todd said.

"Next question: where will my friend be taking you?"

"Not sure yet – I need to make some calls," Todd admitted.

"Do that. I do as well, which reminds me – did I correctly infer from one of your comments that you'd slipped Chip Keller one of those private phones?"

"Yes, I did."

"How handy. Please send me that number so I can contact him."

This Todd did, then rang off after assuring Gerald that he'd call Steve immediately.

"That's two down," Gerald said to Jason.

"We're approaching Harbor Beach," Jason said. "I know I go north of here, but I don't recall exactly which road I take west away from the lake. The night I drove to the lakeshore, I wasn't attending to the road signs."

"Don't worry about it. Just go north until you see Nathan Road, then turn west," Gerald explained as he keyed in the number that Todd had sent him.

"Hello?" answered an unfamiliar voice.

"Hello…Chip?" Gerald asked hesitantly.

"No, this is Shawn. Chip's right here, though." The phone was handed over.

"This is Chip – is this Todd?"

"No, this is Gerald."

"Gerald! What are you doing on this network?"

"Long story," Gerald replied. "Listen, I think we've hit on a way to get the feds to congregate. Is there a spot near the woods on Nathan Road that's suitable? Somewhere off the road?"

"Sure. There's a big fallow field immediately to the west of the woods. There's some scrub springing up, but it's mostly meadow grass. You could pull into it without problem."

"Good. That's where we'll go, then, and just wait for them."

"We'll be right along," Chip assured him, then rang off and turned to Shawn. "That drone your aide is bringing – does it have Global Location Network locking?"

"If it's a bell or whistle, I'm sure this drone has it," Shawn assured him.

"It's a pretty standard feature on high-end drones. Tell him to take the drone to the corner of M-53 and Nathan Road and launch from there. He'll want to fly it due east to some coordinates I'll provide. He'll be able to see the cars in the field. He should start filming everything the minute he arrives."

"Filming everything? Are the feds going to show up?"

"Probably. And us and my deputies as well. And when we all do, I expect things might get a little…tense."

"Okay," Shawn said as he called David.

"While you're on that, I'll contact the dispatcher so she can let everyone know where the party is," Chip said, reaching for the radio microphone.

*   *   *

Meanwhile, Todd was making a call of his own as the van passed through Gagetown. "Pippin?"

"Yeah, Bree, we've almost got it for you," came the exasperated response.

"No, I'm calling with a change of plan," Todd replied.

"A change of plan? Great!" Steve snarled. "What now?"

"We've got…that is, a water pickup has been arranged."

"A water pickup?" Steve asked. "Like a boat?"

"Yes. At Caseville. The party making the arrangements is suggesting we all go. There will be room on the rescue vessel."

"Wait – this is moving too fast. What boat? Who's at the helm?"

"Pippin, we don't have time for a full vetting. A boat will be taking us off the pier at Caseville, and we need you to tell us where it should drop us off!" Todd said sharply.

"Right. Boat pickup," Steve was muttering on the other end of the line. "Actually, if you can pull it off, that's a better solution that what we'd...boat pickup...Northfarthing, think Northfarthing...let me get back to you on just where in Northfarthing."

"Fine, just don't take too long."

*   *   *

"You may be losing sleep, but at least you're getting some night hours in, Ms. Lock," Lcdr. Dunne commented as the Jayhawk helicopter worked its way up the Lake Huron coast. Since they'd cleared the Blue Water Bridge, he'd turned the controls over to her so she could get the experience.

"True, and I appreciate it, sir," Lock confirmed as she checked the dash gages and the coastline below. Dunne barely glanced at the glowing readouts – Lock was a responsible officer and a superb pilot. As far as he was concerned, he was just along for the ride.

"How are you doing back there, Fleury?" Dunne asked casually, and after a bit of silence asked again, "Fleury?"

"Yes? Ah, yes, sir? Fine back here," came the abrupt response. How anyone could doze off in the bay of a flying helicopter was beyond Dunne's comprehension, but somehow flight mechanics managed it with regularity.

"Message coming in, sir," Lock alerted him just as he caught the radio hail. He flicked a switch to cut off Lock's headset so she could concentrate on flying. The message was brief, but caused him to grimace and roll his eyes.

"Copy that, Station," he acknowledged, then announced to his crew, "Our lords and masters at DTD instruct us to keep special watch upon Harbor Beach, and possibly Port Austin, for any suspicious vessel activity. They're still vague about what they mean by 'suspicious', but by jiminy, if we see it, we should report it."

"Perhaps smuggling, sir?" Fleury suggested.

"Possibly, but in that case the request would have probably come through Border Patrol or DEA," Dunne replied.

"We're not likely to see much of anything," Lock pointed out. "There are freighters out in the lake, but only the die-hard pleasure crafters even have their boats in the water this late in the season, and few of them are out this late at night."

"True, which should make our flight easy," Dunne acknowledged. "But – if we see any pleasure craft that look suspicious, you be sure to report them!"

"Understood, sir," Lock said with a grin.

*　　　　　*　　　　　*

"The target is continuing north, ma'am," the voice in Captain Touma's earpiece said, and the flashing red dot on her display moved a bit further up the coastline.

"Understood," Touma replied sharply, her mind churning. What was the target up to? It hadn't stopped in Harbor Beach, so the idea of a connection at the harbor there was blown. Perhaps Port Austin? It made little sense, but that was the next major harbor along this road.

Or, perhaps, the target had no plan. Perhaps they were just running randomly in blind panic, seeking to escape by dodging and dashing. For some reason that image fired a predatory excitement inside her, and she bared her teeth in a feral grin. Let the target try to run. There was no place for it to hide.

"TacComm, have all free units converge on area bounded by M-25, M-53, and M-142," Touma instructed. "Ensure units are actively watching M-53 at the Huron County line and M-25 at Unionville. Stand by for further orders. Touma out."

"Should we stay on M-53, ma'am?" Sickles asked. They were on the outskirts of Bad Axe, approaching it from the west.

"No," Touma replied, examining the map on her tablet. "Go through the city, but continue east. We'll turn north at Verona, whatever that is. We'll try to box them in."

"Yes, ma'am."

*   *   *

Todd's private phone rang again with a familiar number.

"Gerald?" Todd asked.

"Hi, Todd. Where are you now?"

"Northbound on Caseville Road, just approaching M-142 west of Pigeon. Less than ten miles from Caseville."

"Good. I just had my last talk with the party picking you up. He's not far from Caseville now. His name is Lean Bear and I'm sending you his number so you can talk directly."

"All right."

"We're approaching...the end of our journey here. You keep to the plan no matter what happens," Gerald said.

"I...okay, sure," Todd replied. "You guys are...I mean, you're all right, aren't you?"

"We'll be fine, but if you don't get away safely, all our work will be for naught, so stay focused."

"I will," Todd assured him.

"Park the van somewhere out of the way and tuck the keys inside it. I'll pick it up later."

"All right. Thank you for all your help. May God bless and guide you."

"Indeed," Gerald replied, and rang off.

"What's up?" Patrick asked. "Any changes?"

"No, we stick to the plan. Make it to Caseville, stay under cover as much as we can, expect pickup on the jetty," Todd replied. Just then they came to where M-142 crossed Caseville Road, and even as they were waiting at the stop sign, a pair of dark DTD vehicles came roaring through the intersection, their blue lights flashing. For a moment everyone's heart stopped, but the vehicles continued eastbound, taking no notice of them.

"Wonder where they're going?" Bethany asked in a frail voice.

"Not Caseville, which is what matters to us," Todd replied jauntily, but he was recalling the ominous phrase Gerald had used.

No matter what happens.

Just then the phone rang again, this time with a call from Steve.

"Pippin? We're almost to Caseville and the pickup is on schedule. Whatcha got for us?"

"Not much. Head north to Oscoda, if possible. Depending on the boat's speed, that should take two, two and a half hours. If you can't get to Oscoda, call back and we'll work out something else."

"Great. What then?"

"Working on it."

"Working on it?" Todd snapped. "That's all you have? Get to Oscoda?"

"Listen, these last-minute changes mean we have to start from scratch. We were planning two or three parties being driven out of Eastfarthing, not five coming by water! We were hoping for a stealth exit, but instead we have to assume constant surveillance and at least warm pursuit! This isn't as easy as it looks!"

"Yeah, yeah, sorry, Pippin," Todd acknowledged. "We copy that we head for Oscoda once we're safely away. Keep us posted as you can."

"Will do."

"And could you offer some prayers for our companions? They made sure we got away cleanly, but might be finding themselves in a tight spot."

"I'll do that, too," Steve replied, then rang off.

"Developments?" Grace asked.

"Yeah, such as they are," Todd replied. "Once we're on the vessel, we head for Oscoda."

Hasty Arrangements

The ring of the phone awakened the light-sleeping Luke first, so he slipped out of bed and took the phone to the kitchen in hopes of letting Felicity continue to sleep. He guessed that it was a medical issue that he could just talk the caller through and follow up on in the morning.

It didn't take Felicity long to notice Luke's absence. She waited in bed for a while, guessing that he'd return soon, but when he didn't, she pulled on her bathrobe and went to the kitchen, where she found her distressed husband sitting at the table looking glumly at the phone.

"What's wrong?"

"Not so much wrong as difficult," Luke replied. "That was your dad. They're putting out an emergency call for resources and...suggestions, I guess."

"Suggestions?" Felicity asked.

"Yeah, it's a crash situation. They're having to do an emergency evacuation from Eastfarthing. Looks almost as bad as last May – troops in the field, certainly drones in the sky. Todd and Grace are involved."

"Grace?" Felicity gasped. "Is she in danger?"

"Gil didn't tell me much, but I presume so," Luke replied. "They were working on evacuating a couple who were being pressured to abort their child when something dire happened and they had to scram. Apparently, this couple has been on the run for hours. Fangorn had been cooking up a plan to stealth them out of the district, but that went right out the window, and for a while things looked pretty desperate. Then somehow a boat escape was arranged, and they're being plucked off a jetty in Caseville."

"A boat escape? Great to get them off, but water is wide open, no cover at all. They'll be visible for miles," Felicity pointed out.

"That's what we're contending with," Luke confirmed. "A boat rescue just moves the desperation point. The plan is to bring them to Oscoda, but then they have to be picked up as stealthily as possible, and –" Luke began, but was interrupted by a knock at the back door. A puzzled Felicity opened it to find a disheveled but grinning Bob standing outside. He'd been sleeping in the stable for a couple of nights, but was clearly awake now.

"Howdy," he said cheerily. "I wouldn't've disturbed ya, but I saw the light on an' wondered if I could nab a little bread 'n' butter, and maybe a glass of milk."

Luke gave Bob an exasperated look but Felicity just grinned and opened the door, waving him toward the breadbox and refrigerator.

"So," Felicity asked, sitting down beside Luke and taking his hand. "What kind of suggestions was Dad looking for?"

"He was…ah…" Luke stammered, uncomfortable with continuing this conversation in Bob's presence. "Any kind, I guess. Specifically, he asked about the ATV I've been using, but that's essentially useless. Not only is it a lightweight that can only carry one rider, it's almost out of gas. He's calling everywhere to see what he can round up, but the time pressure is intense."

"What kind of timeframe are we looking at?" Felicity asked.

"Less than three hours to get something thrown together and down to the pickup site, wherever that will be. Stealthily."

"Three hours?" Felicity exclaimed. "That's barely –"

"Mmm," Bob gave an almost obscene moan of pleasure as he bit into a thick slice of bread generously smeared with butter. "Miz Felicity, your bread is to die for."

"Thank you," Felicity replied distractedly.

"If y'don't mind my sayin' so, you folks seem a mite upset," Bob added, leaning against the counter as he munched his bread and sipped his milk. "Anythin' I can help with?"

"Thanks, Bob, but –" Luke began in an impatient tone, but Felicity laid a hand on his arm and gave him a glance. He made to say something to her, but then just closed his mouth and waved to her to speak.

"In case you haven't yet figured this out, Bob, we and some of the people we know are here in the backwoods because we're kind of…on the edge of the law," Felicity explained. "We aren't doing anything immoral, but some of the things we've been forced to do to help people have gotten us in trouble with the authorities."

"I figgered somethin' like that," Bob admitted, sitting down at the table with them. "What authorities? State or federal?"

"Ah…federal," Luke said, a bit surprised that Bob would know to ask.

"Damn feds. Always stickin' their long noses everywhere they don't belong," Bob grumbled.

"Right," Felicity agreed. "Currently there's a group that needs to escape the Thumb area, and things are tense over there right now. If they can elude capture long enough, they'll be able to board a boat at Caseville and head for Oscoda. The most pressing concern is active overhead surveillance. We have to presume that they'll not only be visible for their entire trip across the lake, but once they land as well."

"So they escape capture in Caseville just to get arrested in Oscoda," Bob observed. "Then they sure can't be picked up on a pier by a van. How many people we talkin' about?"

"Five," Luke said, and Felicity looked at him in surprise.

"Five? Who's the fifth?"

"Not sure," Luke admitted. "In the past, we'd try to pick them up in things like ATVs or UTVs or even dirt bikes, then transport them by covered paths to safe locations. This area has plenty of cover, but we don't know the trails well enough to traverse them in the dark, and we may not be able to assemble enough trail-capable vehicles in time."

"Got a map?" Bob asked. Luke opened his tablet and brought up a map of the area. "I know the trails real good, but your plan wouldn't work even if you got ATVs."

"Why not?" Luke asked.

"Michigan DNR does regular drone flights over these parts, especially this time o' year," Bob explained. "They use look-down infrared cameras to spot ATVs runnin' through the woods. They'd be sure to spot a group of 'em an' swoop in to investigate."

"Why would DNR be interested in tracking ATVs through the woods at night?" Luke asked.

"Poachers use 'em," Bob replied.

"Well, that's great," Luke grumbled. "We can't use the roads and we can't use the woods. Maybe we should just tell them to turn back now."

"Now, now, keep yer chin up," Bob admonished, peering at the map. "How tall is th' boat?"

"How tall?" Luke asked.

"Clearance above th' water," Bob explained. "How tall is it from waterline to highest point? 'Cause if it's low enough, it'll be able to get under th' West River Road bridge here on the Au Sable just west of Oscoda. They should be able to do that unless they're in a tall cabin cruiser. If they can, it opens up all kind of options."

"What kind of options? You just said that ATVs can be spotted and tracked," Luke asked.

"Can they ride?"

"Can who ride?"

"These people comin' ashore. Can they ride horses?"

"Horses?" Luke blustered. "What do you mean –"

"Yeah, horses," Bob answered. "Y'got a whole stable full of 'em back there, and th' tack to saddle 'em."

"What good –" Luke began, but Felicity patted his arm again.

"Grace can certainly ride, as can Luke and I," Felicity explained. "I'm sure Todd will be able to get by, but I'm not

sure about the other three. One will be a pregnant woman –
well, Grace is pregnant, too, so that's two."

"Pregnant? How far along?" Bob asked.

"Just a few months."

"Shouldn't matter, then," Bob waved dismissively.
"Anyone can sit in th' saddle of a walkin' horse. If we get th'
horses saddled, I can lead y'all down to the lower Au Sable
by trails in the woods. There are spots where the trails lead
right down to th' water, so if th' boat can make it past that
bridge an' get close enough to the shore, we could get 'em
off an' under cover quick enough. May call for some wadin',
but that's just wet feet."

"But won't the DNR drones spot a herd of horses as
readily as a bunch of ATVs?" Luke asked.

"Nope," Bob replied with a smug grin. "DNR has to set
its cameras to look for higher temps, like engines. If they set
them low enough to find body temperature, they'd be
flaggin' every deer and possum in the woods. That's one
reason poachers are usin' more horses these days."

"You...ah...seem to know quite a bit about the activities
of poachers," Felicity said with a smile. "But could you do
this at night? Get us and a small herd of horses down to the
lower Au Sable by covered trails?"

"You got headlamps?"

"Yes, quite a few of those," Luke said.

"Then sure, I can get you there and back," Bob
announced proudly.

Felicity and Luke looked at each other with a mixture of
astonishment and disbelief. "This is...hare-brained," Luke
muttered.

"Perhaps, but it may be our only option," Felicity pointed
out. "And it has the advantage of being completely
unexpected. Who's going to anticipate a night pickup by
horses?"

"That's a very slender advantage," Luke replied.

"I'm open to any alternatives you have to suggest," Felicity countered. "What – two hours and forty minutes now?"

Luke shook his head and took her hand. "I concede. Best plan we can find in a tight situation. I can think of about a hundred ways it could go wrong, but I can't think of even one alternative."

"Bob, you're a hero," Felicity said. "Why don't we get on saddling the horses?"

"We'll handle that," Luke said, sliding the phone to Felicity. "You call your dad and explain everything. See what he can do about arranging pickup from here, assuming we bring everyone in safely."

"Take two hours to get there from here by th' trails we got to take," Bob announced, stuffing the last of the bread into his mouth and downing the milk. "An' we should bring blankets – a nighttime trip across the lake, they'll arrive mighty cold. An' be sure to get th' clearance of that boat."

Rescue

The small village of Caseville was as quiet as one would expect in the middle of the night. The fugitives came into town from the south and found their way to the small municipal beach from which the jetty thrust out into Saginaw Bay. Todd let everyone out onto a wooden walkway then drove the van back to the main street where he parked it behind a church. He messaged Gerald the van's location but got no response, then hiked back to the beach, hoping that a guy walking alone along dark streets wouldn't draw much notice. While he was walking, a call came in from Gil Peterson, explaining how the pickup plans were proceeding, and asking about the clearance of the boat.

Todd rejoined the others, who had taken shelter under a pavilion. The air was warm for an early autumn night, but the occasional gusts off the bay threatened chillier temperatures out on the water. Grace and Bethany were huddled around Tyrone, who had come wearing his usual shorts.

"Any sign of the boat?" Todd asked Patrick, who was scanning the dark water for any sign of a vessel.

"Nothing I can see," Patrick admitted. "Can we call him?"

"If we don't see something soon, I think I will."

After several more minutes of peering into the night but seeing nothing more than dim, distant lights, Todd keyed the number Gerald had sent him.

"H'lo?" came the reply.

"Hi, I'm...Bree, a friend of the friend who contacted you," Todd said.

"Hunh," the voice grunted. "You my passengers for the evening?"

"Yes, and we're at the pickup site."

"Hunh. I don't see you."

"Don't see us?" Todd asked in surprise. "Where are you?"

"Approaching the end of the jetty."

"You are?" Todd asked, straining his eyes. "I can't see anything out there."

"Have to know what you're looking for. I've only got my running lights on. I'll flash my forward searchlight." A few seconds later a bright white light flared briefly, illuminating the bow of a low, plain-looking boat just alongside the end of the long jetty.

"There he is!" Bethany nearly cheered. "Should we go out there?"

"No, we need to stay under cover as long as possible," Todd warned, then said into the phone, "Sir – what should I call you?"

"Boat's name is *Marten Clan*," the voice replied. "Do you see me now?"

"Yes. We want to remain under cover until you get closer. Will you be able to pick us up at the base of the jetty, by the boardwalk?"

"I should. This lightly laden, she only draws two feet, so I'll be able to get right up to the pier. There are stones there I have to be careful of, but they'll let you climb down to water level so you can pretty much step aboard. You'll all get a little wet, though."

"That reminds me – how tall is your boat from the waterline?"

"If I drop the radio mast, she clears just under eight feet from the waterline to the top of the radar antenna."

"Thanks, I'll pass that along," Todd said. While he was doing this, the others watched the vessel's progress toward the harbor. When she came to the base of the jetty, where the walkway joined it, she turned in the channel so that her bow was pointed outward then eased up alongside the rocks that formed the jetty. The little party dashed from the pavilion to the water, and a man stepped out of the boat's pilot house to toss a couple of lines ashore. The wind was light from the southeast, but there was enough chop to keep the boat rocking, which almost deterred Tyrone, who'd never set foot on a boat in his life. But the women and the boat's pilot helped him aboard, terrified and soaked to the waist. Lastly Patrick and Todd leapt onto the broad deck, bringing the lines with them, and the man got behind the wheel and eased the throttles forward.

Todd ensured Tyrone and the women were settled before approaching the man behind the wheel. "I'm Todd Beck," he introduced himself.

"Lean Bear, Saginaw Chippewa," the man replied.

"Thank you so much for doing this. I don't know what we would have done without your help."

"You're not home yet. Where are we headed?"

"Can you make it to Oscoda? Hopefully we can get a ways up the Au Sable so we can be picked up under cover."

"Ah," Lean Bear nodded. "Oscoda's no problem, just two hours north across the lake." He reached over to flick some switches on the control board, and some lights about the edge of the hull came on. "Time to look more normal. Sorry there aren't many luxuries aboard, but this is a simple fishing vessel. Make yourselves as comfortable as you can."

"Believe me, we're so glad to get out of that situation that comfort doesn't matter."

"Hunh. It will, but it should only be for a couple of hours."

*   *   *

"Station Tawas, this is Jayhawk six zero four one," Lcdr. Dunne said into the radio as Lt. Lock banked the helicopter to follow the curve of the beach below. "We have cleared Port Austin and are proceeding down the Saginaw shore. Nothing to report."

"Copy that, Jayhawk. Station Tawas out," came the reply.

"And so proceeds our pleasant midnight cruise," Dunne announced. "You doing all right back there, Fleury?"

"Fine, sir. I don't imagine there's a coffee shop we could drop down on?"

"Not along this coast at this time of night," Dunne grinned. "But it is just a short hop across the bay. I'm sure Lieutenant Lock could find a truck stop along I-75 and land us in their parking lot."

"That's fine, sir," Fleury replied as Lock shot him a grin.

"Not many vessels of any kind down there, much less suspicious ones," Lock said, looking out her window at the broad waters of Saginaw Bay. "Some dedicated fishermen near the shore – is it too early for duck hunters?"

"There's a vessel," Dunne pointed to some lights just ahead of a wake. "Just a couple miles east of the Charity Islands. Looks like they're headed north."

"Hmm," Lock checked her radar. "Their transponder is squawking that it's a light commercial fishing vessel licensed to the Saginaw Chippewa tribe."

"Ooh, protected by treaty, even," Dunne said. "Better not mess with them."

"Isn't it kind of late for a commercial fishing boat to be underway?" Lock asked.

"Are you asking if this constitutes suspicious activity, Lieutenant?" Dunne asked, watching the northbound boat. "I've learned over the years never to question the doings of golfers and fishermen, particularly tribal fishermen. They keep their own hours for their own mysterious reasons. Besides, since our DTD masters didn't see fit to provide us with a definition of 'suspicious activity', I can't see how that boat qualifies."

"Neither can I, sir," Lock concurred.

"How about you, Fleury? See anything suspicious down there?"

"Just a whole lotta water, sir," came the reply.

"Then it's unanimous," Dunne announced with satisfaction. "We are flying above unsuspicious terrain. How are we set for fuel?"

"Satisfactory, sir," Lock pointed at the gage that indicated enough for several more hours of flying.

"Think so? Your inexperience is showing, Lieutenant Lock. If you tip your head and squint a little, our fuel situation looks to be approaching marginal. Not dangerous yet, but sufficiently questionable to justify an expedited return to station. Also, I've detected early manifestations of crew distress. I don't want to be responsible for coming between Petty Officer Fleury and his coffee. I suggest we continue down the shore to Bay City, then plot an overland course to return to Selfridge – unless, of course, we spot some suspicious vessel activity along the way."

"Clearly there is much about flying I have yet to learn," Lock grinned.

"I'll advise our overlords of our intentions while you work out that homeward course. Unless they specifically request another coastal transit, we'll plan on a quick return."

"Yes, sir," Lock replied.

*   *   *

"There it is," Gerald said as the shiny security fence along the edge of Nathan Road came into view. "Chip says there's a field just beyond it. There should be an access turnoff."

"Got it," Jason said. They drove past the fence-bound woods and slowed down to look for a place to turn off the road. Sure enough, there was an access, just enough to allow farm equipment to cross the ditch and get into the field for plowing and harvesting. Jason turned onto this and drove into the grassy field, bumping and jostling as the low car crossed the unplowed meadow. Jason brought the car to rest about fifty yards into the field, clearly visible from the roads to the north and south as well as, presumably, from above.

"So – what now?" Gerald asked.

"We wait for them to arrive. If our ruse worked, it won't be long," Jason replied.

"Do we get out?"

"No. We remain in the car. We want to keep them ignorant of the true situation as long as possible. Even now there is almost certainly at least one drone overhead. We show them what they expect to see."

"I get it," Gerald replied, though it grated on his nerves to just sit passively while foes closed in. "I'm going to notify Chip that we're here." He made the quick call, then told Jason, "Chip says they're just a few minutes out. He said to hang tight until they arrive."

Jason just smiled.

After a few more minutes of tense silence, Gerald asked, "Mind if I make another call?"

"Not in the least," Jason replied, so Gerald keyed a contact on his personal phone. It rang until it cut to voice mail, at which point Gerald disconnected and tried again. This time the phone was answered on the fourth ring by a groggy voice.

"Gerald?"

"*Hi, Kim.*"

"Gerald, where on earth are you?" the voice sharpened. "We were expecting you back hours ago!"

"*Still here in the Thumb area,*" Gerald replied in Ojibwe, trying to take it slow out of respect for Kim's inexperience in the language. "*Sorry for the delay – I got entangled in some issues. I need to tell you a few things. I'm here in a rural place with a friend named Jason Pelletier. That's Jason Pelletier. In case anything happens to me, I haven't broken any laws.*"

"If anything happens to you? Gerald, what are you talking about? Why are you speaking Ojibwe?"

"*Hopefully, nothing will happen, but if it does, especially if I disappear, tell the tribal elders at Garden River to push the matter, and not to accept no for an answer.*"

"Gerald, you're starting to scare me," Kim said, her voice edged. "What have you gotten yourself into?"

"Nothing but helping some innocents facing government oppression, Kim. Tell them to talk to Huron County Sheriff Chip Keller. Oh, and Lean Bear as well, though he'd probably contact you first. I owe him for some fuel."

"Gerald, where are you? I'm coming over there –"

"No!" Gerald barked. *"Stay home! Hopefully this will come to nothing, and I'll be home by breakfast. I just needed to tell you this in case things...turn out differently."*

"Gerald –" Kim began, but again he cut her off.

"No time, Kim. I'll be back in touch as soon as I can. I love you, Kim. I'm doing what Mom and Dad told us was important."

"I love you, too, Gerald."

*　　　*　　　*

"Captain, HHS reports the target has stopped," came the tech's voice.

"Where? A residence?" Touma asked.

"No. Along a rural road. I'm updating the display now," the tech replied. Touma zoomed her tablet screen to display the red dot flashing on Nathan Road just ahead of her position.

"Do we have eyes on this yet?" Touma snapped.

"Stand by, ma'am," the tech replied. Touma waited impatiently until the voice came back. "Drone control reports visual contact. They confirm the car matches the target's registered vehicle."

"Well? What are they doing? Getting out? Running?" Touma asked.

"Stand by, ma'am," the tech repeated. Touma sat fuming for a long minute before the tech came back on. "Drone control reports no activity, ma'am. No movement, nobody even getting out of the car."

"What, they're just sitting there by the side of the road?"

"Apparently they're in a field, ma'am."

"In a field? What are they doing in a field?"

"No idea, ma'am. If drone control passes along any details, I'll notify you promptly."

"You do that," Touma said sharply. For some reason her subordinate's ignorance infuriated her. Was a little competence too much to ask? Maybe she'd need to do some housecleaning when this debacle was over.

Captain Touma's attention turned to the target they were pursuing, and her fury intensified. Those ignorant hicks had led them on a chase all across the district and back. She didn't even know their names, but it didn't matter – they were just typical rural scum of the type that made this backwoods post so impossible to manage. All the effort they had to expend just to get people to do what they were supposed to! Damn them! Well, she'd teach these ones not to cross her, and shortly, too – their location was less than five minutes away.

"Can't you go any faster?" she snapped at her driver.

"Yes, ma'am," Sickles replied shakily as he accelerated. She glanced with contempt at his white-knuckled grip on the wheel and the sweat on his face. Clearly speeding down a dirt road in the dark was more than he was up to. Maybe she needed to find a new driver as well.

"What…what's that?" Sickles asked after some minutes.

"What's what?"

"It…it looks like some sort of fence, ma'am," Sickles nodded toward a silvery structure coming into view.

"Is it in the road?"

"No, ma'am."

"Then drive past it. The target is less than a mile ahead on the right."

"Yes, ma'am."

The tech's voice came in her earpiece. "Ma'am, drone control reports no change in status. The target vehicle hasn't moved, and nobody has exited."

"Understood. Don't bother me unless there's a change," Touma replied. They were passing the silver thing now, a tall security fence enclosing a stand of trees. What that was doing here she had no idea, but it didn't matter – the target was nearly in view.

"Slow down, you fool! They're just ahead on the right!" she snapped, and Sickles braked so abruptly that they began to slide on the gravel. He regained control, but drove looking ahead with wide eyes, licking his lips nervously. They were passing the woods and could see beyond them a dark field.

"There they are!" Touma pointed at a car parked in the field, its headlights burning. "TacComm, Touma, what's the ETA for other units at the target location?"

"Stand by, ma'am."

"Turn into the field!" she barked at Sickles. "Get close to them!"

"Where, ma'am? There's a ditch."

"They got out there – find the crossing they used!" Damned incompetents.

"Ma'am, other units report ten to fifteen minutes out," came the response from TacComm.

"Tell them to speed it up, TacComm." Looks like she'd have to make this detainment herself. "There, there's the turnoff, right there! Turn, dammit!" Sickles slammed the brakes, skidding slightly, then turned to drive across the meadow.

As Sickles steered his timid way across the irregular surface, Touma glared at the car parked there. It was an older model, worn and tired like so many in this forsaken region. The targets were hiding inside, not showing themselves. She didn't know if she hoped they'd come quietly or not. She got a certain thrill from the mental image of yanking them from the car, slamming them face down in the dirt to be cuffed, handling them a little roughly on the way to the detainment vans. After all, why should HHS have all the fun with them? An unresisting arrest might be easy, but a resisted one might afford a little diversion.

"There – stop there," Touma pointed at a spot about twenty yards from the target's car. Sickles braked clumsily and Touma got out, walking behind her vehicle as she pulled her sidearm from its holster. Probably unnecessary, but she was in no mood for any more nonsense. It was time to end this, and if that took a heavy hand, so be it.

Still there was no movement from inside the car. She thought she saw two figures, which was what they'd expected, but she couldn't be sure. Protocol dictated that, with support on the way, she should refrain from engaging until backup arrived. But how difficult could two frightened civilians be? Besides, she wanted this over with, and if her damned slowpoke troops had to learn by showing up to find that their commanding officer had done their job for them, so be it.

"All right, you in the car, step out slowly and keep your hands in sight," Touma called. She kept her sidearm lowered for now, but thumbed off the safety and clicked on the targeting laser. There was no response from the vehicle, so she called again. "You in the car! Exit slowly! Now!"

The driver's door, which was closest to her, cracked open then swung out slowly. From the shadowed interior stepped a man, who stood slowly while holding both hands at shoulder height. As he turned to look at her with a serene expression, the indirect light from the headlights illuminated his face. Captain Touma blinked and gasped.

"You!" she cried, her surprise quickly supplanted by hot fury. She snapped up her sidearm, leveling it directly at his chest. The red dot of her targeting laser glowed brightly right over his heart.

"Yes, Captain Touma, it's me," Jason said calmly.

"But...how..." Touma's mind reeled in confusion. Pelletier? Here? But they'd been tracking the targets all the way from their home – and besides, she had it on good, if informal, authority that he'd been vanished after the foul-up last spring. And yet, here he was. "How did you get here? What are you doing here?"

"Just trying to help."

"Help who? Them?" Her rage intensified as she remembered his betrayal, and her grip on her pistol tightened.

"I'm trying to help all of us," Jason explained, keeping his hands raised. "There are factors at work here that you don't understand, factors that are distorting your perceptions and everything we're doing here."

"I don't know what you're talking about! All I know is that you're a sellout, a damned traitor who kneecapped this operation right on the verge of success!" She was trembling with rage as she recalled all the hindrances and obstacles they'd had to contend with since that initial screw-up, all the wasted opportunities and blown chances, not to mention her own personal humiliation and professional setbacks.

All because of him. This double-crosser was the author of all that trouble and failure, and probably much more. Who knew what trouble he was up here hatching now?

"Listen, Captain, I want to explain," he began, but she cut him off.

"Shut up, you! I don't want to hear any weasel talk from a proven traitor!" Her anger was burning so hot that she was almost seeing red – the edges of her vision were starting to close in like a scarlet circle centered on this man, this locus of her hatred. She was dimly aware of someone exiting from the far door of the car, of new lights illuminating them, of cries and slams, but none of that distracted her. Her vision, her attention, her entire being was focused on this miserable man before her, this treasonous worm, this pitiful excuse for a human. Her arms trembled with the effort of restraining her hands from doing what they so longed to do, and still he simply stood there, looking at her quietly, waiting for her move.

*   *   *

"We're nearly there!" Chip called as he roared down Nathan Road.

"Just a couple minutes out, chief," came Angela's voice over the radio. "I'll be coming from the north."

"David reports he's got the drone in position over the site," Shawn said, tucking away his phone and holding onto the armrest as Chip gained speed.

"We're about ten minutes away, chief," Tom Stover said. "Be advised that we saw a couple of DTD vehicles heading in the same direction, presumably converging on the site."

"Copy that," Chip acknowledged with a grimace. "Things might get a little tense, Senator."

"I'm ready," Shawn said with more bravado than he felt.

"There it is," Chip pointed to a field that was coming into view beyond a windbreak. "Could you punch that red button on the box on the dash there? Thanks – that gets the dash cam recording. And just for good measure," he pulled the private phone Todd had given him from his pocket, "turn on video and snap this into that mount in the dash there. That's right, camera outward."

"Two cameras?"

"Never hurt. Besides, that's the phone on the private network. I don't know where it streams to, but I hope it's somewhere safe. And here we are."

Slowing down just enough to manage the turn, Chip steered into the field, bouncing and jolting as he went. Shawn could see that there were two vehicles and some people standing, but all was dim until the cruiser's headlights illuminated the scene.

"What the hell?" Chip muttered in alarm, parking the car and turning on the flashers. Shawn could see the cause of his concern. Full in the cruiser's headlights stood a woman holding a pistol pointed directly at an unarmed man who was standing beside the other car with his hands raised. Neither party was moving, but the situation looked very tense, and as Chip bolted from the cruiser Shawn saw his hand reach for his holster then pull away. Shawn got out and keyed David's number.

"You getting this, David?"

"All of it, boss. The extra lighting helps."

"Stay on it."

Meanwhile Chip was advancing slowly, both hands open and visible, stepping carefully through the grass. He knew tightly wound situations when he saw them, and this clearly was one. "Okay, ma'am, take it easy," Chip called. "He's unarmed, he's no threat, backup's here. Just lower the weapon, nice and slow, and we'll sort this all out." Beyond the woman Chip saw a man standing beside the car, which was clearly a DTD vehicle. The other man had a sidearm but he hadn't drawn it, and looked like he was spectating. Beyond him Chip was encouraged to see one of his deputies arriving at the far side of the field. It had to be Angela, because she had the SUV, and made good use of it as she roared over the scrub toward them. Glad as Chip was to see reinforcements, he hoped Angela would recognize the delicacy of the situation. Her headlights were now illuminating the scene from the other side, and Chip returned his attention to the woman with the gun. She was in DTD uniform, but her face was contorted by some internal struggle. He didn't know what she had against this man, but whatever it was, it was putting her under immense pressure.

Chip glanced at the man she was aiming toward and saw with shock that it was Jason Pelletier. So that was who had been with Gerald – but where was Todd? He shook his head – that didn't matter just now, while this clearly dangerous state of affairs did. He had no idea what dynamics were in play here, but he'd seen people with murder in their eyes, and this woman was one of them.

"Easy now, easy," Chip said in a firm but calm voice, daring to take a few steps closer. The woman was focused on Pelletier, but she shot a quick glance at Chip, who promptly stopped and held out his empty hands. Beyond her he could see Angela getting out of the SUV and unholstering her weapon, but only moving slowly to get in position on the other man, who was still simply watching.

Captain Touma was caught in a tension like she'd never felt. There was more activity in theater – more vehicles, more people. She knew some of her troops would be here soon. Lights were flashing red and blue off to her right. This should reassure her, take the pressure off.

But the rage boiling within her wouldn't let her ease off. Instead she felt a keen sense of a chance slipping away, of an opportunity evaporating, never to be recaptured. The more parties that arrived, the faster the evaporation, until it would be gone forever. She clenched her jaw and tightened her grip on the pistol, keeping the bright red dot squarely on her target's chest.

Chip could almost feel the tension crackling in the air. To his dismay, he saw two black DTD vehicles turn into the field on the north side, where Angela had turned in, and come racing in their direction. Chip didn't know if this would embolden the woman or pacify her, but his guts told him the more variables in this situation, the less stable it would be. It was unlike any negotiation atmosphere he'd ever been in, and he didn't like how things seemed to be tipping.

"Easy now, no need for that weapon. Everything's under control," he said as soothingly as possible, but the woman still ignored him.

Jason felt amazingly calm considering he was being targeted by a weapon in the hands of a bitter enemy. But part of him knew, in a way he'd never known before, that this circumstance was beyond his control. There was nothing he could do, and there was a freedom in that. In fact, there was tremendous freedom in that, and it filled him with such effervescent joy that he almost laughed. All his life he'd been hounded by the conviction that he had to take action to fix things. Here, now, he knew that he could not, so he needn't fret or expend energy trying.

He looked at Captain Touma and knew what he had to say, not for his good, but for hers. "You don't have to do this. There is a better way." She simply glared back at him, her face contorted, seemingly trying to respond.

Then Jason's eyes were drawn upward. The night sky was shrouded by some kind of dim red haze, but almost directly overhead it was being parted by what looked like pure white clouds, bright as if illuminated by a sunrise. Part of his mind was asking how white clouds could be so brilliantly lit in the middle of the night, but as he gazed a figure came from or through them, and began descending as if on an invisible stairway. As the figure drew closer, he saw that it was a woman in a dazzling white dress. When she got close enough, Jason was astonished to find that he recognized her – the short red hair, sparkling eyes, and brilliant smile.

"You!" Jason cried in wonder and amazement as the woman came nearly down to his level.

"Yes," she replied, standing just above him. Looking at him with infinite love she extended a graceful hand. "It is time for you to come with me."

"Damn you!" an agonized voice cried, and Jason heard two sharp pops.

Chip had been braced for any development, but when the shots came, he was still startled. Pelletier had said something in a low voice that only the woman could hear, but it hadn't seemed to affect her at all – if anything, she became more aggravated. Then he'd looked upwards, as if his eyes had been drawn to the sky, and after gazing for a few moments had said something to himself.

It was then that the woman had fired. She was well trained; it was a classic double-tap at nearly point-blank range. Pelletier dropped like a rag doll and Chip's instincts took control.

"Down!" he yelled as he whipped his pistol from its holster. Now it was the woman's turn to be illuminated by a targeting dot. "Drop it! Down on the ground! Drop the weapon or I'll fire!"

The woman was gazing at the sidearm in her hand like it was an alien device. She looked dazed, and didn't appear to be targeting anyone, but that could change at any moment. Chip crouched low, keeping his gun pointed. He was glad to see that the man on the other side of the car, whom he presumed was Gerald, had taken orders and gotten low; he hoped Senator Ramirez had done likewise. On the far side of the DTD vehicle he could see that Angela had the other man kneeling on the ground, his hands behind his head as she kept her gun trained on him and removed his weapon from its holster.

"Drop it!" Chip called again. "This is the Huron County sheriff and you're under arrest for murder! Drop the weapon and kneel with your hands up!" Still the woman didn't respond, continuing to stare at the gun as if unable to grasp what she'd just done with it. Unfortunately, Chip could see three uniformed DTD personnel approaching from one of the parked vehicles, though two others seemed to be hanging back.

"You're under arrest!" Chip called again, trying to break through to the woman. "Drop the weapon and kneel on the ground! I'll shoot you if you don't comply!"

The approaching DTD staff heard that. Looking at the body on the ground, the confused woman, and the sheriff cars, they halted and looked indecisive. But the sight of them seemed to break the woman from her trance. Glancing around with a confused and desperate expression, she found her tongue.

"I...I declare this a high-security area," she called in a shaky voice. "Secure the perimeter and detain all within."

"The hell you say!" Chip barked. "You're under arrest for violating Michigan law! Drop the weapon or risk being shot for resisting arrest!"

"As enforcement officer for the SPD, I declare this a federally sensitive area and order all within it to be detained!" The woman cried again. To Chip's alarm, the three DTD staff made a move toward her. He saw they were all armed, and wondered what they might have back in their vehicles.

"No, you don't!" Gerald cried, rising from behind the car and holding his hands up. Chip could see that they held papers of some type. "I'm Gerald Solomon of the Garden River Ojibwa! I'm a Canadian citizen and a member of the Anishinaabe First Nation! If you detain me, you'll have a diplomatic firestorm on your hands!" He offered the paperwork to the DTD personnel.

"And I'm Senator Shawn Ramirez, representing this district in the Michigan Senate," Shawn came out, his legislative ID held high. "I just watched this woman gun down an unarmed man in cold blood. There was no threat to her or to the SPD. We've got it all on video!"

"I've interdicted all network traffic within the SPD!" the woman called. "Your video feed will be stopped!"

"Not these ones," Shawn replied. "The drone video feed is to private storage, and if I'm detained the video will be shown on the senate floor next week!"

The woman was starting to look panicked. "Detain them! That's an order!"

"You can't give orders," Chip said firmly, stepping toward her. "You're under arrest for murder. Everyone saw it, including your own men. It's on video. This is not a federal matter. Now drop the weapon!"

Chip almost pitied the woman, whose eyes were darting every which way like those of a cornered animal, but he also knew that cornered animals did desperate things. The three DTD troops just twenty yards away still seemed to be dithering, and the two back by the vehicles seemed to be staying put for now. Two more sheriff cars with lights flashing pulled up behind the DTD cars, which reassured Chip but did not resolve things – this situation could still go any number of ways.

"Detain them, dammit!" the woman shrieked. "Set up a perimeter! Seal off the area, I tell you!" She was glancing madly back and forth between where her three troops were still hanging back and where Chip was slowly advancing, his pistol still trained on her. Chip didn't know if she'd yet seen Angela quietly approaching from behind her.

"You forfeited your authority when you committed that felony!" Chip cried. "You are under arrest! Drop the weapon and kneel on the ground!"

"You can't arrest me! You can't!" the woman turned toward Chip, trying to bluster her way out of it. She was still holding her weapon loosely, not pointed at anything. Behind her Angela had closed to within twenty feet, and suddenly she charged, tackling the woman and knocking the gun from her grasp. Angela was no small woman, and her target was nearly winded with the force of the impact. One of the three troops started forward, but a warning glance from Chip halted him. Angela was kneeling on the woman's back and cuffing her, so Chip holstered his pistol and went to pick up the woman's gun. He could see that Gerald was kneeling beside Jason's body, looking for any sign of life while shaking his head.

"Can you tell me who this is?" Chip asked one of the DTD troops, gesturing at the woman whom Angela now had kneeling in the grass.

"That's Captain Katy Touma," the man answered, "and she really is the director of enforcement for the SPD."

"Well, as you all saw, she's also a murderess," Chip replied. "You can contact your authorities about what you all should do next, but she's going to the Huron County jail in Bad Axe until the circuit court judge decides what to do with her."

"Yes, sir," the man replied.

Chip surveyed the scene, not quite certain that matters were completely settled. Tom and Ron were approaching, both carrying shotguns but otherwise not looking belligerent. The three nearby DTD troops were huddled together while the two who had hung back now ducked into their vehicles, hopefully to communicate with their coordinators. Angela had Captain Touma standing beside the SUV and was talking to her, presumably reading her her rights. Gerald was standing by Jason's body, and Shawn was talking on his phone. In the distance Chip could hear an approaching siren, which probably meant that one of his deputies had called for the medical techs. They wouldn't be able to any good for Jason, but Chip would be glad to see them. The arrival of the medics and other clean-up staff facilitated the turning of an important psychological corner at a disaster scene, marking the transition from 'active' to 'settled'. With these leaderless DTD troops hanging around, and hundreds of others just a radio call away, Chip wanted this situation settled as quickly as possible.

Chip walked over to where Gerald was standing. Despite Gerald's somber expression and slight head shake, Chip knelt beside Jason's body and felt for a pulse anyway. There was no movement of any kind under the already-cooling flesh, and Jason's eyes were going glassy. The expression on his face was peaceful, with just the slightest hint of surprise.

"Did you find the answers you were seeking?" Chip stood and asked Gerald.

"Mostly, and a lot more besides," Gerald replied. "The account of what I learned and saw tonight will make many a tale on many a long winter night. He especially should be remembered, for he died a hero." Gerald gestured to where Jason lay.

"How so?" Chip asked. It had taken nerve to face down that maniac with a gun pointed at his chest, but Chip couldn't see how Jason's actions could qualify as heroic.

"He took a chip in his arm to save the life of an unborn child," Gerald explained. "The case that Todd and Grace were involved in was a couple whose child had been diagnosed with a genetic anomaly. They had been scheduled for an abortion, and the clinic had embedded a tracking chip in the mother's arm. No matter where they ran, they'd draw the authorities after them. Jason took that chip into his own arm so we could lead them astray while the couple escaped. Then we just sat here waiting, buying them time, while the predators converged on us."

"Ah, yes – that would be heroic," Chip admitted. "Did the couple escape? Asking unofficially, of course."

"Unofficially, yes, I think so. I'm sure I would have heard by now if they hadn't. They may not have arrived at their destination yet, but they're safely away."

The ambulance had now arrived at the field, and Chip waved them over. "I need to attend to this, if you'll excuse me, Gerald."

"Yes, I need to make a call myself, to assure someone that I'm all right," Gerald replied, stepping aside and keying his phone. Chip directed the ambulance crew to Jason's body then stepped over to where Shawn was just getting off his phone.

"Well," Chip observed as he surveyed the scene. "This'll have some repercussions, y'think?"

"Oh, plenty of them, political but even more legal, I'm thinking," Shawn replied. "I called David to ensure that the footage was clean and safely stored. He's archiving a copy, and sending a copy to your office, the county prosecutor, and the state attorney general."

"Thanks," Chip said. "Plus, we've got my dash cam, and presumably Angela's, and a host of witnesses. I'm afraid we'll need to take a statement from you, maybe not tonight, but soon."

"That'll be fine," Shawn said. "My night is shot anyway, as is a number of other people's. I called the Senate Majority Leader, and he had me call the state AG while he called the governor. I also called Wayne Osterland, and he's calling the other house reps whose districts lie within the SPD."

"So, nobody's getting much sleep tonight," Chip said.

"No. The AG's idea is that we need to hit the ground running so we'll be ready when everybody comes into work tomorrow morning. Present a united front with the complete story: charges, inquests, legislative hearings, the works. The feds are going to be scrambling. My guess would be that they're going to try to bury this initially, ignoring it in hopes it'll go away. Then I'm guessing they'll try pushing back in the courts, arguing policies and jurisdictional issues. That's what we need to be prepared to counter. Your office, as well as all the area sheriffs and prosecutors, could get dragged into that."

"Bring it on," rumbled Chip.

"Tragic as this incident is, some of us are hoping it has the beneficial side effect of precipitating some discussions, maybe even confrontations, that have been hanging fire ever since the SPD was announced. In my opinion, the governor's office and administration have been soft on the whole matter all along. The feds offered the carrot of resources and relief from responsibility, and the stick of threatened lawsuits and regulatory complexity, so the governor has waffled. In the legislature, lawmakers who belong to the same party as the current administration in D.C. have been silent, and those who don't have seen the SPD as someone else's problem.

Hopefully the fallout from this will send them a wake-up call."

"Hopefully," Chip said. "But my instincts tell me that things have only begun to hit the fan. Looks like Angela is ready to go, so I need to get back to process our suspect in. I've got a county prosecutor and a circuit court judge to awaken, which I'm not looking forward to, but I know they'd not thank me for springing this on them in the morning. Are you okay? One of my deputies can run you back to your car."

"Thanks. I'm still not sure whether I'll be going home or just driving straight to Lansing. Good thing I keep a change of clothes in my office," Shawn said. "Good luck with what promises to be a messy morning for you. Call me if you need help."

"Good luck yourself," Chip replied, and got into his cruiser to head back to his office and all the responsibilities that awaited him there.

Refuge

Any lingering reservations Luke might have had toward Bob the leech harvester were laid to rest by his efforts that difficult night. Despite the man's loose-jointed personality and verbal flippancy that bordered on irreverence, Luke couldn't deny that Bob was a diligent and tireless worker. When it came to the arduous task of preparing the horses for the journey, Bob did as much by himself as Luke and Felicity did between them. With unerring skill he led them along darkened paths through the strange woods, with only an occasional glance at the map on Luke's phone to get his bearings. He kept the horses controlled and moving where Luke would have been completely lost. He brought them to the Au Sable right at the point Luke had designated, and they were able to watch the *Marten Clan* barely squeeze under the bridge to make the rendezvous.

The crossing of the lake from Caseville to Oscoda hadn't been comfortable for any of the refugees, particularly since the *Marten Clan* was a low boat with an open pilothouse. Grace and Bethany had huddled close to Tyrone on the sole bench, which was too short for them to be seated comfortably, trying to share their body heat with the chilled and exhausted lad. And though they were all immensely grateful for their timely extraction from the SPD, they were equally grateful to be pulling up to the river bank and bidding farewell to Lean Bear and his noisy fishing boat.

But they still had the long, brisk ride back through unfamiliar woods before them. Again, the indefatigable Bob had led the party, calling them on and encouraging them. Fortunately, Bethany had a little riding experience, and Patrick caught on quickly enough, but it took quite a bit of coaxing to get Tyrone onto a horse. Felicity stayed close by him as they rode, but Bob also would ride back to reassure and encourage him, even getting him to laugh at times. It was a demanding journey for people who'd already had a demanding night, and everyone was grateful when they finally arrived back at the Peterson's small house. Gil had arranged people to be there to take the Becks and the Hoods away, but arrangements were still being worked out for Tyrone, who'd been the unanticipated fifth refugee. Fortunately, Tyrone was glad to bunk anywhere for the time being, and expressed a genuine preference for joining Bob in the hayloft.

As the Petersons saw the couples on their way, Bob single-handedly unsaddled and stabled all the horses. Felicity brought him and Tyrone a loaf of bread, a slab of butter, and a pitcher of hot chocolate for quick rations and offered to cook up a big breakfast for them, a suggestion that was warmly received. But when she returned to collect dishes, both were wrapped in blankets and sound asleep in the hay. She smiled and returned to the house to go to bed herself. It promised to be a quiet day around the Peterson household, though there would certainly be demand for a big dinner.

*   *   *

Lansing was normally quiet this close to an election, with the politicians out campaigning and staffs scattered across the state. Thus, many workers and news sites were surprised to see that the Senate Majority Leader had scheduled a press conference for 10:00 a.m. Curiosity was running high enough that the conference was packed. Standing around the lectern were the Senate Majority Leader Ed Lavoy, Senator Shawn Ramirez, and Senator Connie Rigney. Behind them stood an array of House members. Savvy observers noticed that most of the lawmakers attending hailed from the Thumb region of the state; the canniest of these made the connection that these were legislators whose districts partly or completely fell within the controversial Special Protectionary District.

The press conference had a simple purpose: to announce the introduction of two new bills into the Michigan legislature. Senator Ramirez of Port Huron would be sponsoring a Senate bill that would make it illegal for any party, public or private, to implant any device in any Michigan citizen that would enable the party to track the geographic location of that citizen without the citizen's full knowledge and consent. Representative Wayne Osterland of Huron County would be introducing an equivalent bill in the House. Senator Rigney of Bay City would be introducing what would be termed the Medical Freedom of Choice Act in the Senate, which would make it illegal for any party, public or private, to ban by law or policy any Michigan citizen from receiving medical care from any provider they chose, if the citizen accepted responsibility for compensation. Representative Neal Stahl of Lapeer County was introducing the same bill in the House. Though the precise wording of the bills was still being hammered out, the Majority Leader was enthusiastic about his support, and would be the first co-sponsor of the bills when they were introduced. When asked why these bills were being introduced so late in the legislative session, Senator Ramirez simply alluded to 'disturbing recent developments', and the need to protect Michigan citizens. The Majority Leader was confident of broad support for both bills, swift movement in both houses of the legislature, and quick signing by the receptive governor.

Early in the afternoon another press conference was called in Lansing, this time by the state Attorney General, who had two nicely scrubbed boys standing beside him, flanked by uniformed State Policemen. He introduced them as Isaac and Andrew Bailey of Pigeon. In severe tones the AG announced his intention to file a writ of *habeas corpus* on their behalf for the boy's parents, Jack and Maureen, and their siblings Elizabeth, Catherine, and Rose. The boys' family had been taken in one of the mysterious raids of the prior spring and had not been seen since.

The AG announced his intention to get to the bottom of that and several other unexplained disappearances within the Special Protectionary District. In fact, he'd received intelligence that SPD agents had staged after-dark raids on homes across the district just the night before, and that anyone who had a friend, neighbor, or family member suddenly disappear should call the number or contact the address provided.

The content of these press conferences made some of the news sites, though the import of them was almost lost in the chaff of pre-election coverage. Only a handful of observers wondered if there was any connection between these unexpected conferences in the state capital and the bizarre, almost unbelievable account of a woman in Huron County who was being charged with gunning down an unarmed man in full view of the county sheriff and some deputies. There was a rumor that the woman was a federal official, but there had been no confirmation of that.

*   *   *

A few days later, Shawn called Chip with an update. "In case you haven't heard, the state police have begun augmenting the Tuscola County sheriff's watch on the old mental health site outside Caro."

"I hadn't heard, but Amanda will be relieved," Chip replied. "Her staff is stretched enough without having to watch that gate around the clock. Will the troopers be sending over drones?"

"No need," Shawn replied. "There's nothing that drone footage will show us. It's the road traffic that matters. Besides, then we don't have to test the no-fly zone declaration."

"Good thinking. I caught that on the clip of your press conference in Lansing – how you carefully avoided mentioning specific entities or incidents."

"It's a skill you learn in the world of politics," Shawn replied. "It's easier for the other guy to back away from a challenge that has only been hinted at, not fully issued."

"True," Chip laughed. "Are the troopers spotting anything down in Caro?"

"I haven't got a full report, but I understand that any traffic happens in the dead of night. Vans, buses, and supply trucks arrive and back into that covered landing dock. Then they draw the drapes across the entry before loading or unloading, so there's no way anyone can see what's coming or going."

"There has to be a way to get in there," Chip said.

"If there is, the Attorney General will find it. He's obsessing about the place, and has half his staff doing research for filings. He's preparing for a battle royal."

"I'm not sure he's going to need it," Chip replied. "There's been an interesting development up here: Captain Touma has retained a private defense attorney."

"Really?"

"Yes. Her initial visitors were anonymous attorneys who talked to her at length, then she goes and hires this renowned defender from Metro Detroit."

"So she's not being defended by government attorneys," Shawn observed. "What do you think that means? That they're disavowing her actions?"

"Seems like it, though we'll have to wait for developments. I'm guessing the feds will have a hard time completely distancing themselves from what happened, given that Touma was wearing a government uniform and driving a government vehicle on a government mission, and killed Pelletier with a government bullet shot from a government gun. Oh, and speaking of that, what are you doing around lunchtime the day after tomorrow?"

"I'll check. What's up?"

"Jason Pelletier's funeral. We're burying him in the township graveyard. It'll just be me and Erin and some of the office staff, unless you can make it."

"What, no family? Couldn't you run down some details about his life?"

"Our researchers did their best – Erin's particularly good with that sort of thing – but found nothing. His prior employer is, obviously, no help, and without any personal details we had no idea where to begin looking. He probably lived in the D.C. area, but could have come from anywhere."

"So he'll be buried in an unmarked grave, unknown and unmourned. No man should go like that."

"He'll be recognized at least, and a few of us chipped in to get a grave marker, so he won't be unknown."

"What did you put on the stone, given how little you know about him?" Shawn asked.

"Just his name, date of death, and a Bible verse."

"Which verse?"

"John 15:13. That was Angela's idea."

Shawn grabbed his Bible and found the reference. "Good choice," he smiled.

"I thought so."

"I'll see if I can make the funeral and get back to you. Talk to you later, Chip."

*   *   *

The atmosphere in the conference room was tense enough before the arrival of the DHS delegation, and it was not improved by their emphatic arrival. From their almost lock-step entry to the manner in which they took their seats, it seemed clear they wanted to dominate the proceedings.

"What the hell is going on here?" Roy Nicholson plunged in without preamble. "We seem –"

"Please, Roy, let's begin with introductions," Cynthia interrupted smoothly. "Not all of us are familiar. Roy

Nicholson of DHS, with Gretchen Killian and Michael Zhou, also of DHS. This is Pete McMillan of HHS, with Natalie Griggs and Stacey Lang, who have been coordinating the effort up in the Special Protectionary District. Mr. Soren here is an observer from Director Miller's office." She gave a nod over her left shoulder to a dark-haired, stone-faced man who sat behind her and did not acknowledge her introduction.

"Great," Roy snapped. "Now that we've dispensed with the pleasantries, how about some answers? Like how did a chip with a supposedly secret geolocation capability end up in the wrong person? Our troops ran all over the District thinking they were tracking a party who turned out to be somebody else! Anyone want to explain how that happened?"

"We…are still gathering information about that ourselves," Pete replied. "It's been very difficult getting information out of the District. The local authorities have…not been cooperative."

"And they won't be, I can guarantee that! Which brings us to another question: what the hell was going on with the ex-director? I thought that was a settled issue, that he'd been taken care of, and here he turns up in the middle of the district! I was given the impression that an HHS program had taken charge of that matter, and supposedly neutralized him as a factor." He glanced quickly at Cynthia, then glared at the HHS reps.

"We're still reconstructing the sequence of events –" Cynthia offered, but Pete interrupted, rising to the provocation.

"While we're asking questions, how was it that a DTD officer who'd been recalled and investigated for insubordination and losing control of her operation not only ended up back in the District, but in charge of the Enforcement arm?" He glared back at Roy, who seemed poised to respond when Cynthia broke in more firmly.

"Please, people. Acrimony and recrimination won't get us closer to resolving this. We're having trouble enough getting a handle on what actually happened, and when."

"True enough," Roy jibed. "Especially when the Director of the District finds out about the problem only a couple of hours before the locals announce their response to it. We've been playing catch-up ball ever since – typical HHS competence."

"Director Buchanan was agreed upon by all parties involved in the District initiative!" Pete snapped defensively.

"You know full well that Buchanan was a compromise that DTD conceded on! Had it been up to us, a colonel would have been in charge of the whole operation!"

"Yes, and considering what one of your captains did, I can only imagine how much havoc a colonel would have wreaked!" Pete rejoined hotly.

"People!" Cynthia interrupted sharply. "This is getting us nowhere. We're here to determine how we should respond to local provocation, and how we should configure the District going forward. Blame shifting and finger pointing isn't accomplishing that." She glared at both men until Pete nodded and Roy leaned back in his chair, crossing his arms and looking sullen.

"One thing's clear: the bills introduced into the state legislature were carefully crafted to directly challenge core elements of our initiative," Pete ventured. "But beyond that and some court filings, the response of state lawmakers and executives has been quite measured. I don't know how much of a fuss we want to make."

"Screw 'em, I say," Roy pronounced. "We're the federal government. Let them pass their bills and then defy them to enforce them within the District. Our laws trump their laws, simple as that. Frankly, I think they're playing chicken, and we ought to call their bluff. I mean, I know the immediate situation is a major cluster, but they may not. It's not like they're making a big deal about it."

"Yet," Mr. Soren said in a cold voice. "Not yet." The conversation stopped and everyone looked at the silent but ominous attendee.

"Yes...ah, Mr. Soren is quite right," Cynthia added after a moment of uncomfortable silence. "The fact that the embarrassing details of the shooting incident have not yet attracted much attention doesn't mean they couldn't. If they do, they could spark difficult questions that could reach to Director Miller's office and beyond. Very difficult questions." Cynthia managed not to glance at Mr. Soren, whose brooding presence reminded her keenly that following this meeting she was due for a tense interview with Director Miller that was sure to cover a broad range of topics.

"Are you suggesting that the locals are suppressing information in an attempt to pressure us into responding as they wish?" Roy asked. "Screw 'em, I say."

"I'm not suggesting that I understand their motives, but I am trying to grasp the implications of what they have and haven't done, in light of what they *could* do, and explore the potential ramifications," Cynthia replied. "I would also advise you not to underestimate their intelligence and abilities."

"If I may suggest," Pete interjected, "the primary benefit of the SPD was always intended to be on the HHS side. While DTD and other agencies could make good use of the District for their own purposes, even from its embryonic form the District has been mainly an HHS initiative. Considering that, we have some suggestions to make." He smiled at Natalie Griggs, who nodded back.

"What suggestions would those be?" Cynthia asked.

"The HHS staff is in agreement that we've gotten substantially what we were seeking out of the District. We've tried a variety of procedures and protocols, and our field staff has gained valuable experience. We've learned much about what policies work and what don't. In our estimation, we could scale back or even abandon operations within the

District at this point and still consider ourselves to have met our operational objectives."

"You mean...back down?" Roy snarled. "Give them the satisfaction –"

"I mean make prudent decisions regarding the allocation of scarce resources," Pete corrected him. "For our part, sure, we could hone and tune our operations for another two years if that was an option. But since we've achieved most of our goals, if packing up and moving on is the sensible choice – particularly if the local environment has been rendered operationally toxic – that's fine with us."

Roy snorted his disgust at this, but Cynthia looked pensive. "Are you sure? After all, the District has barely been in existence for six months. That hardly seems time enough to conclude any significant testing."

"The SPD concept was intended from the outset to be nimble and responsive. We've leveraged that in many ways during our implementations, and have gleaned an impressive amount of data and experience. Could we use more? Certainly, but if the operational resistance is becoming prohibitive, we're satisfied with what we have. We'll be years digesting and incorporating the results of our work within the SPD, which will better prepare us to deploy the concept in higher-population areas – which has always been the primary goal." He looked at Roy with a smug smile, which Roy mimed back.

"Well, if you're certain," Cynthia said. "What about DHS? You're the largest other player in the District. What are your operational objectives? How would they be impacted if we dialed back our activity within the District?"

"As Mr. McMillan has pointed out, the District has largely become a test bed for HHS ideas. Our role has been supportive of that. Sure, we've ironed out a few kinks and added a few pages to our Urban Ops Policy manuals, but if there's nothing left to enforce, we have other theaters in which we can deploy our assets," Roy answered.

"Well, then," Cynthia looked around with satisfaction, "if that's the consensus, then we have a framework for moving forward. Our legal and policy people can address specifics, but the broad direction is settled. Agreed?" There was a general murmur of at least concession, if not enthusiastic assent. "Very well then, I'll draw up the notification to send to Director Buchanan. If you could have your staffs prepare more specific procedure lists and get them to me by the end of the day, we can begin preparing an implementation schedule for the wind-down. As you're aware, Director Miller wants this matter expedited, so we want hours, not days, people. Thank you for your time."

Everyone stood and packed away whatever they'd brought. The DHS contingent fairly marched out the door, and the HHS staff was not far behind them, leaving Cynthia gathering and packing away her scant materials. Over her loomed Mr. Soren, who stood silently by. When she'd finished, she looked at him with a thin smile.

"Should we go, then?" she asked.

"The Director is waiting," Mr. Soren replied, gesturing toward the door.

*　　　　*　　　　*

The incoming call was from Kelly, who was holding down the office in Lansing. "Hey, boss, you might want to check out the link I'm sending. It's a live stream of a press conference being held right now there in Port Huron."

"Sure, Kelly," Shawn replied, opening the link to see a small conference room that was about half-full. Behind a nondescript lectern stood a woman in uniform reading a statement. The text at the bottom of the screen identified the woman as Lt. Bonnie Hammond of the Domestic Terror Division. To Shawn's eyes she looked like she'd rather be anywhere else, but was continuing dutifully.

"…have determined that a restructuring and refocusing of priorities for the Special Protectionary District is warranted. Effective immediately, SPD staff will be curtailing operations. Citizens who have come to rely on staff for vital services will be redirected to other providers. Though there may be some adjustment issues, nobody will be denied prompt, suitable care. Above all, citizens of the SPD should not feel endangered. This decision was made in part because the threat of domestic terror was deemed to have been suitably dealt with. In short, we have largely completed our mission." The lieutenant looked up from the lectern with an unhappy finality.

"Ms. Hammond, is this move in response to –" called a voice from off camera, but the lieutenant's response was curt.

"As I explained at the outset, I will be taking no questions at this time." With that she turned and strode from the room. Shawn closed the link.

"So, they're folding up already? That was quick," Shawn commented to Kelly.

"Oh, it's even faster than that. Connie's staff is reporting some strange rumors out of Tuscola County that are still being checked out."

"What kind of rumors?"

"One thing we know for sure is that in the middle of last night a big black bus pulled into the Caro site, escorted by two unmarked black SUVs. The bus backed into the canopied landing bay while the SUVs loitered about with nobody getting out of them. About half an hour later the bus pulled out again and drove down to M-46 and over to I-75, where it turned south. Sheriff Morris detailed a car to tail them that far, but we're not sure where they went from there."

"If they were DTD, then possibly down to I-69 and then to Fort Wayne," Shawn speculated.

"That's what I think," Kelly agreed. "But that's not the kicker. About dawn this morning people start wandering out of the facility, looking confused and blinking in the daylight.

When the deputies and state police troopers approached them, they told of being detained in the building by guards who wouldn't say who they were or who they worked for. They were never given any reason for their detention, and were never allowed to leave the building. The windows were all blocked off, so they had no idea where they were. But when they woke up this morning and nobody came to take them to breakfast, they tried their doors and found them all unlocked. They just walked out of their rooms and out of the buildings. The place was deserted except for the detainees. The staff was all gone – guards, cooks, administrative staff, everyone."

"By dark bus in the middle of the night, no doubt," Shawn suggested. "Are these are missing people, then?"

"That's what Connie's staff is thinking, though things are still being checked out."

"Holy smoke – to think this is going on in America," Shawn mused. "Listen, I want you to get David on this. Have him run over to Caro and get involved with the sheriff's office or whoever's handling these people. Render all aid and assistance, of course, but I want him to focus particularly on our constituents. I want him talking to everyone there, getting personal information, seeing they have whatever they need. Ensure Ed and Wayne's staffs get notified of this, too. I want a list of all our constituents who were held in that prison in my hands by tomorrow morning, understood?"

"You got it, boss."

Shawn rang off and sat trying to contain his temper. His constituents, American citizens, detained without charges or representation or even communications? Oh, somebody was going to catch it for this. Somebody was going to catch it hot.

*   *   *

Gerald's phone rang, and he saw it was Kim.

"Hey, Kim," he answered, "everything all right?"

"Hey, Gerald. We're fine as a family, but I thought you'd want to know: Esther died in her sleep last night."

Gerald nodded. "It doesn't surprise me. I hope she found peace."

"I think she did. She'd been resting well over the last few days, particularly since you returned from that crazy visit. Her nights have been good."

"No distressing dreams or visions?"

"None that she told me of. She did mention that she had the same dream a few times, of a torn and tattered spider's web blowing in the morning breeze. She said it was a very peaceful dream."

"I'm glad. She was a wise woman and a true prophetess of the Anishinaabe. May her soul find rest."

"Indeed. Are you planning to come back down any time soon?"

"Not unless I'm needed. The Huron County prosecutor took my deposition, but I told him that if they needed me to testify, I'd return. Are you hearing any word from over there?"

"No. Most of the sites are still obsessing about the upcoming elections. Some of the smaller sites are tracking developments, but there aren't many."

"Give it a few months," Gerald advised. "The people I know won't let it rest. The implications of what was attempted there in the Thumb go to the heart of American freedoms. Whether it'll be ignored, or serve as a wake-up call, will say much about where America is headed."

*   *   *

"Hey, Brady," Steve said as he answered the knock at his front door. "What brings you up here?"

"I had to show you this," Brady gloated, pulling his phone from his pocket, "I just had to show you – this is so cool."

"What is it?"

"Well, I've been trying to figure out how to stymie these broadcasting chips. We can't get the government to undo the patches to the phones and other devices, because that would require them to admit what they've done. We can't get them to remove the chips, either, for the same reason. We can't advise people to mess up their geolocation features like we've done with our phones, because people need them. And only a few people are going to be willing to dig the chips out of their arms."

"Right on all counts," Steve said, sitting the excited Brady down on the couch. "So, what have you come up with?"

"You'll love this. It's elegant, but we'll have to convince people to participate in order for it to work."

"I'm sure we could do that. What does it do?"

"It's a simple little program that I've already posted for download. The cover is that it's a free timer program – stopwatch, alarm, timer, all the basic functions. It does all those things, which is trivial, but it also captures all the detected chip IDs when they're broadcast and keeps a running record of them all. It then rebroadcasts those chip IDs at regular intervals until the device is shut down or restarted."

"So...wait," Steve shook his head. "The phone captures and retains the chip IDs and continues to rebroadcast them? How is that good?"

"It's good because it cripples the critical component of their construct, which is proximity broadcast!" Brady gushed. "Can't you see? It'll totally torque their framework, and they probably won't even be able to tell what hit them!"

"I guess I'm still not getting it," Steve admitted.

"All right," Brady said patiently. "Let's say you've got one of those chips implanted, and I'm carrying a typical phone. Let's also say that you and I cross paths here in Ubly at 1:00 p.m. My phone would pick up your chip's signal and broadcast it. The government would then know you were in Ubly at that time. Good so far?"

"Got that," Steve assured him.

"But if I continued on to Bad Axe while you went to Sandusky, my phone wouldn't continue to broadcast your chip's ID once I'd moved out of range. But if you wandered into a supermarket over in Sandusky, one of the other shopper's phones might pick up your chip's signal and broadcast it. Now the government knows you're in Sandusky at, say, 1:40 p.m."

"Got that."

"But let's say my phone has this little program installed." Brady was almost bouncing in excitement. "It would pick up your signal in Ubly and broadcast it, but it would also keep track of your chip ID. As I drove north to Bad Axe, my phone would continue to broadcast your chip ID and its location every five minutes. So, if I happened to stop into the Sugar Bowl, and I'm sitting there at 1:40 p.m., my phone will broadcast your chip ID and location at the same time you're in the supermarket in Sandusky."

"So the government would be getting two different signals putting me in different places at the same time," Steve said slowly.

"Right! And my phone would keep broadcasting your chip ID no matter where I went. Furthermore, let's say that while I'm having lunch at the Sugar Bowl, I pick up three more chip IDs from other diners. My phone records all of those as well, so now I'm regularly broadcasting four chip IDs. Then I return to Port Huron, while those other diners go back to Pigeon or Bad Axe or Harbor Beach, and I keep broadcasting their IDs for days."

"That would certainly screw up their system," Steve said, the light dawning. "Brady, you're right. This is elegant, and clever as hell."

"The diabolic cleverness of their system lay in its simplicity, and how it leveraged common infrastructure,"

Brady explained. "This patch exploits that simplicity to frustrate their assumptions, and there's nothing they can do about it without exposing their scheme."

"Does it work? The chip you removed from Mom's arm is long dead – how did you test this?"

"Testing proved all too easy," Brady sighed sadly. "There are plenty of these chips deployed across the Thumb. I thought I'd have to hang out near hospitals or medical offices to pick up enough signals. It turned out that supermarkets and donut shops were more than sufficient. I'd guess that one in five, maybe even one in four, area residents have had these chips implanted, including teens and children."

"So even though the SPD is being scaled back, those will still be in place, broadcasting their IDs?" Steve asked.

Yes – and the phones will still be transmitting their locations," Brady replied. "A little silver lining for the government to the dark cloud the SPD turned out to be. It wouldn't surprise me if the chipping program is one of the things the government expands from here."

"But...your program should help cripple that, right?" Steve asked encouragingly.

"It should, and we should get word out as far as we can, but penetration will be light even then. Getting my program on one phone in a thousand would be wildly successful, but there are still cars and cash registers and workstations to deal with," Brady said glumly.

"But still – it's something, and it can serve as a template for other programs," Steve replied. "We can get the word out through as many underground channels as we can, start spreading the link. We may not be able to take them down, but we can bruise their shins."

"Yeah," Brady brightened a bit. "Yeah, that's true."

*   *   *

Luke returned to his home later than he'd expected from the medical calls that he'd gone out on the day before. He was tired and cold and hungry, and a bit resentful of the first commitment that had kept him away from his home and wife overnight since they'd been married. But Felicity had kept a dinner plate warm for him and listened sympathetically as he poured out his frustrations. She left the dishes for the morning, figuring that her husband needed to be put to sleep, but despite her best efforts he was still tossing and turning an hour after they'd gone to bed.

"What's on your mind, sweetheart?" she asked, nestling against his side.

Luke sighed and was silent for a while. Felicity waited patiently – she was learning his ways, and that he needed time to gather his thoughts and courage before discussing a difficult topic.

"It's just...I don't..." he stammered, then sighed again. "This isn't the kind of life I envisioned providing for you. I mean, I hardly had time to dream about providing for you, but as far as providing for my wife, and especially since that wife is you...I'm not saying this very well."

"Don't worry about it," Felicity chuckled. "What kind of life did you envision providing, and how does our life fall short of that?"

"Well, I wasn't anticipating living in an old, poorly insulated cottage with badly fit windows that don't keep the drafts out. I wasn't expecting to have to constantly watch the propane level so the stove doesn't cut out in the middle of cooking dinner, or be stingy with the gas to run the generator because it needs to last the entire week. And I guess I was hoping to have a regular job, with a paycheck we could count on."

Ah, Felicity sensed they were coming close to the heart of the problem. "How did your visits go? Anything you couldn't deal with?"

"No, not this time. They all went well enough, I suppose."

"I'm sure they were grateful for your help."

Luke snorted. "Oh, they were exceedingly grateful. Gushing with gratitude. Couldn't thank me enough."

"Was that all?"

"Oh, I was given some cash here and there – about seventy-five dollars in all. About three hundred dollars' worth of fuel chits. And a few pounds of butter and two jars of homemade maple syrup."

"Really? Butter and syrup? I'll make pancakes for breakfast."

"Yeah. And lots of 'we owe ya, doc' and 'we'll make it up to ya'. Plenty of those. It's becoming my most common form of payment."

"Well, they deeply appreciate your help."

"I'm glad, but I wish I had a bit more to show for my sacrifices – not so much for me, but to provide you a better life," Luke said.

Felicity smiled in the dark and kissed his shoulder. "To set your heart at ease, I'm perfectly satisfied with the life you're providing for us. There's nobody I'd rather share my life with than you, and nowhere I'd rather live than with you, even if it means living in a small cottage with drafty windows. I'm sure everything will work out over time."

"Thanks," Luke murmured, not sounding totally convinced.

The next morning Luke went out to do morning chores in the stables, a task with which he was assisted by Tyrone, who was still bunking down in the hayloft. Another foster home was still being sought for Tyrone, the challenge being finding a family that was both willing and able to continue his education. In the meantime he was happy to continue sleeping in the hay and help about the homestead as he could. For their part, the Petersons were glad to have him. He was cheerful, helpful, hardworking, and a natural with the livestock. Felicity worked with him on informal lessons. This morning he and Luke finished chores quickly and came in together for breakfast, which was fluffy buttermilk pancakes slathered in butter and swimming in homemade maple syrup.

"Honey, I noticed a worked up patch down on the flat portion of the meadow," Luke said. "Were you doing something down there? Or was Bob?"

"No, that was the team of men," Felicity said with a sly smile.

"Team of men? What was a team of men doing here?" Luke asked, a little alarmed.

"They showed up in the morning the day before yesterday. They were here to dig a well."

"A well? On our property? Whatever for?"

"I guess they thought we needed one. I could hardly gainsay them – they just showed up with a truck and started drilling."

"Oh," Luke said, trying to make sense of this. "You didn't schedule a well drilling, did you? 'Cause I sure didn't."

"No, I didn't."

"I can't say I think it a bad idea – our current well certainly has too much iron in the water. But why sink it down there on the flats instead of closer to the house?"

"They said it was the sensible place to dig it, all things considered. You can discuss it with them – they said they'd be back today. In fact, I think I hear them now," Felicity said.

Now completely befuddled, Luke went out the kitchen door to find a truck backing a big trailer down his driveway. On the trailer was a small skid-steer utility vehicle, and the truck bed was loaded with cinder blocks, a variety of pipes, and a small hi-lo for unloading. A couple of pickups were parked in the yard and work teams wearing hard hats were piling out and grabbing their tool boxes from truck beds.

"C'mon, guys, we got to get the site cleared and leveled so they can start laying pipe! The foundation pour is scheduled for tomorrow afternoon!" A man with a tablet was hollering to the others. Luke recognized him as Jerry Bleeker, whose daughter Luke had helped through a bout of pneumonia last summer.

"What...what on earth is going on?" Luke asked.

"Andy, once Mack gets that trailer placed, can you help him unhitch it so we can get that forklift going? We've only got this truck for a few hours, and a lot of stuff to unload," Jerry continued his bellowing.

"Felicity?" Luke turned to his wife in mystification.

"They're building us a house, Luke," Felicity gushed, unable to contain herself any longer. "They showed up the morning you left, blueprints in hand – I've got them inside. They've been planning this for months. They said it was the least they could do, and besides, they want you to stay in the area."

"Wait...a house?"

"Yes! It's simple, but beautiful. Twelve hundred square feet, which isn't a mansion, but more that the six hundred or so we've been limping by with."

"But...we can't afford a house!"

"We don't have to. They're giving it to us, as a thank you gift. Or you can think of it as a form of payment, if you wish. Apparently, they've been stockpiling materials for a while, and finally accumulated enough." Felicity was grinning and bouncing on her toes.

"A house? Really?" Luke was so surprised that he could barely speak.

"Yes, a house. These people love you, Luke, and appreciate how much you've done for their families. It'll have a big kitchen, and a living room, and three bedrooms. You can have one of them for a study and office, but we're going to need the other one."

"For what?"

"For a nursery – Dad."